One moment Carshing back her hair.
The next she wa   and
onto the bed. Th   her
head, smashed d   king
into helpless de   her
knees, her legs,   as a
scream . . . a terrible, te   own.
There was no one else in the room.

Novels by Frank De Felitta

The Entity
Audrey Rose
For Love of Audrey Rose

Published By
WARNER BOOKS

the Entity

a novel by

Frank De Felitta

WARNER BOOKS

A Warner Communications Company

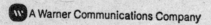

en-ti-ty (**ML** entitas) *BEING, EXISTENCE: something that has separate and distinct existence,* real or imagined.

For Raymond, my son

Acknowledgments

A number of people helped me in one important way or another to write this book. These people are Steven Weiner, who worked on all of it; Barry Taff, Kerry Gaynor, and Doris D., whose lives inspired part of it; Dr. Jean Ritvo and Dr. Edward Ritvo, who generously shared their knowledge and imagination; Dr. Donald Schwartz, who contributed helpful information; Barbara Ryan, whose unique and special insights provided encouragement; Ivy Jones, for her skill at dramatic re-creations; Michael E. Marcus, Tim Seldes, and Peter Saphier, for their continuing support and cogent input; William Targ, my editor, whose perceptive criticism helped to make this a much better book than it was; and Dorothy, my wife, for her constant faith, love, and cheerful good nature.

I would also like to express my gratitude to Dr. Thelma Moss, whose distinguished writings and seminars in parapsychology gently led me through the looking glass and made of me a firm believer in the probability of the impossible.

March 23, 1977—Statement made by suspect, Jorge (Jerry) Rodriguez, booked on first degree assault charge, taped in the presence of Officer John Flynn, #1730522.

R: *Yeah, look, look, I'm finished. We're finished. I mean, that was too much, I didn't dream it. There was something . . . something going on with Carlotta. Something was going on in that room. I . . . what do I tell you? I didn't see, exactly, something. But I saw what it was doing to her. And you've got to understand she was . . . she was in the bed . . . I just came from the bedroom and I was . . . getting ready, you know, I was getting ready to go to bed with her. I turned around and I saw her . . . first I heard her; I heard her first, and she was . . . you know, moaning . . . she's making noises like, love noises but scared too, like she's not liking what she's feeling, I don't think, and I turn and I think it's a put-on, like a put-on for me, you know, like "I'm ready for you, poppa." We were very, very close, we had a good relationship always. So I turn around and I look and . . . I see this . . . like something is pressing her . . . now . . . uh, understand what I'm saying here, it's pushing . . . her . . . she's got no clothes on, and I can see her breasts, they're being . . . touched . . . now, how do I say it, like, it's not her own hands, you understand, and I think I'm going bugs. I look at this and I say, Jesus Christ, what has she got me, crazy? All of this crazy talk with those kids from the university, am I seeing something? Am I dreaming? So I shake my head, you know, and I look a little closer, I say, you know, this is a put-on, this is a put-on. It's something she's doing. I say, "Hey Carlotta, Carlotta . . ." But she doesn't answer, and her moans are growing louder, and she's like . . . in pain . . . more pain, and I look closer and I see that . . . that her breasts, they're being pressed and squeezed, by fingers . . . only I can't see the fingers, the fingers are pressing them, you know, the nipples are being pressed down, I see her body, like . . . uh . . . you know, it's jumping, as if someone is on her, pumping away. Oh, my God, I say, Jesus Christ, what the hell is going on here? Then I see her legs, ripped open, pushed open, they're pulled apart, and she starts screaming, but all the while she's holding . . . holding . . . someone . . . or something. Her arms are around something. Well, by now, I say, Jesus Christ Almighty, she's being attacked. I can't see it, but she's being attacked. I'm half out of my skull. I don't know what to think. You know, believe me, I didn't know what I was doing . . . uh . . . the first thing that come to my hand, I . . . suddenly I find myself standing over her with. The . . . the . . . I went over there with this wooden chair and I smashed it . . . I had to get this thing off her, I had to save her. You gotta understand I love her, at least . . . I loved her. I didn't want to hurt Carlotta, but it's that thing, that thing that was on her, that was pressing on her, okay, that was screwing, fucking her. And she making all those noises, and I . . . brought the chair down on them. I smashed it. (Weeps.) I swear to God, as God is my witness, that's what happened. I saw something. At least I saw something that she was feeling. Something on top of her. I couldn't see it with my eyes, but there was something there, you gotta believe me, there was something there. I tell you, I'm out of my mind.*

(Weeps.) If I ever get outta this mess, I tell you I'm gonna take the hell off. She was a great girl, Carlotta . . . I liked her. We had something going for a while. But . . . she's got something there . . . something there with her. I tell you she's in trouble . . . She's in bad trouble. Something's got hold of her. Something. I don't know what it is, but . . . Carlotta is in trouble.

ENDS

PART ONE
Carlotta Moran

. . . Come, you spirits
That tend on mortal thoughts, unsex me here,
And fill me from the crown to the toe, top-full
of direst cruelty! . . .

—Shakespeare

1

10:04 p.m. October 13, 1976

THERE had been no warning. No way to predict. Nothing at all. She had gotten out of her car. Her back was hurting. She remembered thinking: welfare is a good thing, but it makes you do what they want. Now she had to go to secretarial school. Not that she minded, but it was funny somehow. Why it was funny, she couldn't define. It hurt to close the car door.

She had to cross the street to get to her house. It was because she always returned home from the school from the northern end of Kentner Street and it wasn't worth the bother to turn the heavy Buick around. The garage was Billy's. He needed it for his engines, his cars, who knew what. So she crossed the street, her back hurting. She had hurt her back the year before, helping the bus boy lift up a tub of dirty dishes. Too stupid.

The wind was dry, picking up little brown crisp leaves and rolling them across the pavement. The leaves never decayed in West Los Angeles. They just seemed to roll around in every season, dead little things that seemed to have a private life of their own. It was so dry you

13

could feel it in your throat. That bleak dryness that comes out of the high desert and makes you depressed as hell.

Carlotta looked down the street as she crossed. The Shell station looked about a mile away in a bright spot of lights. Like looking through the wrong end of a telescope. How far away was every human activity. All the houses were dark. Even silent. Regular, small tract houses with tiny lawns, fences for dogs. But even the dogs were asleep. Or quiet. Only the distant rush of the freeway, like a faraway river, could be heard over the dark neighborhood.

Kentner Street was a court, a dead-end street terminating in a bulge of pavement where you could turn your car around, and that's where she was, at the end.

Entering the house, she heard her son, Billy, in the garage. The radio was humming softly. Carlotta closed the door behind her, and locked it. She always locked the door. Billy had a side entrance from the garage. She removed her beige vinyl jacket and sighed tiredly. Her eyes wandered about the living room. Nothing out of place. Her cigarettes on the table by the couch. Her shoes on the floor, her clothes and magazines, a coffee cup, a broken heater vent that banged when the thermostat changed—it was like slipping into an old pair of shoes. It was comfortable. It was Carlotta where she relaxed. Where there was no outside world. The world stopped at the door. Welfare paid the rent; but it was Carlotta's place. It was like a thousand built on an identical plan all over the city. Just another cracker box. But it was hers. The place where she and the kids came together as a family.

She went into the kitchen and switched on the light. The bare bulb overhead turned the walls very white. Inside the refrigerator there was no beer. She would have liked a beer but there was none. She sat a moment in the bleak and bone-white kitchen, then went to the stove and settled for some re-heated coffee.

It was 10:00. A little past, because it took about twenty minutes to come back from the school. But not yet 10:30, because Billy would have come in by then and gone to bed. They were very strict about that. It was an agreement they had come to. He got the garage, if he was in by 10:30. Billy was very good about it, too. So it was between 10:00 and 10:30 at night. Wednesday. October 13. Tomorrow was secretarial school again. A day like all others. Nine to one: typing. Steno: twice a week in the evenings.

Carlotta rose from the kitchen chair, thinking of nothing in particular. She turned off the light and walked down the narrow hallway to her bedroom, pausing a moment to look in on the girls.

Julie and Kim were sleeping like it was very serious business, with only the little night light—a furry animal with a light bulb inside—softly illuminating their faces. They looked like twins, though two years apart. Different father from Billy's. Pretty as angels. Someday, God, Carlotta thought, no welfare. None of this. Something better. She closed the door on the sleeping girls and went to her own bedroom.

The bed was unmade. That huge, preposterous bed which the last tenant couldn't have moved from the house without ripping apart every door in the place. It had four posts and carved tendrils and angels on the headboard and baseboard. The joints were glued and there was no pulling it apart. It was a labor of love, built from scratch, in the room. The builder must have been a master craftsman, an artist, a poet. How he must have hated leaving the bed behind. Carlotta loved the bed. It was unique, an escape from the humdrum. Jerry loved the bed. Jerry. Confused, nervous Jerry—wondering what the hell he was getting himself into. Poor Jerry—Carlotta's mind lost the train of ideas.

She took off her clothes, pulled on a red robe, and went to the window. She locked both the windows in the bedroom. She checked the swivel catch behind the studs. It was because of the wind outside. If you don't lock the windows, they rattle all night long.

She took a few pins from her hair. The black hair fell to her shoulders. Carlotta looked at herself in the mirror. She knew she was pretty. Dark hair, clear skin, soft and

15

vulnerable, but her finest feature was her eyes—quick and dark. Jerry said they were "flashing dark." Carlotta combed her hair. The light—now behind her in the mirror image—was behind her head, so that an aura of light bathed her shoulders, illuminated the dark lapels of the red robe.

She was nude underneath the robe. Her body was small and soft. She was light-boned. There was a natural softness in her walk and movements. Men never treated her roughly. There was nothing hard about her which men wanted to break down, to reduce. They appreciated her, this vulnerable quality, the fine shape and its suppleness. Carlotta studied her small breasts, the slim hips, seeing herself the way she knew men saw her. Now she was a month away from being thirty-two years old. The only lines on her face were around her eyes, and they actually looked like laugh lines. So she was pleased with her appearance.

The closet door was open. Inside, her shoes were neatly arranged—Carlotta's sense of order. She was thinking about a shower as she looked for her slippers. There was no hiding place in the closet; it was rather like a small box built into the wall.

The house was deathly quiet. It seemed to her the whole world was asleep. This was what she remembered thinking—*before it happened.*

One moment Carlotta was brushing her hair. The next she was on the bed, *seeing stars.* Some knock, like being hit by a charging fullback, plummeted her across the room and onto the bed. In a blank mind, she realized that the pillows were suddenly around her head. Then they were smashed down over her face.

Caught between breaths, Carlotta panicked. The pillow was being pushed down, harder and harder. The cotton was being shoved into her mouth. She couldn't breathe. The force of the pillow was awful. It was forcing her head down deep into the mattress. In the darkness Carlotta thought she was going to die.

It was instinct that made her arms grab the pillow,

punch up over it, twist her head violently side to side. It was an instantaneous eternity. It lasted a lifetime, but too short a time to think. She was fighting for her life. A yellow heat swam in front of her eyes. The pillow covered her entire face, her eyes, her mouth, her nose, and her flailing arms couldn't budge it. Her chest was near bursting.

Her body must have been thrashing without her knowing it, because now it was grabbed and grabbed hard.

Carlotta was sinking into helpless death but she felt huge hands on her knees, her legs, the inside of her legs, her legs which were pried apart, pulled wide and open, far apart, and then some knowledge floated like a shot up through her consciousness and she understood and it filled her with energy. It filled her with a savage strength. She bucked and kicked. Her arms flailed, and when she bucked again to kick, to kill if she had to, a searing pain ripped through her lower back, rendering her powerless. Her legs were spread, pinned onto the bed far apart, and, like a pole, a rough, crude post, this thing entered her, distended her, forced its way into her until there was no stopping, just a thrust of pain. Carlotta felt ripped apart inside. She felt herself being torn apart in repeated thrusts. It was the cruelest weapon, repulsive, agonizing. It was ramming its way home. Her whole body was sinking into the mattress, pressed down, pushed down by this ramming weight which was turning her into a piece of raw meat. Carlotta jerked her face, her nose felt air, her mouth gasped and sucked in oxygen at the side of the pillow.

There was a scream. It was Carlotta's scream. The pillow was smashed back into her face. This time she could feel the imprint of a huge hand, its fingers pressing through onto her eyes, over her nose and mouth.

Carlotta sank into darkness. She had seen nothing. Only the far wall—not even that, only its vague color through the sparks and spirals which danced before her eyes—before the pillow had been thrust back onto her. So she sank, her strength ebbing. Carlotta was dying. She

17

would be dead soon. Already darkness was growing and pain mounted over her and was unconquerable. Was she dead?

The light was on overhead. The main light. Billy was at the door. His eyes were staring out of their sockets. Carlotta bolted upright, sweating, looking at Billy with glazed eyes.

"Mom!"

Carlotta grabbed a sheet, covering her battered body. She was whimpering, half moaning, not quite sure yet who Billy was. A fiery pain filled her chest. Circles and stars still danced in the air before her; her eyes felt like they had been gouged in.

"Mom!"

It was Billy's voice. The pitifully, tender fright in his voice brought forth some instinct in Carlotta, some need to take over, to mentally focus, to act.

"Oh, Bill!"

Billy ran to her. They embraced. Carlotta wept. Nausea filled her. Now she became conscious of the pain which inhabited her private parts and spread into her upper thighs, even into her abdomen. It was as though she were destroyed inside. An inflammation grew within her —which knew no stopping.

"Billy, Billy, Billy . . . !"

"What is it, Mom? What's wrong?"

Carlotta looked around. Now she understood the worst thing of all: *There was no one else in the room.*

She whirled around. The windows were still locked. In a panic she spun around to face the closet. Only shoes and clothing. Too small to hide anyone.

"You see anybody?"

"No, Mom. Nobody."

"Is the front door locked?"

"Yes."

"Then he's in the house!"

"There's nobody here, Mom!"

"Billy, I want you to call the police."

"Mom. There's nobody in the house."

Carlotta's mind was reeling. Billy was almost calm. He was only frightened at seeing her like that. His smudged face was scrutinizing hers, with the tender fright of a child, with the tender concern of a very young man.

"Didn't you see anybody?" Carlotta said. "Didn't you hear anybody?"

"Only when you screamed. I ran in from the garage."

Julie and Kim were now standing at the door. They were terrified. They looked at Billy.

"It was just a dream," Billy said to them. "Mommy had a bad dream."

"A dream?" Carlotta said.

Billy was still talking to the girls. "You've had bad dreams, too," he said. "Now Mommy had one. So go back to bed."

But, unmoving, the girls stood frozen in the doorway, looking at Carlotta.

"Look in the bathroom," Carlotta said.

The girls turned like automatons.

"Well?" Carlotta demanded.

"There's nobody in there," Julie said. Carlotta's behavior was frightening her to the point of tears.

"Look, keep quiet," Billy said. "Let's all get back to bed. Come on, now."

Carlotta, unbelieving, mechanically pulled the sheet around her, tucking the ends around her sides. She tried to control her shaking. Her mind was confused. Her body was beaten. But the house was calm.

"Christ, Billy," she said.

"It was a dream, Mom. A real humdinger."

A consciousness returned to Carlotta as though it had been, after all, a dream. A kind of waking up, a kind of rising out of hell.

"Christ," she murmured.

Carlotta looked at the clock. It was 11:30. Almost. Maybe time enough to have fallen asleep. But Billy

19

was still dressed in his jeans and T-shirt. What had happened? She tried to sit at the edge of the bed but she was too sore.

"Get the girls into bed, will, you Bill?" she said.

Billy hustled the girls out of the room. Carlotta reached for her robe. It was crumpled and on the floor in a red heap. Not even close to the chair where she always left it.

"Let's get out of here," she said.

She put on the robe, sitting at the edge of the bed. Her body was drained. She looked at her arms. Welts were rising in a flanneled series above her elbows. Her little finger felt sprained from the struggle. Struggle? *With whom?*

Carlotta stood up. She could barely walk; she felt almost disemboweled. For just a moment, she had the eerie feeling of not being able to tell if she were dreaming or if she were awake. Then it passed. She probed within, and felt a slight moisture. Not blood. And nothing—no sign of—She slowly tightened the robe around her and left the room. For the first time the bed seemed monstrous, an instrument of torture. Then she closed the door.

Carlotta had no doubt she had been beaten and raped. She sat on a chair in the kitchen. Julie and Kim were drinking milk and eating Oreo cookies. Billy sat uncertainly near the door. Shouldn't they go to bed, he must have been thinking. Or was something still wrong?

It was a little like having a death in the family, Carlotta thought. You knew it would get better, everything would return to normal, you would forget it all, but in the meantime you had to live through that feeling of being alone in a dark pit. Of being lost and frightened. And you didn't know how long it would last.

"Easy on the cookies," Carlotta said. "You're going to get sick."

Kim's chocolate-lined mouth twisted up at her. Julie drank her milk slurpingly. To Carlotta they seemed so very vulnerable.

"Let's go watch TV," Carlotta said.

They sat on the couch. Billy turned on the set. Some movie stars Carlotta couldn't quite place were seated formally in what seemed to be an expensive New York penthouse. Billy sat in the easy chair by the ventilator. Everything looked normal, but felt unreal. It was like looking through a glass which somehow made everything look strange, distorted.

Carlotta was a realist. Her outlook was grounded by necessity and by her own experience. There were few or no illusions she had about herself or where she was going. Some people lived in a kind of make-believe, trying to be what they weren't, not too sure what their lives were all about. But a little poverty, a little bad luck and hard times, and you got to know who you were. What bothered Carlotta the most now, besides the physical pain, was being unable to figure out what was real and what was not.

"Hey! That's Humphrey Bogart," Billy said. "I've seen this film."

Carlotta put on a smile. "You weren't even born when this was made."

Billy looked at her defensively.

"I saw it. At the YMCA. You watch. He's going to get shot."

"He always got shot in those pictures."

Billy slumped back in the easy chair.

"I know all about this film," he mumbled.

Carlotta looked at the girls on the couch. Like two little dolls half wrapped in a blanket one of them must have dragged from their bedroom, they slept, oblivious to everything. They sucked their thumbs, so seriously, so intently.

"Lower the sound a little, Bill," she said.

As the night went on they slept. Fitfully. Carlotta with her feet propped up on the coffee table. Billy in the plump easy chair, one leg draped over the arm rest. Only the flickering television set, nearly silent, gave a semblance of life to the house.

Carlotta jerked. Her body snapped awake. She stared at the bright rectangle of sunlight against the wall beside the ventilator. Billy must have turned the television set off sometime during the night, because it was off now and he was in his own bed. The girls still slumbered on the couch, Julie's leg lying on Kim's stomach. Carlotta looked at the clock in the kitchen. It was 7:35. In half an hour she had to leave for the secretarial school. The thought depressed her.

Her head felt leaden. One of the worst night's sleep she'd ever had. She began to think about the night before. Was it only last night? The feeling, the repulsion of it all, came back to her, and with it, nausea. She struggled to her feet and went to the bathroom, where she brushed her teeth for fully five minutes.

By the hallway leading to the bedroom there was a basket of clean but unironed clothes and she dressed herself from what she could find in that rather than go to the bedroom closet. Bra, panties, a blue denim skirt. All the blouses were wrinkled. She pulled one out and put a sweater over it, hoping it was not going to be a hot day.

The alarm by the bed buzzed. She listened to it, watching the girls squirm. Billy came out, half awake, and crossed the hallway in his underwear and silenced it. Then, without looking at her, stumbled back into his own room and sat on the bed, yawning, working up the energy to get dressed.

"Thanks, Bill," Carlotta said.

What was she going to do? Every muscle in her body was sore. There was no time for coffee. Welfare was going to be mad as hell if she missed even a day of school. Carlotta felt miserable.

In the kitchen she put a bowl of fruit and a box of cornflakes on the table for their breakfast. Before leaving she wakened the girls for school. The house was stuffy, claustrophobic. She stepped out into the bright light of day, got into her car, and drove off to the secretarial school.

22

2

CARLOTTA slept in the huge bed. She woke, hearing micelike noises through the walls. Scratching and coming on through. Then she smelled something terrible. It was the stench of meat left to rot. Carlotta sprang upright.

She was struck on the left cheek. The blow spun her half around, almost knocking her over, and she put out her arm to brace herself. Then her arm was pulled out from under her. Her face was forced into the blanket. A great pressure was on the back of her head, the nape of her neck, pushing her down from behind.

She kicked behind her, touching nothing. A powerful arm grabbed her around the waist and pulled her up, so that she was on all fours. Her nightgown was lifted up over her back and—from behind—she was violated. The intense thing—the giant dimension of it—the pain of it finding so quickly the entrance and thrusting so fast inside, ramming away like that's all she was, that place, and not a human being at all.

This time the blanket onto which her face was pushed was not so perfect a gag as the night before when she had nearly suffocated under the pillow. She could half-scream through the fistful of wool. Try as that hand would, it couldn't silence the gasping, frightened half-cry of a woman in agony.

She heard a laugh. A demented laugh. Neither male nor female. Lewd, lascivious. She was being watched.

23

"Open, cunt—" the voice chortled.

Carlotta bit the hand. Was it substance she met? Yes, the teeth went into a flexible substance, but it drew away easily. A blow on the back of her head sent sparks shooting into her eyes. Why didn't he finish? The whole bed was rocking.

The light was on. Just like last night. Only this time instead of Billy with his hand on the light switch she saw their neighbor, Arnold Greenspan. Greenspan looked ridiculous. An old man with knobby knees, an overcoat thrown on over his pajamas, a tire iron in his hand. What was he going to do with that iron, a feeble old man like that? He looked scared to death.

"Mrs. Moran!" he was shouting. "Mrs. Moran!! Are you all right?"

He looked so strange, bellowing at the top of his lungs, when he was only three feet away. Why was he shouting? It was because Carlotta was screaming. She tried to stop, but her body shook in spasms and gasps.

"Mrs. Moran!!" was all he could say.

Now Billy's terror-ridden face poked in from the door under Greenspan's elbow. Carlotta was gazing blankly at both of them, shivering and quaking like some dumb beast. Greenspan was looking at her breasts, swollen and reddened, like they had been wrenched at.

"Billy," Greenspan said. "Go call the police. Tell the operator—"

Carlotta tried to clear her mind.

"No," she said. "Don't."

"Mrs. Moran," Greenspan said, "You've been—"

"I don't want the police."

Greenspan lowered the tire iron. He approached the bed. His eyes were moist. Concern seemed to tremble in the very tone of his voice.

"Wouldn't it be best to speak with someone?" he said. "They have women police."

Greenspan had no doubt what had happened. It was no nightmare as far as he was concerned.

24

"I don't want to go through all that," Carlotta said. "Leave me alone."

Greenspan watched her. The confusion in his own mind mounted. Billy came to the bed.

"The same thing happened last night," Billy said.

"Last night?" Greenspan said.

Carlotta was coming down from her hysteria. Bit by bit rational thought was weaving its way through the dark labyrinth of fear in her brain.

"Oh, God!" she wept. "God in heaven!"

Greenspan was peering hard at Carlotta.

"I remember hearing something last night," he said. "But I thought—my wife said, it was—you know—men and women, they were just fighting. I thought it was something else, but I—"

"That's all right," Carlotta said.

Only now did she become aware that the elderly gentleman was in the presence of a naked woman. She drew the sheet around her, pinning it against her side with her arm. There was an awkward silence.

"Wouldn't you like some coffee?" Greenspan said. "Some hot chocolate?"

His voice was changing. It had lost that tone of emergency. His kindness was coming through. Why did that bother Carlotta?

"No," Carlotta said. "Thank you."

"You're sure? Something? Please, Mrs. Moran. You and the children. You come over to our place. We have the room. You sleep there tonight. Tomorrow we can talk about it. You should see somebody . . ."

"No," Carlotta said. She was rational now. "I'm all right."

"Last night it was even worse," Billy said.

Suddenly Carlotta knew what was bothering her. Why had Greenspan put down the tire iron? Why didn't he think that somebody was in the house? In the closet. Why wasn't he checking the windows? She spun around. Of course the windows were still locked tight from last night. Why wasn't an old man like that afraid anymore? Why hadn't he dashed into the bathroom, slamming at something unknown behind the shower curtain with that silly and impotent weapon of his?

"You've caused yourself some harm, Mrs. Moran," Greenspan said. "You ought to be attended to."

That was it. Greenspan no longer believed the same thing he had when first he had flipped on the light and, terrified, had seen his neighbor obviously raped and beaten. Now he was too solicitous, and his concern was slightly too gentle.

"Mrs. Greenspan—she can make you something nice. She can stay here with you if you like."

He thought she was drunk. Doped up. You could see it in his eyes. They were curious, observing the symptoms, as it were, of this odd and unusual malady. She hated him for this.

"What time is it?" she said.

"Two o'clock," Billy said.

"You've been alone all evening?" Greenspan said.

"Just the children," Carlotta said. "Look. I'm fine. One of those damn crazy nightmares. Scared the daylights out of me. But I'm all right now. Really all right."

She slipped on the robe, turning modestly away from Greenspan, dressing over the sheet and then letting the sheet fall back to the bed. Christ, she had needed some sleep, she thought, as she tightened the cord around her waist.

"Let's get out of this room," she said.

They went through the hallway into the living room.

"Go on home, Mr. Greenspan," Carlotta said. "Everything is fine."

"Fine? Look, I'm not so sure—"

"Really. Fine. Absolutely."

Greenspan looked at her directly.

"Of course, I'm much older than you, but I know a lot about life. So does Mrs. Greenspan. About things. You have to talk to someone. You have to explore this

26

thing. I want you to feel free to come over and have some coffee with us. And talk. About whatever you want."

"I will," she said. "Goodnight, Mr. Greenspan."

After he left, Carlotta closed the door and locked it again. Billy looked at her. They were both silent for some time. Carlotta didn't know what to do, what to say. Her mind was reeling around and around, like a slow carousel.

"I didn't mean to kick him out," she said. "I just wanted to think by myself for a while."

"Sure, Mom."

"You think I'm going crazy?"

"Oh, Mom. Of course not."

She drew him to her. Good old Billy, she thought. Good kids were hard to find, but she had one.

"What am I going to do?" she said.

There was no answer.

It was a grisly repetition of the night before. The girls stood at the entrance to the living room. This time they were sniffling as though they were sick. Scared sick.

Carlotta sat on the couch. Her breasts felt like they had been pulled out from her chest. Billy lay down in the big easy chair, but nobody turned on the television set. Carlotta did not sleep. Because it had happened and it hadn't happened. It was and it wasn't. She had been awake and yet she had awakened from it. Her body was sore in all the tender areas. Now her mind searched through the events of the last two nights, trying to piece together an answer.

The arm—she had felt the arm. The penis—only too real. Urgent, but not really warm. But hard as could be. The weight on her. That she was not so sure about. It felt more like a pressure than an actual physical weight, more like an incredible down draft, an overwhelming gravity. There was no real sensation of something like a body on her, except for the hands and the penis.

Carlotta jumped awake. She knew she would nev-

27

er really sleep tonight. Two nights without sleep. Her head felt like it was stuffed with cotton. Every sound, every movement of the children, every buzz, creak, and scratch in the house snapped her awake.

What about the voice? The demented old voice? It came from a smaller body, it seemed, like a—she pictured a crippled old man, without legs, though she had never seen anything, either night. Had she heard the voice? Had she imagined the voice? Was there a difference?

The darkness turned to a grayness and then a slow rectangle of light was forming on the wall. Daylight. The alarm went off. Billy awoke in the easy chair, but he was too tired to move. Carlotta could not, would not rise. The buzzing continued like a soft and very angry fly. Slowly it whimpered off and went silent.

Carlotta looked at the kitchen clock. It was nearly 8:00. She had to move fast. The school took attendance and reported you for absenteeism. Her neck felt bruised. She drew the cord of her robe more tightly around her. She thought about Jer. Where was he? Six more weeks on the road. Six weeks before she would see him again. She needed him. He was solid. She needed somebody now. It was like a premonition. Life was turning over, going terrible all of a sudden. Why? She lay down heavily, folded her arms, and fell asleep.

She woke up. Billy was gone. Her groggy mind tried to piece things together. She sat on the edge of the couch, her body aching dully. It was nearly 4:00. The girls had returned from school and were out playing. She could hear them outside on the sidewalk. Then she turned and saw them through the window, writing with chalk on the cement. She went to the kitchen and reheated some coffee.

It was extremely still. She could hear the buzz of the clock on the wall. Then, everything seemed so strangely silent, like a lull between tornadoes. She thought rationally as best she could; if this thing happened one more time . . . Then what? She paused, the coffee cup suspended before her lips. Then she would clear out, that's what. Leave the house. She had the feeling that the root of all this was the house somehow. Yes, if it happened again, they'd leave—just pick up and go. Where to? Cindy? Cindy Nash would take them in. A day. Two days. Make up some story. The house has termites and they're spraying. What the hell. Cindy was a good friend. She needed no stories. They could stay there a week if they needed to. Maybe Jerry would come home earlier. He did that occasionally. He'd just drop in between cities. Quick layover for a night—sometimes a weekend. Carlotta smiled wanly. Damn. Why didn't he leave a number? Or ever think to call her? She drank the coffee. It was already lukewarm. What if Cindy couldn't take them in? What if George objected? What if? Carlotta furrowed her brow, but no answer came. There was no answer to that. Just have to wait and hope that nothing—

Billy came up the walk from school. The rest of the world was coming home from work and she was just waking up. A growing feeling of darkness hovered in her mind, as though something, perhaps her whole life, was sliding into an abyss if she didn't watch out and make exactly the right moves.

"Hi, Mom," Billy said.

"What's making *you* so happy?"

"I'm secretary of the auto mechanic's club. Down at school."

"Terrific. No kidding. I never got past B-squad cheerleader."

Billy held up a beaten, heavy gray notebook, evidently used over many semesters.

"My official ledger, see?"

"Do they know you can't spell?"

"Oh, Mom."

"Just kidding. Hey, don't throw it on the couch. I'm sleeping there tonight."

There was a silence. Billy put the books on the easy chair. He went into the bedroom, to change into old jeans

29

so he could continue to work on the engine block in the garage.

She drank some coffee. It was cold. Tonight it was going to be the couch. If that didn't help . . .

That night they watched television. Billy had gone to the store for milk and cheese crackers, which they all ate. Carlotta had undressed the girls for bed and tucked them in.

Around 11:30 she lay down on the couch and drew the blanket over her. Billy said nothing, but he left the door to his own bedroom open. Carlotta lay still, thinking about the last two nights. As time passed, she grew more and more worried. About the noises in the house, the unfamiliar sight of distant automobile headlights tracing distorted rectangles over the hallway, and she could not sleep. Then she realized the couch was hurting her back. Every possible position either hit a button or a bulge; there was no flat, hard surface. Her muscles were being strained no matter how she lay. She finally tried lying on her right side, staring into the darkness.

At about 2:30 she must have been dozing because she jerked awake. It was the ventilator. A tiny *ping* as the thermostat dropped off. She listened intently. Nothing. She could hear the children breathing in their rooms. Outside—nothing.

She closed her eyes but could not sleep. Slowly she drifted in a semi-consciousness, an awareness of half-formed images rising up out of the retinal chaos. Then she slept.

Through the next day, Saturday, a faint optimism prevailed in the house. Nothing unusual had happened. Except for a sore lower back, Carlotta was in good spirits. She took them all to Griffith Park, several acres of high wooded hills which, in Los Angeles, passes for wilderness. With all the families out there, Carlotta felt once again a part of the human race, doing what everybody did, feeling the way everybody felt. Even the kids seemed in an unusually lively mood. Billy found a softball game to throw himself into. They returned exhausted, late in the afternoon.

Sunday, too, passed in a normal way. Carlotta cleaned up, except for the bedroom. Billy was out with some mechanics, building, taking apart, who knew exactly what? The girls watched TV. Carlotta practiced her shorthand. It was boring, but necessary. So the hours passed. A normal day. Even the night was uneventful.

But with Monday the mood changed. Mr. Reisz, the incredibly thin and demanding instructor in shorthand and typing, called attention to Carlotta's score. Her accuracy and speed rate were dropping. She hadn't even noticed. It bothered her, because she had been doing so well. What if she couldn't make it as a secretary? What if that turned out to be a rougher road than she had pictured? Was she getting trapped in some kind of failure, some kind of system designed to frustrate her? Was there some limitation in her make-up? Suddenly, it was disturbing her, this little problem with her accuracy and speed rate. Suddenly she was afraid of not being able to cope.

When she walked into the house that night the children were in a rotten state of affairs. Tension was filling the house, but nobody could tell why. Julie and Kim were scrapping on the floor. In retrospect, it all had some incredible, ominous significance, but at the time it made no particular impression on Carlotta.

"Julie hit me with the ashtray," Kim wailed.

"I did not!"

"She did!"

"Did not!"

"Shut up," Carlotta said. "Let me see."

Sure enough. An angry red mark was rising along the back of Kim's neck.

"See? She threw it at my head!"

But Julie protested her innocence. Carlotta knew, the way a mother knows, that Julie was telling the truth.

"Don't look at *me*," Billy said. "What do you think, I get my kicks beaning little kids with ashtrays?"

"Okay. Okay," Carlotta said. "Let's all scream at

each other. Look. Mother is not in the mood to handle this sort of thing, so silence is the best idea for a while. All right?"

A moody silence prevailed.

"Well, *I didn't*," Billy muttered.

Two days with no problems at night. But on that couch, her back was going to go out permanently. Carlotta hated doctors. It always meant more pain with them. Besides, with a good night's sleep on her own firm mattress, it would probably repair itself. This wasn't the first time. Carlotta opened the door to her bedroom and peeked in.

The sight of the enormous bed with its heavy carved wood, its ridiculous European angels, now took on a sinister aspect, a kind of mocking, grinning look. The covers and sheets were still on the floor from the last time she had slept there. With only a slight trepidation, she entered the room. No odor. Nothing out of place besides the sheets. She stripped the bed and made it afresh.

It was 11:10. She needed rest. She needed to improve her score at school. She needed to impress Mr. Reisz. She had to show herself she was back on the right track. She slipped into the cold, fresh sheets and closed her eyes.

Time passed very slowly. Her body felt comforted by the hard mattress, suspended, tranquilized. Yet she dozed fitfully. Her eyes kept opening. She had left the door to the hallway open. And she knew that Billy was leaving the door from his room open, too. Just in case.

It was probably around midnight. The light bulb behind the clock face had gone out. Had it blown out? Carlotta peered at it through the darkness. Why had she awakened? She listened.

Nothing. She gazed in front of her in the darkness, could dimly make out the vague form of the dresser, the mirror, and the distant reflection of the bed in the darkness.

She breathed deeply. Nothing. No smell. Nothing wrong. Then why had she awakened? Then she had a premonition, a kind of impression. That *something* was com-

32

ing. Coming to her from many miles away over a broken-up landscape, and it was going to be there in a fraction of a second. She bolted out of bed.

"Bill!"

Billy scrambled out of bed. Carlotta leaped into the hallway, draping herself in a dress, buttoning buttons. She met Billy by the door.

"There's something coming," she said.

There was a crash behind her. She turned. The lamp had toppled from the nightstand. Now the nightstand was heaved against the wall. She slammed the door behind her.

"Let's get out of here!" she cried.

The whole bedroom behind the door was crashing with thrown furniture. Then the sound of the mirror as it smashed into tiny pieces.

"Mom—" Billy was staring at her, terrified.

"Grab Kim," she yelled. "I'll take Julie!"

They ran into the girls' bedroom. Billy swept up Kim, the blanket draped over the little girl's legs.

"Should I take the blanket?!" Billy yelled.

He was panicked.

"Yes! Yes! Take it! Get out!"

Something—shoes—a dressing table full of cosmetics—slammed against the inside of the door. As they ran into the hallway she could see the door bulge and a crack begin to form in the cheap wood.

"Holy Christ!" Carlotta said.

They ran into the living room. It sounded like the bedroom was being torn apart, piece by piece, as fast as possible. Not like an explosion, but like someone systematically doing it, one thing after the other, angry, venting his fury on the objects at not finding Carlotta there. Suddenly the draperies—heavy cloth draperies—were ripped like tissue paper and the sound reverberated through the house.

"Damn! Damn!" Carlotta cried out.

Tears of fear and rage coursed down her cheeks. She was at the front door, but with Julie in her arms she

33

couldn't slip the bolt. She leaned forward, pinning the girl against the door. Julie involuntarily whimpered in pain. But it gave Carlotta the chance to pull the bolt. Something shot against the closed bedroom door and splintered into fragments.

"*CUNT!*" roared the voice.

They ran out into the night and got into the car. Behind them it seemed as though the bedroom—what was left of it—was being broken apart, as though a wrecking crew were attacking it inside with a ball. Carlotta slipped the car into reverse, shot backwards into somebody's shrubbery, recovered, and spun the tires, squealing and roaring, out into Kentner Street.

"Christ did you *hear* that, Billy?"

Billy said nothing. Petrified, Carlotta whirled on him.

"Didn't you *hear* it?"

"Yeah, Ma, yeah."

Billy was looking at her, strangely she thought. His eyes glistened with tears.

Carlotta shot through a red light, past the lonely intersection. There was nobody around. She drove without thinking through a labyrinth of streets, past similar looking dark, shaded houses.

"Slow down, Mom," Billy said. "You're going fifty."

Carlotta looked down at the speedometer, then eased a bit on the accelerator. The panic of the flight had blinded her to what she was doing. She was operating in a vacuum, by pure instinct, like a frightened animal.

"Where the hell are we?" she said.

"We're near Colorado Avenue," Billy said. "It's over there, behind the factory."

Instinctively, she drove to Colorado Avenue. She slowed down a little more. To forty miles an hour.

"Listen, kids," she said, checking the hysteria in her voice. "We're going to be all right. You got that? You guys okay?"

She turned and over her shoulder saw Julie in the

back seat. She was silent. Sick—scared and silent. In the front seat, still wrapped in her blanket, Kim gasped, too petrified to even cry. With amusement through the fiery panic, Carlotta saw that Billy was in his underwear.

"Better wrap that blanket around yourself, Bill," she said. "I'm going to Cindy's."

She drove up Colorado, turned north, and was driving, now within the speed limit, toward the bright lights of the movie theaters and motels which signified West Hollywood.

"Where the hell—"

"Turn left," Billy said, tucking the blanket around himself. "It's almost all the way into Hollywood."

Miraculously, as though driving by itself, the car found its way into the streets which looked familiar: dark, cracked, crowded single-dwelling places being over-run with large apartment blocks.

"There it is," Billy said.

Carlotta pulled up in front of a huge pink building. It said *El Escobar* on the front. That was about the only thing which distinguished it from the other apartment complexes down the street. And the red and blue globes which were somebody's idea of exotic lighting, now making the palm trees in front look like horrible, sickly plants.

They climbed up the stairs, Billy holding the blanket to keep from tripping.

"Listen," Carlotta said. "Let me do all the talking. Whatever I say, that's what happened. If anybody ever asks you about anything when I'm not around, you say the same thing." She looked around. The girls nodded.

"Sure, Mom," Billy said.

Carlotta pressed the doorbell. What a ridiculous appearance they were going to make, she thought. The sound of the doorbell—a buzzer—seemed to split open the night. But no one came. She pressed it again. What if no one answered? Then a hand parted the drapes slowly at the window. Immediately the door opened.

"Carlotta!" Cindy said. "Billy! What—"

"Oh, Cindy!"

"Don't cry, honey. Come on in. Everybody. Come on in."

Cindy was in her bathrobe, her hair in high, huge curlers, but to Carlotta she seemed beautiful. Especially now. In the tiny apartment, the gold carpet, frayed at the edges, the walls which cracked in two years, the look-alike chairs and table in the kitchen—the kind of apartment multiplied by tens of thousands all over the city—it seemed like the most desirable and blessed of havens to Carlotta.

"What was it?" Cindy asked. "A fire?"

"No," Carlotta said. "We . . . got thrown out of our place."

"You got thrown out? By who?"

"We—just had to get out . . ."

"Had to . . . I don't get it. What happened?"

The girls started to cry.

"Aw, kids. Look," Cindy said. "You want to stay here, is that it? Sure."

Cindy stirred from the chair in front of Carlotta. She went to the hall closet and returned with an armful of blankets and a few pillows. In the open doorway to the bedroom Carlotta could hear Cindy's husband George snoring grumpily. Miraculously, he had slept through the whole thing.

"Thanks, Cindy," Carlotta said. "I don't know what I'd have done—"

"What are friends for?" Cindy said.

She put the girls under two blankets on the couch. Billy curled up into some huge pillows nearby. Cindy leaned over and whispered to Carlotta.

"It's man trouble? It's Jerry, isn't it?"

"No, no. He's out of town for another six weeks."

"You want to tell me alone? When the kids are gone?"

"Okay. I'd appreciate that."

Cindy tucked in the girls. Carlotta slipped off her dress and lay on the floor.

36

"You going to survive like that?" Cindy asked anxiously.

"It's actually better for my back."

"Okay. Listen, you guys. The bathroom is right there. Go ahead if you want."

"God bless you, Cindy," Carlotta said. "I'm so sorry—"

"Nonsense. We'll talk about it in the morning."

"Goodnight," Julie said. It was so absurd. As though she were camping out, being polite, knowing nothing of why she was there.

"Goodnight, doll," Cindy said. "You all get some sleep."

"Goodnight, Cindy," Carlotta said.

Through the thin walls of the bedroom Carlotta heard Cindy telling something to George. George grumbled a bit but she silenced him after a while. In the silence of Cindy's apartment Billy was already asleep. So were the girls. The panic was relaxing its grip on Carlotta. She felt increasingly drained of energy with every passing second. Then tears began to form in her eyes. Tears of exhaustion, frustration, fear. She was crying, but making no sound. Then she was through, too tired for tears, or for thoughts. She fell asleep. They all slept. Without dreams.

3

THE sunshine brightened the daisies on the kitchen table and made the floor glitter. Cindy sat perplexed.

"You actually saw these things come through the wall?"

"I didn't see them," Carlotta said. "It felt like that. I sensed it."

"These animals?"

"I don't know what they were."

"So what did they do?"

"Not much," Carlotta lied. "They just, you know, walked all over, tried to touch me—"

"Jesus!"

"Scratched on the wall. Knocked things over."

"You sure you were awake?"

"Cindy, I swear. I was awake as I am now. Don't you think I've thought of all that a thousand times? I was absolutely awake. I was sweating scared, bug-eyed, awake."

Cindy shook her head and whistled.

"How long has this been going on?"

"Almost a week. It happened twice, then it started happening again last night and I freaked out. I grabbed the kids and ran. I just couldn't stand it anymore."

"I don't blame you," Cindy said.

Cindy furrowed her brow in thought.

"Well," she said finally, "you're not insane. I

know you pretty well. If you were scared, there was a reason. You're one of the most stable persons I know."

"Then what do you think it is?" Carlotta said. Cindy remained staring into her coffee cup, and she said nothing for the longest time. Then she looked up at Carlotta.

"Jerry."

"What?"

"It's Jerry. He's at the bottom of this, sure as I'm sitting in front of you," Cindy said.

Carlotta inhaled from the cigarette. On the television screen a master of ceremonies smiled at an audience of middle-aged women from the Midwest, but the sound was low and it was only a silent blue flickering presence, absurd, erratic, and meaningless.

"You don't buy that," Cindy said.

"No."

"Look. When somebody caves in, it's from some central problem. I mean, people don't just decide that Thursday would be a good day to have a breakdown, do they?"

"I don't know."

"Of course not. It's always one big thing, something basic to their lives which is eating at them."

Carlotta squinted at the tiny television screen. Then she turned back to Cindy.

"What exactly are you trying to say, Cindy?"

As though given the signal to release her pent-up philosophy of life, Cindy leaned forward and began talking rapidly and forcefully.

"You are suffering and you don't know it. You've been avoiding it. You've been pretending everything is fine and dandy when it isn't. And Jerry is at the bottom of it all."

"I don't see the connection—"

"Of course not. It's never direct. Think of my aunt, the one who flipped out. What connection was there between talking to the nonexistent FBI in her living room and her real problem? None. Her real problem was being rejected by her daughter, that stinker, Jewel. The dumb kid had run off with an artist, lived in the midst of garbage and wanted money. Threatened suicide if she didn't get it. The whole seamy works. Drove my aunt crazy. But you see, there was no direct connection. It's always indirect, kind of around the corner. You've got to be able to see into the real problem. You've got to know what's really going on inside you."

"How does what's happening to me tie in with Jerry?"

"He wants to marry you, doesn't he?"

"I couldn't tell you, Cindy. Our relationship was never that . . . defined. You know, we just had fun together. We like being together. I don't know if Jerry wants to get married. But we're kind of in it together, maybe a little more than we had thought at first."

"Yes, but having fun is one thing. Being married is another."

Carlotta sighed softly.

"You should be a psychiatrist."

Cindy beamed.

"I know. That's because I read a lot," she said. "Look. Don't be afraid. These decisions get made. If you're smart, they get made in the right way."

"Well," Carlotta said, "maybe it's good to get it all out into the open. I honestly never thought about it just like that. I mean, who knows, you may have a point."

Cindy put a hand on Carlotta's arm. To her surprise, the arm was warm, almost perspiring. A wave of pity stabbed Cindy's heart.

"You just think about it. There's no problem you can't face. Just be honest with yourself."

"Okay. It seems very remote, but I'll think about it."

"Everything will come out all right," Cindy said.

On the television screen a well-dressed man in a business suit stood behind a lectern. It appeared that he was selling something with his white smile, and then he held up a huge Bible and thrust it at the camera. It seemed to Carlotta that he had thrust it at her.

In the night Carlotta woke. Bones ached. Headache. Where was she? George snored softly in the next room. The lights from cars passed over the living-room wall. There was Billy, his hair falling in his eyes, screening his face. The girls asleep in the shadows. How peaceful. Not a breeze stirred. Only vague thoughts. Thoughts beneath words. How did it come to this, that I am sleeping on Cindy's floor? Yes, I remember. I am still sore. What is going on in me? Outside of me? What am I anymore?

But she was safe here. It was impossible that anything could happen here. There were too many people. Cindy would come to the rescue. While George slept. Everybody but George would witness it. Witness Carlotta's insanity. She saw herself surrounded by doctors in a long corridor, struggling, screaming. Was that how it was? When you went over the edge, were you yourself anymore? Did you know your name? What were you then?

So the images of the last nights danced about in her brain: the flashing lights, the taste of cotton stuffed in her mouth, the overwhelming sensation of—of—that—that—Carlotta could no longer tell. It was neither dream nor reality. And who in the whole apartment, who in the entire city of Los Angeles, could tell her what it was?

The following day passed pleasantly. Carlotta skipped school. Instead, she and Cindy went shopping. Cindy bought a leather purse on Olvera Street, where Mexican crafts lined the ancient cobblestone road in a festoon of piñatas and colored pottery. They went home and played backgammon till it was time for Carlotta to make the long drive to West Los Angeles to pick up the kids. All in all, a pleasant day. Relaxing. The autumn sun had been good for Carlotta, like a health cure, almost. The air almost clear, fresh, and the cries of the children and the festive Mexican music—it was cheerful again. Only a small stone in the bottom of her mind, which neither of them talked about.

But as night came on Cindy could see a personality

change right in front of her eyes. Carlotta became nervous, afraid. Was there something more on her mind? More than even seeing things in the dark? Cindy wondered.

Then George came home. His shirt was ringed under the arms. He hesitated when he saw Carlotta. Then he went without a word to the bathroom. There was a rumble of pipes and then the shower began to roar. Its sound was furious.

"Is he mad at me?" Carlotta whispered.

"No, that's just George," Cindy said.

"Look. If it's inconvenient——"

"Not at all."

"I mean it——"

"Love your company. Stay as long as you like."

"It seemed like George——"

"Forget him. He came out of the womb with a frown."

Cindy seized the moment. She gestured toward the door with a barely perceptible toss of the head. Carlotta was puzzled.

"I have to speak to you," Cindy said. "Let's go outside."

They went out the door and closed it behind them.

Cindy looked Carlotta in the eye.

"There's something you haven't told me," Cindy said. "What is it?"

"I've told you everything."

Cindy saw the evasive look in Carlotta's face. Whatever it was she was keeping back, it had a hold on her. But how far can you push your friends?

"The only thing in the world I want, Carly," Cindy said, "is to see you pull yourself together. You believe that?"

"Of course I do."

"If you don't want me to help you, I can't."

"Honest to God, Cindy. I'm being straight with you."

42

But Carlotta's eyes hid some dark, evasive truth, and if Cindy wanted it, she was going to have to pry it out.

Cindy pulled Carlotta further from the apartment door. Down below the pump gurgled water over the rocks of the imitation Hawaiian waterfall. Over the alley roofs behind the building two cats ran hissing and spitting across the red tiles. The sun was going down, a distant orange ball through the haze. Carlotta shivered in the strange and sudden chill.

"Are you on drugs?" Cindy said softly, afraid.

"Drugs? Me? Heavens, no!"

Cindy looked into Carlotta's eyes. She searched them quickly.

"People take drugs, and then they see things," Cindy said. "Even when they don't want to, sometimes."

"God is my witness, Cindy. I never touched a thing."

"Franklin Moran was hooked."

Carlotta balked. The memory of that rough, rugged face with its little-boy grin came into her mind. That and the sick-weird nights, followed by the sweet-sad mornings—

"But *I* never did," Carlotta said softly. "I never took a thing. That was one thing that came between us. The first thing," she added with a touch of bitterness.

Cindy hesitated.

"Then what is it?"

"It's nothing. I mean I don't want to talk about it," Carlotta said.

"I don't mean to push, Carlotta, but you can't hide this thing because it will destroy you if you try."

Carlotta suddenly looked up. She had been trying to light her cigarette, but the cold breeze snuffed out match after match. When she looked up there were tears in her eyes.

"I was raped," Carlotta said.

Cindy's hand went instinctively to her mouth. She was stunned.

"Raped," Carlotta tried to say again, the unlit cigarette quivering in her mouth, but the word came out almost inaudible.

"Oh, dear God," Cindy whispered.

Carlotta turned away. Would this feeling of being rotten never leave her? Once again she felt soiled from head to foot, immersed in it, and there was no way to get clean.

"Dear God," was all Cindy could say. Then the tears appeared in her eyes, too, and she reached out gently and put her hand on Carlotta's shoulder. Then the two women embraced. "I'm sorry—I didn't know—I didn't even guess—oh, baby!" was all Cindy could manage.

"Oh, Cindy," Carlotta wept, "it was—I feel like— ruined—just ruined all to hell inside—"

"Baby, baby—oh, my God! How could it happen?"

"I was all alone in my room and something grabbed me—smothered me—I nearly fainted—the whole world went dark—"

Carlotta pulled back from Cindy. She seemed to grow strangely cold. The night breeze blew her hair, lifted it gently across her forehead, the dark eyes suddenly far away and cold from Cindy.

"You don't understand, do you?" Carlotta said.

"Of course, I—"

"I wasn't lying about the thing coming through the wall."

Cindy only stared at her.

"What in God's name are you talking about?" Cindy whispered.

"Don't you see? It was and it wasn't—I was raped and beaten, but there was nobody there—I nearly died and when they turned the lights on I was all alone."

Cindy could not comprehend.

"Did you call the police?" she whispered at last.

"Cindy, Cindy, good old normal Cindy! I was *alone* in my bed—when they turned the lights on. This—man —whoever, whatever he was—vanished—gone—just simply gone like a bad dream—"

Cindy's hand remained immobile at her own throat, in the posture of one who cannot understand the simplest points of the most extraordinary phenomenon even when she is hearing them.

"I don't understand," Cindy said. "You were—attacked, or you weren't—?"

"Of course I was. He beat me. He almost strangled me. Then he used me—terribly. And when the light went on he vanished like—like he was never there."

Cindy leaned against the railing. She could see that Carlotta had told the truth. She could tell by the way Carlotta tried to avoid her eyes, the pretty face hidden in shame and humiliation, the memory of the assault still burning in her imagination, and now a terrible fear began to fill her eyes. Carlotta whirled on Cindy.

"You see? You see?" Carlotta implored. "There's no answer, is there? It's true and it's not true. It happened and it didn't. I flipped out! I flipped out, Cindy! Twice!"

"It happened again?"

"The next night! Why do you think I ran the hell out of there when it started the third time?"

"But now, when you're here with me—?"

"Everything's fine with you. But I don't know how long it's going to last. I'm afraid to go home. I'm afraid to be by myself."

"Of course," Cindy said. But she was confused. "I don't blame you."

For a long time neither spoke. Even though it was cold, they remained standing in silence. The blue night was now illuminated by the red and green bulbs in the palms below. Carlotta was shivering with cold. Cindy, usually so sharp and quick, was lost in the endless labyrinths of her own thinking. There was simply no way to figure it out. No way at all.

"Then you stay here, Carlotta," Cindy said. "As long as you need to."

Carlotta nodded. She gazed vacantly out into space, trying to will her mind into focus once again. She blew her nose into a small handkerchief. She straightened down the hair lifting up in the cold breeze.

"But I think," Cindy said, "that you should see a psychiatrist."

"I can't afford a shrink."

"You can go to a clinic."

"Not for mental problems."

"You are definitely wrong. You can go to the clinic at the university. Payment is strictly optional, and if you're on welfare, the payment is zilch."

Carlotta nodded. She smiled.

"You think I'm loony?" Carlotta said.

"I don't know. But it scares me."

"Okay. What do you say we go inside?"

Cindy nodded. The two women held hands as they turned and walked to the apartment door, then dropped them as they were about to enter.

"Don't tell George," Cindy said. "He's a bit strait-laced about things."

"I wouldn't have told anybody in the world but you," Carlotta whispered back.

"Okay. Smile. Here we go."

And Cindy opened the door. Inside Billy and the girls looked up. Suspiciously, Carlotta thought. Searching her face for hidden signs. They seemed to know instinctively when she was involved in that—horror—almost as though they could read her mind, and then they returned to the Jr. Anagrams game spread out on the kitchen table. George came in with a folded newspaper, looked briefly at Carlotta and then at Cindy.

"Is it possible to eat in this place?" he said.

"Just a minute, George," Cindy said.

"Christ," George mumbled.

George fiddled with the television dial. Billy dropped several anagram pieces on the floor. Carlotta felt in her purse for a paperback, sat down, and pretended to read. It seemed like every time she talked about it, thought about it, it was there again, dominating her life, her entire world, like a haze that surrounded her. Malevolent. Bad-smelling. Cindy humming in the kitchen was the only sound of cheer.

Thursday passed. Friday. A slight smell of ozone entered the evening air. It depressed Carlotta.

Julie and Kim slept on the couch. Billy slept against the wall beside the television set. George grumbled as he stepped over Billy in the morning. Supper was silent and moody. George shoveled peas onto his fork and mashed them down with a knife.

Carlotta did not go to a psychiatrist. The problem was becoming more remote. The world was re-forming itself into something less fearsome, more friendly. She felt good physically. Sleeping on the floor was better for her back. Being with Cindy was a good thing. It made things whole again.

During the day she sat stiffly behind an enormous typewriter at the Carter School of Secretarial Arts. The tall, thin Mr. Reisz, whose crew cut had grown considerably thinner since the long lost days of his youth, walked up and down the aisles with a stopwatch in his hand. The room was filled with the clatter of forty typewriters in feverish activity.

"And . . . stop!" Mr. Reisz called. "Thirty words. Who typed thirty words a minute? Thirty-five? Excellent. Forty. Did anybody type forty words?"

Carlotta raised a hand. Mr. Reisz strolled over. He studied her results.

"Watch the capitals," he said. "Firm. It's a firm, sharp hit."

Across the aisle another girl answered for her friend.

"Juanita," she said. "Juanita typed forty words, sir."

Mr. Reisz strolled behind the desk. He frowned.

"Tell her the little finger is still weak," he said. "Don't turn the wrist. Just give it a short, firm hit."

It was translated into Spanish. Mr. Reisz returned to the desk in front of the rows. The school was under sub-

47

contract to the County of Los Angeles. Most of the girls, a lively, giggling bunch, were on welfare, several of them pregnant again.

Carlotta looked out the window. Some lanky adolescents were jump-shooting basketballs into the hoop on the adjacent blacktop yard. Their faces shined with perspiration. It was a lazy, hot day, smelling inside of old sweeping compound, a faint aroma of mildew, and the fine dust which sifted from nowhere onto the desks and windows.

How beautiful life is, thought Carlotta. Who would have imagined that a minister's daughter from Pasadena would be happy banging out capital letters for the welfare board? Yet she was happy here. She liked the girls, the angular Mr. Reisz, so absurdly formal and yet considerate, and she liked to improve herself, day by day with a numerical score. When all is said and done, thought Carlotta, it's the simple, ordinary things that make for a good life. The things Bob Garrett had believed in, and had taught her. The little details that you can embroider into a rich and full way of feeling.

The nightmare of the last week passed into an imperceptible cloud, hanging farther and farther away on the mental horizon, and with it, any thought of a psychiatrist.

Carlotta was afraid of psychiatrists. People who went to them never got any better. Here, with Cindy, she was safe. She was in a fortress of security with walls ten feet thick. She had time to think things through carefully, to reconstruct the past. She lay in the bathtub, and the soft light came in through house plants hung at the window, throwing cool rays over the sparkling bubble bath.

What was the condition of her house? It might be a charred ruin by now, with only the toilet and refrigerator poking up out of the blackened rubble. She could envision Mr. Greenspan rushing around in his underwear, trying to direct the firemen. Crowds standing by watching

48

bricks and pipes flying around in space. But her thoughts seemed incredible to her. They seemed like something a mental case might conjure up in her worst seizures. The world was not like that. Carlotta felt like a giant bird, circling and circling, gently approaching the earth once again. Now everything was back in focus, back to reality, and there were no more fantasies.

She stepped out of the tub and dried her shoulders with an enormous yellow towel. Her brow was furrowed, thinking: She ought to find out. She ought to go to the house. Should she wait to pick up Billy at school so they could go together? Or should she go now with the sun still full in the sky? She slipped on her bra and panties. In the bedroom she dressed in a shirt and jeans borrowed from Cindy. She had no clothes of her own at Cindy's and couldn't afford to buy any.

Carlotta combed her hair. In the mirror her face seemed pretty once again. Tranquility had returned the softness to her small features. She felt confidence returning. So she went out the door, car keys in her hand.

She stopped the car a little before the dead end of Kentner Street. The exterior of the house looked completely normal. She stared at it for a moment. There was not a thing out of place anywhere. Then she got out of the car.

When she opened the door, she was struck by the dry heat which filled the house. It was oppressive, stifling, breath-sucking. She went to the thermostat. It must have been jostled the night everybody ran, because it stood at 93 degrees. She turned it off. It was quiet inside. A few flies buzzed around the unwashed dishes by the kitchen sink.

Julie's slipper lay on the hallway floor, where it must have fallen that night. Carlotta peered into the girls' bedroom. Only the teddy bears, a few books, some underwear on the chair. She picked out several things for the girls from the drawers. It seemed even more quiet there.

Not even a sound of traffic could be heard. Then she went out into the hallway and stared at the closed door of her own bedroom.

She studied the door. No cracks. No burn marks. Nothing. She eased it open with her foot. Inside the sheets were fallen from the bed. A lamp lay on the floor, the shade stepped on and bent. She pushed the door wider. A bottle of cologne lay on the hardwood floor. The room smelled of violets.

She went inside the room a few feet. It was a little cooler there. The windows were open. Had she left them open? Now she saw that the night table was tipped over against the wall, and a scratch showed where it had scraped against the plaster. Several more bottles of lotion could be seen behind the bureau. Where was all the torn plaster, the gouged walls, the exploded ceiling? It looked like the material remains of one person's panic. Somebody had freaked out from bed, knocking over the night table, smashed into the bureau, and had dragged the sheets halfway to the door. That was all. Amazed, Carlotta circled slowly through the room.

It looked so very normal. In the sense that there was nothing inhuman about it. She could see very plainly what had happened. She was almost sorry for the frightened person she had been, to have reacted in that way. She slowly closed the windows and locked them.

Carlotta opened the closet door. It was dark inside. She couldn't find the little metal chain for the light bulb, so she had to lean forward, peering into the dark maze of skirts, jeans, and dresses. She selected a few and laid them over her arm carefully.

She heard a distant growl.

She stood erect. She listened. Nothing. She turned around. Nothing. She keened her senses. She smelled the room. Nothing. She waited. A bird called from the hedges outside. A boy went by on a bicycle. She turned cautiously back into the closet. There was a distant sound, a low, metallic rumble which vibrated the window pane. Carlotta whirled again and stepped out of the closet. The

50

sound intensified, was guttural. It seemed to be trying to articulate, with great difficulty, some kind of human sound. Carlotta backed to the door, which was closed. Fumbling behind her, she found the knob.

The growl subsided. Carlotta opened the door a crack and listened. Was it in the hallway? She was afraid to leave the bedroom. She slowly pressed the door closed again, leaning against it, listening with her ear against the door. Then it rose again, a low, rumbling, belching sound which wavered and changed pitch, but which made no sense.

Carlotta ran to the window. High overhead, two white trails arched over the Southland heavens, the jets invisible, but their roar like a double, demented thunder which shook the window pane, growing louder and louder.

Carlotta looked up at the unending blue sky. It seemed so pure. So deep. Like an infinite sleep. The vapor trails slowly disintegrated, leaving feathery billows fading into the pale blue depths. The sun was warm and friendly on her face.

So it was jets. No voice. No voice at all. I made it into a voice. Am I dreaming? Or have I awakened?

She moved away from the window and went into Billy's room. She picked out several T-shirts, underpants, blue jeans, and some plaid shirts. She carried the bundle of clothes to the car and piled them into the back seat. The slender trees wavered briskly in the fresh breeze as she drove away.

When Carlotta and the children walked into the apartment she could sense there was something on her friend's mind. But all Cindy said was, "You sure look fit as a fiddle."

"I am," Carlotta said. "I feel good."

"Great. That's great."

An awkward silence hung in the air. Cindy smiled uncertainly at Carlotta then turned to wipe her hands on a towel hanging from a rack. Cindy began to grate cheese.

51

Later that evening Billy said, "Hey, Mom. When are we going to go?"

Carlotta tried to ignore the question, but Billy persisted.

"I got stuff in the garage. I can't just leave it forever."

"It's not forever."

"Then when are we going back?"

Carlotta sighed. "Soon."

That night Carlotta lay on her back, watching the ceiling. A thin strand of dust wavered in a cross-current of air, dangling near the cut-glass chandelier. She heard muffled voices from the bedroom. She turned her head. A light was still on inside, though the door was closed.

"Well, why *didn't* you tell her?" George grumbled.

"Oh, George," Cindy whimpered. "I couldn't."

"I warned you, Cindy."

"She's got no place to go, George."

Carlotta rose up on her elbow, straining to hear. There was some indistinct mumbling.

"Shhhhh!" Cindy said.

"I don't care if she hears," George said.

Cindy began to sniffle.

"Oh, Christ," George murmured.

"I'm sorry, George," Cindy whimpered.

"Jesus."

"See? I'm not crying."

Cindy sniffled several times. She blew her nose. The room was silent. Then the light went off inside. Carlotta knew that the protection of Cindy's apartment was beginning to fade away like a morning dew.

"You know what to do?" George said.

"Yes."

"When?"

Cindy mumbled something.

"When?" George repeated.

"Tomorrow," Cindy said. "In the morning."

"Well, just make sure you do."

"Oh, George."

52

"I got to get up at seven. Some of us work, you know."

Then it was silent. Carlotta lay back on her mattress of blankets. She looked at the ceiling and bit her lip. What the hell? she thought. Now what?

The morning sunshine radiated through the grimy windshield causing Carlotta to squint her way through the familiar streets of West Los Angeles. Billy sat silently at her right. In the back seat Julie and Kim fussed noisily.

"Hey, cut that out," Carlotta said over her shoulder. "No fighting."

She breathed a sigh of relief when she let them off at their school corner. Relief followed by a tinge of guilt for messing up their lives so.

She would be late for her own class this morning, but it couldn't be helped. There was this thing she had to do first at Cindy's.

Cindy was ironing when Carlotta returned to the apartment. Their preliminary exchange was forced, unnatural. Then Carlotta said: "I really got to thank you, Cindy. For all you've done."

"My pleasure. You know that."

"I mean, it's been a week and all. I didn't think it would be that long. Honest."

"Look, Carlotta, I wish I could—"

"I feel really great again. And I don't think those nightmares are going to happen anymore. I think it's time we split. You know?"

"Really, I don't know. If you feel okay . . ."

"I do. I really do. Just fine."

"Because you're welcome here, you know . . ."

"I know. I know I am. But it's been long enough. The kids miss their home. I didn't mean to move in, for heaven's sake."

"George, you know, he has his problems—"

"George is really fine, to let us stay. Tell him that. We really appreciated him."

"I'll tell him."

There was another silence. Carlotta clearly did not want to get up and begin packing the children's clothes. Cindy stirred her coffee, though it must have been cold by now.

"You going home?" Cindy asked.

"I think it's best."

"I don't know. I've been thinking, Carly. Maybe you should move out of that house."

"That's impossible."

"Why?"

"I have a lease. If I don't honor it, welfare will."

Cindy shook her head. "So you're stuck there?" she said.

"I don't think it's the house, anyway. I think it's me."

"I'm not so sure. Nothing's happened here in a week. Everything's been fine here."

"For which I thank you, Cindy. You've given me the chance to get my head together."

Cindy sighed. "Still, I worry about you."

"I'll be all right. Tell you what. I'll spend a couple of days with my mother."

"Your mother? Carlotta—"

"Sure. A couple of days in Pasadena. A big house like she's got. Room for the kids to run around. Julie and Kim have never met my mother."

"I know."

"Couple of days. Big breakfasts out on the patio. You know, the works. That's all I need."

"Well," Cindy said uncertainly. "You know best."

It was silent again. But this time Cindy was softened. She knew exactly what Pasadena meant to Carlotta. She blew her nose.

"I'm sorry, Carlotta. I just wish—"

"Forget it, Cindy. I really enjoyed being with you and George, now it's time to go. That's all there is to it."

"Okay, okay," Cindy said, looking away, putting her chin on her hand, then more abstractly: "Okay, okay . . ."

Carlotta rose from the table. She looked at the jum-

ble of pajamas, borrowed from Cindy and George, looking improbably large on the couch right now. The thought
of moving filled her with dread.

"Wasn't there a case for the sleeping bag?" Carlotta
asked.

"Yes. It's in the closet. I'll get it."

Cindy walked to the closet. The clock on the wall
bonged a mournful hour. Neither spoke. Carlotta felt herself sinking into a depression.

4

FIFTEEN minutes from Pasadena Carlotta began to recognize the old estates, the dry hills with their strange,
withered brown grass, and the high concrete embank-
ments covered with ivy. The night seemed to condense a
peculiar fog that made the houses look evanescent. As
the freeway rumbled by under the car, Carlotta became
more and more aware of the darkness closing in, as
though the road and the night together were forming a
tunnel in front of her.

Up the fourth ramp, she knew, was the road that
arched over the dampened concrete bridge, dripping in
the fog. It led, dark and narrow, down to Orange Grove
Boulevard. Then the road widened, and on both sides
were the preposterous, imposing houses, broad lawns,
and immense palm trees. There, too, she knew—she
could almost smell them in the wet air—were the bitter
lives, the grasping, uncertain ghosts with the elusive and
ambiguous smiles.

Smells came to her, as her memory roamed the dark
rooms, the heavy curtains, the hallways that led from the
grand piano to the patio, and then, on the other side, to
the rose gardens. At night the rose gardens smelled like
dust and chemical spray. Her mother would work in the
garden at night, her gloved hands sprinkling white poison
in the roses. Carlotta wondered why her mother waited
until night to tend the roses. She only came back in when
her father snored—a soft, wheezing snore. She never

went to bed when he was awake. Nor did they speak. Their lives were as perfectly silent as the moonlight that glistened off the snails and the thorns.

But it was in the gestures that they communicated. Sharp, erratic, nervous gestures. Broken dishes, smashed glasses communicated some mysterious tension that ran like a river through the house. And somehow, it was Carlotta's fault. Somehow, the shadows all leaned on her, the silence folded itself on her, and the bitterness screamed inaudibly that it was her fault.

So sparkling white the china on the table, the Limoges platters, the Waterford decanters—proud symbols of her mother's inherited wealth. Glistening in the sun! The Sunday morning alive with bird songs, people chattering on the lawn. And she—dressed like a sunflower in her yellow gingham dress—carried hors d'oeuvres on pewter plates to the ladies. She curtsied, she smiled, a dimpled, charming smile, and they took delight in her every movement. A mechanical doll. With the pale flesh of rare porcelain moving in perfect response to the formal, slow manners, the delicate laughter as soft as the summer breeze. And the voices of the men! Like a gentle thunder, sonorous and far away, like gods in the clouds. That man—it seemed impossible that he could really be her father—he opened the Bible and read from it: ". . . And thou shouldst have one to comfort thy soul, and cherish thy old age . . . who loveth thee . . ." A musical voice, a grumbly, deep voice like twisted metal banging in the wind. So distant he looked from them all, like a shadow afraid of the sunlight that bathed them all. Each Sunday they would meet, fashionable ladies and gentlemen, some of them famous, many of them rich, to perform in a ritual of perfect grace. Carlotta did not believe in it. It all seemed so false. Yet she dared say nothing.

Late one night she was awakened by voices—*their* voices—resounding through the house. It frightened her. Never had such sounds reverberated through the immense rooms. Her father leaped from his desk and threw the black ledger—the financial ledger—at the gray wall.

Or was it at her? What were they screaming about? What was a mortgage? What was a zoning law? Somehow he had done evil. It had to do with that black ledger. Now he saw her watching him. She had not meant to. Only she had been awakened by the noise. He struck her. Her mother screamed. Two months later a lawyer came to visit them. What was a divorce? Why did her mother want one and not her father? But the lawyer told them not to get one. Because of Carlotta.

From that time on, nothing made sense. Things they said and did, with no purpose, only with an anger nobody could mention. But their divorce, which they continued to discuss in short, angry bursts under the sun umbrellas, unaware that she saw and heard them from the garden—that divorce did not materialize. They stayed together because of Carlotta. She was the only thing they had in common. In her, they would exorcize their hostility. They would find a reason to exist. They were all chained together in the same darkness.

With every passing year, the sterility increased. Her mother moved her bed into the room at the end of the corridor. Her father grew thin and bald, his skin erupted in rashes, and he fought for power in the church. Then Carlotta's body began to change. It was something she tried to prevent, but there was nothing she could do about it. Her chest grew tender, hair began to grow where her legs came together, and one day there was blood. She buried the underpants in the rose garden, but it happened again, and then again.

Alone in her bed, hearing the silence of the empty house, strange feelings floated through her, as though a friendly stranger had come into her. And the gentle spring night, the moonlight coming in through the window, touched the European oak furniture and the cut flowers and made them dance for her, improbable animals that cavorted with a silver sheen.

It was not in her imagination that she discovered the curves, the soft concavities of her self. Her feelings suddenly focused there, almost painfully, and they mounted higher and higher, faster and faster, until, exhausted, she saw in her mind's eye the moon and stars bursting into a thousand molten fragments. Slowly she caught her breath, wondering what had happened. Where had she been? Had they heard?

Then there was the night her mother's hoe came upon the dirt-encrusted underpants, the blood spots, dried and rusted. And for once she heard them converse in muted tones.

They undressed her and tried to bathe her, but she could not stand the thought of them touching her, and drew away. "Carlotta—turn thy face to me . . ." At night, in their bedroom, they discussed the changes in her body, but it nauseated her to hear it from their mouths. The touch of her father's hand became a cold and repulsive thing to her.

Suddenly they were watching her. Somehow there was something obscene in the way they watched her. What were they watching for?

By the time she was fourteen she felt like a grown female stuffed into the shape of a child. They had battered her into a different form. She ran away. They brought her back. They prayed for her. They threatened her. They told her of the great evil that was in her, why it was she ran away.

They bought her things—child's things. A dollhouse with tiny people and furniture, floppy-eared animals made of cloth, a world of make-believe. They wanted her to be a child whose charm and intelligence would ward off the desire that had come to invade her. She would never be ruined, never be tormented, never be forced to live a hellish existence because of those feelings . . .

The feelings that stirred her in the sunset, with her friends, listening to the soft music of the radio, the lights of the waves sparkling at the beach—those feelings became paralyzed, became a cloud of buzzing voices, each transforming her into *their* image. She wanted to live, but she was confined in *their* closet. She could almost taste life, all around her, so close, and yet so maddeningly out of reach.

Her instinct led her to boys, rugged boys, older boys. Only they had the courage to take her away from the spiderweb her parents had fashioned around her. She loved the thrill of forbidden wine with them, their rough handling. She wanted the dollhouse to break, the people to disintegrate, and live human beings to rise in their place.

One day, outside the high school, she saw an older boy drive up on his motorcycle. He was too old to be in school. But he liked the girls there. His name was Franklin Moran—

Franklin, she thought. You are strong. You can take me away from them. She lay on the wet sand at the beach and whispered in his ear. He kissed her lips. A wild fire swept through her. She wanted so badly to live. Her body took over again. She was stirred by that forbidden fire, that delirious ecstasy of his body. She felt his chest rising and falling against hers. Time, like an awful cloud, was threatening her. There was no time. Franklin, she whispered, Franklin, take me, take me now . . .

When she returned, her hair wet with sand and salt spray, Franklin waited outside in his car, not certain whether to come in. He heard them screaming in the kitchen. Carlotta was in tears. Franklin shouted that they were getting married. Her parents shouted and dismissed him from the house. But she went with him, both scared, both pursued by curses and hatred, both wondering what the world would do with them now. But in the darkness, Carlotta knew, as Franklin shifted gears and drove away, that the spell was broken. Whatever she would suffer now, whatever the universe would send her way as retribution, it was the legitimate cost of her independence.

As far as she knew, her parents from that day on were dead inside her. As far as she knew . . .

Now as Carlotta drove up the broad avenues, she wondered whether death had ever eased the soul of her father. Whether annihilation ever really soothed a self-loathing, confused soul like that. Perhaps all along he had really desired annihilation more than anything. Certainly more than life with that nervous, hostile woman who had accidentally borne him a daughter.

The palm trees floated by, dream-like, in the night. No one was awake. No lights were on. Even for Pasadena it was unearthly quiet. In one of those long houses, stuck back on a sculptured estate, was her own mother. A stranger now, thin, embalmed in her own self-denial and fear. Would she greet Carlotta at the door? Would she take in the illegitimate children? Or would she scream, as though visited by the legions of the demon himself, and slam the door? Certainly age would have softened her, bent her to a charitable heart—

But the closer Carlotta came, recognizing more and more of the avenues, the gardens, the landscape, memories piled up. Agonizing memories of a twisted mechanical doll fighting for her life. How could she bring her children into such an atmosphere? How could she sacrifice everything she had become, had learned the hard way to be? And what was left of her mother? A broken, humbled woman? A bitter, stunted old lady, with white hair and suspicious eyes? Wasn't it better to leave the past in the shadows? How could it help anymore? With her eyes grown warm and moist, Carlotta turned the car and slowed, and then saw the house.

Large and brooding, firmly anchored to the ground with pillars and massive roofs, it stood as it always had in her memory. But stranger, more ghostly. One light was on in what must be the kitchen. Was that her mother sitting alone? The stars above the house seemed to twinkle malevolently. It was the cause of everything, Carlotta thought. Everything in her life, every decision she ever made, no matter where, came out of this house. Here they had made her, formed her, reformed her once again, until

61

they were satisfied she had been made in their image. And now she had come back again. Wasn't that proof that they had won? The dead had won. The living dead had won. Now, pursued by her own nightmare, Carlotta was about to run back into the shadow world that she hated. She would disappear, become twisted—she would fight it no longer.

With a desperate twist of the wheel, not knowing what she was doing, Carlotta jerked the Buick around. The house receded. Disappeared. The familiar avenues receded. They were gone. Carlotta found herself breathing easier as they cruised down the embankment of the old freeway, and shifted into the fast lane, driving hard out of Pasadena for the last time.

Carlotta's hands gripped the wheel more tightly. She drove toward Santa Monica, exiting in West Los Angeles, and wound around the factory district there. Life as a marionette is worse than no life at all, she concluded to herself. The familiar trees and alleys which ran into Kentner Street approached. She drove up the last block.

"Hey, Mom," Billy said rubbing the sleep from his eyes. "I thought we were going to Pasadena."

"Not this trip."

"I want to go to 'Dena," Kim said.

"Shhhhh," Billy warned. "You'll make Mommy mad."

". . . 'Dena," Kim said.

"Shhhhh," Billy repeated.

The girls were getting edgy. You could feel it in the car. Like a cold wave of electricity. Bill was itchy, too. Now Carlotta saw that the city crews had cut all the trees in Kentner Street in half. All that was left was a row of weird, white-topped trunks, with the branches stacked into enormous piles in the gutter, marked off by red flags and ropes.

"God in heaven," Carlotta exclaimed. "Will you look at that? They just butchered the entire street."

"How come they cut all the trees down?" Julie asked.

"Half the trees," Billy corrected. "The top half. They were probably sick or something. Looks stupid."

Carlotta pulled to a stop. The house loomed in front of them. Behind the roof, darkly silhouetted against the blue and gray and rosy waves of the evening sky, the palm trees rose in a series of menacing isolated clumps. This was no more the friendly house of a month ago. The shadows were long, radiating outward from it toward Carlotta. The inner depths were lost in darkness.

"Who knows?" Carlotta said. "Who knows what's going on anymore?"

They took their belongings inside.

The house was stuffy. Very quiet.

"Open a window, will you, Bill?"

On the kitchen counter, flies crawled sluggishly over a forgotten cookie.

"What a mess!" Carlotta said.

The night was cold. The leaves rustled outside. A bit of wind was rising.

"Hey!" Billy called from his bedroom. "My radio is broken!"

"Your what?"

"It's all smashed on the floor!"

"Must have fallen," Carlotta answered from the kitchen.

She reached under the sink for some detergent. Damn it! Bugs. She pulled out the soap and closed the door underneath. Billy came in from the living room, holding parts of plastic, wiring and some metal grids.

"Gosh, Mom," he whined. "I made it myself. Remember? Seventh grade. Now it's all busted."

"You can't solder it back together?"

"No," he said, disconsolately. He walked out of the kitchen, his shoulders slumped dejectedly. "It looks like somebody ripped it apart."

Carlotta turned the faucet. It gurgled, sputtered,

then the water came out. Brownish at first. Then it warmed. Steam rose. The windows began to cover at the edges with a thin, ghostly film of vapor over the glass. It was growing colder outside.

From the bedroom came the sounds of Kim and Julie fighting.

"I've had it with them!" Carlotta said to herself.

She turned. A glass toppled over. It smashed over her arm in a shower of splinters.

"Damn," Carlotta said, half out loud. Suddenly the house was silent. Her heart was pounding.

Billy stood in the doorway, a wrench in his hand.

"It's a glass," Carlotta said. "It fell. What'd you think it was?"

Julie poked a tear-streaked face around the corner of the kitchen door. Then Kim, her hair half out of its braid.

"Now you go back to your room, Kim. Get dressed for bed. Julie, I need your help in the kitchen. Come on. Move!"

Julie looked inquiringly at her mother. She was scared.

"Move, Kim!"

Carlotta took a threatening step toward her. Kim scampered off into the bedroom. She could hear her slamming the drawers petulantly as she dressed.

"And *don't* slam the drawers!"

It grew quiet.

Julie dried the dishes that Carlotta washed. Billy could be heard from among metallic sounds in the garage. Dried bits of dead tree bark were dropping on the roof as the wind picked up. A dry, empty wind.

The doorbell rang.

Carlotta and Julie exchanged glances.

"Go to the bedroom, Julie."

The doorbell rang again. Julie went into the bedroom, closing the door softly behind her. Carlotta went to the front door. She opened the door—far enough to see

64

a vague form blocking out the street lamp overhead. Her heart was racing.

"Cindy!"

"Trick or treat!"

Carlotta fumbled with the latch and bolt and finally pulled the door open.

"Gee, I'm sorry," Carlotta said. "Come on in. I didn't know it was you! What on earth are you doing here?"

"It's okay?"

"Okay? You're a feast for sore eyes. I just didn't expect you."

"I knew you wouldn't go to Pasadena," Cindy said.

"Can't fool old Cindy."

They stood in the kitchen. Carlotta beamed.

"Coffee? Beer?" Carlotta offered. "There's nothing else. This is scrounge night at the Moran residence. What you got there?"

In Cindy's hand was a small overnight bag.

"I thought you could use a little company. I was thinking about how it would be, the first night back, and so I—"

"What about George?"

"As far as he knows I'm with my sister in Reseda." Cindy laughed. "Not that he gives a particular damn."

"Well, God bless you, Cindy. I *was* feeling a little, you know, strange about the whole thing. I sure am glad to see you here."

"I could just use your couch."

"Wonderful. Wonderful."

So the night passed peaceably. Cindy, Carlotta, and Julie played cards: Old Maid. Julie won. It was time for sleep. They tucked in the girls. Cindy watched Carlotta kiss them goodnight. Cindy waved a kiss to them from the doorway. They turned the lights off, leaving the girls in total darkness.

"Pleasant dreams," Cindy whispered.

In the living room they sat for a moment. Only one lamp was on, throwing a soft glow against the corner and

65

the wall, where Cindy sat on the couch and Carlotta lay back in the easy chair. The rest of the room was full of long, black shadows.

"Cold for you?" Carlotta said.

"A bit."

Carlotta went to the thermostat and turned the wheel up a notch.

"You feel scared?" Cindy said.

"Not in my mind. It's not like I have this feeling in my brain, like it's going to fall apart or anything. Just a kind of sensation in my body. A kind of premonition. That's all. Scares me a little. I can almost sense it coming."

Cindy watched Carlotta's face, silhouetted in a dreamy light. It was the face of someone who had fought for her life before, and who knew once again she was in a battle, and that the stakes were high.

The pipes clanked under the house. In the garage Billy was scrubbing the grease from his hands, dipping into a bucket of white soap. He wiped his hands on a dirty towel by the light switch. He walked into the house, nodded at Carlotta and Cindy, then went into his bedroom.

"He's so grown up," Carlotta whispered.

Cindy nodded.

"Makes me feel so old," Carlotta said. "Good Lord, Cindy. That was sixteen years ago. Sixteen whole years. I'm an old lady."

"You still look pretty good."

"Yeah, but I have to work at it. All the time."

Cindy chuckled.

After a while they heard the bed springs rustle under Billy's weight as he lay down. Then a light went off. There was the sound of sheets moving, then it was still.

"I suppose," Carlotta said, "it's time for bed."

She didn't move.

"It's eleven-thirty," Cindy said.

"That late?"

"I'll take the dishes in. You just go to bed."

66

Carlotta still sat motionless in the chair.

"Tomorrow is school again. I'll never be through."

In the kitchen Cindy put the glasses into the sink. She turned, her figure a loose dark form in the obscurity.

"Go to sleep, Carly. I'll be right here on the couch."

"Okay."

"You want to sleep on the couch?"

"No. It kills my back. I'll be all right."

"Just leave the door open."

Carlotta rose reluctantly.

"Sleep tight, Cindy. And thanks again for everything."

"You get some rest."

"Right. Goodnight."

"Goodnight, dear."

In the bedroom the air was dry and not so warm as in the living room. It could have been the way the house was constructed. The bedroom was a later addition and must have been made of different materials. More plaster, less wood. Anyway it was always cooler in here. She stood in front of the mirror and quickly undressed.

In the shadows her breasts defined small dark hollows. Only the small nipples rose into the pale light reflected from distant exterior lights. Her soft belly curved away into the darkness and the pubic hair totally mingled into the black areas of night. It made a shadow of her, carved out of the substance of the night. Even to herself she looked vulnerable.

She pulled back the blankets and slipped into the cool sheets. Soon the bed warmed. She looked up at the ceiling. She did not sleep. She sensed Cindy sitting on the couch, unfolding a blanket, and then lying down, nestling a while, and then it was quiet. Billy snored and then stopped. Slowly Carlotta became drowsy. The pipes murmured under the floor boards, a low, rumbling thunder which died away into several clanks. She opened her eyes and looked at the ceiling. Nothing. She closed her eyes, nestled her cheek into the smooth cotton pillowcase and drifted away into the night. She slept deeply.

7:22 a.m. October 25, 1976

Carlotta smelled something. Meat. No. Yes. Different. Bacon. She rose quickly. Sunshine streamed in through the window, throwing sparkles over the cosmetic bottles by the mirror.

"Cindy!" she called. "What are you doing?"

"Breakfast," Cindy called from the kitchen.

Carlotta slipped on a robe and slippers and stumbled to the kitchen.

"Hey," she said. "You don't have to do that! Where'd you get the bacon, anyhow?"

"Bought it."

"Already? What time is it?"

"About seven-thirty."

"You're a wonder."

Carlotta yawned and rubbed her face.

"I must look a fright," Carlotta said.

"A little informal, I'll admit," Cindy laughed.

Julie scampered in, wearing a sleeping gown. Behind her was Kim, clad only in underpants, smiling uncertainly, sleepily, rubbing her eyes. She dragged a worn stuffed dog across the floor.

"Well, look who's up," Cindy said. "Sit down, ladies. Cornflakes on the table."

"Listen, Cindy," Carlotta said. "I have to get dressed. Be right back."

Carlotta went back into the bedroom. She carefully picked out a plaid suit. It had wide lapels. Over a white blouse it made her look small and busty. She loved it. Billy walked into the kitchen, hitching up his blue jeans.

"Good morning, Mrs. Nash," he said.

"Good morning, Mr. Moran."

"What's for breakfast?"

"Sit down, Mr. Moran," Cindy laughed. "I will serve you personally."

Billy sat down. He stared out the window at the perfect day. His bare feet tapped against the linoleum floor. The sunshine poured in through the windows. Outside, the leaves showed a yellow-green, bright where they

68

stretched up out of the shade of the house. And over the roofs was a clear blue sky.

"Nice day," Carlotta said, returning.

"Perfect," Cindy agreed.

Cindy picked up the dishes and bowls and carried them over to the sink.

"Hey!" Carlotta said. "What do you think you're doing?"

"You go to school. I'll get the kids off and clean up."

"Nothing doing—"

"You're going to be late."

"Cindy—"

"I mean it. Look at the clock. It's after eight."

"My gosh. You're right."

Cindy dried her hands on an apron.

"Listen," Cindy said. "About tonight. Maybe I should go back."

"Sure. Of course," Carlotta said after the slightest pause. "And listen. I'm so grateful."

"I got a kick out of it. Now, you go. And drive carefully. I'll get the girls dressed."

"You're a real angel, Cindy."

Carlotta picked up her spiral shorthand book and a larger, faded gray loose-leaf binder from the kitchen table.

"Well, goodbye, everybody."

There was a chorus of goodbyes.

Carlotta walked into the sunshine. The breeze whipped briskly, stirring the leaves over the shaded walks. The car was still cool. She got into the car, waving to Mr. Greenspan drinking his coffee, European style, from a tiny cup on his tiny porch. He waved back, brandishing a half-eaten piece of toast, nodding and smiling. She reversed the car, turned around, and drove off.

She fiddled with the radio dial. She turned it off. She passed a green light. Stopped at a red light.

There is a slight difference between Santa Monica and Los Angeles. A visitor wouldn't notice it. But the trees are older, bigger, shadier. More elderly people on the sidewalks. Some of the buildings go back to before the Depression. In the bright sunlight, when you cruise down in a big Buick, it's like an avenue of creamy color and blue sky. Nothing like it in the world. The morning crisp, cool air just makes the lawns and flowers stand out in the sun. And far away, very far away, so you have to know where to look to see it, a vague blue rim low in the sky: the Pacific Ocean.

"Good morning, cunt!"

Carlotta froze.

Carlotta looked through the dusty windshield. The hot wide avenue stretched endlessly through huge shady trees and gas stations on distant corners. Everything she did she did slowly. Cautiously. Waiting. It couldn't be. Not in broad daylight! She felt the radio dial. It was off. She looked to the side.

Two male Latin faces looked down at her from a beat-up truck in the adjacent lane. Their sun-tanned faces, both darkened with small mustaches, scrutinized hers. Their eyes fell down past her neck, her shoulders, her breasts, and hips. The car behind her honked. She pressed the accelerator. The pickup truck turned left. She saw it disappear through the rearview mirror.

"Hit her! Poke her!"

Carlotta's heart raced. She whirled around. The voice was just above her head. Behind her head. No one in the back seat. She righted the wheel, caught in the morning traffic, and touched her lip, puzzled.

"Get her on the palisades!!"

"Drive her off the pier!!"

Carlotta's head spun about. Her eyes wide and filled with fear. Watching. Searching. But there was no one in the car. She opened the window. Her foot pressed down the accelerator. She tried to lift her foot. A force was pushing her foot down on the accelerator.

"Drive her off the cliff! Off the cliff!"

"Break the steering wheel! Fuck her on the shaft!"

Two crackling, demented voices that sounded like

70

creaky doors. Now the car was picking up speed, moving down Colorado Avenue, beginning to pass cars.

"Stop it! Stop it!" shrieked Carlotta, holding her hands over her ears.

"Ha ha ha ha ha ha ha ha!" multiple laughter, raucous, commingled in her ears.

Now a groan, a deep twisted voice, whispered into her ear.

"Remember me, cunt!"

The steering wheel slipped through her hands. The car turned right. Carlotta grabbed at the wheel, but could barely budge it. The Buick fishtailed onto the main artery of Santa Monica, on its way to the ocean. Little mice hands were pulling at her hair.

"Pinch her! Pinch her!" shrieked a voice.

"Poke her!" yelled an insane, sibilant voice.

Now the wheel was locked like iron. Carlotta could not lift her foot from the accelerator. Either it was paralyzed or it was held down from above. In any case, it was immobile, dead-weight heavy, pressing down the pedal.

"Dear God, dear God," Carlotta wept, fumbling for the seat-belt latch. But it was stuck into the crevice of the front seat. "O God, my God."

The lock snapped down on the door with a sharp click. The automatic window rolled up with a gentle hum. In the crosswalks pedestrians hesitated, then moved back, glaring at her as the Buick sped by them.

"I'm sorry, dear God, I'm sorry for everything I ever did, please—"

"Shut up!"

"Burn her! Shove the lighter up her crotch!"

The cigarette lighter snapped in and began to heat.

Carlotta screamed. You know the end is coming. Your soul wants to fly, but it is trapped inside the body. Ahead, the statue of Santa Monica, the crude white stone shining in the sun. Beyond it the roses. Then the blue sky. Two hundred feet below, the Pacific Coast Highway, like a concrete ribbon, hugged the rocks.

"Harder!"

Something smashed her foot down to floor the accelerator. The car jumped ahead. Her brain buzzed; the blue edge of the cliff raced forward.

"Farewell, Carlotta!"

Carlotta shrieked.

Suddenly, she twisted the wheel so hard the car screeched in an arc and flew toward the last row of buildings.

"Get back, you bitch!"

The wheel rapidly turned back. But the front tire caught the curb and the Buick careened over the sidewalk. Two unemployed men, lounging in the shadows of the alley, seemed to fly backward in slow motion as the car lunged forward. In an abstraction in which Carlotta was left in all eternity, she saw the patrons on the second floor of a bar only now begin to look up from their tables.

"Please don't let me die," Carlotta prayed, without hope.

The window broke in like a wave. Behind closed eyes she felt the shards spread over shoulders and face like a soft, stinging rain. The metallic dull buckling of the grille and fenders, and the interior engine parts torn and thrown from the ripped hood. Violently thrown forward, her stomach felt torn by the seat belt which slammed her back into the seat. Nausea filled the world. Everything was a long, drawn out flash in the sound of exploding metal and glass, and the aura of pain was all that there was. She noticed then that everything was still.

A man pounded on the door.

"Better get her out. It's smoking."

"Don't touch her."

"It's smoking!"

"Leave her alone. She'll sue."

"Call an ambulance."

"Don't panic."

A face peered in through the shattered window. It was friendly, scarred, tough.

"I'm not going to hurt you, ma'am. But the engine is smoking. If you can, you should get out of the car."

Carlotta wanted to tell him that everything was really quite fine, and yes, she would, thank you, get out of the car, if you would please move out of the way, but she couldn't open her mouth. All the words died in some incalculably vast and empty desert in her brain. She only looked stupidly at him.

"I think she's in shock."

"She's just dazed."

"Open the door."

Together, the two men pried open the smashed door.

"Get the seat belt off her, Fred."

"Can't. It's jammed. No. There. I got it."

"Easy does it."

Carlotta felt herself being lifted from the car. She tried to tell them to put her down. She wanted to go home. But all that happened was that she clung to the man's neck and wept.

"She's all right. Only some scratches."

"A miracle."

"That Buick's a mess."

Carlotta saw the world flow by in uncertain, curious faces.

"They're trying to kill me," she wept, being carried to a booth in the bar. "They're going to kill me."

PART TWO
Gary Sneidermann

What the hammer? What the chain?
In what furnace was thy brain?
What the anvil? what dread grasp
Dare its deadly terrors clasp?
                    —Blake

5

WALLS were covered in an orange glow. It was the sunset. Overhead fluorescent lights flickered, casting a green-white light on Carlotta's hands. In a window, a deformed reflection, herself, in a jacket and skirt, folding and unfolding her hands.

There was a buzz of voices. A door had opened. Carlotta turned. A tall boy walked in, wearing a white jacket. His hair was long, dark, and it bunched over his collar. He closed the door.

"I'm Dr. Sneidermann," he said.

He smiled. A perfunctory, polished smile. He gestured to a chair in front of a desk. Carlotta sat down slowly as he went behind the desk, neatly tugged his pants up at the knees, and sat down. He leaned forward. A handsome face, boyish, gray eyes.

"I'm one of the staff psychiatrists at the clinic. I was on call for emergencies tonight."

Sneidermann watched her face. It was cut all over with fine lines. A bruise darkened her chin. Her eyes were dark, watching him like a scared animal. She seemed on the edge of losing control.

Carlotta squinted at him, as though peering through

a fog. From time to time she moved her head abruptly. Was there anyone else in this tiny office? What happened to the people with all the papers? She forgot how she had come to the clinic.

"I think we can get along just fine," he said.

She looked at him suspiciously.

"Are you cold?" he asked. "Sometimes there's a draft from the outer lobbies."

Carlotta vaguely shook her head. She turned around. The door was still closed. No one else was in the room. She turned back to Sneidermann. She wondered where the doctor was. Instead, this boy was smiling, a composed, artificial smile.

"Have you seen a psychiatrist before?"

"No."

The fact that she answered relaxed him. He cleared his throat. He was not certain exactly how to proceed. He moved his chair from behind the desk, to be closer to her.

"How do you prefer to be called?" he asked.

"Car—Carlotta."

"Carlotta. Good. Very good."

Suddenly there was a disturbance, outside. In the lobby, she heard voices. Somebody was out there. Nurses' voices? Carlotta watched the door.

"Carlotta," he said.

Somebody was calling her. She turned. Who was this boy in the white jacket? How did he know her?

"What we have to do, Carlotta, is talk. You have to tell me what's going on inside you, what you're afraid of. This is the way we find out where the problem is."

Carlotta looked at him strangely. She bit her lip, thinking of something else. Then, something frightened her, because she turned in her chair, looking toward the window.

"Where are you now, Carlotta?"

"In the clinic."

"Yes. Very good. Why did you come here?"

Carlotta turned back slowly. Her body was weighed down. It was sore from the accident, tense with fear, her face flushed under the bruises. Her fingers were stiff, white, and cold.

"Because they were all around me," she said in despair.

"Who was?"

"In the car."

Sneidermann nodded, but she missed the gesture. Her fingers absorbed her interest. They locked in her lap, intertwining, back and forth, back and forth.

"Can you tell me about the accident, Carlotta?"

She unloosed her fingers. Sat up straight in the chair. In front of her was a young man in a white jacket, leaning forward toward her. She studied his face. Square, intense, not lined. Younger than she was.

"Carlotta?"

"What?"

"Could you tell me what happened in the car?"

Slowly, very slowly, like water over cold earth, her eyes misted over. The nostrils flared. If she was going to cry, it would relax her. But she only shook her head.

"Is it difficult for you to tell me what happened?"

She nodded.

"That's all right, Carlotta."

It occurred to her that now she was safe. Why was that? Because the door was closed. Because it was quiet in here. It was different in here. The doctor faced her, encouraging, professional, friendly.

Sneidermann's finger, moving slowly along a crack in the desk top, was the only indication of his uncomfortableness in the impasse. Then he caught himself. He was completely still, his face a mask of impenetrable competence. Yet his thoughts were whirling as he watched her.

Carlotta looked down at her lap. Her head had the heavy quality of one who has not slept. She felt trapped. She could not tell the doctor what had happened, and she dared not leave.

"Was there someone with you in the car?"

"No—not at first—"

"But after a while?"

76

Carlotta nodded. When she looked him in the eyes, he smiled. A restrained, practiced smile. She had no confidence in him. She had imagined someone entirely different. It was like talking to Billy.

"After a while they were in the car with you?" he said.

"Yes."

"Did they speak with you?"

"Yes."

"Can you tell me what they said to you?"

She shook her head.

"It would be difficult for you to tell me what they said?"

"Yes."

"That's all right, Carlotta."

She seemed to have relaxed. At least her body no longer was tensed. Carlotta began to realize this was no normal conversation. The doctor never let go of what he wanted to find out. He manipulated her with words.

"Perhaps the voices came from the radio."

"No. The radio was off. They were around me."

"I see."

She pulled a wrinkled tissue from her purse. She felt humiliated. She was afraid to look at Sneidermann.

"They wanted to kill me," she finally whispered.

"But they didn't succeed. We're going to make sure they don't come back."

"Yes."

"Very good."

For the first time, Carlotta felt a contact with the figure in white. Behind the mask, the pose, something had made a contact. He seemed to care. She looked at him more closely. It was true. His small gray eyes watched her with concern.

"Is this the first time this has happened?"

"No. The first time it was different."

The vein in her neck throbbed. Her fist crumpled the tissues into tiny balls. Her breath trembled.

Sneidermann watched her pretty face. The dark eyes,

77

afraid. Once flashing with dark fire, with fear and hostility, now they were two deep wells, leading down into her private misery.

"Can you tell me about that time?"

"It's not something I like to talk about."

"You find it difficult?"

"Yes."

"But this is a doctor's office. There are no secrets here."

Carlotta inhaled. *They're* listening, she thought. *They'll* take off your clothes and poke at you. Now she was completely isolated. Slowly, she turned back to the doctor.

"I was raped," she said, inaudibly.

Her eyes blurred and became warm. She lifted her face to Sneidermann. He looked like a soft white form.

"I was raped," she repeated, not knowing whether he had heard.

"In your home?" he asked gently.

Surprised that he made no response other than that, she only nodded. She watched him closely. Behind his mask he seemed not to have changed. Again it dawned on her this was no ordinary conversation.

"I see," he said. He was studying her now.

She bit her lip. She tried not to cry. It was no use. Her face only twisted into a grimace, a distortion of remorse. Like a black flood it all came out: the terror, the repulsion, the humiliation. She tried to cover her face with her hands. She wished the doctor were not watching her, but she could not help it.

"It was so repulsive," she wept. "So ugly!"

She inhaled in quivering gasps. The ugliness surrounded her. She could feel it, taste it, everywhere.

"I'm so dirty!" she said.

The crumpled tissue dabbed uselessly at her eyes. She was slumped in the chair, weeping helplessly. A stab of pity pricked Sneidermann's heart. Gone was the ladylike, petite woman who had entered. She was transformed into a girl without dignity.

78

The crying ceased. Little by little. The clock hummed on the wall. Sneidermann waited at the corner of the desk, in the same position as before. The growing silence flowed around them both, uniting them.

"I just want to die," she said, softly.

Sneidermann opened his mouth, then stopped. He decided to wait another moment. He congratulated himself on having kept a perfect calm thus far.

"Did you call the police?"

"How could I? There was no one in the room."

Sneidermann was caught off guard. For an instant, the mask dropped off. He looked at her, not believing he had understood. He tapped his finger on his lip and leaned back slightly. As best he could, he adopted the mask of the doctor once again.

"Can you tell me what happened?"

"I was raped. What more is there to tell?"

He cleared his throat lightly. His brows were furrowed in concentration. A thousand possibilities swirled in front of him. Now he had to go carefully.

"You were alone in the bedroom?"

"Yes."

"You were raped by whom?"

"I—I don't know—" A long pause. "There was no one there."

"Tell me, Carlotta, when you say 'rape,' what do you mean?"

" 'Rape' means rape."

"Can you be more precise?"

"What do you mean, *precise?* Everybody knows what rape is."

"Sometimes people use it in a metaphorical way. I was raped in a business deal, or something like that."

"Well, that's not what I mean."

He did not confront her now. He wanted her to know he was on her side.

"Could you tell me what happened?" he asked gently. "It might be difficult but I have to know."

Carlotta retreated from him. Her voice dropped, lost

its flexibility. She became cool. She became impersonal about herself.

"I was combing my hair," she said, "in front of the mirror. In the darkness, I think . . ."

"Yes."

"And he grabbed me."

"Who grabbed you?"

"I don't know."

"Then what happened?"

"What happened?" she said bitterly. "What do you think happened? I thought I was going to die. He was smothering me."

"He choked you?"

"No. The pillow. He had the pillow over my face. I couldn't breathe!"

"Did you try to resist?"

"I tried. But he was too strong."

"And he forced himself."

"I told you. Yes."

"Completely."

"Yes."

"Then what happened?"

Carlotta's eyes flashed angrily at him.

"What happened?" she said. "What happened? After he used me—sexually—he disappeared."

"He ran away?"

"No. He was just—just—gone."

"Out the door?"

"No. The door was closed. One minute he was on me and the next he was gone. Then my son came in."

Sneidermann nodded abstractly. He thought a moment. Then he turned back to Carlotta, listening more than watching her.

"Your son—did he see anybody?"

"Just me. He ran into the bedroom. I was screaming."

"Then what happened?"

"We—the girls, too—stayed in the living room. I was scared."

"You were afraid he was still in the house?"

"No. He was gone."

He looked at her now in the silence. Carlotta could see that he did not know what to make of it.

"Tell me, Carlotta," he said slowly. "What makes you think it was not a real man who raped you?"

"He just—evaporated—when Billy turned on the light."

"Maybe he jumped out the window."

"No. Windows were locked. He just disappeared."

"You felt him in you, though?"

"Definitely."

"He felt like a man?"

"A big man."

"You were in pain?"

"Yes. Of course."

"All right. What happened afterwards?"

"Nothing that night. But the next night—"

"Did the same thing happen?"

"This time from behind."

Sneidermann rubbed his brow. He looked even younger than when he had walked in. Carlotta thought he must be very smart to be so young and to be a doctor.

"What did your son think?"

"He came in with a neighbor. They thought I was hallucinating."

"Why would they think that?"

"Because I was screaming and there was no one there."

"Have you ever taken drugs?"

"Never."

"All right. What did you think?"

"I—I wasn't sure. I—I knew I was sore. I felt terrible inside. You can't mistake that. I could smell him all over me—"

"You smelled him?"

"Yes. He was foul."

"I see."

"I'm not sure if he—if he—"

81

"Ejaculated."

"Yes . . . I think he did. But when the light went on I felt I was waking up. Coming up out of the darkness. And nobody else was scared. They never thought there was anybody there."

Sneidermann nodded. He seemed to have found a grip on Carlotta. Now he watched her again: the facial signs, the body language, the tone in her voice. He wanted some confirmation for what he was thinking.

"You said it happened a third time."

"Not exactly. I heard him coming. I smelled him from far away. I ran out of the bedroom."

"What happened?"

"I grabbed the kids and ran out, fast as I could. We drove to my friend's house."

"And then?"

Carlotta shrugged. "Then nothing happened. I stayed with Cindy for a week. I felt better. We all did. I couldn't stay there forever. I went back home with the kids, yesterday. Cindy stayed with me last night. Everything was fine. I woke up, we had breakfast, and then I got into the car. I was driving to my secretarial school in West Los Angeles."

"That's when you heard the voices in the car."

She nodded. She seemed to have relaxed. Only her eyes, like a rabbit's, caught his now and then for some kind of assurance.

"So what do you think?" she said. "Go ahead and be honest. Tell me."

She fumbled for a cigarette. Lighting it, her fingers still trembled. Sneidermann waited until she was through. He had to keep her confidence. Without lying.

"Well, Carlotta," he said. "Of course, it's very serious."

"Do you think I'm insane?"

"Insane? That means different things to different people."

He smiled at her. But Carlotta saw he didn't give an

82

inch. He was still the professional, hiding his feelings. He never relaxed.

"Do you have someone who can stay with you?" he asked.

"My son, Billy."

"How old is he?"

"Fifteen."

"What about your friend, Cindy?"

"Not tonight. Maybe after a few days."

"Because I'd like you to be with someone, Carlotta. At all times. I don't want you to be alone."

"All right."

"Now, we have to take some medical tests. A few psychological tests. They don't hurt."

"Right now?"

"We can do it tomorrow."

"I have to go to the secretarial school. I'm on welfare, and they take attendance."

"Let's talk to the nurse at the desk when we go out. Usually we can work something out with welfare."

She ground out a half-smoked cigarette.

"So there's nothing you can do?"

"Not until I know exactly where the problem is. I have my ideas, but I need the other tests to make sure."

"In the meantime, I'll be dead."

"No. I don't think so."

"They tried to kill me today."

"I think if you're with someone you'll be all right."

She pushed her hair from her forehead. Distant echoes of voices were heard beyond the door.

"I don't know what to do," she said, simply.

"I think you've done a very good thing by coming to the clinic."

"You think so?"

"Definitely. It's a first step. And the hardest."

There was an ominous silence. They waited a moment. Carlotta simply stood up, straightening her skirt. They walked to the door.

When the door opened, a maze of corridors glittered brightly. Carlotta did not remember having seen them before. To the left was the reception room. Sneidermann leaned forward on the deak, talking to a nurse. Carlotta did not remember having seen the reception room either.

He came back to her, across the orange carpet. Suddenly, he was the only familiar face to her in the entire world. "Here's a card," he said. "It has the number of the clinic. They'll find me if you need me. Any time of day."

She put the card into her purse. Her manners were those of a well-bred young lady. Yet she was on welfare. It intrigued him.

"Thank you, doctor," she said softly.

"Sneidermann," he said. "Let me write that on the card."

Then he watched her leave, uncertainly making her way into the corridors with strips of colored tape along the floor. She disappeared. Sneidermann finally exhaled. He was exhausted.

"You were in there a long time, Gary," said the nurse.

"What? Oh! Listen, are you sure she's never been to another psychiatrist?"

"That's what she wrote down."

"No drugs."

"If you believe her."

"Incredible."

He poured himself a styrofoam cupful of black coffee. He was still absorbed in Carlotta.

"I'll be in the library," he said. "I have to write this up."

He walked quickly down the hallway, gulping coffee. Under his arm was a black vinyl folder, but no notes in it as yet. His footsteps echoed over the lonely tiles of the medical complex.

Sneidermann lit a cigarette, exhaled a cloud of smoke, and took off his jacket. He rolled up his sleeves, revealing muscular forearms. His recall was excellent. The entire meeting played before him at will. He wrote it down in the black folder, on which he had written her name.

Far away another resident pored over several large texts, as oblivious to Sneidermann as Sneidermann was to him.

It was a huge, old library, with tiles on the floor and wooden carvings on the doors and stairways to the upper levels. It was quiet. This late at night the medical complex was nearly deserted in this wing. Sneidermann stood, put a foot on the chair, leaned forward, and examined what he had written.

She had made her opening moves. This was no housewife with a career frustration. It was no obese secretary whose loneliness translated into overeating, bulimia. Sneidermann's other cases fell away from his consciousness. He almost could not believe what he had in front of him. He wanted to keep it to himself, to work it through before the others found out about it. He trembled with excitement.

He pulled a text from a high shelf and carried it back to the reading table. Hallucinations which were visual, tactile, aural, *and* olfactory were quite rare. Most likely, they were manifestations of either a psychosis or a hysterical neurosis. Sneidermann felt pleased that he had calmed her down, had ridden down her hysteria until she made contact. He had gotten her to speak rationally with him, something he had doubted was even possible when he first laid eyes on her, standing, lost and helpless, in the middle of the room.

He knew his work was cut out for him. He knew he would have to search in the classical literature for the fullest descriptions of such multiple hallucinations. Then he consulted his notes. Her voice had gone flat when she described the attacks, as though they had happened to a total stranger. Therefore, there had been dissociation. Possibly, classical grand hysteria. Otherwise, he thought, her ego seemed intact—good reality testing, once he had brought her down.

His next thought was psychosis. The hallucinations had been so extreme, her delusion so complete, that she must have lost contact with reality. But the longer she talked, the more she calmed down, the more rational she had become. He decided to hold off on that diagnosis until he learned more of her history. Psychosis, schizophrenia, usually show indications by the early twenties.

His curiosity grew, making him restless. The psychic violence of part against the whole, trying to re-organize itself into a new constellation. For what purpose? Why now at age thirty-two? The case ahead was wide open, an unexplored continent, and he was anxious to begin.

Alone now in the library, it suddenly occurred to him that he could have hoped for nothing more. To be curing the broken and the twisted, in a discipline he deeply respected, under the best conditions, the image of his father came to his mind. A shrunken, defeated man, the smell of cleaning fluid on his hands. There, but for the grace of God, Sneidermann thought. In a strange city, among strangers, Sneidermann found himself thrown into his cases to avoid those thoughts.

He rubbed his eyes, closed the textbooks, and threw his cup into the wastebasket. He willed himself to concentrate on the case before him, but weariness made the thoughts evaporate, slide meaninglessly into one another. He picked up the casebook and left the library.

The loneliness of resident psychiatrists is a secret to anyone outside the profession. The isolation, the empty, formal corridors, the tasteless seminar rooms and purely professional relationships, and the competition everywhere never lets up even for a minute. As he walked through the deserted courtyard with the fountains turned off and the pools silent, the sounds of the city rumbled eerily through the night. He walked back toward his quarters concentrating on Carlotta Moran.

Billy leaned over her shoulder. He touched a small towel, dabbed in disinfectant, to her skin. Her neck was streaked in gentle lines of pink, as though an invisible claw had reached for her.

"It's a miracle you're alive," he said. "The Buick's a wreck."

"You think you can get it back together?"

"Sure. Probably. With some parts. That fan just disintegrated."

Carlotta winced when he touched the lacerations under her ear. In the mirror the tender concern showed on his face. She watched him, and behind him, in the mirror, through the open window, the street lamps filled a vacant lot with brightness. The weeds were grown high and yellow, rustling in the night breeze.

"How much is it going to cost?" she asked.

"Couple hundred."

"Which we don't have," Carlotta groaned.

The girls were at the door, watching. Their eyes were wide with wonder.

"Did the doctor hurt you?" Julie asked.

"No, honey, no. Not at all. Mommy just talked."

"You going again?" Billy asked.

"Tomorrow. After school."

She gestured to Billy to stop. She stood up.

"Listen, kids," she said, "there's a card on the desk. It's got the number of the clinic. If something happens, you call. Okay? His name is," she consulted the card, "Sneidermann." Kim laughed at the sound of the name.

In an hour the children were in bed. Carlotta slept on the couch. Billy had sawed a wide board and placed it under the pillows. On top of the pillows they had put Julie's old mattress pad. It covered the buttons and hollows. Not perfectly, but she slept. Not well, but nothing happened.

She passed the first night in the strange realm of the ill where all the rules are reversed. Somehow the doctor had confirmed it. Anxiety was like a dark cloud that grew over her, until she forgot what life was like without it.

"Billy," she said softly.

It was morning. Billy sat up in bed, the sun shining over the rumpled sheets.

"What?"

"If Jerry calls, for God's sake, don't tell him anything. You got that? Make sure the girls get it, too. That's all I'd need."

"You mean he's coming back?"

Billy sat up straighter, fully awake. Hostility, confused but unmistakable, rolled from him like a river. He sat against the headboard, his arms hanging loosely at his side. But his handsome face was a man's face, in dead earnest, and the stocky shoulders were squared back.

Carlotta took a step toward him. Her voice was gentle.

"Look, Bill, I know how you feel. But understand something. I like Jerry. And he's trying to like you. You owe him that much in return. And besides, it doesn't matter what you think about him. He's my friend. Do you know what I mean? We're a good pair together. Maybe it'll be permanent. You'd better think about that. Because it could just be permanent. And as long as you live here, you're going to have to adjust to it. You agree?"

"It's your mistake, Ma."

"Let's leave it at that. My mistake. I let you make yours."

Billy picked up a checkered shirt from the chair. He sat on the edge of the bed, putting it on. He avoided her glance.

"You want me to come with you?" he said.

"Thanks, Bill, but it's only to the school."

"You're sure?"

"Sure. What can happen? I'm taking the bus."

"Okay."

He stood up, took his pants from the same chair, and stepped into them. He buckled his belt.

"Because I can get a car. Jed drives. You call if you want a ride home."

"Okay. We'll see how I feel."

He followed her to the front door. She carried the notebook in her arm.

" 'Bye, Mom," he said.

She held onto him a moment. Then she walked out into the sunlight. At the end of Kentner Street the bus turned a lazy, heavy corner. After she paid the fare she saw him, still standing in the shadow of the door. Then he turned disconsolately and went into the house and the door closed.

"Did you sleep well?"

"Fairly well."

"In the bedroom?"

"On the couch. In the living room."

Sneidermann nodded. She seemed far more relaxed, seemed to have placed herself in his hands. It pleased him greatly. The thing he wanted now was to get going as rapidly as possible. There was a brief momentum from the day before, and he tried to enlarge it.

"No nightmares?" he said.

"No."

He smiled. He was genuinely encouraged. She saw it immediately. She decided to let him do as he wanted with her.

"It was a good idea, Carlotta. To sleep on the couch."

Somehow the doctor seemed to have remembered every detail of what they had said the day before.

"Are you here alone?" he asked.

"Yes."

"I'd prefer it if someone came with you. Your son, for example."

"He's in school until the middle of the afternoon."

"Well, we could meet at a different time. What about four o'clock? Would that be all right for both of you?"

"What about you?"

"I'll change my hours. I can do that."

Carlotta nodded. She hesitated at placing her trust in him. The youthful appearance of his face troubled her. He should have been twenty years older.

"Then we can meet at four o'clock," he said.

"Tomorrow?"

"Every day."

"Is that necessary?"

"Yes."

The prospect of such full-time treatment was far from what she had expected.

He shuffled several papers on the desk. She exhibited none of the tenseness of the day before.

"I told you yesterday about some tests," he said. "These are very routine. You've had most of them before. Blood, urine, a few are psychological. A psychologist is going to show you some pictures. You make up a story around them. Things like that. Nothing hurts. No surprises. Could you take them now?"

"I suppose. If you want me to."

"Good. Let's go."

He stood up rapidly. Carlotta was a little afraid at the speed with which things were happening. She stood up slowly, taking her purse from the floor.

"I'm going to take you to the laboratory," he said. "It's a big place down there, and you could get lost."

Together they walked out the door and into the noisy labyrinth, Sneidermann nodding to doctors and nurses. They crossed several lobbies, several laboratories full of technicians. He was tall, his long legs walking quickly, hard to keep pace with. They turned a corner, found a place in front of the elevator doors, and waited with a gathering crowd.

"You're not a real doctor, are you?" Carlotta said.

Sneidermann blushed. He laughed.

"What makes you say that? I'm a resident, which is a doctor. But I do have a supervisor."

"You just look young, that's all."

"Well, I'm not that young."

The elevator opened, disgorged patients and men

delivering supplies. They got in. He pressed a button. On the ground floor he led her through a series of corridors and swinging doors. The walls were lined with several old men and women, coughing in their wheelchairs.

"This is Mrs. Moran," he said to a nurse behind a window. "From NPI. I want a complete physical work-up. I want the orange form, the green one, and the yellow one."

The nurse chuckled.

"We have other colors."

"Give me the whole rainbow."

The nurse checked off several boxes on the typed form in front of her.

"Just have her sit down. We'll get to her in a minute."

Sneidermann walked back to Carlotta. The alien smells of the chemicals made her nervous. It was colder down on the ground floor. There were dials, tanks, and tubes in racks everywhere. Suddenly it grew larger in her mind. It dwarfed her, the metallic and glass gleam of the rooms, the sick old men in the corridor.

"Now don't be worried," he said. "I know this isn't a pretty place. It's like a garage down here. But listen, you've had a blood test before, haven't you? That's as painful as it gets. I wouldn't lie to you. Mostly it's just boring. It takes about two hours. Try not to fall asleep."

She smiled nervously.

"I'll be upstairs when you're through. If you want to see me, have them show you to NPI."

"NPI?"

"Neuro-Psychological Institute. They'll know."

"All right."

He turned to go. Then he turned back. She was still nervous. She hated to see him go.

"I'll be there and we can talk if you want. It'll be up to you. How you feel. All right?"

"Yes."

In the office, for all his youth, he had seemed authoritative. It was the nurse who had brought out the boy-

91

ish quality in him. Seeing him flirt had unnerved Carlotta.

"Mrs. Moran," said the nurse, "will you come in, please."

Carlotta resigned herself. She entered a room full of tubes, cylinders, bottles of dense and ugly liquids. Whirling machinery inside steel containers made a humming sound. Technicians were sliding racks of blood across the counters. She shivered. She was dehumanized, a piece of the great medical machine. Even the light here was green and cold. Everybody looked strange. The nurse held open a curtain. Carlotta went inside and took off her clothes.

6

A LIGHT drizzle fell outside the house on Kentner Street. Carlotta had not returned from the clinic. Dark birds sang a cheerless note, over and over, in the hidden parts of the trees. The house was cold and had an empty feeling.

Billy stood at the sink, vaguely aware of his sharp reflection in the black window. Since Carlotta had become ill—or whatever it was—Billy had taken to washing the dishes, dressing the girls, and making his own lunch. He knew sooner or later he might be called upon to do more. But right now, he did the only things he could, the tiny gestures that might ease her burden.

There was nothing shameful in being mentally sick, Billy thought. It struck like the flu or a dozen other diseases. It was just that there was no medicine for it. You couldn't put it under a microscope and identify the bad cells.

His face tightened. Thinking about microscopes and cells reminded him of school, and biology, and all the things he hated. The smelly classrooms, like prison cells. The weird teachers, who got their kicks out of embarrassing you in front of the class—small-minded creeps with tiny lives and no hopes for anything better. How he hated them.

He hadn't attended school in more than a week, but it didn't bother him. He didn't give much of a damn what they said or did to him. Anyway, what could they do? He was on the way to being sixteen, and soon he'd be able to cash out entirely—legit.

Still, Billy was pricked by worry. The timing was bad. Especially now, with his mother sick. He hated adding to her troubles. But after all, what did she really know about him? What his thoughts were—his dreams? What do parents ever really know? All she knew was that he was a car freak. She even made jokes about it with Cindy. Well, it was more than wrenches and grease that made him spin. He wasn't going to end up in the pits. He had a goal. A big goal. And cars were just a tiny stepping stone toward getting there.

Billy's eyes glazed. His hands remained idle in the soapy water as he considered the future—even bigger and better than Jed's Uncle Stu. Now there was a success story. Not yet forty and the sole owner of the biggest used-car dealership in Carson. A six-acre lot with a fantastic turnover. Sometimes, more than a hundred cars on a single weekend. Uncle Stu made a fortune just sitting behind his desk, buying and selling. Yes, that's where Billy was headed—his own dealership one day. And not way out in Carson. Brentwood, Westwood, maybe even Beverly Hills.

Billy looked out the window. Through the drizzle that streaked the glass he saw the blue bus turn onto the corner. No one got out. He looked at the clock. It was nearly six o'clock. What was keeping her? He hoped nothing had happened to her on the bus. Like getting one of her spells and seeing things. How awful to be sick that way. Billy knew from stories he had heard how people's personalities changed. Sweet, tender people became twisted, silent, brooding figures, lost in the shadows of the house, never went out, even began to smell bad. That was the horror: not the sickness, but the changes in the person. The person became different and you could grow to hate her; you could want to stay away from the very person you used to love.

Billy pushed the thought out of his mind. He could never leave her, no matter what.

His face stiffened as his thoughts gravitated to Jerry. Goddam beaner. Trying to act like he was somebody big. Bouncing around the country like a Vegas hot-shot, then coming in on a one-night stand and using his mother like a—yeah, like a whore. Why did she let him? What the hell did she see in him? What was the big attraction? Damn greaser—

A dish smashed on the linoleum floor.

"Holy shit!"

Billy stooped to pick up the pieces. They were sharp and cold. He scooped them into a paper bag and dropped the bag into the trash can near the stove. He looked for other remnants on the floor.

A second dish smashed on the floor.

"Christ!"

What the hell was happening? Hurriedly, he piled the pieces onto some newspaper. The pieces were icy cold. The shards seemed to bounce around, almost weightless. He dropped them into the can. They clattered, broke, and bounced for a while. He put the lid firmly on the can.

"Billy!"

He turned. Julie looked at him from the shadows of the living room.

"What?"

"Look at me!"

Julie walked into the doorway between the kitchen and the living room. Her eyes were strange, pixie-like. Her hair stood out on end.

"What the hell you do that for?" Billy said. "Go comb it down."

"I didn't do it. It did it by itself."

Billy stared at her disgustedly.

"You did, too," he said. "Now go comb it down. I'm in no mood to play and Mom sure as hell won't be when she comes back."

"I didn't—"

"Julie!"

Julie stared at him with an injured expression. Then her eyes glinted. She pointed at Billy.

95

"It's happening to you, too," she giggled.

Billy reached for his own hair. It wavered, distended, grew out from his head.

"You look like a clown," Julie laughed.

"Goddam rain," he muttered, combing his hair down.

"It still looks funny."

He grabbed Julie by the arm, dragged her to the kitchen sink, and wet his comb. He ran the comb vigorously through her hair.

"Ouch! Billy!"

The front door opened and Carlotta entered. She looked tired, her whole body sagged, and water dripped from her coat and face. The sockets of her eyes looked lost in the shadows. She tried to smile, but found herself unable to.

"I'm sorry I'm so late, kids, the doctor—"

"That's all right, Mom," Billy said. "I bought some frozen ravioli. Got some milk, too."

Carlotta nodded a weary thanks. She took off her coat and sat heavily at the kitchen table.

"How are you, doll?" she said to Julie.

"Okay," Julie said, catching Billy's warning glance. "Me and Kim were just playing."

"Good, good," Carlotta said, abstractly.

In her mind an endless series of nurses, doctors, and technicians walked around her while she lay on a cold leather table waiting for reasons she had not understood. She was glad to be home. The children gave her strength. But she was bone tired, hardly able to keep her mind on the meal in front of her.

She chewed slowly, hardly conscious of the food. The darkness at the window seemed to grow. The girls snapped at the crisp celery—a gift from Mrs. Greenspan's vegetable garden. Carlotta leaned forward to quiet them, when she froze.

"Did you hear that?" she whispered.

Billy's fork stopped halfway to his mouth. He listened intently.

96

"No. What?"

"Under the house. Under the floor."

Julie and Kim watched her. They wondered if it was a game. They quickly understood it was not.

"I didn't hear nothing," Billy said.

There was a low groaning in the foundations.

"Well, that sure wasn't my imagination," Carlotta said, a trifle shrilly.

They went outside. The water dripped from the eaves, the clapboards, and the windowsills. In the darkness the rain water flashed eerily as it fell. The water swirled under the house, where the foundations raised it off the muddy ground.

Under the house mold, decayed cardboard, and wet rope dangled from the soggy rafters. Billy squirmed beneath the narrow crawl-space; his flashlight made a beam of light shoot through the pipes and cement blocks, picking out pieces of wire and insects trapped in the glare.

"There's nothing here, Mom!"

He stuffed rotted cardboard in the places where the pipes touched each other. Sawdust fell on his forehead. Sweat ran down his forearms. He grimaced, the insects crawling up his arms.

"It sounded like it was under the bedroom!" Carlotta called.

Billy made his way deeper into the darkness. He pushed the bricks, metal springs, and rusted pipes away from him. He leaned against a support. A low, metallic groan angrily shook the house.

"Billy! Are you all right?"

"Sure, Mom! It's the bedroom supports!"

He leaned in, trying to find where the pipes and supports bent together. He stuffed old newspaper and clumps of cardboard into the joints. Then he leaned against the support. Nothing. No sound. It was deathly quiet in the darkness.

After half an hour his shirt was soaked through. His face was lined with dust and cobwebs. Strange mold clung to his trousers, a smell of something alien, like dust from metal. He extricated himself with difficulty through the opening and stood up under the umbrella Carlotta held. The rain fell around them both, holding them in its quiet, insistent patter.

"What was it?" Carlotta asked.

"The pipes against the support. I leaned on it and it made that sound," Billy replied.

"Then what leaned on it before?"

Billy shrugged, brushing the cobwebs from his hair. Carlotta's pretty face was softened by the distant street light, catching her forehead at an angle. She pulled a wet piece of cardboard from his shoulder. Billy looked closely at her face, her eyes, the expression deep inside them. He began to realize the depths of what she was going through.

"It's an old house, Mom," he said. "It probably shifted."

"It sounded like somebody was moving in," she said nervously.

Billy laughed.

"It stinks under there," he said. "A rat died. Something's rotten."

They went inside. Billy changed his clothes, showered. Everything felt different. The house had changed. They were no longer alone in it.

Carlotta kissed the girls goodnight. She saw Billy go into his bedroom. She could not get over the unmistakable impression that things were different now. The atmosphere seemed thicker, charged in some way.

She turned off all but one light. The skirt and blouse slipped from her body. The doctor had warned her to get as much sleep as she could. It was no problem now. She felt like lead. She crawled between the sheets and closed her eyes.

Slowly she relaxed. Like a drug, fatigue made her limbs even heavier, her thoughts even slower. The impressions of the house faded farther and farther away from her. Only the heater made a noise from time to time. Shadows drifted quickly through her mind. Peculiar shadows, distorted and angry.

Carlotta drifted down into the core of herself. People she had known, things she had done, rose up about her, silhouetted, twisted, looking for her. A great lassitude enveloped her. She knew they were looking for her. Down through the corridors and empty yards, someone was looking for her. She saw his face, outlined by the strange lights. He saw her, came toward her, smiling . . . called her by name . . .

"Carlotta!" Franklin Moran said. "Well, whaddya think? Ain't much, but it's ours!"

Now they were legally married. Carlotta looked at the tiny room, a large bed jammed under the windows, a tiny kitchen visibly leaning in toward the bed.

"Come here, babe!" he said. "Let's celebrate!"

"Jesus Christ, Franklin! It's two-thirty in the after—"

"Ha ha ha ha ha ha."

He playfully threw her down on the bed. She was only sixteen. Sometimes his hands got rough with her. The rugged face, lined already, square and tough, became strange in front of her. It almost frightened her.

"Oh, baby," he sighed later. "You are one swell—"

"Shhhhhhh. Don't say that."

He grinned. His muscular chest rose and fell evenly in the golden light. At times like these she loved him madly. She loved his vitality, his self-reliance, his muscular quickness.

"Okay," he grinned again, patting her softly. "But it's true. You are."

There were two windows, both cracked. It was summer, and they kept the shades down. It was dark inside, but also mercilessly hot. Franklin liked to walk around in his shorts. Outside came the sounds of hammers, welding torches, and a radio which never stopped.

"How do you like this, huh, babe?" he said. "Beats Pasadena by a mile, don't it?"

"Yes. I told you."

"Then why do you look so sad?"

"I'm not sad. I'm just—"

"What?"

"Nothing. Money. What are we going to do for money?"

"Don't worry," he laughed. "Have I ever let you down yet?"

"No, but—"

"You better believe it," he said, his eyes flashing.

Carlotta sensed she had best say nothing. When he felt good, he was one step away from losing his temper if anybody crossed him.

The bathroom was behind the storage shed of acetylene tanks downstairs. To get to it, Carlotta had to walk through the racks and the rags and endure the stares of the two mechanics. She had to knock on the wall before she turned the corner, because often they used it without closing the door.

Then she became pregnant, and her belly was swollen.

"Hey, minister's daughter," said Lloyd, the mechanic with the wool cap. "You sure you ain't never been kissed?"

"She only sixteen?" asked the shorter mechanic.

"Franklin sure got himself some young pussy," Carlotta heard.

She went upstairs quickly. It had been three months since she had left Pasadena with Franklin. At the time, it seemed adventurous. But the two mechanics below frightened her, and they seemed to drag even Franklin down into a mud that threatened her, too.

Franklin's job was to procure used parts any way he could. Then they rebuilt large auto parts and sold them as new. They had to quickly size up the prospective customer and figure out how much trouble he might cause.

As Carlotta's belly grew larger and larger, she stayed

inside more and more. The illness confined her to bed for longer and longer periods. Franklin grew restless. He wanted his girl back. She was no fun. She wouldn't do it any other way except the way she couldn't now.

"Hey," he coaxed. "Come here, babe."

"No. I can't."

"Why not?"

"The doctor said."

"Fuck the doctor. You're not that pregnant."

"I am. I don't show it, but I am."

"What's with you? You never used to be like this."

"Things are different, Franklin—"

"Damn right they are."

Somehow it was a relief, being separated from him in this way. Yet when he took his clothes off, the light golden, streaming in through the closed shades, she could not help but appreciate his body. His stocky shoulders, a powerful neck, and squared head. His legs were long for his torso, his hands large and strong, his genitals full and weighty. She liked to run her fingers over his chest. She liked the changes she caused in him.

But the pregnancy was hard on her. The doctor told her she should have waited a couple of years. She felt she was invaded, bloated from the inside. She felt she was being transformed into something else. At times she could not bear being touched.

Slowly Franklin's temper grew shorter and shorter. She became almost frightened of him. It occurred to her he knew other girls. Yet what could she do?

One night he came in the door reeling.

"Pastor Dilworth's daughter," he said. "I would like to show you something."

She knew immediately he was drunk. Or worse.

"You're loaded," she said, disgustedly.

He took off his clothes. He was proud of his erection.

"How about that?" he said, swaying. "Hah?"

"Look at you. You can hardly talk right."

"Come on, babe. I want you and me to—"

"Leave me alone. You think I'm going to take that

101

stuff when I'm eight months pregnant? Is that what you think?"

"Oh, Jesus," he said, stumbling into the room, knocking over a lamp. He laughed at the sound of the crash. "I married me a frigid wife."

Carlotta leaned back against the wall. For the first time the sight of her husband, sitting on the bed, ready for love, naked, disgusted her. It was grotesque, repulsive. Suddenly she wanted to go home. But there was no home for her anymore.

"Come here, Carlotta," he whined.

"No, I can't. Leave me alone—"

"Jesus," he said, suddenly lying down on the floor.

He pulled the blanket down from the bed, wrapping it around his shoulder.

"Frigid," he mumbled. "She's frigid, Franklin. Poor Franklin."

Gradually he fell into a deep slumber. She felt the life stir within her. It, too, seemed grotesque suddenly. She was trapped. Her whole life had suddenly squeezed itself into no future at all.

Across from the machine shop was a dusty road and, across from that, a wash: a concrete ditch twenty yards wide. The banks were also slabbed with concrete. The only water which trickled by was in a slimy green groove in the center. It was here that Franklin picked up their money. On Saturdays they raced their bikes for a fifty-dollar pot, and Franklin usually won. The only worry was the police.

One day two patrolmen came to see Lloyd. He was suspected of dealing in amphetamines. There was a search warrant. Lloyd leaned against the vise, twirling the handle, while the police searched the drawers. There was an infinite number of drawers, cabinets, files, not to mention the screws, bolts, machine parts, and rags in fire-proof cans.

Carlotta heard their voices while she lay on the bed inside.

"Let's see what's upstairs," said one patrolman.

"You better not," Franklin said. "You only got a warrant for the shop."

"I got a warrant for this address, kid."

Franklin ran up in front of them.

"You stay out of my house, you bastards!"

She heard one patrolman say to the other, "I didn't care for that remark, did you?"

"Not at all. Listen, punk. You going to open the door or am I going to use your head to open it?"

Inside it was dank, dark, and it smelled of stale beer. Clothes and bottles, overturned ashtrays, bits of package dinners covered the floor. From the bed she could see the policemen trying to adjust to the darkness.

"Who's that?"

"That's my wife."

The policeman pushed the door open wider with his truncheon. On the bed, drenched in perspiration, shivering, Carlotta sat upright, leaning against the headboard.

"She's just a kid."

"What am I supposed to do about it?"

"You got her on mescaline too?"

"She's pregnant."

The second policeman stepped into the room, adjusting his gaze to the darkness. He smiled at Carlotta, who tried, but could not, smile back.

"Franklin?" she said. "What's wrong? Why are the police here?"

"Nothing, ma'am," said a policeman. "We have a search warrant. We won't disturb you."

"I think we should get her to a hospital, Roy," said the other.

The second policeman stepped closer to the bed. He examined her face. Her eyes had dilated, her face twitched in a spasm of pain.

"Call an ambulance," he said.

"That's *my* wife! She's having it here!"

"Shut up, kid."

103

"It's all right, Franklin," she said weakly. "Don't fight them."

She saw Franklin fuming between two policemen. She was aware of being carried somewhere. She thought she saw him in an ambulance. She was not certain of anything. She heard the scream of sirens all around her.

Franklin held the infant high over his head. The room stunk with diapers and the smell of vomit.

"God," he said. "Did I do this?"

"Not all by yourself, you didn't," Carlotta said.

"I did the important part."

He nuzzled her behind the neck.

"Just kidding," he said.

"Hey! What are you doing? I'm feeding the baby!"

"Well, he can only use one, can't he?"

"Franklin—don't you ever grow up?"

Suddenly his smile froze on his face. He knew now that the six pounds of squirming, helpless flesh at his wife's breast had come between them. Forever. She had been so quick, so lively, somebody he had picked out a year ago as being somebody special. Now she was covered with baby stink. The whole room was wretched with it. The nightmare of being trapped in it overwhelmed him.

"Where are you going?" she said.

"Where there ain't no baby shit," he said at the door. "No minister's daughters, no cops, no—no *nothing*."

He slammed the door behind him. She knew where he was going. Amphetamines. That's what picked him up. She hated the sight of him, the eyes flashing, the quick, jerky movements, the wired-up sense of humor.

He became rough with Carlotta when she could not come through for him. Then he became gentle with her. He wanted her to give herself. He wanted that kid who used to sleep with him on the beaches. Who used to ride down the streets of Pasadena with him, causing shock in all the squares, and bald old men to pop their eyes with burnt-out desire. But she had slipped away from him. Something was permanently different. Try what he did, it

104

was all gone. And Carlotta could only sit by and silently watch the destruction of their relationship.

Franklin became dependent on drugs. His nervous system was being destroyed. In only a few months he lost twenty pounds. In some way Carlotta had held up to him a mirror in which he had seen the superficiality of his soul, and it sickened him.

The money grew short. Franklin won fewer and fewer races, took more chances, began to deal in drugs. He turned more and more away from her, staying out late in the bars, drinking beer and joking with the girls there, the shadows growing ever deeper in his eyes. By the time the autumn had come, and the dusty cool weather grew dry and abrasive, Carlotta began to wish desperately that she could escape.

"You're going to get busted!" she screamed. "What the hell are we going to do then?"

"Ain't going to get busted."

"Grow up, Franklin! You're not the only one in the house!"

Franklin went to the refrigerator. He pulled out a can of beer.

"You mix uppers and beer, and they're going to find you—"

"A stinking, goddam, fucking hole!" he suddenly yelled, tears in his eyes. "That's all you ever were!"

She looked at him, hatred filling her eyes, making her tremble from head to foot. Suddenly she wished him dead. He glared back at her, helplessly caught in his own despair.

"What happened to you, anyway?" he yelled, louder. "You used to be a real fine kid, a—"

"It's all over, Franklin! Can't you get that through your head? The fun time is over! Billy—"

"Fuck that kid—I wished he'd never been born—"

"I wish *you'd* never been born! I wish you'd—"

Suddenly the room was quiet. Carlotta held Billy in her arms, stood there, the sun outlining his thin arms, the square head, in a rim of gold. He was a silhouette, an adolescent at the age of twenty-five. He had burned himself out, trying to stay young, and nothing had come to fill him from the inside. As far as Carlotta knew, he was dead already.

"Stinking, goddam hole!" he yelled.

Suddenly he flew into a rage. He threw the beer against the wall, splashing the liquid over them both. He dragged the shades from the rollers. He kicked the one chair through the room, again and again, until it cracked apart against the door.

"Shit—shit of a life," he bawled.

Suddenly the room was quiet. Carlotta held Billy in her arms. Franklin turned slowly, his muscles tensed. He pointed at her, staring into her frightened, dark eyes.

"You'll pay for this," he said quietly. "You're going to know what you did to me."

He went to the door. He stopped and looked at her again. He looked like he was going to cry again.

"I'm going to show you, Carlotta," he said. "I'm going to *show* you."

Clumsily, he went outside and slammed the door.

Carlotta sat on the edge of the bed, crying. At that age, she did not know what it was that a woman gave a man, to fill him from the inside with confidence, with the love of life. Much later she knew. But then, holding Billy on her lap, she only hated Franklin, wished him far, far away. The only thing she prayed for was to start all over again.

He did not come back that night. Nor the next night. The third day she asked the mechanics. Lloyd glinted at her, his eyes examining her figure under her blouse. Franklin was gone to race. Something he wanted to show them all. No, Franklin was not sober. Carlotta went back upstairs and locked the door behind her.

The fourth night Franklin still did not return. Carlotta called out the window at midnight to Richard, who looked up from the lathe. No, Franklin had not called.

Carlotta spent the night alone, trembling. She had the unmistakable premonition that something terrible had

106

happened. She could not shake the notion from her head. She woke, perspiring, yet no one had called her. No news had come from anywhere.

On the fifth day, late in the afternoon, she was certain something was wrong. Richard and Lloyd stood in the dusty road, their faces white and ashen. From time to time they looked up at the apartment. Then Richard made his way up the rickety stairs. He knocked slowly. She hesitated a long time. Then, making her way through the mess, she opened the door.

"Franklin's killed," Richard said clumsily.

"What?"

"He's dead—"

"You're sick, Richard. What kind of a joke is this?"

"No, it's true. He broke his back—"

Numbness spread through her limbs. As bad as it was, her life fell into a deeper abyss. She saw Richard through a black tunnel, hardly understanding what he was saying.

"He took too many chances—not like him. He was —he was just going crazy—"

"Richard—"

He caught her. She realized she had been fainting. He carried her to the chair. She shook her head, trying to throw off the nightmare. But when she opened her eyes, Richard knelt before her, his hair wild and tangled.

"He kept rolling!" he bawled. "He wouldn't stop rolling!"

Now suddenly her body was filled with stones and she, too young to know what to do, felt thrown into the dark waters. The room seemed to be dark, suspended in the void.

"Oh, my God, Richard, don't cry. What am I going to do?"

She stood uncertainly, looking into the room, the mess that her life had become. She could not bear to think of Franklin being buried. The burial of everything she had once believed in. She threw some clothes into a bag. She picked up Billy in her arms and looked one last

107

time at the tiny, dank apartment. Now it had that dusty odor of autumn, a kind of mildew everywhere. She stepped back, out onto the wooden porch. She closed the door. She closed it on Franklin. In the room were bad smells, amphetamines, mescaline, and hashish. Cracks in the walls and under the stained carpet. Behind the door now were the screaming arguments, the hatreds, the jealous accusations. It was all there, locked up behind her. There was suddenly a chance to be free.

"Richard," she said, "drive me to Pasadena."

Richard looked up at her.

"You sure?"

"Very sure. Get in the car."

So she moved back into the rolling estates on Orange Grove Boulevard. This time she had an infant. The family sat around the dinner table as before. They had Sunday brunches as before. But she did not speak with them. And they loathed the infant. They wanted it put up for adoption. Quickly. But in her dreams Carlotta still remembered Franklin. He cruised up the boulevard to knock at her door, so boyish yet so rugged. He wanted to speak with her. But he was dead. Somewhere she saw the motorcycle, cartwheeling over the oil drums at the edge of the course. He rolled and rolled, entangled in the spokes and the dust, spinning around and around. For nearly a year she had those dreams. Then she only had dreams about the smelly apartment, a kind of violence that took place in a dark room far away. Then Franklin disappeared from her memory altogether, a strange void, and he finally ceased to exist completely.

The ground shook.

Carlotta, deeply asleep, felt rather than heard a strange, metallic rumble. She knew it was no earthquake. She opened her eyes cautiously.

The wall seemed to glow. A lonely train whistle echoed from the darkness. She raised herself slowly from the couch. A glow hovered against the wall, moved, and then slid along the surface toward the window. The train bellowed fiercely, like a great animal in pain.

"Bill!" she whispered.

There was no response.

She glanced into the hallway. It was dark. Billy was either asleep or still in the garage. She stood up and backed toward the far wall, away from the light.

"Bill!!"

The area of light quivered and distended. It had reached the window. The lamp on the table was glowing. Behind it the rectangle of light held still about three feet above the floor.

"Dear God!" she whispered.

The lamp exploded, plunging the room into darkness. A blue glow began to form until it hovered over the broken wire frame of the destroyed shade. It formed and re-formed like a ball of jelly in the black room.

Carlotta screamed.

The two lights flowed into one another. They formed a kind of green flow between the wall and the table. The room filled with the eerie light. Carlotta saw her hands illuminated in the cold light.

Then together the lights dissipated slowly. They grew thin. They became transparent. Then they were gone. It was completely dark.

Billy's door banged open against the wall.

"What is it, Mom?"

Carlotta found herself pressed against the far wall, unable to speak. Her forehead was covered in cold perspiration.

"Where are you, Mom? I can't see you!"

Carlotta turned, shaking, and looked into the hallway. Somewhere in it was a form, half-defined, of her son.

The light went on overhead. Billy stood blinking in the light.

"What happened, Mom? Did it happen again?"

"Nothing happened."

"I heard a crash."

"It was the lamp."

Carlotta came out of her shock to see Billy reach for the broken light fixture on the floor.

"Don't touch it!"

He picked up the pieces.

"It's *cold*," he said.

Carlotta felt herself suddenly chill. She shivered.

"Hand me the blanket, will you, Bill?"

He put the blanket over her shoulders.

"You want me to call the clinic?"

"No. I'm all right now."

Billy looked uncertain, self-conscious all of a sudden.

"Are you sure?"

"Yes. I'm all right. Now you go to bed."

"You're sure?"

He went down the hall to his room. He left the door open. Carlotta tried to sleep sitting up in a chair, the blanket wrapped around her, facing the broken lamp on the floor.

Sneidermann lit Carlotta's cigarette for her, putting the lighter back into his pocket. She seemed calmer now than when she had first come in. She was intelligent. He knew now what her IQ was—125. Her black eyes followed his every movement, not certain what to believe. He spoke in a very relaxed manner, matter-of-factly. It was a technique to reduce her anxiety.

"Everybody gets into a situation at some time that we call a panic," he said. "When your car crashed, for example. You told me that everything seemed to hang in space before you hit. That's a typical way to experience panic."

"Yes. I remember."

"Now, when you woke in the middle of the night, you were in a panic. Well, it's the same thing. Your mind was going incredibly fast. Very sharp. Everything looked slowed down."

110

Carlotta inhaled slowly. Her eyes had the gleam of one who does not believe what you are saying. Yet behind the facade Sneidermann could see her hungry for any kind of assurance.

"Do you remember what you told me?" he said. "You said there was a sound."

"No. I screamed, I think."

"Before that."

"I don't remember."

"Think. You told me when you first came in today. A sound as the lights died away."

"It was an animal. Far away."

"No. You described it as something else."

"I said it was a lonely sound, like a train."

"Exactly."

"Oh, come on, Dr. Sneidermann! Even you don't believe that."

"Consider it a possibility. Don't forget your state of mind."

Carlotta shrugged. "All right," she said.

"You were awakened by this strange noise. By the rumble underfoot. Your mind is racing away. Your thoughts are shooting around with the speed of light."

"So what?"

"That's how you described it. Those were the words you used when you came in today."

"Okay, go on. I'm listening."

"Are trains common in West Los Angeles?"

"No. Rare. Very rare."

"See? Once in a blue moon. They come out of the factories, I believe."

Sneidermann watched her. Belief and disbelief struggled for possession of her mind.

"And there it shines," he concluded. "This bizarre rectangle of light against the wall. Of *course* it's a rectangle; it's coming through the window."

"But it changed shape."

"Curve in the tracks."

"And the blue light?"

111

"The lamp was on the edge of the table. Train shook the ground. It fell, smashed, blue flash, went out. Now, in your perceptual state, everything was extended. Slowed down. It *seemed* to you that it hovered in the air a long time. Of course, it really was only a fraction of a second."

"You're very convincing."

"Remember how slowly the glass seemed to break when you hit the telephone pole? That really happened in a hundredth of a second. It's your mind that made it seem different."

Sneidermann smiled. "Am I making up science fiction?" he asked.

"No."

"I wasn't there with you. But what I just suggested —wouldn't that be a possible explanation?"

"I suppose so."

"Now, being invaded by outer space—that's a second explanation. Which seems more reasonable?"

Carlotta sighed. She was convinced. There was no need to answer.

"Of course it all makes sense now," she said. "Now I can think clearly. Here, with you. But when something happens there, it's a different world altogether."

"I understand, Carlotta. But you don't want to live in an unreal world."

"No, of course not. But what happens if I don't *act* from reason? You know what I'm trying to say? What if I throw something at the kids, for example? Thinking they're something else."

Sneidermann nodded.

"I know what you're getting at," he said. "Of course. But I can tell you I don't think that will happen."

"Why not?"

"There's a medical explanation. I could put it to you like this: Your case is not the kind where you would mistake something as important to you as your children for anything else."

Carlotta straightened in the chair, smoothing her

skirt. It was a gesture she made when she was thinking very intently. Already she was accustomed to losing herself in her own thoughts while Sneidermann waited. She had grown accustomed to the ground rules of the sessions.

"If my mind has this power," she said finally, "to make me *see* things and *feel* things, things which *aren't* there, or only half there—then I get this chill inside of me. I get a feeling as though some demon has got Carlotta in the palm of his hand, just laughing at her."

Psychosis was the worst road to travel, Sneidermann thought. It was long and hard and hell all the way. These hallucinations had pointed straight to full-blown psychotic episodes. But now, leaning back in the chair of his apartment, he saw many indications that were more hopeful.

In the first place, Carlotta Moran's medical history was now available to him. There had been no prior treatments for any kind of psychological disturbance. It is not impossible for schizophrenia to suddenly blossom at the age of thirty-two. But the odds are against it. Normally there is some kind of sign by the early twenties.

Going over the latest meeting also gave Sneidermann hope. The perceptual distortion of the train light had grown out of a highly charged emotional situation. This was more characteristic of hysteria, not psychosis.

It was true that she had a feeling of unreality about herself. Estrangement from reality is a crucial indication of psychosis. Yet, once she calmed down, she seemed to respond to his questions with a full sense of self. Hadn't she been genuinely concerned for her children at the end of the session? What this meant was that these feelings of unreality were attributes of the attacks, and not a permanent dissociation.

The more Sneidermann looked through the texts piled on his desk, the more he checked his own notes of the interviews with her, the more he searched for an overall, tentative pattern, the better the situation seemed to appear. Hadn't she even complained of peculiar feelings

113

inside her during the attacks? That, too, was a symptom of hysteria, not psychosis.

The door opened. Jim entered. Sneidermann's roommate smiled in a friendly way, then began to throw things into an overnight bag.

Sneidermann watched. Being the only Jew in a dormitory of highly competitive males, most of whom were in surgery, general, or dentistry, he kept himself polite, friendly, but withdrawn. Out of all first year residents, only a few are invited to join the staff—a goal he sought. So Sneidermann abstained from the Southern California social gambit and concentrated on making his way to the top of the class. The free and easy ways in the sun remained for him nothing more than a pleasant view from the window.

"Jim—aren't you scheduled to take the late afternoon shift next semester?"

"In three weeks. Why?"

"Would you trade?"

"You crazy? Sure. What's the reason?"

"Nothing. I like the patients on it."

"It's your life. It's a deal."

"I appreciate it."

Jim waved with a large grin and left. Down the hallway were girls with tennis rackets, laughing with their boyfriends. Sneidermann softly closed the door.

The more Sneidermann thought about Carlotta Moran, the more she intrigued him. He could not get her out of his mind. He sat down. Then, restless, he stood and paced the floor.

Fears, yes. But not phobic. Her fears centered around something very specific. Obsession, compulsion? None at all. Sneidermann paged through the texts, making notes. Nor is she depressed. She may be later, but at the moment there is no depression. Anxieties? Certainly. He penciled the words "hysterical neurosis" lightly at the bottom of the page of notes. He slowed down, considering it carefully.

Neurosis, because it was controlled unconsciously,

and she hated it. Hysterical, because the signs and symptoms began and ended in periods of intense, sexually tinged emotions. Then she calmed down. Once she calmed down, her thought processes seemed normal. Sneidermann rubbed his eyes. His thoughts proceeded almost by themselves.

Somehow, she was like those buildings which one finds in the poor parts of Los Angeles. Something wrong in the construction—they stand ten, twenty years with no problem. Then comes a tremor. Every other building stands firm. Hers goes down in a cloud of rubble, leaving naked girders in what had been a stable personality.

What was it? And why now?

He tried to concentrate on his other cases. He tried to write a letter home. He could not. He finally threw his gym shoes and a sweatshirt into a handbag, went to the gymnasium, and for an hour bashed a handball against a wall.

8:16 p.m. November 11, 1976

An unexpressed darkness settled around the tract home on Kentner Street. It swallowed them all like a black fog, during the day and during the night. It seemed nothing would pierce that fog. It cut them off from reality. Anything outside—a mailman, a child on a skateboard—looked far away, outside the cave they were in, hopelessly distant and illusory.

Whether the television was on, whether Billy was in the house, whatever Carlotta did—it made no difference. They were no longer alone in the house.

On the evening of November 11, Carlotta sat on the couch, sewing patches on shirts and trousers. The girls lay on the floor, coloring. Billy rummaged through a basket of clean socks, looking for a pair.

"Damn," Carlotta said.

Billy looked at her.

"Look up there," she whispered.

115

Billy turned. A crack had formed in the ceiling. Plaster dropped in tiny streams to the rug below.

They all watched it, transfixed. Because the crack was growing. Longer and longer. It grew snakelike in a pattern; then it stopped. The ceiling was covered in a black design, incomplete, and the plaster sifted like flour from the wound.

"Jesus," Billy whispered between his teeth.

Carlotta finally looked down from the ceiling. The house seemed so fragile. Now the night was all-powerful.

"Does that mean something, Bill?" she whispered.

"No, it's just cracks. Lines."

"God," she said, "it looks so—"

The thought dangled incomplete in her brain. The girls were caught in the labyrinth of fear.

"Mommy," Julie whispered, "there's somebody at the window."

Carlotta whirled.

"Where?"

The blackest of nights reflected her own image, hand held to her own throat, ready to flee.

"I don't know," Julie answered, uncertainly.

"What do you mean, you *don't know?*" Carlotta hissed. She kept her eyes on the two windows of the far wall.

"I—"

Billy went to the window. He leaned forward. He cupped his eyes against the reflection. Then suddenly he yelled and threw the windows open, waving his arms. Dead silence. He leaned carefully out. Only the crickets made a noise.

"She just got spooked," he said, swinging around at Julie.

"Listen, Julie," Billy scolded. "We're not playing a game. Do you understand? Mommy doesn't want to hear anything unless it's for real. Okay? It's too important now."

"I wasn't playing," Julie said.

Carlotta shivered. She went to the thermostat.

116

"Now, Julie," Billy said softly. "Did you really see something or not? You were playing, weren't you? Wasn't it make-believe?"

"I—I—don't know—"

"Billy," Carlotta called.

The thermostat was moving crazily. The dial revolved visibly in the metal container, back and forth, bending inside. Billy stood behind her, looking over her shoulder. He reached his hand forward.

"Don't!" Carlotta cautioned.

He stopped, withdrew his hand.

"I don't know," he said. "I don't know much about temperature gauges. It's not the heater. That's steady. Maybe the metal band inside got warped or rotted—"

"Metal doesn't rot."

"Corroded. You know what I meant. What that little strip in there would do."

"What do you mean, 'would do'?"

"How it goes haywire when it breaks. That's all I meant."

"Well," Carlotta said, "it's steady now. See?"

The dial stabilized at seventy-two degrees, dipped slightly, then returned.

"I guess it's working now. That's normal, isn't it? Seventy-two?"

"Close the windows, Bill," she said, turning away.

"Right. See? A cold draft."

He closed the windows. Carlotta sat in the easy chair, biting her lip.

"And pull the shades, will you? All the way."

He did so. Now it was silent. Their ears rang in the silence.

"I'll plaster the ceiling," he said. "Tomorrow. I can get some plaster in the afternoon."

"Good."

But Carlotta was withdrawn from them all. Her face was taut and her heart pounded.

"Hey, Julie," Billy said. "Let's play a game of Hearts."

117

They produced a pack of cards and dealt out the hands.

"You know how to play," he said. "You get rid of your hearts."

Carlotta watched them, heard their voices a thousand miles away.

"The Queen of Spades is the witch," he said. "Get rid of her."

"Oh, dear Christ," Carlotta breathed.

"Okay. You have the two of clubs. Put it down."

"Dear Christ, dear Christ."

Carlotta sank back in the chair. Her face was swallowed in the shadow. She barely heard them playing. Waiting.

7

AN iridescent, long, red fish slid like an eel through the green weeds. The ocean was vast, translucent, and warm. All at once the fish rolled over and entered a canyon of blue coral rocks, shimmering on the sandy floor. It was looking for something . . . In the mouths of the caves were bright stones, pearls glittering in the blue water . . .

The telephone rang.

Carlotta bolted upright, holding her head. The sunshine poured in through the windows. Billy sat in the easy chair, eating cornflakes and watching the auto races on television.

"What was—?"

The telephone rang again.

"I was dreaming," she muttered, shaking her head.

She stood up from the couch. She tried to remember the dream. Where was the fish going? Why was everything so beautiful? The telephone rang a third time. The dream disappeared.

"Jerry!"

She pressed the receiver as tightly as she could to her ear.

"Where are you? Saint Louis? You're supposed to be in Seattle! What? . . . End of the year audit? Well, don't put anybody in jail . . ."

She twirled the cord in her fingers. To Billy she looked like a school girl excited about a date. The sight disgusted him in a vague, undefined way. He turned away.

"Oh, Jerry!" she said, smiling, but her voice tensed. "That's *next* week! The nineteenth! . . . What? . . . Oh, I see . . . Of course . . . I'll meet you at the airport."

Now she was fully awake. Excited, she nevertheless felt anxiety. She felt her reserves would hold for several days at most. Flustered, she waved at the television, a gesture for Billy to turn down the volume. But the roar of the crowd and the racers remained loud.

"Oh, it's so good to hear your voice! . . . What? Oh, yes. Me too! . . . I can't talk . . . I'm not alone."

She laughed. Billy switched off the set and left the room.

"Julie wants to say hello," she said.

Julie took the receiver in both hands. Her eyes were shining with excitement.

"What?" Julie whispered. "I can't hear you! . . . Playing jump rope . . . *Jump* rope! . . . with Kim . . . Yes . . . I miss *you!* . . . Here comes a kiss. Ready?"

She blew a kiss into the receiver. She listened intently.

"He wants to talk to Kim," Julie said.

Carlotta held the receiver to Kim's ear.

"Say 'hello, Jerry,' " Carlotta whispered.

" 'Lo, Jerry."

Jerry's laugh came through the telephone.

"Say 'How are you?' " Carlotta coached.

"How *are* you?" Kim repeated in a trembling voice.

Carlotta took the receiver from her.

"You sure?" she said. "He's right here. Just a minute."

She turned. Billy was not there. She covered up the receiver with her hand.

"Bill!"

"He went to the garage," Julie said.

Carlotta's face clouded. She uncovered the receiver and smiled again.

"I guess he's gone, Jerry. What? No. I was mistaken. He wasn't even in the house . . . Oh, yes . . . I miss you so . . . Oh, I do, I do . . . Oh, Jerry . . . Please be careful. I'll be waiting for you . . . Oh, don't . . . I hate to say goodbye . . . 'Til next week." Her voice sank to a whisper. "I love you . . . Goodbye!"

She held the receiver in her hand. Slowly she let it down. She sighed.

"Mush," Julie giggled.

"Yeah," Carlotta laughed.

Her mind spun with details. To buy a new blouse. A skirt. Something with embroidery. Where was the money to come from? A blouse, then. Something cheerful. In her imagination she saw Jerry step from the plane, waving at her in that boyish way, stepping down, holding her. They would drive someplace. Other images with Jerry came to her . . . She smiled.

Carlotta crossed her legs. She looked uncommonly pretty today. A suntan had darkened her forehead and cheeks, her arms and legs, and her dark eyes seemed darker than ever. She looked forthrightly back at Sneidermann.

"All right, Doctor Sneidermann," she said. "You have the tests back. What's going on?"

Sneidermann swiveled in his chair. It was a gesture his supervisor made. Instead of making Sneidermann feel at ease, however, it only made him feel awkward. He tapped several files on the desk and opened the first of them.

"I don't have all the answers, Carlotta. But we do know there's nothing wrong with you medically—physiologically. And as far as we can tell, your intellect seems to function as well or better than normal."

"So?"

"That leaves only one area."

"What's that?"

"Psychological development. Emotional development. Here the tests and what you've told me do begin to add up."

121

Carlotta smiled. Sneidermann observed that something had happened. There was an inner vitality. Her demeanor radiated a sense of confidence. For the first time, she had a sense of humor about herself. He wondered what was the cause of her new-found determination and optimism.

"Do you mind if I tell you, Dr. Sneidermann," she said, "that this sounds exceedingly remote to me."

He chuckled in spite of himself.

"Of course not. The general idea is that certain phases of our lives never really die. They continue to exist within us. For certain specific reasons, they come back. By coming back they cause delusions, anxieties, even hallucinations."

"So simple."

"Not at all. It's as though ourselves, the part that walks around during the day, is full of holes. Shot through with holes. The conscious mind has no problem. Orders hamburgers, reads the newspaper, yells at the kids. But some deeper experience, some kind of structure, crawls up like a magician through a trap door and takes over at very specific moments. For very specific reasons. For reasons we don't know yet."

Carlotta smiled. But her hands dropped nervously into her lap.

"What are you going to do?" she said. "Give me a shock treatment?"

Suddenly pity stabbed Sneidermann.

"No, no, Carlotta," he said. "Nothing like that. Look—think of it this way. We're going to put a patch on an inner tube. But it's your conscious mind which has to find out where the hole is."

Carlotta's eyes were moist. The idea of sickness penetrated her and filled her with shame. Sneidermann realized that there was nothing he could say to expel that notion from her mind. She stood. He escorted her to the door.

"Goodbye, Carlotta. I'll see you tomorrow. Tomorrow, we'll get started."

"Goodbye, Dr. Sneidermann."

She smiled vacuously, but walked briskly out the door, and was gone before he could say another word.

Sneidermann spent the next hour in the office bringing his notebooks up to date. It was near the supper break, but he wasn't hungry. A group conference with five in-patient cases—one, an autistic boy of seven—was currently in progress down the hall. Sneidermann decided to poke his head in, for a while, at least.

Leaving the office, he detoured through the main lobby to pick up coffee and a candy bar from the public vending machines. Pushing open the door to the outer vestibule, he saw Carlotta standing at the glass doorways grown black with night. Her reflection was almost full size, as she stood so close to the glass. She seemed afraid to go out.

"Carlotta," Sneidermann said in surprise, "is everything all right?"

Carlotta turned, startled. "Oh, yes—of course—my ride—I don't know where my friend is. She's always on time—unless she's had car trouble—"

Sneidermann thought for a moment. He was supposed to remain on duty for the entire evening. Otherwise, he could drive her home.

"Would you like to telephone her?"

"Yes. Thank you."

Carlotta went back with Sneidermann to the desk. She punched Cindy's number and waited. No answer. Then she hung up. She looked at Sneidermann helplessly.

Sneidermann considered. He could suggest a cab, but neither of them could afford it. He checked his watch.

"You live in West L.A.?"

"Way out near the freeway."

Sneidermann leaned over the desk.

"Tell Boltin I'll be gone for half an hour," he said to the nurse. "I'll owe him one."

123

Sneidermann walked quickly into the lobby with Carlotta. He held open the door for her.

"I'm terribly sorry," she said.

Sneidermann waved away her apology.

Carlotta sat in the torn bucket seat of the tiny MG. Sneidermann got in, slammed the door shut, and turned on the ignition. The MG roared out of the parking lot, swerving around several parked cars.

"Now is when I find out how much my patients trust me," he said, smiling. "I drive fast."

Carlotta remained silent. He felt a tinge of embarrassment trying to joke with her. They drove toward West L.A. in silence, the MG swerving through the traffic like a ballet dancer. The traffic bottled up near Wilshire Boulevard, where skyscrapers were rising up every month, as though the city could not grow fast enough to suit its people.

"Are you a native Angeleno?" Sneidermann asked.

"Excuse me?"

"I said, are you from Los Angeles, originally?"

"Close. Pasadena."

"You know?" Sneidermann said, fumbling for cigarettes, finding none, "you're the first person I've met who could say that. This city is full of millions of people and all of them are from someplace else."

Carlotta removed a package of cigarettes from her purse and offered him one. They both lit up. With the canvas top down, the breeze ruffled through their hair. Sneidermann cast a glance at Carlotta. She did look rather pretty in the front seat of his car.

"Well," she said. "I did live for a time in Nevada."

"Las Vegas?"

"No. The desert."

"Really? What were you doing out there?"

"Living."

Carlotta inhaled deeply on her cigarette as she relaxed back in the seat, her head resting on the vinyl bolster.

Los Angeles raced by them. Sneidermann took a wrong turn, trying to cut around the factory yards. He cursed softly, then had to retrace his path toward Colorado Avenue.

"Pasadena, huh?" Sneidermann said. "That's supposed to be a wealthy community."

"Parts of it. Parts of it are very wealthy."

"What about the part you come from?"

"Very wealthy."

Carlotta spoke quietly. She was more relaxed outside the office. Sneidermann suddenly realized that there was a whole new rhythm to her, something that had never surfaced in the artificial setting of the office. Was he getting the real Carlotta in the office? Or only a formalized one? A Carlotta who was frightened by the alien sounds and sights of the hospital.

"I'd like to ask you something," Sneidermann said. "Just out of curiosity."

"Okay."

"You live on welfare," he said politely. "That's what you wrote on the form."

"Yes."

"Why is that necessary?"

Carlotta looked at him strangely.

"I ran out of money."

Sneidermann chuckled, a trifle embarrassed at the poor show he was making.

"I—meant, your parents. Couldn't you ask them for help?"

Carlotta considered for a moment, then shrugged and looked out the side at the oncoming traffic.

"I didn't want to."

"A matter of principle?"

"No. I just didn't want their help."

There was a long silence. Sneidermann felt she had said all she was going to say. Strange, how different she was out of the office. Not nervous; deep down, perhaps, but no surface gestures that betrayed anxiety. For a moment he felt out of his element. He almost preferred meeting people—especially women—in the formalized confines of the institution. Then Carlotta sighed.

"When I lived in Nevada," she said, "I had the opportunity of being with a very wonderful person. Julie's father. And Kim's. And I learned it was better to be independent of most people." Carlotta looked at him. "Welfare is only temporary, Dr. Sneidermann. Soon I'll graduate from school. I'll get a good job."

Sneidermann smiled. "I'm impressed."

"By what?"

"By everything. Your independence. Knowing who you are and what you want." He glanced at her. "Keeping your family together. And doing it the hard way."

Carlotta's eyes lowered, almost demurely, he thought. Then she smiled. "I'm glad you approve of me," she said softly.

Sneidermann said nothing, but something inside him was churning. His perception was undergoing an overhaul. He realized he needed to know more about Carlotta. Not as a therapist, but as a human being. In these few moments, in this brief ride through the darkening byways of West Los Angeles, he discovered in her other dimensions, dimensions only hinted at previously. If you ask a thousand questions in a formal situation, you get only a fraction of what you get when you just spend time with a person. It changes the way you speak. It changes the way you relate. It cuts through all the artifice.

"Dr. Sneidermann."

"Yes?"

"This is a long-time proposition, isn't it?"

Sneidermann thought a moment. In the office he would have given her a quick, incisive answer. There he believed that honesty was the best policy. Let the patient know the worst right away. Now, tonight, he wished he could find some glimmer of hope, some way to say it so she would not be frightened.

"It may be," he finally said.

"Months?"

"Maybe longer, Carlotta."

She bit her finger and looked away. "I don't have months," she said in a whisper.

"Why not?"

"Jerry's coming back."

"Who?"

"Jerry. My fiancé. He's coming back next week. For one night. But soon it will be permanent."

"Don't you think he'd understand?"

Carlotta shook her head. "He's very skittish about insane people. His mother committed suicide."

They drove in silence up Kentner Street. Carlotta gestured to the house at the end. A nondescript house, Sneidermann thought. The scene of all her terrors. Now it was dark inside. He wondered where her children were. To his surprise, Carlotta still sat there, unmoving. He turned off the ignition.

"Dr. Sneidermann . . ."

"Yes, Carlotta?"

"I don't understand what's happening to me."

Such a simple thing to say. What horrible depths it revealed. Sneidermann was stabbed by pity for her.

"I must be totally insane," she said softly. "To see and feel these things . . ."

She looked up at him, almost shyly, vulnerable, waiting for an answer, testing him.

"There are many patients, Carlotta, who have seen things. Felt things. Things that could not be."

"That's hard to believe."

"You'll discover that I never tell lies. Listen, Carlotta. In that clinic where we meet, there is a fifty-three-year-old woman who speaks to a baby that isn't there, nurses it—I'm serious—diapers it, and it doesn't exist. There's a seventeen-year-old boy who climbs steps that aren't there, who goes around knocking on doors that aren't there, who scratches at windows that don't exist. There's a seventy-year-old man who is afraid of a Renaissance prince who follows him around, even into his dormitory room. You see what I mean, Carlotta? It happens.

127

Much more often than you think. And each patient swears that what he sees, smells, and feels is no hallucination."

Carlotta was silent.

"Then I'm no different," she finally said.

"There is one difference."

"What's that?"

"They have to live in an institution. You don't."

Carlotta turned to him.

"Don't you think I will? Someday? Like them?"

"Not necessarily. Why should you? You've already made the commitment to get better. While you're still fundamentally healthy."

Carlotta trembled slightly. Then she smiled gratefully.

"Thank you, Dr. Sneidermann. Somehow, you make it seem better."

"I'm glad, Carlotta."

He moved to open the door for her, but she was already opening it and stepping out. An independent woman, Sneidermann thought.

"Goodnight, Carlotta."

"Goodnight, Dr. Sneidermann. Thanks."

He waved, turned on the ignition, and drove off. For a fleeting moment he saw her small image in the mirror; then he turned the corner and she was gone. Sneidermann felt better than he had in a very long time.

The rising moon hung like a red-orange paste-up over West Los Angeles. Long streaks of brown clouds sliced through the sky.

Between the purple sky and the dark streets Carlotta walked with Julie and Kim. The green lights of the street lamps were turned on, chemical lights that turned their flesh white and their lips black.

Yet the sky was deep purple, iridescent. There was the sensation that it was all abnormal. The long shadows from the palms, the dark recesses of the tract homes, all grew darker and darker. The glistening foliage looked

128

sickly. The walks bloomed with red poinsettias bobbing silently in a breeze, and fences glittered, cold and wet, beside them.

"Where is Billy?" Carlotta muttered.

As they walked, the steps echoed in the night. They were near the corner of Kentner Street. Carlotta was afraid to go into the dark house.

After Dr. Sneidermann had driven off, she had climbed the porch steps and had discovered Julie and Kim huddled together on the tattered floater, just sitting there in the dark. They had been afraid to go in without Billy. They told Carlotta that Billy had left right after coming home from school. They didn't know where he had gone.

"He said he'd come back," Julie said, holding Carlotta's hand.

"I'm scared, Mommy," Kim said.

Carlotta turned around and walked a few paces in the other direction.

"Of course he'll come back," she said. "But he knows he's supposed to be home now."

"How come?" Kim asked.

"Because Mommy is not supposed to be left alone. That's how come."

Carlotta now saw her house at the end of the block. And even though Dr. Sneidermann had convinced her that her demon was not within the house but within herself, the dread which it inspired in her—unlit, a black rectangle against the banked earth of the dead end, a tiny wooden structure leaning in from the alley behind it— was indescribable. She knew that if Billy, for some reason, did not come back, she would walk the streets the entire night. She would never go without him back into that house.

"Mr. Greenspan," she called softly, rapping on the door with the European-styled heavy knocker. "Mr. Greenspan!"

There was no answer.

"I guess they're out," she said.

129

She went back, distractedly, to the sidewalk.

"There he is!" Julie said, pointing.

"Where?"

"Up the street."

Under the darkened elms, now black with night, Billy walked forward, his familiar slouch barely defining him in the shadows. He slowed, looking ominously at the group waiting quietly for him. His face was bleached by the intense street lamp overhead. His black lips twisted into a nervous grin.

"Where have you been, Bill?" Carlotta said.

"Junk yard. Car parts. For your Buick."

"You know you're not supposed to leave me alone! I told you! That's doctor's orders!"

"I'm sorry—"

"*Sorry?* What do you expect these kids to do if something happened?"

"Nothing."

"That's right, Bill. Nothing. Now you listen to me. You are the man of the house. You start acting like one. You're not a kid anymore."

"Well, heck, Mom. It was your Buick I was working on! I didn't wrap it around a telephone pole!"

Carlotta took both girls by the hand.

"Let's go inside," she said. "It's cold out here."

They entered the house. The lamps failed to dispel the sense of darkness. Carlotta was still angry and, the girls could tell, still afraid.

"We need some more light in here," she said.

The living room, in which they stood uncertainly, was cluttered with Carlotta's clothes. Some magazines and cosmetic bottles lay on the table. She never went into the bedroom anymore. If she needed something, Bill got it. Or Julie. The clutter was a sign that her daily life, because of the nightmares, was getting tattered around the edges.

"Don't stare at me, Julie," she said. "Haven't you got some other place to go?"

Julie stared at her, perplexed. Both girls waited.

For something. A signal, maybe, that everything was all right now. Now that Billy was home. But the signal never came.

"Well?" Carlotta said.

Julie went off to her bedroom, feeling she had done something terribly wrong. She knew Mommy wasn't to blame. She knew Kim wasn't to blame. Then who was?

Carlotta sat in the chair, put her feet on the footstool, and lit a cigarette. Billy stood purposely in the center of the room. Kim wandered through the hallway and ended up in the bedroom. With Julie there would be solace.

"Jesus," Carlotta whispered softly. "I've become a real nice person, haven't I?"

"No," Billy said.

He sat on the edge of the couch in the poorly lit room, one leg over the other.

"I wasn't asking you for an answer," she said.

Carlotta puffed on the cigarette. The house was quiet. Billy remained immobile, poised for an expectant blow, girding his defenses.

"This whole thing sort of sickens you, doesn't it?" she said. "Isn't that why you stay out late?"

Billy said nothing, playing with an ashtray.

"Admit it," she said. "Your mother is crazy and it shames you."

"It doesn't shame me."

"What? I can't hear you."

"I said, I just feel sorry for you."

He was silent, moody. She could not decipher what was inside his brooding head. The muscles of his forearms rose and fell as he twirled the ashtray. The shadows ate into his eyes, dark sockets lost to her gaze.

"You were out late last night, too," she said.

"I was in the garage."

"No you weren't. Cindy had to stay until six o'clock."

"I was in Jed's garage."

Carlotta turned away from him, inhaling, then

131

ground out the cigarette. Involuntarily, his eyes were caught by the red glow of the dying ash.

"Listen, Bill," she said softly. "I need you. I don't care if it's repulsive to you. How do you think *I* feel? But I'm not doing this for kicks. You understand?"

"I know."

"You'll have to be tough, Bill. Don't run out on me. Because, you know, this is the first time, the first time ever, that I've had to ask you, I mean in a serious way, to take care of me. Because I have almost nobody else to turn to."

"I know, Mom. I said I was sorry."

"Jerry, Cindy, and you. Maybe Doctor Sneidermann. That's it. I couldn't count on the Greenspans."

"I meant it when I said I was sorry."

"Okay. I'm not angry. You just have to let me know your schedule and keep to it. It doesn't mean you're necessarily trapped here. We'll work it through together."

Carlotta smiled at him. In some way he had passed a test. He had accepted his responsibility like a man. Billy sat there, legs crossed, thoughtful and sincere.

"You sore at me?" she asked.

"No. Only it was *your* Buick I was working on. That's why I was late."

"I just needed you here, Bill. I got a little high-strung. I'm sorry."

Billy sat for a while and watched TV, then shut it and stood up heavily. He looked vacantly at the clutter in the room for a while, then at Carlotta.

"Goodnight, Mom," he said, and kissed her.

" 'Night."

When Billy was in bed she walked to the door of the girls' bedroom. Julie had undressed Kim. Now they both lay in their underpants on their separate beds. Carlotta looked at them sadly. What were they going through? Kids always feel responsible for everything. This whole thing had become a tunnel that had finally swallowed them all up. She tucked them under their blankets and kissed them tenderly on the foreheads. Julie smiled in her sleep.

"Keep the door to your room open," Carlotta said toward the dark bedroom that was Billy's. "You sleep like the dead."

"Okay, Mom," came his voice.

Carlotta turned off all but one lamp, the one which had fallen. Now the shade was repaired with masking tape, the wire refashioned, a new bulb put in the socket. The soft, yellow light made the room look less dingy. The house was quiet. She slipped off her skirt and blouse, put on a nightgown and wrapped herself in a robe. She waited for the drowsiness to set in.

This was her prison, she thought. Unable to go anywhere alone. Impossible to sleep at night. Dark shadows. Isolation. A bus ride to the school, then to the clinic, then to the house. Then more isolation. It occurred to her that, without Jerry, there would be no relief to it. Her thoughts became less bitter, more diffused, and finally she felt her arms and legs grow heavy.

She took off her robe and slipped into the sheets on the couch. She wore the blue nylon nightgown, the one Jerry loved, the one she always wore when he came home. Against her skin it felt like a warm and protective memory of him. She felt herself drift around, looking for the channel that led down into the vaults of sleep.

Vague ideas floated through her head. She saw Sneidermann in a tiny white office. She saw the bus wending its snail-like way to the secretarial school. Other forms came and left. Lustrous images rose and fell behind her eyes. She drifted down.

The odor came first. It flowed in from the hallway, a cold, stinking, invisible lava. It rolled through the darkness of the living room and covered her. It coalesced around her, solidified. Paralyzed her limbs with cold. Bright lights flashed behind her closed eyes.

He chuckled. *He* was moving in on her, lifting high the nightgown. Her limbs felt like lead, unable to rise.

133

Now *he* held the nightgown over her face. *He* pinned it down, imprisoning her arms around her face. A weight, a different weight, held the nightgown down. *He* moved down, a warmth-sucking cloud, over her breasts.

"*Crazy,*" whispered a distorted wind. "*Crazy, crazy . . .*"

Carlotta kicked. But her legs were heavy, without power, as though under the sea. *He* chuckled. A hand-like form, invisible to her, pressed her soft belly in its fingers.

She gasped spasmodically. She tried to scream. The body on her face pushed the nightgown deep into her mouth. Mucous ran from her nostrils. She twisted from side to side, unable to see anything.

"*Easy, easy,*" the faraway voice whispered. "*Soft and easy . . .*"

Something in her sent a feeling like pain, but disturbing, through the belly to her breasts, rising to her sore nipples.

"*Be nice . . . Be nice . . . So easy now . . .*"

A lick of tongue. Carlotta threw herself violently upward and was brutally slammed downward again. The nylon fabric pressed hard against her face. She thought she saw colored lights on the other side. Forming. Changing. Forming again. Giddy lights swirled in her brain. Vomit began to rise in her throat. Hot, choking, with a taste of bitter acid.

"*Come on, bitch . . . cooperate!*" the senile voice screeched.

Suddenly *he* was in, forcing the cold shaft in, a wide, rough pole, and she began to faint. Every sound became more and more indistinct, farther and farther away, leaving her with a feeling of pain. Interminable, plunging, pain.

"*Ahhhhh!*"

There was a convulsion, and then he paused. She felt it. Gluey, cold, and stinking. A wave of nausea accompanied her to the abyss. She heard a sultry whisper, rough and windy at her neck.

"Nice . . . nice . . . Tell the doctor you're a sweet cunt . . ."

It was gone. The weight was gone from her body. The nightgown fell back from her face. She moved her arms down, slowly. Her face was drenched in perspiration, her skin covered with raised bumps, cold and clammy. She pulled the nightgown, trembling, over her damaged body. She did not know if she had lost consciousness. Or for how long, if she had. She tried to cry out. But there was no strength in her. She felt like death itself.

"Bill!" she whispered, hoarsely.

But there was no answer. The darkness of the room was complete. She realized she was nearly inaudible. She wondered that the lamp was off. Had *she* done that? Billy would know. She took a step toward the hallway. Collapsed, thinking of Bill. That was how he found her in the morning.

Sneidermann looked with dismay at the bruises around her eyes. Worse, he saw the panic in her eyes. Carlotta would not calm down. This was an emergency.

Gone was the intelligence that grasped ideas quickly. Now it was distorted, reaching blindly for any answer. He had known immediately something was wrong when Cindy had accompanied her to the lobby. Now all he could do was try to calm her down, get her to talk about it, get a picture on what had happened.

Carlotta foundered, looking in vain for words.

"It was like a wave," she said. "That's all I remember."

"Why do you think it wasn't a dream?"

"I . . . No! It got *on* me and I woke up! So it couldn't have been a dream!"

"All right, Carlotta. Then what happened?"

"He held me in his arms."

"He? Carlotta, before you said, *'it.'* "

"What are you talking about?"

Sneidermann leaned forward and spoke softly.

135

"You said, *it* was like a wave. Now you said, *he* held you in his arms."

Carlotta looked at him, her eyes filled with horror. She gripped the edge of the chair.

"He, it—what difference?" she said. "I couldn't breathe! It was on my face!"

He gave her a white cup with water. Her hand trembled so violently, he helped her drink it. The touch of his hand on hers seemed to restore her thoughts for an instant.

"Thank you."

"Did he speak with you this time?"

"He called me a name."

"What name?"

"A—cunt."

"You said something was on your face as well. Do you remember what that was?"

"A dwarf."

"A dwarf? Why do you say that? Did you see it?"

"No. I—just had the impression that it was a dwarf."

Sneidermann hated to see this regression in his patient. She was in a worse state of anxiety than the day she first saw him.

She watched him watching her. But at times her gaze seemed to go right through him. She had lost all confidence in herself, in him, in their working together.

"He told me to cooperate," she said blankly.

"What did he mean?"

"You know damn well."

"Sexually."

"Yes."

Her voice was bitter. Repugnance overflowed her being. Yet Sneidermann felt she had been brought back into the interview situation. He was not certain, but it seemed she could sustain a dialogue with him now.

"Did you?" he asked.

"*Did* I? What the hell do you think I am? I wanted to kill him!"

"Did you strike at him?"

136

"I told you, I couldn't. I was pinned down."

"But you resisted . . .?"

"I kicked."

"And it didn't help?"

"He wore me out."

"I see."

"I gave up."

A shot of anxiety flowed quickly through Sneidermann's veins. They were the most ominous words he had heard.

"What do you mean," he asked softly, "you gave up?"

"There was no point in fighting it any longer. It was hopeless, completely hopeless. *Nobody* was going to help me."

"But you didn't feel that way the first times?"

"No. Now I knew it was no use. I just—I—there was nothing to do! He was too strong for me."

She had settled into a kind of fatigue. Obviously she was sorely in need of sleep. He wondered why she had waited until their normal appointment hour to come to the clinic. There was a tone of flatness in her voice. Her eyes regained their flashing brightness from time to time, but they only looked out from a bruised and defeated body.

"Are you badly bruised?" he asked.

She said nothing. Mechanically she unbuttoned her blouse. She lowered her head, exposing the nape of her neck. Raw red bruises lined the neck down to the shoulder. Several pinched areas. Tiny puncture marks.

Without being asked, she removed her bra, exposing her milk-white breasts, the blue lines of tiny veins running to the nipples. Around the nipples were angry red and brown areas, indented impressions of tiny teeth. Sneidermann was momentarily flustered. He knew he should have taken her to an examining room, had her put on a hospital gown, and examined her only with a nurse present. But Carlotta had moved too fast for him.

"Lower down, too," she said, lowering her skirt and

panties. When the examination was over, she dressed. She stared at him. He sat down in the chair behind the desk. He tried not to show how worried he was.

"It's real, isn't it?" she whispered.

"The bruises? Yes. Very real."

"They're not in a place where I could bite myself, are they?"

"No."

"Then they're *real*."

"I told you, Carlotta. The bruises, the bites, are real. Your feelings are real. The rest I need more information about before I can explain it to you. Until I have that information, there are a few things that you *must* do."

She looked at him dubiously. He thought he saw a mocking smile appear on her lips.

"In the first place," he said. "I don't want you to sleep alone. I mean, without at least one other person in the room. Because these attacks will *not* occur if there is someone near you."

"That's what you said about sleeping on the couch."

"I said I thought it was a good idea. I didn't say the attacks *couldn't* happen there."

"Admit it, Dr. Sneidermann. *You didn't think it would happen there!*"

"All right. I'll admit it. I thought it would be better for you."

"That doesn't make you very smart, does it?"

"Listen, Carlotta. What about Billy? Is there a way he can sleep in the living room? Maybe roll the bed in? A cot, maybe?"

"I suppose."

"Here," he handed her a tiny bottle of pills. "I want you to take these tranquilizers. They won't knock you out, but they do reduce anxiety and that can be as bad as the delusion itself. Take two just before you go to bed."

"If you think that will help, Dr. Sneidermann."

He could not miss the sarcasm in her voice.

"But the most important thing is this, Carlotta," he

said. "Thursday there is going to be a case conference. I want you to be there."

"A case conference?"

"Several staff psychiatrists. They'll ask you some questions. It's a way of getting a consensus about your diagnosis."

"You're *really* scared, aren't you?"

"Absolutely not. It's perfectly routine."

"It is not. You're afraid of losing your patient."

"Carlotta, I can show you the clinic rules. It says there, in black and white, that there must be a diagnostic conference for every patient. It's the regulations."

She straightened up in the chair. He observed, despite his being flustered, that her anger at him had channeled her mental energies. In short, she was in control of her thoughts and her speech once again.

"Well," she said. "Maybe *they* can figure it out!"

"Certainly. It's the same in all parts of the hospital. You call in other doctors for consultation."

Carlotta was silent for a moment. Then, by mutual consent, they rose. Sneidermann saw how frightened she still was. Her eyes searched his, afraid to find out what she was certain they contained: a negative judgment on her.

"Here, Carlotta. This is my card."

"What? I have your card."

"No. This is my private number so you can reach me any time."

She looked at it. She looked at him, smiled, and put the card in her purse. She seemed to visibly relax before him.

"Thank you, Dr. Sneidermann. That's very kind of you."

"All right," he said. "Have Cindy drive you home. Take a long, hot bath. Relax. Get the kids in bed early. And remember, keep Billy near you. I want you to sleep. Is that clear?"

"Yes. Goodbye, Dr. Sneidermann."

"Goodbye."

Sneidermann felt exhausted. Why had he given her his personal telephone number? He knew it was wrong. Why had she thrown him off his guard? Why did he need to break the rules to restore her confidence in him? Had he dealt with her, in this tiny way, as a woman instead of a patient?

He cursed himself for even this tiny breach of—what?—ethics? Of course not. Of discipline. He had been a little panicked. His instinct took over. That was what bothered him.

Sneidermann was in a state of confusion. He had to restructure in his mind what he had done and why, and make sure it never happened again.

8

Moran, Carlotta Alicia Dilworth. Born April 12, 1944. Pasadena, California. Presbyterian, nonpracticing. Childhood diseases: chicken pox, mumps, measles. Problems with school authorities: none. Problems with legal authorities: none. Current address: 212 Kentner Street, West Los Angeles, California.

Current occupation: Supported through Los Angeles County Disability. Child support, A.D.C., Los Angeles County Department of Welfare. Secretarial arts training school, tuition also paid for by Los Angeles County Welfare.

Marriage: 1960, to Franklin Moran, used car parts salesman and professional motorcycle racer. Unstable personality. Alcohol, drugs, explosive temper. Abusive. Deceased December 1962, of injuries due to racing course accident. One son, William Franklin.

Common law marriage to Robert C. Garrett, Two Rivers, Nevada, 1964. Rancher. Deceased April 6, 1974, of cardiac failure. Two daughters, Julia Alice (born 1969) and Kimberly Anne (born 1971).

Previous psychiatric illness: none.

Hallucinogens: none. Alcoholism ruled out. EEG: no disturbances. History of epilepsy, etc.: none.

Thought processes: no blocking. Reality testing: intact. Memory: excellent. No loosening of associations. Slight flattening of affect when discussing symptoms. Tested IQ: 125. (WAIS)

Onset of symptoms: October 1976

Symptoms: auditory and olfactory hallucinations; somatic delusions (sexual abuse, penetration); possible suicidal impulses; multiple bruises, scratches, minor lesions on breasts, thighs, lower back; anxiety, panic reactions; generalized hostility; beyond individual attacks, no significant estrangement from reality.

Preliminary diagnosis: psychoneurotic reaction, hysterical type.

Gary Sneidermann sat nervously in his supervisor's cramped office. Dr. Henry Weber looked over the page once more, said nothing, and dropped the paper on the desk. He lit his pipe with the monstrous flame from a translucent lighter, puffing vigorously.

"Okay, Gary," Dr. Weber said. "Why couldn't this wait until Thursday?"

"I wanted to get a good fix on this case before going into that meeting. Some things are not clear."

"Fair enough."

Sneidermann cleared his throat. Dr. Weber's craggy face, lined around the eyes and jowls, watched him sympathetically. The moments with the senior psychiatrist were treasured, but they put Sneidermann on the block. Dr. Weber demanded precision. It was grueling, but that was why he had come to West Coast University.

"These bruises," Sneidermann said. "They are quite severe, and I wonder if they aren't the result of psychotic self-abuse."

"Could be hysteria. Hysteria can raise welts, cause blindness, loss of hair. I've seen open sores and loss of feeling in the fingers and toes. All induced by auto-suggestion."

"But direct bruises? Bite marks, puncture wounds?"

"Certainly."

"I would be relieved if that was true, sir. The thought that she was taking a knife to herself—"

"She expresses through her body what she cannot express any other way. She's boiling inside."

142

Sneidermann felt immeasurably relieved. He picked up his notebook and rapidly paged through it. He found what he was looking for.

"Then there was something strange," he said. "In her personal history. I'd hoped you could shake it clear for me. Find some pattern here."

"Shoot."

"It happened after Franklin Moran was killed. She went back to Pasadena with the infant. Ran away again within the year. This time to a town in Nevada."

Dr. Weber listened carefully. He watched the pipe smoke lazily rise and fan out under the ceiling. Sneidermann tried to examine the facts of the case through his supervisor's eyes.

"She works as a waitress in a cafe. Meets a retired rancher there, named Robert Garrett. Much older. Sixty-four. She takes up with him."

"How old is she?"

"Nineteen."

"What does she do, look after him?"

"No, they sleep together. He gives her two daughters."

"What happened then?"

"He died," Sneidermann said. "A natural death. It was during the spring floods. The second man to die on her. But this time she's cooped up in the tiny cabin. Cold outside. Can't get out. Water all over the roads. Isolated. Three kids, two of them infants. And he just lies there, dead."

Weber frowned. "I don't get what you're driving at."

"You see, these attacks are preceded by the smell of rotting meat."

Dr. Weber looked directly at Sneidermann and shook his head. He wasn't buying.

Sneidermann persisted. "It's such a direct connection."

"Precisely. But in the unconscious there are rarely direct connections. Maybe once in a while something gets

143

cooked up into a dream symbolism. But this sort of hunt-ing almost never pays off."

"But you see, an idealized relationship like that one. She repressed the negative aspects of it, which had to exist. And now—"

"Let it go, Gary. Maybe there's some connection. Right now, you want to be sensitive to the whole pattern."

"Yes, sir."

Sneidermann sighed.

"Look, Gary," Dr. Weber said. "Most of the time it goes way back. As far back as you can get, to the infan-tile neurosis. Something very basic. It may manifest itself in different ways, but it shows up in every relationship she's ever had."

"What do you mean—shows up in every relation-ship?"

"Well—take a good look at what you just described to me. This adolescent she fell in with. A typical over-grown kid. They play at sex. Then the old man. That's safe sex, Gary. She's consistently avoided the real thing."

"They gave her three children."

Dr. Weber waved away the objection. "It doesn't take sex to make babies. Not real sex. You want a con-jecture? I'll give you a conjecture. She's masturbating. That's all. This entire circus that she's invented—it's to cover up what every little girl does."

"Why would she have to go to such extremes to—"

"That's what you're there to figure out."

Dr. Weber smiled. Sneidermann began to see Car-lotta in a different light. What he saw in front of him now was a complete, tormented personality, a little girl in a woman's body.

"Of course," Dr. Weber added, "this is conjec-ture. Could be a hundred percent the wrong direction. That's what keeps psychiatry from being boring."

Sneidermann always wondered how Dr. Weber saw humor in such situations. He wondered if the time would come when he, too, would be so tough, or would be forced to develop such a hard facade.

"Perhaps, sir," Sneidermann said. "In any case, she went back to Los Angeles with the children."

"To Pasadena?"

"No. No communication with her mother. Father dead already. Stroke. She moved to a place in West Los Angeles."

"This brings us up to date," Dr. Weber said.

"Yes, sir. She's worked in various nightclubs. A few boyfriends. Nothing serious."

"Prostitution?"

"No, sir."

"You sure? You ever met a prostitute?"

"Me?"

"I'm not talking to anybody else."

"I don't believe so."

"What are you so embarrassed about? Either you have or you haven't."

"I have never met a prostitute, sir."

"Then you don't know Carlotta did not engage in sex for money."

"She still has a lot of Pasadena in her. In many respects she is a little lady. In spite of herself. I don't believe she would sleep with a man for money."

"All right. You may be right."

"Last year she met Jerry Rodriguez. Very stable, ambitious type. Self-educated. Works with a fast-moving firm. Banks and real estate."

"Is this a serious relationship?"

Sneidermann coughed lightly. He felt himself under the direct gaze of his superior again.

"There seem to be some complications," he said. "The worst is between Jerry Rodriguez and Carlotta's son, who is now fifteen. There have been some sharp words, even a fist-fight or two."

"A triangle," Dr. Weber said.

"Exactly. The problem is, when he comes to town, he stays with her in the house."

"Sleeps with her?"

"Yes."

"Pleasant situation."

"He and the son came to blows the last time. It nearly ruptured the relationship."

Dr. Weber swiveled slowly in his chair. He seemed to wait for Sneidermann to catch something, but Sneidermann could only sit in his chair, feeling inadequate.

"This happened before the symptoms began?" Dr. Weber asked.

"Yes, sir. Then he left town. Promised to think things over."

"You see? This is the crucial moment for Carlotta. This is precisely the kind of situation that can energize a breakdown."

Sneidermann watched Dr. Weber. The older man seemed to enjoy his discovery.

"This Rodriguez," Dr. Weber said. "Mature man. He wants the real thing. No more playing around for Carlotta. No more faking with kids and old men. Faced with the real thing, she buckles. She goes back to her infantile reality."

The case was becoming clearer to Sneidermann. Dr. Weber was pushing him toward daylight.

"My only advice," Dr. Weber concluded, "is to be flexible. Don't force anything on her. For whatever reason."

"Yes, sir."

Sneidermann suddenly realized that the room was insufferably hot. His shirt was wringing wet. He felt limp. On top of that the pipe smoke had filled the tiny office and he felt a desire to get out, to run on the beach, to stretch his lungs and forget the tension of the last two weeks.

Sneidermann stood and gathered up his notes. He had the impression that Dr. Weber wanted to say something but was withholding it now.

"Will that be it for now, Dr. Weber?"

"Don't overextend yourself, Gary."

"What do you mean?"

"I heard you were trying to transfer one of your cases to another resident. That's possible in the program you're in, but it's not a good idea. You need the cross-fertilization of different cases. Different kinds of problems."

"Yes, sir. I'll consider it."

November 15, 8:40 p.m.

Carlotta sat on the cold cement steps in front of the house. The night was calm, oppressive, still smelling of the smog that had infected the day. Black leaves rustled beside the porch light, casting shadows on her feet. Far away was the sound of children running, then silence.

Her own childhood seemed a dream, so far away it almost had never existed. A pale girl, frightened of the shadows the sun drew across the deep green carpets. Running through the rose garden, bright and glistening, sharp with thorns. Neither the tall man inside nor the nervous woman in the garden spoke to her. Twisted, insubstantial shades, both of them. Carlotta felt the fear rising again in her, after all the years.

It was poverty which had broken her, remade her into something more basic and stronger. Unreal things no longer frightened her. Men, work, and loneliness. Life was a very basic proposition. Then why was the old fear rising now?

Because now in her life there was something twisted again. Something insubstantial, yet more powerful than she. Carlotta poked her finger along the chips and cracks in the cement. That was the similarity, she thought.

"Mommy!"
Julie ran from the door, stopping short at Carlotta.
"He's hurting Kim!"
They ran inside. In the hallway Kim crawled along the floor. Her lips were bleeding.

147

"I fell," Kim whimpered.

"She did not!" Julie said. "He pushed her! She was standing in the bathroom, and he—"

Carlotta picked up Kim, cradling her, rocking her.

"Her tooth is chipped," Carlotta said.

Kim coughed, choked, and Carlotta wiped the blood from her chin. She rocked the little girl in her arms.

"It's all right, Julie," Carlotta said. "Where's Billy?"

"He didn't do it!"

"Then who did?"

"*He* did!"

Carlotta looked at Julie. She recognized the same frightened glaze that had covered her own face in the mirror. Was Julie getting sick, too? Was she infecting her own children in some strange way?

"Come here and sit by Mommy and Kim," she said.

Carlotta wiped away the last of the blood from Kim's lips. Kim seemed deathly tired. She fell into a trembling, exhausted sleep.

"Why do you say—"

But she felt it unmistakably in the room. A pressure in the atmosphere. A vague sensation of odor. And now she was completely awake.

"Do you smell it, Julie?"

"He's back, Mommy!"

"Oh, Jesus!"

There was a click. Carlotta turned. The window was locked. Had it just locked itself?

"Where's Billy?" she hissed, clinging to Julie's arm.

"You're hurting me, Mommy!"

Carlotta felt the rising chill in her spine, creeping into her brain. She heard the sound of creeping timbers, of a metallic groan. She stood, holding Kim against her chest.

"Billy!"

She felt the great suction of the air. Her skin prickled. The hair on her arm stood on end. She backed slowly toward the kitchen door.

"Billy!"

148

The door from the garage jiggled violently.

"Hey, Mom! Open up! It's me!"

Carlotta grabbed Julie. She did not remember having locked the garage door. That door was never locked. Suddenly the shadows undulated all around her.

"Ha ha ha ha ha!"

"Mom!"

On the couch, the blanket and sheet were being pulled back. For her. She reached for the knob on the kitchen door. But, like a bad dream, it, too, was locked. She fumbled for the bolt.

Suddenly there was the sound of glass shattering. Shards burst over the floor, scuttling down to where she stood. Like a living wave of glass. There was the presence of a body. It grabbed her arm.

"Mommy!" Julie screamed.

Carlotta found herself dragged forcibly toward the couch. She twisted, found her arm bent up against her back. She flailed. Was flung onto the couch.

"Billy! Oh, God—he's got me!"

Billy ran in from the hallway. His forearm was cut in many places. He watched his mother, writhing on the couch, her legs kicking at an invisible attacker. He leaped forward, grabbed her by the shoulders, tried to pull her off. Suddenly she was incredibly strong. He could not recognize the twisted grimace on her face.

He braced his feet against the floor, panic-stricken.

"Oh God! He's got me—Billy—I'm going to *die*—"

Billy tried to grab her with both arms. But she twisted out of his grasp. She wrestled violently. The girls were screaming. It was suddenly cold in the room. But he saw nothing.

"Save me—Bill! Save me—"

He leaped forward, tears flowing from his eyes. He beat the air in front of her. Nothing! He yelled at the top of his lungs. But Carlotta did not stop. Her face was twisted in pain.

"Look, Mom! I'm driving him away! See? I'm sending him off!"

Billy beat his fists in the air. He made a terrible racket. Carlotta sank against the wall, her body shivering, merging with the shadows.

"Oh, Bill—it's the worst it ever was! He's so strong —"

"Yell!" Billy shouted to Julie. "We'll drive him away! You too, Kim!"

The girls shouted, waving their arms, not certain what else to do.

"Louder!"

The children jumped, created a bedlam, were carried away in their fear and hysteria, throwing incredible shadows across the carpet to Carlotta, who leaned back against the wall, her eyes glazed and black.

"Oh, Bill," she whispered. "I'm afraid! He's going to kill you! He's too strong for you!"

Then Billy was sucked into the center of the room, spun and turned about like a piece of cardboard in the wind.

"Bill!"

"Mommy!"

Something seemed to batter at him. He covered his eyes with his hands. He crouched over, then knelt on the floor, trying to protect himself.

"Bill!"

The punches seemed to pummel him, shaking his side, bringing him lower with each blow.

"The candlestick!"

Billy looked up. For a brief instant everyone, including the girls, was frozen into silence. The candlestick hung in the air, nearly five feet off the ground. It neither rose nor fell, but hovered in space. Then, with a murderous velocity, it crashed down on him. He threw up his hands in front of his face. The candlestick struck him on the left wrist, making a cracking sound.

"Billy!"

Then he stood, his eyes flashing in delirium, his hair distended and wild. His body moved strangely, jerkily,

150

angrily. His useless hand dangled at his side. His face was twisted in pain.

He picked up the lamp from the table, swung it back and forth in front of him. The shadows roared over the walls, long distorted black beings that swung high over them all. Carlotta saw the tormented features of his face lit from below, the unnatural shadows snaking up from his nostrils.

"I ain't afraid of you!" he yelled at no certain point in the room. "Go away! You bully! Leave us alone!"

"Bill—don't! He'll kill us all—"

"Go away!" he bellowed. "We don't want you here!"

"Don't do that, Bill!"

"See?" He turned to Carlotta, his face flushed and the eyes vivid. "He's gone! He's scared!"

Carlotta came to him uncertainly. His body was trembling like a leaf. She had to help him into a chair.

"Ma, we got to fight him! Here and now!"

He spoke hoarsely, almost moaning. Carlotta was frightened that he was no longer the same.

"Shhhhhh—"

"I ain't afraid, Ma! He can't kill me!"

"Shhhhhh—"

"The bully!"

"Bill—"

"The bastard!" Bill screamed into the darkness. "Son of a bitch!"

Slowly he became aware of the girls watching him the way they had once watched Carlotta.

"It's okay, Billy," Julie cried. "He's gone."

He groaned, put a hand to his face, withdrew it, moved in the chair, leaned his head back, then groaned again.

"Oh, Mom!" he wept. "We've got to stick together!"

Carlotta wiped the tears from both their faces. She put her finger on his lips. She brushed down his hair. Slowly he seemed to come down. Their eyes looked into each other's, neither certain of what had happened.

"Your hand," Carlotta said softly.

"It's okay."

"No. It's broken."

"That was the candlestick that broke. See? I can move my fingers."

He moved his fingers painfully in front of her.

"What happened, Billy?"

"I don't know, Mom," he said quietly.

The house rang with the infinite silence. Of the four, none knew what was happening to them. Now Carlotta saw her sickness spread like a foul contagion to all members of her family. She felt guilty for them all. She had brought them to the same abyss. They breathed the infected atmosphere together.

She soaked Billy's hand in icy water and bandaged his wrist tightly. They'd see a doctor in the morning. She dared not speak of what had happened. She dared not ask Billy. What if he no longer knew what was real and what was not?

They slept in the living room. Billy wrapped himself in a green blanket. The girls huddled with Carlotta on the couch. No one slept. There was no way to distinguish perception from hallucination. The walls gave way around Carlotta in a fear of madness. What were they all thinking, each one too frightened to say it out loud?

"Her son is sensing this thing now, too," Sneidermann said.

Dr. Weber nodded, leaned forward toward the urinal, and considered. The white porcelain reflected his face, the metal pipes sparkled above him.

"Folie à deux," Dr. Weber said. "The madness of two."

Sneidermann felt abashed at having intruded on Dr. Weber. But such conversations were normal. In a gruff, masculine way it suited Dr. Weber's sense of humor. It amused him to see residents shy.

"Do you think I should bring in the boy?" Sneidermann asked. "Find out what is going on in his head?"

Dr. Weber shook his head.

152

"He'll tell you exactly what his mother will tell you. What do you expect him to say? Lock up my mother, she's crazy?"

"No, but—"

"It would only confirm the reality of these delusions to her. She would be quick to realize that she had a corroborating witness. That's going to make it that much harder for you."

"Yes, but—the evidence for this thing existing independent of her is mounting up. Last night, all hell broke loose with the son playing a leading role. Even the girls took part in the delusion."

"Folie à trois, folie à quatre," Dr. Weber said, a peculiar smile playing at the edge of his lips. "The children are protecting their mother. They are giving her support. Absolutely. Family bonds are stronger than anything on earth. Very touching, what kids will go through to protect a parent."

Sneidermann thought a moment.

"Isn't there danger in this? To the kids? Going through something like this? Her son injured his wrist during last night's episode."

Weber shook his head.

"If I understand the case correctly, the answer is no. Because if there are real causes for delusion among the kids, they go back to much earlier problems than the mother's hysteria. In which case they should be treated accordingly. But this seems to be a direct response to Carlotta. You know, she is really demanding that they support her. She needs them to support her ego. She's terrifically frightened of the isolation that insanity represents to her. So in a way this support from the children, bizarre as it seems, is really a lot better than if they cut her off completely."

Sneidermann sighed.

"Okay," he said. "I'm relieved."

"It's going to be a bit of a madhouse down on Kentner Street for a while. But I think that as the mother improves the children will return very quickly to a normal

153

relationship with her. You know how it is—Mommy is sick. The kids are really scared. It's a terrible thing when you're real young.

"But," Dr. Weber continued, brushing his hair down, examining it in the mirror, "the thing is this. You have to be sure that there is no other reason for the altered relationship."

"I'm afraid I don't catch what you are saying, Dr. Weber."

"It's nothing specific. But suppose Billy had some interest in supporting this illusion? Could be that the relationship is not so innocent as you supposed?"

"That's an interesting thought."

Dr. Weber turned.

"Billy is the only male in the house, and probably sexually active. It's a situation that did not exist a couple of years ago."

"Right. The son is fifteen."

"Maybe to the kid, this is a chance to act out his own feelings. This Rodriguez, a sexually more powerful rival, threatening to enter the house. Maybe it's a way to say: 'See, Mom? I can take care of you myself. I'm with you on this. That other guy—he doesn't know anything about it.' It's not something that is seriously going to retard your case, but it is a complication that you have to consider."

"Yes, sir. I will. A very good idea."

"On the other hand," Dr. Weber added, in a measured tone, "it may be that Carlotta is not who you think she is."

November 16, 11:05 P.M.

The street lamps along Kentner Street glowed dimly. In the fog they radiated a cruel blue light. The moisture swirled in a visible mist. Currents of droplets rose and fell into larger currents, and through it all was the cold smell of the distant sea.

"There's no point in sleeping here," Carlotta said. "Not anymore."

She gestured to the couch.

"No," Billy said. "I guess not."

"I mean, if he wants to come back he will. Won't he?"

"I guess so."

Carlotta desperately needed to ask Billy what he had seen. What he had felt the night before. Yet she was horrified to even try.

"The doctor told me to sleep on the couch. With someone near me."

"But you got sick there, too."

Got sick, Carlotta thought. Billy thought it was sickness. She looked at him. He avoided her glance. He was dissembling about something. Or else he didn't know himself what to think.

"I mean, I might just as well sleep in the bed. Where I'm comfortable. If I'm going to be sick anyway."

"Sure," he said softly.

"What's the matter, Bill?"

"I don't know what's going on, Mom."

The simple truth struck Carlotta's heart. They were in the same fatal ambiguity. Neither knew what was real or what was not.

"What about the doctor?" he said. "Doesn't he have any ideas?"

She shook her head.

"All sorts of ideas," she said. "None of them fit."

"Then you might as well sleep in your bed, Mom. I don't see what difference it makes on the couch."

Carlotta's heart sank. Sneidermann being wrong about the safety of the couch, it now seemed there was no choice but to endure as best as possible what the future held. And try to survive.

"Then I'm back where I started," she said.

She gathered the blankets from the couch. Billy watched her cross the floor to her bedroom. Without a word he took the pillows in his arms and followed her.

With her foot she moved open the door. It was cold inside.

"Everything looks the same," she murmured, almost to herself.

"It's cold in here."

"Billy, if I asked you something, would you promise to tell me the truth?"

"Sure."

Carlotta put the blankets on the unmade bed, pretending to be as casual as possible. She turned on a lamp, the glow illuminating her face softly. She looked at Billy, her eyes lost in the darkness. She looked at him sadly, with confusion, depending on his answer.

"Did you smell anything last night?"

"In the living room? No, Mom. I don't remember anything."

"You'd be honest with me? No matter what?"

"Yes."

"All right. I need to sort out some things in my own head."

Carlotta, confused, sat on the edge of the bed. Billy handed her an ashtray. She tapped a cigarette against her wrist, but did not light it.

"But you smell it a little now, don't you?" she said.

"I—I don't know, Mom."

"How could you not know?"

"I'm confused, Mom. I know what *you* smell. Sometimes I think I do, too. But maybe it's only because you told me."

"So you don't know? Right now?"

"I *think* I do. I—"

"What does it smell like?"

"You know."

"What?"

"A human smell. A flesh smell. Dirty."

Carlotta put the cigarette back into the package, her fingers trembling. Billy thought it was a *human* smell. That had never occurred to her.

The windows were completely black. Tiny rivulets of fog dribbled down the exterior of the glass. Carlotta watched the movement of light in the water. Then she turned slowly back to Billy.

"Maybe we should go back to Cindy's," she said.

"They don't want us, Mom. George would hate it."

"Maybe. Maybe you're right. I don't know what to do anymore."

Billy stood awkwardly, his body outlined in the strange window light, over her. Carlotta never felt so alone.

"Want me to stay in here with you?" Billy said softly.

Carlotta smiled. Only there was no joy in the smile. Just a sad, utterly hopeless smile that broke Billy's heart.

"*Last* time we scared him off."

"You're the dearest thing to me in all the world, Bill. I don't want you to be hurt."

He was not certain how she meant that. Everything was so confused. He was afraid even to kiss her goodnight. He left, his footsteps faintly pattering into his bedroom.

The fog condensed into a light rain, then cleared and stopped. She undressed, her figure throwing long, oblong shadows against the wall. Billy opened the door of his room. He saw that she had kept her door open. He saw her shadows, undulating against the wall.

There was no answer, she thought. Not from the doctor, not from Billy. There was no rational prop either way. Suspended between two equally bleak alternatives, her mind began to spin in random, unconnected thoughts. Was it real or was it not?

She slept with the table lamp on beside her. She was astonished when she woke in the middle of the night and the light was off.

"Bill?"

"*Shhhhhhhhhhhh.*"

Before she could make a sound, a cold hand clamped down on her mouth. She kicked, found her leg caught, her arms pinned behind her.

"Shhhhhhhhhhhh."

She was held down. A weight pressed down on the edge of the bed. Her eyes widened in horror. She saw nothing. A cold feeling on her thigh. A cool caress. She struggled violently.

"Shhhhhhhhhhhh."

A fingertip traced the outline of her breast gently.

She twisted her head violently, gagging. A hand held her hair tightly at her forehead. A warning. She knew not to make a sound. For an instant nothing happened. It was totally black, and she saw nothing, not even the near wall.

"Who are you?" she hissed.

She felt fingers along her belly, going down.

"Where do you come from?" she spit out.

"Shhhhhhhhhhhh."

Her legs were parted. Delicately. Something held down her feet. Something different from the caress along-side her thigh. She felt a relaxation in the night. As though the air around her warmed. She felt the hairs on her arm begin to stir, then her skin prickled all over with count-less needle points.

"Who *are* you?"

She breathed with difficulty, her breath coming in large gulps.

In the black bedroom she thought she saw herself in the mirror. Then she realized that the air in front of her was coalescing into a transparency. It glowed. A vapor began to rise over the floor in front of her.

"Oh, my God!" she whispered.

It congealed, a substance like smoke, but denser. A cold, clammy green light spread out from it; deathly.

"Shhhhhhhhhh."

A musculature—a forearm—like a hiss of air, twisted and hoarse, it expanded, then glowed. Her body was illuminated by the green light, her thighs lost in the shadows it created.

"Shhhhhhhhh."

A neck—powerful shoulders—the veins—standing out—ears—

Carlotta pushed herself back against the headboard of the bed, trying to lose herself in the shadows.

"Shhhhhhhhhh."

The face that looked down on her—from so high—smiled lewdly.

The walls around them both glowed. Seemed to expand, until Carlotta had no sense of space, no feeling for depth, only the rising, rolling light that was more than light in front of her. She grew delirious. Hot. Weary. Empty. She gasped for breath.

The shadow of the nostrils—flared—with delight at her—cruel lips—the eyes—the eyes—the eyes were slanted—almond-shaped—bored through her—knew her carnally—knew everything about Carlotta—

His long finger was on his lip. He was complete.

"Shhhhhhhhhhhh."

She crawled, dumbly, trembling, across the bed, not knowing where she was or where she was going. Then her limbs failed her, felt like rubber, and she tried to call out, but she was voiceless. Her body was heated and flushed.

A hand on her waist. Turned her softly, like a flower. It seemed that galaxies were spinning in her brain. Everywhere was a green warmth. She pressed upward into it, dissolved upward with unimaginable force, until she no longer existed.

"Oooooooooooooooohhhhh."

"Shhhhhhhhhhhhhhhhhhh."

A black shudder of revulsion swirled upward through her spine. Consciousness fell away.

In the morning she lay nude, crossways on the bed. The door was still open. She had no strength to rise.

Gradually the sounds of daylight outside filled the bedroom. She heard Billy stirring in his room behind the wall. She opened her eyes. She sat up slowly at the edge of the bed. The windows were dry, streaked in lines of dirt from the last night.

She went into the bathroom, closed the door, and showered. She showered for nearly an hour.

On Wednesday, November 17, Sneidermann felt some anxiety. He had transferred one of his cases to another resident. With the extra time to explore the Moran case, he had come up with some interesting historical material. Soldiers had hallucinated entire regiments. Old men had spoken to horses, on their way to funerals. All manner of people had experienced all manner of delusions under periods of emotional stress. But their reasoning power had always returned. The violations of their sense perceptions did not permanently infect the functioning ego. So when Carlotta failed to appear that afternoon, and when Sneidermann called the secretarial school and found out that she had not attended for a week, a dim premonition began to assail him.

He called Carlotta at home.

"Oh, Dr. Sneidermann," she said. "I guess I missed our appointment. I don't know what's happening—"

Her voice had the unpleasant, vague quality of one who is removed from what she says. There was a pause.

"I was sleeping in the bed last night. There didn't seem to be any point—sleeping on the couch—after what happened with Billy—and I woke up—and he was on me—"

"Are you all right?"

"Yes—I—I just don't know what to do—"

"Where's Billy?"

"Oh, he's here. He stayed home from school—"

"All right. Do you want to come to the clinic?"

"No. I mean, what's the point? What good does it do?"

Sneidermann tried to picture her, clutching the telephone cord, trying to remember who he was, Billy watching her from some distant part of the room.

"Carlotta . . . Can you tell me what happened?"

"Yeah—I mean, I've told Billy, so I guess—but it's so—"

160

"It's nothing to be ashamed of. It's like telling me a dream."

"Yes—but I—he—I saw him."

"You saw him?"

"My God! Yes—"

"Visibly? I mean, did you—what—could you describe what you saw?"

"I really did, Dr. Sneidermann. It was—incredible—"

Sneidermann tried to suppress his impatience. Now she had given visible form to this delusion. Further strengthening it, making it that much more difficult not to believe in it. Sneidermann could not but grasp the tenacity with which she had constructed and clung to this thing.

"What did he look like, Carlotta?"

"Tall—six feet—"

"How do you know?"

"His head came over the door—that makes him taller—seven feet—and—" She paused.

"Yes?"

"He was Chinese—"

"Chinese?"

"Yes. He had the slanted eyes—high cheekbones—that kind of face. It flashed through my mind—he must be Chinese."

"Why not Korean? Japanese?"

"I don't know what he was, Dr. Sneidermann. I'm only telling you what I saw."

"Of course. Of course. What else?"

"His eyes were blue-green. He was very muscular—veins in his neck—like an athlete—"

"What was he wearing?"

"Nothing."

"Naked?"

"Absolutely—"

"Was he sexually excited?"

"He was—not exactly—sort of in-between—"

"Yes. I understand."

"He—you know—was very large. That's what frightened me the most."

"Yes. Of course."

"He kind of said, 'Shhhhhhhhh.' Like that. Whispering. With his finger over his lip. Like he was showing me a secret."

"Which was himself?"

"Yes. Exactly. He was showing me himself."

"Why do you think he did that?"

"Because I asked him to."

Sneidermann paused. He concentrated fiercely, trying to get a drift of what she was saying behind the words. Sometimes he felt her, as a dynamic personality, pushing up masks and fighting for control, and sometimes she fell away from him, leaving only the words she spoke.

"Well," she said. "I didn't *ask* him. I sort of shouted, Who are you? What do you want? Something like that—"

"Of course. That's what anyone would do."

There was a long pause. Sneidermann licked his lips. It was plain that there was more to tell. But she wanted him to draw it from her.

"And then what happened?" he asked.

"Then he followed me onto the bed . . . and . . ."

"And he had intercourse with you there?"

"Yes. Completely. Then I . . . I sort of fainted. It was too much. I was dissolving in this light—this light that was really him—a green, cold light. I guess I blacked out—"

"And how do you feel now?"

"Burned out. I feel dirty—in my mind and body—soiled—"

"Yes, Carlotta. Understandable. Of course. It's a very difficult experience. Do you want to come to the clinic?"

"No, I don't want to see anyone. I need to clear my head—"

"I can send a car. I can come down myself."

"No—I don't want to see you—not yet—"

"But you'll come tomorrow?"

"Tomorrow?"

"Yes. Tomorrow is the case conference."

"The what?"

"I explained to you there would be a case conference on Thursday. It is important for me to get consulting opinions. And for you, too."

"Yes—all right."

"I can send a car for you. You just have to call the clinic. We do this periodically."

"You don't have to. I'll be all right."

"Okay, Carlotta. Now listen. This is important. I explained to you that the attacks would not occur if there was someone else in the room with you. Do you remember how it went away the night Billy helped you in the living room?"

"But—"

"I *strongly* suggest you bring Billy into the room. On a cot or something. I know it's a disruption of your routine. But you don't want to face this sort of thing again."

"I'll do what you suggest, Doctor."

"Good. And listen. The secretarial school called here. They asked me to confirm your sessions here. Your instructor told me you'd missed nearly a week of school."

"So?"

"I'm not checking up on you, Carlotta. But I wondered if there was a reason."

"The reason is, there's no point in going."

"What do you mean?"

"I'm in no condition to concentrate. And what's welfare going to do, throw me in jail?"

"No, of course not, but—"

"It's all so far away from me."

"I'd like you to attend."

"I'm too far behind."

"They'll take that into consideration. You'll catch up as best you can."

"It makes no sense to me."

The flat, listless tone, the uncaring quality of Carlotta's voice, was straight out of the textbook. *La belle*

163

indifférence, was the psychiatric term. She was dissociated from herself. She no longer cared about herself. She no longer resisted. He tried to contact her through the fog of her indifference.

"The reason is this: these skills that you are picking up help to discipline you. They also make you confident in your abilities. You'll be in a much better position when you graduate from the school."

Carlotta said nothing for a while. When she did answer, her voice was subdued.

"If it makes you happy," she said.

"Very good, Carlotta. You'll thank yourself very soon. So—we'll meet tomorrow. Come to my office and I'll take you to the conference room."

"Okay. Tomorrow."

She hung up the telephone. Sneidermann sat at the desk, scribbled several final notes, inserted them into the casebook, and looked at the clock on the wall. The room was his for another hour. He decided to concentrate on the hallucination she had just reported. Then he decided to get some coffee from the lobby dispenser.

Her mind was giving her strong and explicit images. Why? What was this thing to her? How did her unconscious come to fashion this elaborate and exotic creature for her? And how much longer would it take until he knew her well enough to even begin to guess?

Carlotta's personality—like any human personality—was built on a series of layers, each resting on the one below. But, like the geological layers in the earth, at the bottom was the core. And the core of Carlotta's personality was Pasadena, in the crucible of her parents' psychological drama. There were upper layers, Sneidermann reflected, the relationship with Jerry, with Billy, with Bob Garrett and Franklin—but they rested on the fundamental organization of her psyche. And that had formed many years ago, in Pasadena. *There* was the key. For the moment, it was veiled even from Carlotta's own consciousness.

He took a cigarette from the nurse at the desk. Then

he walked back into the office. Holes, holes, holes in the structure, he mused, flipping through the casebook. When would they be filled up? For an hour he sat at the desk. For every thought that came to him clearly, there were a hundred that obscured and entangled his understanding. His thoughts fell away into areas that were still unknown. He tried to map the case, to discover where it was he needed to go the most.

He impatiently awaited tomorrow. Perhaps the staff psychiatrists would fill in some of the holes.

9

SNEIDERMANN and Carlotta sat on red vinyl chairs in a small room. It was cold inside. From the elevators outside a group of nurses and male patients emerged.

"One of the doctors is actually famous," he said. "Comes from John Hopkins. Like Einstein in psychiatry."

Carlotta smiled perfunctorily. She lit a cigarette, waved out the match, and crossed her legs. She looked at the clock on the wall. The seminar rooms were located next to the administration offices. There was no smell of medical chemicals here, no noise of public address systems, no shuffle of the public through the lobbies. It was very calm. The white walls absorbed all sounds.

"I never knew so many things could go wrong with a human being," she said.

"The mind is unbelievably complicated. But I'll tell you something, Carlotta. You didn't know it when you walked in, but this, right here, is the finest clinic of its kind on the West Coast. So don't worry."

Carlotta smiled again. He noticed that her smiles had consistently become vacuous, mechanical. She was one step farther from her feelings than the day she first walked into the clinic.

The dark brown door in front of them opened. An elderly nurse with tortoise shell glasses appeared.

"Dr. Sneidermann?" she said, smiling. "Are you ready?"

"Certainly."

The nurse held the door open. He leaned closer to Carlotta and spoke softly.

"Listen," he said. "I have to go in and give a report. Lasts about twenty, twenty-five minutes. Then she'll come for you. Okay?"

"Okay."

He stood, smoothed his hair, made sure his pen was upright and not leaking ink into the pocket of his suit coat. He straightened his tie.

"Dr. Sneidermann."

He turned.

"What?"

"Good luck."

He grinned broadly.

"Well, thank you, Carlotta. I appreciate that."

He went into the seminar room. Carlotta craned her neck. There were several men and a woman in there, one of them rather old, with long white hair. There was a murmur of greetings. Then the door softly closed.

She was out of cigarettes. The vending machines were outside the tiny waiting room in the corridor. She dug some change from her purse and purchased a red pack. The nurse at the desk down the hall was watching her and Carlotta knew it. She lit the cigarette and walked slowly back into the waiting room.

Several muffled sounds came from down the corridor. She turned, looking out the open door, but could see nothing. It had sounded like a physical struggle.

Now, there are places in Nevada, she thought, where people have hard times, get sick, even die, but they do it the way the shadows fly over the canyons. Inevitably. No tubes in the nostrils. No hypodermic needles. No television monitors aimed at your heads.

She looked contemptuously down the corridor. Several suave, energetic administrators emerged from a conference room. Behind them were three elderly nurses and a secretary. Not a trace of spontaneity, she thought. Not an ounce of real humor. Not one person there in touch with himself. Smart as hell maybe, she thought, but out of touch. Like Sneidermann. And now *they* were treating her.

Go to a place like the high desert, for example. There the weeds break and roll in balls into the barbed wire. There the sunrise fills the canyons like long red fingers poking up over the rock. There the cattle thunder through the creek in early spring, sending up a silver spray of cold water and fragile ice crystals.

Yes, in a place like that you might suffer. You might have to fight the earth. Everything could go wrong. But you fought it as a whole person. Because you were part of nature. It was big, and it was part of you. There were no specialists. No corridors. No false expectations. There was no hopelessness.

Carlotta dropped the cigarette into the sand of a stand-up ashtray.

Maybe the day would come. She would go back. Someday. It could happen. No, Jerry would not go. He was a city person. Maybe they could work out something. He was reasonable. Until then, she thought, until then— what? Her heart sank. What was she doing here? Why didn't she just run? Get the hell out?

The cigarette ignited a candy wrapper. Startled, she covered the tiny flame with sand. She picked up several magazines from the table. Women's magazines. Old, tattered love stories for old women. She dropped them back under the table.

She knew very well why she could not leave. Or if she did, why she could never go back to Nevada again.

With the last of her money, Carlotta had bought a Greyhound ticket to Carson City. It was the next bus leaving. She and the infant Billy watched the landscape give way to a more rugged series of valleys and plateaus. Before she got to Carson City she saw a small town, called Two Rivers. It was so peaceful that when the bus stopped there for lunch, she stayed behind.

It was on a road high over a long, sloping valley.

From time to time the ranchers came in for the one movie theater, for a supper at the cafe, for the billiards and beer at the taverns. She worked for the Two Rivers Cafe. She lived in a room behind the cafe with another waitress, who resented Billy. The room became a mess. The ranchers propositioned her continually. By late autumn the skies clouded over, the winds blew the dust through the town, and the valley became bleaker and bleaker.

An older rancher came into the cafe. His hair was white, his denim jacket lined with wool, and his face deeply lined and tanned from the weather. His frame was slender, and he moved with the grace of one who is in touch with his deepest self. She guessed he was sixty.

"Yes," he said, when she asked him. "I know of some places. There are some cabins down by Rushing Springs."

"Could I move in there?"

"For a price. I know the owner. Tell him Bob Garrett sent you."

The cabin was tiny and totally isolated. The owner looked dubiously at her. What did this city girl know about living out in the desert. But Bob Garrett's word was good for him. Carlotta moved in, bought a '54 Chevy with the hubcaps and fenders missing, and drove to work, ten miles, every day. The cabin was not insulated well. During the storms the electricity was erratic. Carlotta wanted the rough land, the moody, uncommunicative people, to make her into someone new. She suppressed every thought of Franklin Moran and Pasadena.

"How's your new home?"

"Oh, Mr. Garrett," she replied. "Fine. Thank you. A little cold. That wind blows right through."

Garrett chuckled. A Navajo turquoise glittered on a silver bracelet. His hands were gnarled, like an old man's, but the forearms were sinewy, and the veins rose up from the muscles like rivers in a brown landscape.

"Nail some carpet on the wall," he said. "Ain't pretty, but it keeps you warm."

169

"I'll do that. Thanks again."

"That owner has got some in his shed. Tell him to give it to you."

Carlotta watched him get up and walk to the cash register.

He always seemed to be thinking of something far away, his eyes twinkling in a strange way, as though he found something vaguely humorous in the people all around him.

"Say, Mr. Garrett," she said, hesitantly. "You wouldn't know anything about cars, would you?"

"I've put a couple engines together. Why? What's the problem?"

"Well, it's my Chevy. Ever since it turned colder it dies. Right on the highway."

Garrett looked at the pretty waitress. She had such frank, trusting eyes, yet he could see behind them a deep suspicion of people and places. She was vulnerable and wary at the same time. She was so determined to be independent, and yet she knew nothing about cars, about the desert, or about the men and women who lived there.

"That's not too serious," he said. "Take it to John. He's the mechanic at the crossroads."

Carlotta hesitated, saw that Garrett was about to go. She leaned forward over the counter, speaking softly.

"Mr. Garrett," she said. "I don't like him."

"John? Why, he's—"

"He gives me strange looks."

"I'm not surprised. He likes pretty girls."

"It's so dark in that garage. He gave me the creeps."

Garrett looked perplexed. He saw the fear behind her eyes. He was not certain what to say for a while. It was his custom not to say too much. But she was helpless, and she trusted him.

"You know," he said, "you needn't be afraid of people out here. No one means you any harm."

"I have my own opinion."

He said nothing, put his hat on, brushing down his white hair. His face looked preoccupied for an instant.

170

This kind of doubt in people bothered him. It did not have to be that way.

"I'll tell you something," he said. "There is a way in which no one can hurt you."

Garrett fell silent. He seemed to be looking for the right answer. He judged how to say it best. Carlotta later found out that he could be silent a whole day if he could not find the right words for the right ideas.

"A person who knows who he or she is," he said, "that person is not afraid of other people."

"Perhaps. In that sense. But I'm still not going to see John."

Garrett sighed. He found her stubbornness amusing and troublesome.

"You got your Chevy here? Bring it to the front. I'll take a look at it."

"Good heavens, Mr. Garrett—I didn't mean for you to—"

"No trouble. I'll be back in a few minutes."

"I—thank you—yes, I'll go get it now."

The autumn froze into a period of snow flurries, one after the other. Carlotta and Billy, confined to the cabin at night, found themselves unable to endure the isolation of the long bleak nights. She began to wonder more and more if there were any more places to run to.

Then the valley became a field of white. The horizon disappeared in clouds of white storm. Suddenly Carlotta realized the folly of her escape out of Two Rivers. She had never experienced a winter like this. Her clothes were not warm enough. The chill of the wind came through. When she bought new coats, her money was nearly gone. Then the cafe closed. It was New Year's. The storm continued. The highway filled up. The Chevy stood under three feet of drifting snow.

The prospect of starving in a cabin in the middle of no place seemed ludicrous. Her whole life was on the verge of becoming a ridiculous and wasted adventure. The snow only came down, softly, piling high outside the windows. The wood supply became low. The owner of the

171

cabin stayed in Two Rivers. The food supply became low. Her child could no longer suck milk from her breasts. Carlotta became afraid of the freezing weather. First the pump froze and it was difficult to unstick it with boiling water. Then the pipes into the sink froze and she could not find them under the house. Metallic groans intermingled with the bitter winds outside. Day and night she and Billy waited for the weather to break.

In the morning she felt the hunger in the pit of her stomach. She was afraid that Billy, his resistance lowered by the cold and the poor food, would get sick. But worst of all was the awareness that she was stuck, dangerously close to starvation, barely ten miles from town. The snow covered the road until there was no way to know where it was. Everything seemed to verify the hopelessness of her attempt at independence, her unworthiness to exist. Franklin Moran was right. He knew what she was good for. That and nothing else. Her parents were right. She was a harmful child, with no right to make claims on the world. Now their voices buzzed in her thoughts late at night. Each morning the clouds rolled over the white fields, dropping snow still higher.

There was the sound of a motor. After a while it came nearer. She looked out the window and saw the owner of the cabin in a motor-driven sled. He waved to her from the entrance to the yard. She weakly waved back.

"I met Bob Garrett over by the junction," he said. "He guessed you'd got yourself caught short. Being new out here."

"Oh, bless him—I did—I feel so completely stupid —"

"No harm, Mrs. Moran. Happens now and then."

He unloaded several boxes of food into the house. Somehow the presence of a man in her tiny cabin made her nervous. She was anxious for him to leave. But he brought in more firewood from his own locked shed, checked the pump and the pipes, and then left. With relief, Carlotta watched him go. To her, all men, except

172

the old rancher, Garrett, were bestial, and it frightened her to be alone with them.

During the spring the mud ran like water through the dismal streets of Two Rivers.

Garrett came into the re-opened cafe. He wore his plaid hunting jacket, his sharp pointed boots. She smiled to him.

"Thank you so much, Mr. Garrett," she said. "You saved my life."

"I knew you weren't the practical type," he said.

"Oh, I just—it was so terrifying—"

"You have to watch out for yourself, Carlotta."

Outside the melting snows ran into the mud. Mud caked every car, every sidewalk, and it clung to the feet of everyone outside. Yet when he called her by name she felt better. Somehow there was a contact with this land, some part of it that was not hostile, and that contact came through the white-haired rancher sitting by the checkered curtains.

"I've never been able to," she confessed. "This place is so hostile. It's as bad as Los Angeles."

Garrett looked at her with a pained expression. He said nothing for a while. She thought he had not heard her. Then, after his coffee, he turned in his chair. They were the only two persons in the cafe.

"I'm going to show my ranch to a prospective buyer. You want to see it?"

Carlotta looked at him strangely. Suddenly she wondered about him. There was nothing suggestive in his voice. Yet she slid behind a veil of indifference.

"From over the town," he said, "you'll get to see the whole valley."

"Oh, Mr. Garrett. I—"

"Just going up the mountain road. It'll improve your opinion of this country."

"Well, I have an infant in the back—"

"We'll only be gone twenty minutes."

After the cafe closed Carlotta sat with a middle-aged

couple in the cab of Garrett's powerful little truck. She held Billy on her lap. As they climbed higher and higher, Carlotta's heart began to fill with wonder. She had never been so high, never seen the landscape the way it looked from up there. Valley after valley dropped into view, the shadows of the spring clouds looked like puffs of white smoke far away, and she could see two forks of a river winding slowly through the cactus far below.

"It's so beautiful up here!" she said.

"Ain't Los Angeles, is it?" Garrett said.

She laughed. She held Billy up to the window.

"Look, Billy! That's an eagle! You've never seen an eagle before!"

"Hasn't now," Garrett chuckled. "That's a hawk."

When they got out of the truck, Garrett pointed out some things to the couple. Far away, like a vision it was so far away, nestled in under red plateaus, was a tiny ranch, almost yellow in the dappled sunlight. A creek ran beside it, and farther away, the highway rose over the dry hills.

The crisp air twirled her hair. Her heart was pounding, not from the altitude, but from a strange thrill. Something she had never known before.

"Oh, I wish I could build a cabin up here!" she exclaimed. "I'd live here forever!"

Garrett smiled.

"I told you that you weren't practical. There's no water up here, and you'd freeze in the winter."

She laughed.

When she got out of the truck at the cafe, she thanked Garrett. She got into her Chevy, drove back to the cabin swimming in a sea of mud, and in her mind's eye was the vision of the yellow ranch far away.

In the early summer the dust and pollen were thick in the air. Billy began to wheeze and cough. She covered his face with a wet handkerchief, but it was something else that was wrong. He began to grow a fever, his face became alternately pale and flushed, and his eyes had a delirious quality. Neither the owner of the cabin nor anyone in the cafe knew what was wrong. The only doctor

174

was gone, traveling in his jeep up the north fork of the river.

Billy was infected. His breathing came and went, sounded like a file rasping on a board. The tiny eyes and nose ran with mucous. He struggled for breath, twisted on the bed, crying. She went back to the doctor's office. A note said he would not return from the North Fork area for two weeks.

The dust howled through the trees. Dead leaves from autumn were flattened against the cabin walls.

She drove the Chevy down to the north fork, guiding the car as best as she could over the rutted roads. Beside her Billy wheezed in three torn blankets. He was propped up against the seat, coughing and spitting. Far away she recognized the ranch she had once seen from high over the town.

She drove into the gate, stopped the car, and got out with Billy in her arms. An old couple told her the doctor had gone around the other side of the south fork, around the canyon, and there were no telephones to the area.

They sat her down on an overstuffed sofa inside. The man went to a telephone and wound up the crank.

"Bob? Jamison here. Listen, a woman here with a sick infant . . . No, not me. Somebody from town. Can you make it down here? . . . What . . . Good, good. We'll be waiting."

Carlotta shivered on the sofa. Evidently she had not been eating well. She looked pale, clammy. They thought she needed a doctor as well.

"Now listen," the man said, "don't worry. Somebody's coming who knows a lot about medicine. Learned it from the Indians. So you just wait 'til he comes."

After an hour a truck was heard rattling down the mountainside. Carlotta stood, realized she had a fever: her legs felt leaden, heavy. Garrett stepped from the truck outside, carrying a small bag.

"Mr. Garrett," she said weakly, smiling, holding out her hand, "I haven't seen you in ages."

"Carlotta! I didn't know—then it's Billy?"

Without another word he went into the darkened bedroom. They boiled water, mixed in several herbs, and Garrett spent the night on a chair watching over the infant. Carlotta sat in the bedroom, then forced herself to eat something, then sat in the room again. Billy slept fitfully, moaning hotly, his face bathed in perspiration, his eyes glazed. Then he slowly drifted into a deep slumber. Carlotta bent over to look. Garrett started, awakened.

"He's sleeping," he said.

"He looks burning with fever."

"It's the worst now. By morning he'll cool down."

Toward sunrise Carlotta fell asleep. Garrett covered her in an Indian blanket lying nearby. The couple slept on the sofa in the front room, stirred, and prepared breakfast. Billy slept through it all, oblivious to every noise.

"See?" Garrett said. "His forehead is cooler."

Garrett prepared several herbs, bathed the child and listened to the breathing. After several more hours he noticed that Carlotta was suffering from a terrible fatigue.

By mid-afternoon it was apparent that Billy was better. His face lost the flushed appearance, and by suppertime he opened his eyes. Garrett drove Carlotta and Billy back to their cabin, the man and woman bringing up the Chevy and driving back in their own car. Garrett took one look at the tiny, dirty cabin and shook his head.

"This is no good," he said softly.

He leaned over the stove, opened the lid, and peered in. Then he looked at the flue.

"You have no ventilation here," he said. "No wonder you get sick. And the roof is in bad shape. You're going to get rain right through it in the fall. What're you going to do when the snow falls?"

Carlotta stood in the corner, watching him inspecting the cabin.

176

"This is just no good," he said to himself. "I never thought it had deteriorated like this."

"I was afraid to ask the owner," she said.

"Do you have some other place to go to?"

Carlotta hesitated.

"No."

"You're going to freeze like a popsickle in five months."

"I—I'm not sure what to do."

Garrett kicked the small woodpile. The rotted wood fell apart in soft chunks. He knew now that the woman depended on him.

"Well," he said, looking up, "I can put up a couple of new rafters for you."

"Oh no, Mr. Garrett. You mustn't—"

"You should have told me a long time ago," he said, almost angrily. Not angry at her, but at himself. He had seen that she was vulnerable, without a man.

"I didn't know—"

"You have to trust people, Carlotta," he said. "Out here we depend on each other."

They buttered bread and covered it with thick slabs of ham. Carlotta seemed to wait for Garrett to decide what to do. Fatigue and the isolation had eroded her confidence in herself. Now she had no place to turn except to this white-haired man who was lost in thought.

"There's no harm in running away," he said softly. "Provided you know what you're running toward."

She said nothing. There was no artifice in what he said. He was not trying to be something he was not. She, too, felt the need to be honest, to be direct, for the first time in her life.

"I was afraid of staying where I was," she said simply. "Anything was better."

Garrett boiled some water and made tea. The tap did not close properly, and he shook his head.

"Life goes forward," he said. "Not backward."

"You're religious?" she asked.

177

He broke into a pleasant laugh, the even white teeth shining.

"No. Not at all. Not as it is conventionally known. I love the land. Life itself. That's my God."

"My father was a preacher," she said distastefully. "I don't think he ever knew who his God really was."

Now the sun was down. Garrett kicked over a wooden box and sat down on it. They drank their tea, sweetened with honey and lemon. Slowly the hour passed by. Carlotta told him about her father, the inward, striving man who was so bitterly disappointed in life.

"Life apart from yourself is hard, Carlotta," Garrett said. "You need somebody to teach you to be on your own."

It relieved her, to hear him speak. It was like removing a cancer from her soul. She found herself telling him private things about herself. She found that a human being whom she could trust was the greatest treasure that the earth provides. In him she saw a different standard of values, something closer to the human. Modest and self-reliant. Self-contained. From that peaceful vantage point she surveyed the wrecked life that had been hers. She condemned it all, this time with the certainty that it would be defeated. She could find a new life. Here. Out where the natural struggle molded you in a different image.

"I believe the sun is rising," he said softly.

"It is. How beautiful! It looks so clear—"

"By mid-summer it will be rising over Twin Peaks. You see how it changes during the year? Everything moves in a long cycle. Everything becomes renewed."

She looked at him. She realized she was staring. She was no longer a little girl. She no longer needed to be one. Between two people there could be a natural relationship.

He, too, was looking at her. Frankly. Penetrating her glance with his. The unspoken hung in the air. She went to the bed and picked up Billy.

"His breathing is normal," she said.

Her own heart had begun beating more rapidly. It

was something akin to desire. But it was more refined. A feeling more delicate, so subtle that she was afraid it would dissipate and leave her the same Carlotta who had run away, fleeing herself. She turned, found him standing behind her, unafraid. He reached his hand forward, his fingers gently lifting the curls at the side of her face. He smiled, a sad, intelligent smile, hidden with the sorrows of loneliness. It was a strange face, she thought. Deeply lined, tough, yet the eyes always found something to find joy in. Now she felt, for the first time, that a human being, a man, knew her as a human being, and he wanted her in a way that she also desired.

"You'll have to take care of yourself, Carlotta," he said softly. "Or else you'll not live as you were meant to."

She smiled, uncertainly at first. She did not know what to do. She was not certain what he meant. So far from the city, from other people, there was only herself to rely on. There were no codes of behavior, no rules, no false thoughts. There were only the two people in the room. The sunshine was bursting through the window, streaking the wooden walls.

"It's only twenty miles up the canyon," he said, his eyes following hers. "By the river."

Carlotta felt a thousand thoughts go through her mind.

"Yes," she said quietly. "All right. I'll get my things."

From the cab of the truck she took a last look at the cabin, so poorly constructed, and the Chevy stuck in the mud, glistening. Farther up the road, all but a few telephone poles out of sight, was Two Rivers. She turned around, holding Billy on her lap. In front of her was a new landscape, a more desolate, more rugged series of valleys and canyons. She had never seen such a wild land before. She never looked back.

Garrett's ranch was on a small plateau. Below it were two creeks fed by springs in the canyons. Beyond a small pasture rose enormous red rocky mesas. They cast their protective shadows over the ranch in the day, and in the winter kept the winds away.

Carlotta decorated the interior of the rooms with fabric from town. She learned how to cook simple meals of corn, peppers, and fruits. She fed the chickens, the few pigs, and milked the cows. Her face became tanned, her movements natural and unhesitating. She forgot what it was like to be afraid.

Garrett believed in nature. If a man cut himself off, he was lost. He lost his spirit, his joy, his sense of being alive. In each thing he showed Carlotta, there was a lesson. The narrow fish in the weeds of the pools. The wildflowers and the ferns. The lizards darting through the crevices. For man was as wild and transient as they, but gifted with awareness.

He wrote poetry that described the breakup of winter. The ice that slid down the face of the rock walls. The tracks appearing in the soft mud. The yellow flowers poking through the melting ice. And each poem he worked over and over, until it became hard and perfect, precise and simple, like the pebbles on the bottom of a mountain stream.

One day they rode to the edge of the canyon. Far below the smoke trailed up from the Indian settlements in the valleys.

"But you have to know, Carlotta," he said, "that there was something only you could have given me. Something I can't explain. As though a river suddenly had a second source."

"Oh, Bob," she said, smiling. "You gave me life itself."

"You always had that gift. You were with people who didn't. Who denied it to you."

"But they don't exist anymore. Not to me."

Garrett watched the smoke from below bend into the breeze and disappear. They walked over the red sand, their faces warmed by the setting sun.

"Those people," Carlotta said, "even to themselves, they never really existed. I know that now."

"Forgive them. They were trapped. They didn't control their own lives."

"I do forgive them. Still, I don't ever want to see them again."

Garrett looked at her. He disliked seeing anger. Nevertheless, he knew the scars were deep. So he said nothing, assuming that time and the desert would heal her wounds.

Carlotta became pregnant. He found a new vitality in everything he did. He brought colored ears of corn and wildflowers and put them on the gates and on the doors. He delivered the child himself. For three days she lay in bed, nursing the infant girl. Then she rose and went to work, Julie in a sling across her back, Indian-style.

From time to time she visited the Indian women across the mesas. She learned how to dye her own cloth. How to cure the girl's rashes with herbs. How to decorate shirts, though her fingers remained clumsy compared to the Indians. She never thought any more of the life before Bob Garrett. There was no life before then. Now there was only the sun, the mesas, the children, and the ranch. Garrett saw her change.

"I see it in you," he said to her once. "Something akin to the rivers and the winds outside. Perhaps it's the soul. I have no words for it. But it moves inside you now, and there is no fear—of life."

She smiled mysteriously.

"What's so funny?" he asked.

"Something is moving inside me."

"What are you—"

"Gather some Indian corn, Bob."

"Are you sure?"

"Yes, of course."

"Oh, Carlotta! This is the most wonderful thing—"

"It will be a boy," she said. "Another you. That's what I want the most."

It was late at night. Outside the coyote wailed. Garrett laughed, his face excited by the news.

"Do you hear him?" he said. "He's so lonely. He has no one."

She reached for his face, placed her hand on his cheek.

"But we do," she said. "We always will."

He kissed her fingers gently.

"Always," he murmured, finding it difficult to speak.

And so their second child was born—a girl—delivered by Bob. And the seasons passed. There was no other life. Carlotta knew nothing else. There was no other Carlotta than the one Garrett had made of her. She gave herself to him, and he had fashioned something fine and delicate out of her.

In the early spring of 1974 Garrett found himself leaning against a fence post. The snow was still on the ground in patches, and the barbed wire hung from his gloved hands. The melting trickles of water swam in his vision.

He went inside the ranch. Carlotta had never seen him look tired.

"Oh, Bob!" she wept, when he lay down on the bed, looking white.

"It's all right . . ."

"I'll get a doctor!"

"Shhhhhhh. Let me just rest a moment."

He slept through the day. Toward evening a rain began to fall. His breathing became deeper and deeper, slower and slower.

"I love you, Carlotta," he said weakly. "Don't ever forget."

"Oh, Bob—don't. I'll go now—the doctor in Two Rivers—"

"No, no. Just stay beside me. For a few more moments."

Then he passed into a delirious sleep. He called out to her, as though looking for her. He opened his eyes from time to time, but seemed not to see her there. By early morning the children were sitting in chairs near the bed. Waiting.

182

"Carlotta," he whispered.

She leaned forward.

He tried to say something. The words buzzed like demented bees in her ear. They made no sense. They sounded angry, wild, and disconnected—a choking death rattle, like he was strangling on his own saliva.

"Carlotta—I—can't—breathe. Don't—don't—leave —me. Don't—leave—me—"

The chest no longer rose and fell. He was gone into a darkness. Only the body remained, a curiously heavy, pallid, unfamiliar body all of a sudden. Now that the soul was gone from it, it looked alien, even frightening.

"Oh, Bob!" she wept.

But the dead man's chest felt heavy and hollow to her. There was something repugnant about it, treacherous. She felt guilty for those thoughts. Yet it was true. The bedroom had taken on a sinister aspect. Something vaguely familiar.

She went into the kitchen to wash her face. The children watched her, not knowing what to do, aware only that a great change had come to their lives. Slowly, as she watched the rain pelt the yard, turning it into a muddy plain, Garrett began to remove himself from her. What he had taught her began to evaporate. For the first time in nearly ten years she did not know what to do.

In the night it occurred to her to wash and dress the body. She stripped off the shirt, then closed the door behind her. The moon shone eerily through the rain-wet windows, glistening. The face of the old man now looked withered and gaunt. Only hollows for the eyes. She took a soft sponge and water, cleansed the old man's body, the lean hips, the long legs, and the sinewy arms. It was like washing dead wood. Where was the soul that had animated her own life?

She dressed the body in Garrett's best clothes. A black suit he had worn only once. The day he had married them both by the creek. Now it was a cruel remnant of the beginning of that life. She was conscious only of the rain beating down on the roof. She could hear the water trickling around the foundations of the house. She closed the door as she left. Did not sleep that night.

At dawn she realized that it was a big storm. The rain had not let up at all. Nor would it for a week or more. The truck was sinking into the mud. She had enough food and wood to stay for a long time. But she dared not. Not with the dead body in the bedroom.

At first it was only a disinclination. Then it grew into a feeling of anxiety. She went to the bedroom and opened the door. To prove to herself that she was the new Carlotta, the Carlotta that was afraid of nothing. Inside, the light fell vividly, a sickly, silver light, on the white hair, the eyes looking strangely crossed, almost slanted. She bent over, closed the lids.

Suddenly it occurred to her that if she stayed in the cabin for a week he would begin to decay. A black chill flowed up her spine, like a wave of nausea. What if the rains never let up? She knew she was beginning to pull apart inside.

That night she slept only fitfully. The children wrapped themselves in Indian blankets on the living-room floor. Where could she go? She wanted to run into the bedroom, shake Garrett and wake him, beg him to lead her out once again from the hole into which she had fallen. But this time there was no one to lead her out. The Carlotta that Garrett had formed began to slough away, like the skin of a snake. In its place was the old Carlotta, the Carlotta who needed to run away. And who had succeeded only too well. She no longer knew who she was, nor why she was there.

As the day came on the third morning and the yard flowed with five inches of water, she knew she was trapped. Nature was going to get its revenge for all the good years. It was going to kill her. But first it was going to exact its payment. Never had she experienced such indifference, such monstrous and alien indifference, in the forces of nature.

Now she knew she was in danger. It was not the food, the firewood, the drinking water. It was not the rain

184

and the mud. It was her mind. It was giving way. She had to act, and act fast. But what? Already she felt afraid to enter the bedroom, could not bring herself to enter that room. The children sensed she had changed. She became afraid of the sounds of the wind and the rain.

Late at night she smelled it. It flowed like a wave from the bedroom. She bolted upright, holding her head. Or was she dreaming? The night had never looked so black, a strange, impenetrable darkness. But there it was. Surely it was in the air. Or was it in her mind? A gentle, but unmistakable scent of flesh gone bad. Only three days, she thought. But the rooms were warm. She gathered up the children and a few belongings and bundled them into the truck.

She wanted to open the bedroom door. Kiss Garrett one last time. But he was not there. Only a hideous substitute that changed and almost moved in her imagination. She wondered if she could trust her own perceptions. She relied on Billy to tell her where the road was in the roaring night. It gave him a thrill, to be counted on like a man, but he was also afraid. Together, they maneuvered the truck up to the highway. It was monstrous, obscene, all the purity of those ten years cruelly and hideously transformed into a grotesque reminder of life's horror.

The children looked out at the dismal scene. Carlotta looked up the canyon. The land everywhere was under water. The only crossing point was swirling with dark, angry waters. She backed up the truck. The headlights picked out a dead animal, turning around on its way downstream. She pressed down the accelerator and then let out the clutch.

The front wheels gripped the broken asphalt under the roaring stream. A branch from upstream crashed against the cab door. The engine whined, sputtered, and the wheels slipped sideways under the impact of the flood. The headlights showed only splashing water, black, with foaming white spray over the hood.

She was afraid to go back, afraid to stop. The engine roared. It was too late, she thought. In the darkness she saw nothing. Then the truck climbed, rose out of the water, and they sat, shivering, on the rise beyond the flooded part of the highway. Down below was the ranch. Only a glimmer was in the kitchen, a red glow where the stove was still giving heat to an empty room. In the bedroom it was black. She could not see even the bedroom windows. Garrett was in there. In her mind's eye she tried to picture him as he had been—the hunting jacket, the boots, the tanned chest—but all she saw was darkness.

"Mrs. Moran?"

"What?"

"Mrs. Moran, the doctors would like to see you now."

The elderly nurse stood, smiling artificially, at the door. Suddenly Carlotta remembered where she was. She was among flat people in a flat, white world.

"Yes," she murmured. "Of course."

She entered the seminar room. At first she saw Sneidermann, seated far away, against the wall. Then, standing before her, were four doctors, one of them a woman.

"Won't you sit down, please?" said Dr. Weber. He began by introducing himself, then the others. The woman was Dr. Chevalier. A white-haired old man, to whom everyone deferred, was Dr. Wilkes. The last was Dr. Walcott, a hefty, nervous man. Carlotta sat on a hard chair. She crossed her legs.

"Perhaps we can move our chairs closer together," Dr. Weber said. "I don't want Mrs. Moran to feel she is being cross-examined."

There was a shuffle as the doctors moved their chairs. Carlotta thought they all looked pale, even anemic. From their pinched faces, they looked privately unhappy, obsessed, and lonely.

"Have you had breakfast?" asked Dr. Chevalier. "Perhaps you would like some coffee?"

"No. Thank you."

It was like being in the office with Sneidermann. You

talked, they listened. But it was not a normal conversation. It was this strange kind of communication which operated according to rules only they understood.

"Tell me, Carlotta," Dr. Weber said, "how do you feel about being here?"

"It's strange. I'd have to admit that."

"You mean it's not like a backyard barbecue, where everyone knows everyone else?"

"Exactly," Carlotta said. "Everybody seems a little strange."

"Strangers, you mean?"

"No. It's something else—"

"Go ahead."

Carlotta paused. She watched them watching her. It was a distinctly uncomfortable feeling. She felt on the defensive.

"The way you're dressed, for one thing," she said. "Bow ties have been out for years."

General laughter broke out. Carlotta had not meant it to be funny, but now she was glad that the tension was broken.

"You know how it is, Carlotta," said Dr. Wilkes, fingering his red bow tie. "We specialists get caught up in our work. We lose touch."

He took off the tie and put it into his pocket.

"You should unbutton the top button," she said.

The men chuckled as Dr. Wilkes unbuttoned the top button of his shirt. He smiled in a kindly way at Carlotta. She began to see them as men instead of doctors. She slowly lost her fear of them. Gradually the room became quiet once again.

"Do you still find us strange?" asked Dr. Weber.

Now the silence was perfect. Things had become serious again.

"Carlotta," asked Dr. Chevalier softly, raising her head. "Do you find us unreal perhaps?"

"Unreal? Yes. That's a good word for it. This whole thing is unreal."

"Do you mean we are only pretending to be here?"

187

"Exactly. I feel I could put my hand right through you."

"As though I were not solid?"

"Of course, I know you are. I'm only telling you what it feels like."

"And the other doctors?"

"The same thing."

"And Dr. Sneidermann?"

"No. I think of him as being solid."

"And you?"

"Me—I—"

Carlotta thought for a minute, oblivious to the doctors looking at her. Then she looked up and nodded.

"Yes," she said. "Even more so. I'm not really here."

"Where are you?" asked Dr. Walcott, in a carefully modulated voice.

"Nowhere."

"Then you don't exist."

"My mind does. My body does. But *I* don't."

"Then the real you—where is it?"

Carlotta shifted in her seat. She had not expected such exacting questions. It was like an examination. The doctors were polite, waiting attentively. But it was difficult to explain to them what the real feeling was like.

"It's as though I remember the real me," she finally said. "The real Carlotta. I liked her, but she doesn't exist any more. I just have a memory of her. Somebody I used to know a long time ago."

"The real Carlotta Moran," asked Dr. Chevalier, making her words clear, "is she dead?"

"No. She just went away."

"When?"

"I don't know."

"When you got sick?"

"Maybe earlier."

Dr. Weber studied the young woman before him. He wondered if she were picking up suggestions about her case from Sneidermann. Residents, even the best of them, have a way of suggesting diagnoses to their patients. He suddenly hoped she would never misconstrue an idea he might accidentally give her. She seemed to be highly receptive to all the doctors, and her mind was racing away, trying to divine what they were thinking and why they were thinking it.

"Will Carlotta ever come back?" Dr. Weber asked.

"Sometimes I don't think so."

"What would bring her back?"

"If she was cured."

"That would bring the real Carlotta back to you?"

"Yes. Then she would be a complete person again. Then the attacks would stop. Then she and I would be one person again."

"Very perceptive, Carlotta," Dr. Chevalier said.

Dr. Weber was now fairly certain that she was repeating what Sneidermann, even without being conscious of it, had suggested to her. It was something he would have to watch.

Again, there was a silence in the room. The windows were closed and it was getting stuffy. They seemed to be waiting for her to say something, but there was nothing to say. Finally Dr. Walcott spoke up again. He spoke in a voice so carefully controlled, so pleasantly modulated, that she felt it was an act, and she became suspicious.

"Who is this Oriental creature, Carlotta?" he asked. "Why does he come to bother you?"

"I don't know, Dr. Walcott."

"Has it been the same creature each time?"

"It's not a creature. It's a man. And he has helpers."

"Now, Carlotta. Even though he has appeared to you, is he real? Is he real in the way that I am real? Or is he real in a different way?"

Carlotta blushed. She felt confused. Obviously, Dr. Walcott was asking her if she was insane or not. It was humiliating. But she decided to give him the truth.

"When he first attacked me, I thought he was real. Then I became convinced it was a kind of dream. When

189

he attacked me in the car, I thought it was unreal until he took over the steering wheel. And then when I actually saw him, I knew for sure he was real."

"What do you think now? In this room—with us?"

Carlotta hesitated a moment. "Dr. Sneidermann explained that it was like a powerful dream."

"Do you believe him?"

"I try to. But I don't."

"Why not?"

Carlotta felt she were being dissected on an operating table. She had not anticipated such a grueling examination.

"Because of the marks on my body," she said, her voice losing its steadfast control. "They're in places where I can't do it to myself. Even in a dream. I'm not biting myself."

"Anything else?"

"My house—you can see the torn drapes, the cracks on the ceiling. *I* didn't do that. Billy didn't do that. Nobody did. The children know he's there. They can hear him. They smell him. And Billy—"

"Yes?"

"He hurt Billy."

Dr. Walcott nodded. "Yes, we know. But didn't you describe yourself as waking up in some way from these attacks?"

"Well, sure—I told Dr. Sneidermann—things sort of glide in, become unreal, and then it happens. Afterwards, it glides away and I think maybe it was just a fantasy or something. But then there are bruises all over my neck and arms, or the drapes are torn or something, or the children see it or hear it. Then I think, even afterwards, that it must be real."

"I see."

Carlotta regained her composure. The whole problem of whether or not it was real confused her. It made her dizzy, because she did not know. Even thinking about that chilled her.

"Do you find it odd that he speaks to you in English,

190

Carlotta?" Dr. Chevalier asked. "I mean—being an Oriental—"

"Quite frankly, Dr. Chevalier, I find this whole thing odd," Carlotta replied.

Dr. Weber suppressed a smile.

"He calls you foul names," Dr. Chevalier pursued. "Why?"

"I—I could tell you. Maybe a doctor like you—a lady—wouldn't know, but—"

"Go ahead."

"Well. Some men—when they—you see, with a woman—"

"Yes?"

"They use these words. Very evil words. Not to hurt, though. It's a way to, you know, sort of, for themselves—"

"To excite himself?"

"Yes. That's it."

"Then why did he try to hurt you in the car? Why did he hurt Billy?"

"He was warning me."

"What was he warning you?"

"To be cooperative."

Under the pretense of sipping coffee, Dr. Chevalier studied Carlotta carefully.

"Why does he attack *you*, Carlotta? Why not someone else?"

"I suppose he chose me."

"Don't you think he has other women?"

"I—I—never thought of that."

"Never?"

"No."

"But why *you*, Carlotta? Why has he chosen you?"

"I don't know," Carlotta said. "I suppose he finds me attractive."

Carlotta was blushing.

Dr. Chevalier waited a moment, then asked: "Would it be a reflection on you as a woman if he left you? If you were cured?"

191

Carlotta sensed she had been trapped somehow by the woman in the tweed skirt. She thought quickly.

"Of course not," Carlotta said. "I hate this whole thing. It's like a nightmare and I can't wake up. I don't give a damn if *he* thinks this or that—I just want to get rid of him—"

Dr. Weber spoke up. He sensed that Carlotta was angry at them.

"Of course, you're right, Carlotta," he said. "We are doing what we can. But it is just not something you can put a splint or a bandage on. It takes a while to find out exactly where the disorder is."

Carlotta brushed an imaginary piece of lint from her skirt.

"I'm not angry," she said. "But I just don't know how much good all this talking is doing."

"Yes, of course. I understand—"

"Talking doesn't seem to help. It hasn't with Dr. Sneidermann."

"Please believe me, Carlotta. We are doing everything that is possible at this stage."

She nodded. But she seemed abstracted, distant. She was clearly losing confidence in their ability. After a few more comments they stood, shook her hand, and the nurse escorted her from the room. The doctors remained inside, somewhat disconcerted by the sudden revelation of hostility and doubt.

Dr. Wilkes stood, brushed back his white hair, and the other doctors looked up at him. He seemed to feel no compunction about directing the meeting.

"Dr. Sneidermann," he said, "would you please join us?"

Sneidermann walked up from the rear of the room. He sat down uncomfortably beside Dr. Chevalier. Dr. Wilkes squinted at the opened casebook on a small table by the door, running the pages over, one by one. Then he turned to Sneidermann.

"What do you think of the original diagnosis?" Dr. Wilkes asked.

"Hysterical neurosis? I still hold to it. Uneasily."

Dr. Wilkes shook his head.

"Things have changed, Dr. Sneidermann."

There was an ominous silence. Sneidermann swallowed nervously and said nothing.

"When she first came to you, there was dissociation only when she described the attacks. You remember? Now she is estranged from reality. She thinks of us as unreal, ghostly figures. That's the first change."

"Yes, sir."

"At first she only heard swear words when she was attacked. Now she has an interpretation. He wants to make love with her. It's an incipient relationship. I don't like that. That's change number two."

"Yes, sir. I see what you mean. Still—"

"In fact, she's rather proud of this creature," said Dr. Chevalier. "It's a testimonial to her sexual attractiveness. That's different, Gary."

"Very important, these changes," Dr. Wilkes said. "This is not some teenager with an identity crisis. It is a highly unstable situation, and it has found no equilibrium whatsoever."

Sneidermann wondered if he had not completely underestimated the danger Carlotta was in. If so, why hadn't Dr. Weber told him? Why hadn't he guessed it, either? Or was it his way of letting a resident learn at a patient's expense? Neither seemed a possibility. Sneidermann began to feel almost queasy. Then he realized it was because the doctors were groping just as he was. Up to this moment, he had assumed that a senior medical staff had finite, distinct answers, as they did in the lecture hall. But now they were all lost in their private conjectures, and Carlotta's eventual cure seemed to become visibly more distant.

"There's another change, too," Dr. Weber said.

"What is that?" Sneidermann asked.

"At first these onslaughts were sudden. Like rapes. In fact, she thought she had been raped, didn't she?"

"Correct."

"Now she described the attacks as sort of *gliding* in and *gliding* out around the actual assault. Those were her words. You see? The zone of delusion has expanded on both sides."

"I caught that," Dr. Chevalier agreed. "I wasn't certain if that was something new."

"It is," Sneidermann admitted.

"And not just changing in a neutral direction," Dr. Wilkes added.

Chevalier sighed. She looked out the window for a moment, as though the sunshine in the courtyard could cheer up the dreary and abused seminar room in which they were.

"Pretty little girl," Dr. Walcott said vaguely. "It grieves me to see her like this."

"Yes," Dr. Weber said.

Sneidermann wondered what was the unspoken thought that hovered in their minds, but from which he was excluded.

"You have a psychotic reaction—a psychotic break on your hands, Dr. Sneidermann," Dr. Chevalier said, looking out the window.

"Definitely," Dr. Weber said.

"I agree," said Wilkes. "Dr. Walcott. What is your opinion?"

"Undecided."

Sneidermann watched them. The thought, like a cold river, flowed through his brain: what if this was more than he could handle? He forced himself to concentrate on their every statement.

"Let's talk about treatment," Walcott said. "A positive transference has obviously taken place."

"Yes," Wilkes said. "That is clear."

"Yes," Dr. Chevalier smiled wanly. "She's falling in love with you, Gary."

"So be careful," said Dr. Walcott.

"It's true," Dr. Wilkes said. "Unrealistic transference is not without some danger to the psychiatrist. A colleague of mine, Dr. Northshield of NYU, was shot by a patient. These repressed emotions are extraordinarily strong."

Again a curtain of silence fell. Sneidermann again had the unpleasant feeling that the precise answers, the invincible confidence of the professionals, was only a facade. Now it was giving way to conjecture, half-certainties, estimations and frustration.

"Then where do we go from here?" Dr. Walcott asked to no one in particular.

"Anti-psychotic medication as a start," Dr. Weber said. "You all know my position on drugs, but I don't like these attacks. They make it harder for her to get back in touch with reality each time. I want her to sleep every night and be free of these horrifying episodes."

"What about suicide?" Sneidermann asked.

"She won't commit suicide," Dr. Wilkes interrupted.

"Why not?"

"She's not trying to destroy herself. She could have done that a long time ago."

"What about the car crash?"

"That just proved she was sick enough to go to the hospital. She wasn't trying to kill herself."

"But what if she changes for the worse some more? Decides to take an overdose?"

"If she wants to kill herself, there is nothing you can do about it. You look surprised. Did that sound callous? Because it's true. You can not prevent this young lady from taking her life if she really wants to."

Sneidermann looked terribly depressed. He sank back in his chair. Somehow the meeting had taken on the atmosphere of some kind of disaster. Not only had he been wrong in his diagnosis, but his patient was in far worse shape than he had thought for over a month.

"This type of psychotic break is not the worst thing in the world," Dr. Weber said soothingly. "Schizophrenia is a hell of a lot worse."

"Perhaps these marks on her body are hysterical symptoms after all," Dr. Walcott suggested hopefully.

"Maybe," Dr. Wilkes said. "I've seen spectacular

195

skin eruptions from hysterical patients. But I believe that she is physically cutting herself and jabbing herself with bottles or coat hangers around the house."

"That would be openly psychotic behavior," Sneidermann said.

"Of course."

The doctors seemed to have come to a consensus. Sneidermann felt suddenly very much alone. He even wondered if he had it within himself to bring Carlotta out of that jungle she had been walking in for months. He wondered if anybody could.

Dr. Wilkes brushed a hand through his hair again, the freckled skin looking oddly out of place beside the craggy face. He gestured to the casebook on the table.

"Your comments here, Dr. Sneidermann, regarding the background of the patient, your speculations regarding infantile sexuality—classically correct. I have no further comment."

Dr. Walcott straightened his tie and stood up. The others followed suit.

"Then we have a consensus on a preliminary diagnosis here?"

"I think so," Dr. Wilkes said.

"Of course, we need to make it more specific. As soon as possible," Dr. Weber added. "She's floating. We're floating just a little."

Dr. Wilkes extended his hand to Sneidermann.

"Good luck, Dr. Sneidermann. I believe you have a better grasp of the case than you think you do."

"What? Oh, thank you, Dr. Wilkes."

"Don't be afraid of making mistakes. My own mistakes would fill a textbook. Be confident."

"I will, sir," Sneidermann said, not certain if he meant it.

They shook hands and the group dispersed from the room. Sneidermann was confused. He had learned it was far more serious than he had thought. They were going to give her major tranquilizers. And all they had told him to do was to dig deeper into her past.

"Dr. Chevalier," Dr. Weber said, "will you be my guest for lunch? Some aspects of this case I wish to speak with you about."

"Certainly."

Sneidermann wondered what was going on. Chevalier was director of admissions. Were they going to hospitalize Carlotta? And what then? His hospital only kept patients for observation periods. Then, if the recommendation warranted, sent them to the state institutions.

"Goodbye, Dr. Sneidermann," Dr. Walcott said. "Cheer up."

"What? Oh, goodbye, Dr. Walcott."

Sneidermann walked down the crowded, noisy corridors, feeling rotten inside.

State institutions were, to Sneidermann, "snake pits." Too many patients, too few doctors. He suspected that most of the time they used drugs to keep patients under control. Sneidermann felt intense anxiety flowing through him. And even if, by some miracle, she survived, what would become of her then? Few patients get better in those crowded compounds. Often, they vegetate in whatever level of psychosis they entered. Never worse, never better. For year after year. The image of Carlotta Moran flashed again in front of his eyes. What was going to happen to her now?

10

THE day was bright, cold, and gray.

Carlotta's heart pounded furiously. It was so small at first. A tiny speck, a black dot against the indifferent sky. Then it banked, the wings flashed once in the dull light, and it grew larger, finally dropping onto the runway. The engines cut off, the wind whipped her hair up into a tangle, and Jerry appeared in the door of the airplane, the first to step out.

"Jerry!"

He was wearing a checked jacket and dark pants. He waved his arm and grinned. A boyish grin which concealed the shyness underneath unless you knew to look for it. Beneath that shyness Carlotta knew the tough determination of someone who had grown up with no one to help him.

"Jerry!"

Jerry stood, almost like a dream, until the stewardess cleared something from the landing steps, and then he came down.

"Carlotta!"

He crushed her to his chest. Carlotta felt herself yield entirely to him, she floated in the first instant of tranquility she had known in over a month. Their lips met, trembling, their emotion making them awkward. Jerry seemed uncertain, as if afraid of losing her.

"Excuse me, sir," said a stewardess. "Could you please move to one side?"

Behind them stood a stewardess and a line of disgruntled passengers.

"Of course. Of course," Jerry said, blushing.

Carlotta laughed.

They walked across the cement for a while, then turned and embraced again.

"How much I've missed you," Jerry said hoarsely.

"Yeah, I know. Look at me. I'm shaking all over."

Carlotta leaned against his chest, closing her eyes. She heard his heart pounding.

"Let me look at you," she said. "Oh, you look so fine. You look like a real executive in that jacket."

"Well, I am. Now. I'm promoted."

He held her close to him again. The slight smell of her cologne, the warmth of her neck, enclosed his senses in a delirious ecstasy.

"Let's go someplace," he whispered.

They went together, arm in arm, toward the ramp where the suitcases were disgorged from the bowels of the airport machinery. Jerry picked out his suitcase and they went outside.

"You look like a dream," he said. "Where'd you get that?"

"The blouse? It's Mexican. I bought it downtown."

Jerry hailed a taxicab. Far away they saw the Holiday Inn, and beyond that, the nightclub where they had met. It all seemed so long ago. When they got into the taxi, he suddenly realized that he didn't know where to go.

"Let's go someplace nice," she said softly. "Where we went the first time."

There was a strange urgency in her voice. It made Jerry pause.

"All right," he said. "Nice it is."

The taxi turned out of the lot, cruised toward the Pacific Coast Highway, then up again to the hills where the road blossomed out in an area that overlooked the ocean. The sun was sinking like a pale ball into the gray horizon. "Sea View Motel" flickered on the sign, and, below it, "Vacancy."

Jerry opened the door of the motel room.

"Kinda crummy, isn't it?" he said. "Not the way I'd remembered."

"It's fine."

"You're sure?"

Carlotta laughed.

"I'm sure," she said.

The drawstring of the Mexican blouse pulled softly through the white fabric.

"Do you want something?" he said. "To drink?"

"Not now."

The dark skirt, its embroidered hem like a green snake, was placed on the chair. Jerry watched her soft body, the way the shadows and the flesh undulated together in the dim light. Embarrassed for a second, then quickly, he took off his clothes.

"You're so beautiful," he said.

"You've lost weight," she said.

"Yeah, traveling," he said. "I forget to eat."

He put his arms around her waist. He sensed her breathing deeply in his arms. His body changed in her presence.

"Maybe things can be more permanent," he said huskily.

She mumbled something inaudible against his shoulder.

"I think I can be relocated to the Southwest. Permanently."

"Really?"

"San Diego. I think it's in the cards."

"Then you could be here—practically—"

"For good. No more traveling."

She listened to his heart beat. She smiled. Her lips looked especially red now, in the setting glow of the west, the violent flare out over the Pacific. The highway far below, snaking in and out through the cliffs, seemed like a dream far away.

"It would all be so different."

"Yes. Very different."

They sat at the edge of the bed. Jerry's hand stroked her soft hip.

"You don't want something?" he asked. "You're shaking."

"Because I'm with you."

His finger traced the line of her body, the soft, wide belly, the smooth contours of her side.

In the gentle glow of the room the walls had become a cream color. The sun was now below the horizon, but the clouds far away had become more orange, a kind of angry fire in streams out over the water. Through the curtain the glow warmed their faces, their bodies, her arms and legs.

"Oh, Jerry!"

Jerry was so much in control, so confident, so considerate. She relaxed in him, no longer knew who she was, or where she was, only that she was different, more intense than ever before. She was carried away in wave after wave of warmth.

"Jerry!"

Jerry pressed her so closely to himself she felt she had been crushed. She wanted to be crushed. She wanted all her bones disintegrated, her whole self broken in his tender arms and remade, made once again into somebody new. Somebody as fresh as she looked but with a new soul, a clean soul.

"Jerry!"

She was unconscious of herself. Sensation upon sensation engulfed her, spread out, left her on a distant shore of dark sands. When she woke, her face was bathed in perspiration. Jerry was looking at her face. Her breasts rose and fell in the darkened glow of the twilight.

She kissed his arm softly.

"I guess I made a lot of noise," she said, blushing.

"I don't care."

"I'll bet the whole motel heard."

Jerry laughed.

"Don't worry about it," he said.

"It was wonderful."

Jerry chuckled silently. He stroked her face. His eyes seemed darkened by maturity now. The boyish look was something she had remembered from before. In reality, his face was more square, more authoritative. Maybe it was the new responsibility of the promotion. Maybe he was tired of traveling. Maybe now, afterward, in this strange but calm blue light, a light that softened her contours as well, he seemed more himself, someone very solid and serious. Their hands played along her breasts, the fingers interlocked.

"You look different," he said.

"How?"

"Your face. It's more serious."

"Yours, too. We're getting old. I'm getting wrinkles."

"You don't have any wrinkles. It's your eyes."

"I missed you."

"I went through hell without you, Carlotta, I really did."

"We shouldn't be apart, then."

There was a silence in the air. Neither wanted to bring it up any more. Yet didn't they have to? Didn't they have to face it now, squarely?

Then Jerry asked casually, "Anything happening on Kentner Street?"

"Oh, they dug up the asphalt. They're tearing down the trees."

"What the hell for?"

"Progress."

Jerry crouched naked over the night table. He poured a little bit of whiskey over ice cubes in two small glasses. Carlotta watched him, smiling.

"To you," he said.

"To us."

The burning liquid felt golden in Carlotta's body. The room now was dark. They kept the lights off. Jerry's naked body glowed red and then purple—the exterior motel lights. He was built squarely, compactly, much

202

more muscular than he looked with his clothes on. Now he was watching her. His dark eyes always seemed to be smiling, no matter what he was thinking.

"You *have* changed," he said softly. "What is it?"

"It's been a long time. Too long."

"Is something wrong? Is it Billy? And me?"

"No. Nothing. I'm only afraid. When you're not here, I'm afraid of losing you."

"You won't lose me."

"I go crazy thinking about it."

"Don't go crazy either," he chuckled.

"What if I did? What if I went crazy?"

"That wouldn't be very good, would it?"

"Would you leave me?"

"You'd still be Carlotta," he said. Then he added, "Wouldn't you?"

There was a strange silence. Jerry scrutinized her face, the face that seemed to have altered under some kind of experience that he did not know about. Maybe it was the separation. He knew it had put him through hell.

The whiskey was in Carlotta's brain. She drank little hard liquor, but she liked it with Jerry. Now, like a swarm of golden bees, it buzzed in her brain.

"Like some more?" he asked.

She nodded.

There was a clink of ice cubes, the sound of liquor gurgling. She watched the powerful male form move with its natural grace in the darkness. Now, he was only a silhouette.

"Oh—your hand," she whispered. "It's so cold."

"I forgot," he laughed. "The ice cubes."

"No, leave it there."

Jerry bent down low, looking into the depths of her eyes. His breath was a pleasant aroma of good whiskey and fine tobacco. A masculine smell. It was almost as dizzying as the liquor itself.

His hand was warm now. Both his hands were warm. She moved higher against the pillows to make it easier for him. Her nipples had grown erect under the

203

bedsheet. She moved her legs. He nuzzled her gently along her neck.

"You smell so nice," he whispered.

She laughed softly.

She grew quiet. They heard each other's breathing in their ears. A faraway ocean of stillness, an insistent sound, regular and deep, growing warmer. The room was warmer now. Totally dark. She could not see her feet at the end of the bed. A distant drone of the highway and the breakers three hundred yards below. Her belly moved, slowly, toward him.

"Yes," she murmured.

In a distant room a radio went on, a popular song, rough but sentimental. Then it went off. A door slammed and somebody drove away.

"Mmmmmmmmmmm, yes."

They pressed themselves so close, the world and everything in it disappeared around them. Only they were left.

"Yes," she breathed, "yes, yes, yes . . ."

Unconscious of the sounds she made, she reached for him, wanted him, let him want her, have her, and she had him. It was as though they were in some kind of underwater world were she fought with him, held onto him, and the flowing warmth spread through her like a gathering fire. It turned her skin soft and glowing, her eyes moist, her heavy breathing turning into soft moans.

"Jerry!" she whispered.

A great peace came to her. She felt him ebbing, far away, with her. Sleepy, exhausted, the two warm bodies were unable to move. She smiled at him. It was too dark to see his face. But she could tell he was sleepy. Feeling a complete, drained, peacefulness.

Now he woke up a little. He edged closer to her, all along her side. They looked at the ceiling for a while, saying nothing, needing to say nothing. After a long while he heard her fumbling for a cigarette. He lit hers with a lighter, then his own. The glow of the lighter made her body shine.

"Hey, Carlotta," he said, looking at her breasts, "what happened? You cut yourself."

"What?"

"There. Down there. Farther down, too."

She blew out the lighter. He flicked it on again. In its yellow glare, Carlotta shrank. The shadows and hillocks of her naked body undulated in the flickering light.

"Don't hide from me," he said softly.

"I don't like it with the light on."

"I'll turn it off."

But he traced his fingers over the small scars and bruises on her breasts, the small of her back, her thighs.

"I didn't do that," he said. "These are old."

"There was an accident."

"What'd you do, go swimming in broken glass?"

"I ran the Buick against a telephone pole."

"Jesus. Why didn't you tell me?"

"I didn't want you to be worried. It wasn't really serious."

"Not even down here? Look. That must have hurt."

"I was sore for a couple of days. That's all."

Jerry believed her. He sank back against the pillows and the headboard. He smiled.

"You know what it looks like?" he said, flicking on the lighter. "It looks like somebody beat you up. That's what those bruises look like."

"Turn the light off."

Jerry extinguished the lighter.

"You know, where I come from, scars prove you're tough. That you can take it. That's what they meant where I grew up."

"I don't want to talk about it, Jerry."

Jerry put a hand on her thigh. Suddenly she seemed distant, a hundred miles away. He felt her start at his touch.

"Would you like to walk along the beach?" he asked softly.

She did not answer.

205

"How about it, honey?" he said. "There's a stairway down the cliff."

Still she said nothing. She got up and went into the tiny bathroom. Jerry wondered what was wrong. He sat a moment on the bed, then got dressed.

Along the beach the moon hung fat and heavy. Nearly a full moon. The waves rolled under a blue-green night, rose out of nowhere. Foamed in a crashing thunder. All along the coast bonfires were burning. They walked, hand in hand, slowly along the wet, compact sand at the water's edge. Far away was the radio music of teenagers in cars parked on the bluffs.

"I think we have to talk about something, Carlotta," he said.

She said nothing, but leaned against his arm.

"You know what I mean."

"Yes," she said softly.

"I couldn't help but think about us, Carlotta. About Billy. All the time I was gone."

"He's sorry about what happened. He's just young. He can't control his feelings. When you come over—"

"I know, Carlotta. I know."

He put his arm around her waist. A lighthouse on the bluffs shot its beam around, a white shaft in the darkness. They stood, unmoving, as the cold, foamy water circled up past their ankles and withdrew again.

"In a way, I don't blame him," he said finally, uneasily. "I'd like to make it right between us all . . . you know what I mean, Carlotta?"

She was silent. Finally it had come. So quickly. In just those few words. Jerry waited for an answer. She raised his hand and kissed his fingers. He found it difficult to speak. He tried for a while, found himself unable to say anything more, not certain if he should. Never had he felt so awkward, so lost for words. It was not coming out as he had hoped, as he had rehearsed.

"Carlotta—I swear—in a few months I'll be in San

206

Diego. That's such a beautiful town. We'll be happy there. All of us."

He found himself unable to say anything more. He only pressed her against his chest.

"We'll be happy, Jerry," she said.

A few lights bobbed over the dark ocean, a tug or a small freighter heading for the port behind the mountains.

"I hate leaving you. Before I've even had a chance . . . to really be with you."

"But you'll be back soon. For good. And I'll be better."

Jerry smiled down at her. He cupped her face in his hands and held it up to him.

"What do you mean, better?" he said.

"Those scars. They'll heal."

Jerry kissed the back of her neck.

"When you come back," she whispered. "I'll be completely healed. I know that now."

Strong spasms shook like waves through her body. An agony or an ecstasy that would not stop. It beat, wave upon wave, like a heat traveling upward through her, and she was delirious. She called out. Her breasts heaved spasmodically. She bucked. It was all like a heat, a slow-motion shock with its center at her private places. She twisted, gasped for air. It would not stop. Her thighs moved forward, unconsciously. Slowly the shocks spread away, came back slower, spread away, came lightly back, and left her. An ocean of pleasure surrounded her. Peaceful air encompassed her. She dissolved in the warmth of the air. She had difficulty opening her eyes. In the bedroom her breasts, nipples erect, rose and fell in the darkness. Perspiration dampened her hair at the temples. Her face was drenched with beads of sweat. She breathed long and hard. She was exhausted. She had never been so completely exhausted.

"Ha ha ha ha ha ha ha ha," laughter: soft, silken, confident.

He was gone.

She slowly turned her head. In the perfumed air she saw, at the foot of the bed, *two dwarfs*. Their eyes deep in impenetrable sockets, their long arms hanging, mis-shapen at their sides, they stood, regarding her without a word. Carlotta felt hot and dizzy inside, her belly sore, her limbs boneless with fatigue. Her glazed eyes watched them drop rose petals, one by one, onto her devastated legs, sweet-smelling petals, that gave off perfume. And slowly, one by one, without a sound, they became lighter, they became transparent, they ceased to exist.

On the morning of December 18, Carlotta felt a heavy sensation in her breasts. She felt heavy all over, and she was inclined to stay in bed.

She felt dizzy. She walked to the living room, then had to sit on the edge of the couch. When she closed her eyes it became worse. Everything inside slowly undulated. She became chilled.

She put on a sweater. Her breasts had grown tender. She carried around some strange illness in the soreness of her body. She went outside to water the garden.

She found herself sitting on the edge of a swing. It hung from the oak tree near the alley. Her face and neck were dripping with perspiration. The white fence along the Greenspan garden rose and fell in a sinister, snake-like movement.

Mrs. Greenspan, as was the agreement, tried to keep an eye on Carlotta. She hated to interfere, but Carlotta looked pale. The aged woman hesitantly put down her knitting and walked through the white picket gate, clos-ing the door quietly behind her.

"Good morning, Carlotta," she said softly. "How are you feeling?"

"Fine. Just enjoying the morning sun."

"You look pale."

"Ever since I've been sick, I stay in too much."

"Well, you get some sun. That's God's own cure."

Mrs. Greenspan went to the far end of her own garden. She began to pull yellowed leaves from the stems. Carlotta's face twisted in agony.

"My God," she moaned. "I'm being pulled apart."

Mrs. Greenspan, not hearing, pulled weeds from between the pansies. Butterflies winked by on tiny golden wings. Then she turned, smiling, but the aged eyes watched Carlotta with concern. Carlotta waved, tried to smile, and rose unsteadily from the swing.

The insects were loud, chirping in a raucous chorus. They seemed to fill the garden, the yard, all the shadows in the neighborhood. They made a buzzing in her brain. She thought she heard voices in them.

"Do you believe in ghosts, Mrs. Greenspan?"

"Of course not," laughed the old woman.

"Not transparent things floating in the air. I mean things from the past."

"Well, you know that the dead live on in us. In our hearts."

"But they don't cause us harm, do they?"

"I don't know, Carlotta. At my age, only experience counts. I would say that the best thing is for you to trust the doctor."

"But he's telling me things when I see the opposite with my own eyes."

"The best thing," Mrs. Greenspan said, "is to trust the doctor. He knows what's best."

Carlotta went back to the front door, in the mad buzz of the insects. These were not the lonely sounds of the crickets outside Two Rivers. These were angry, demonic. More like Santa Ana. The memory of that hot, sweaty apartment and Franklin followed Carlotta inside, and she could not shake it.

By the middle of January it was clear that Carlotta's figure had rounded. Sneidermann guessed it was water retention. He diagnosed it as a secondary hysterical symptom, and as such, not significant. Nevertheless, it could be a reaction to the medication. He took a blood sample. He found no signs of physical pathology.

And yet, she found herself prey to abrupt changes in mood. Even in the office, she snapped at Sneidermann, only to apologize later. She bathed twice, three times a day. The water relieved the awful feeling of heaviness that dragged her down.

"What's wrong, Mommy?"

"Nothing, Julie. Nothing."

"You look so white."

"Mommy is just tired. She's going to lie down now. You go out and play with Billy."

Julie watched her mother lie down on the couch, tucking a sweater over her shoulders. The sight of Carlotta so physically weak frightened Julie.

"Go ahead, doll," Carlotta murmured distantly. "Mommy is just tired."

Carlotta felt an incredible lassitude. All the strength was being sucked from her. Something in her was taking the strength from her bones, turning them into air. She tried to rise, to make supper, to fight it, but the body lay back, being drained.

"Oh, God," she breathed.

She tried once again to rise, holding onto the wall. Then the room began to turn. Faster and faster. Julie, standing at the door, saw her fall, making strange sounds.

Julie ran outside. She saw Billy pushing a lawnmower, sweating in the heat of noon.

"Billy," Julie said. "Mommy's sick."

Billy stopped the lawnmower. Suddenly the sunshine all around the tract house took on a sickened quality.

"What do you mean?" he said. "Did she send you out to get me?"

"She's throwing up."

Billy went into the house. There he found Carlotta in the bathroom, vomiting into the white basin.

"Are you okay, Mom?" he said.

But she could say nothing. She bent farther over the basin.

"Should I call the doctor?"

She shook her head. A violent wrench shook her frame, and she leaned forward again. Billy looked away, not knowing what to do.

"Okay—I'm okay," she mumbled.

Carlotta washed her face, poured water around the basin, gargled with mouthwash. Her face was pale, cold, and clammy, the nostrils flared.

"You better lie down," he said.

But she stood, horror-stricken, looking at her face in the mirror.

"What's wrong, Mom?" he said anxiously. "Don't you want to lie down?"

Billy and Julie watched Carlotta touch her face, looking into the mirror. From time to time she softly repeated, "No—no—no—" Then the silence of the house was deafening.

Sneidermann sat back, surprised.

"Are you certain?" he asked.

"Absolutely. I know the symptoms."

"Have you told Jerry?"

"No. Why should I?"

"Well. Obviously he's going to know sooner or later."

"It's not Jerry's baby."

Sneidermann watched her eyes carefully. He was reading the nonverbal clues, the facial signs, the body as it gestured.

"What makes you so certain?"

"He can't have babies. He was sick. Malaria. When he was in the army. It's hard for him to talk about it."

"Perhaps he was mistaken."

"Dr. Sneidermann, if it had been possible with Jerry, I'd have been pregnant a long time ago."

"Is there someone—"

"I don't sleep around, Dr. Sneidermann. Never."

"Then what are you trying to say, Carlotta?"

"Isn't it obvious?"

"No. You tell me."

211

"I'm carrying *his* child."

"Whose child?"

"Don't be so stupid."

Like a house of cards Sneidermann saw his entire construction, which had taken three months of intense labor, go crashing down. Under that veneer of cooperation she had been harboring the most serious doubts about the reality of it all. Now, under the guise of an hysterical pregnancy, she was trying to buttress her symptoms. He hid his dismay instinctively, and he was certain Carlotta never realized what had gone through his mind.

"Why do you think it's *his* child, Carlotta?"

"Maybe it's just folklore, but—"

"What's just folklore?"

"Bob Garrett told me. In Nevada. The legend goes that a woman does not really conceive unless she—she has an orgasm. That's the sign."

Sneidermann felt even more depressed by the bombshell.

"Then you had an orgasm?"

"Yes," she said softly.

"With—?"

"Yes."

"When?"

"Soon after Jerry left. That was the first time."

"The *first* time?"

Carlotta nodded, blushing. "It happens all the time now. I was afraid to tell you."

"Why were you afraid?"

"Because it's—disgusting—these feelings *he* gives me. I—I try not to let it happen—but—I can't help it."

Sneidermann strove to bury his anguish, forced his mind into more mundane areas. He calculated the time period. Nearly two months. Certainly long enough to build up the symptoms. It was like going back to the beginning again. He almost felt like crying. She looked so pretty, so secure, so normal in every possible way until you realized what she was saying.

"I need an abortion, Dr. Sneidermann," she said.

Sneidermann was absolutely stunned. The whole thing had burst on him without warning, one thing after the other. Then he snapped to. Of course she wanted an abortion. That could eliminate the "fetus." There would be no baby and she could continue to believe in this fantasy creature. He suddenly got an insight into the cleverness with which a psychosis operated. It flabbergasted him. He was going to question her gently now, to find out how much this illusion meant to her.

"Did you have a medical test?" he asked.

"No. I don't need one."

"Why not?"

"I've been a mother three times. I know what the symptoms are."

"I don't believe you're pregnant, Carlotta."

"Believe what you want."

"Could you prove it to me? Would you take a test?"

Carlotta shifted in the chair.

"It's a waste of time."

"It takes a few minutes. Painless. We'd have the results by tomorrow."

"I'm all swollen up, Dr. Sneidermann. I'm sick in the morning. I'm retaining water. What more do you want?"

"Suppose the test showed you weren't really pregnant?"

"I just missed my second period, Dr. Sneidermann."

"But what if the tests were negative?"

"Then I'd really be afraid."

"Why?" he asked softly.

Carlotta said nothing, searching for words. A small expression, almost a pout, of defiance appeared on her lips.

"Because then what's happening to my body?"

"It may be an hysterical pregnancy, Carlotta. You know that—"

"Ha! Sure—it's all in my mind, isn't it? *Everything* is."

Carlotta bit her lip. She looked distraught.

"Will you come downstairs with me?" he asked as

gently as he could. "The laboratory knows me. We could be back upstairs in half an hour."

"But what if it were negative?" she said softly.

"Then you would give up this idea, which even you don't believe in now."

Carlotta, trapped, fumbled for her purse on the floor. She searched for cigarettes, found none, brushed her hair instead. Sneidermann wondered if he ought to push her this way. Still, he wanted to nip it in the bud and get back on the track.

"My God," she whispered.

"What is it?"

"I had the most horrible thought."

"What?"

"What if the test were positive?"

"It won't be."

"But what if it were? Jesus, that would blow everything. That would mean it was for real, wouldn't it?"

Sneidermann realized with dismay that she no longer knew whether she wanted the test to be positive or negative. She had to give up either the symptom or the reality that so frightened her.

"All right, Carlotta," he said. "I'm willing to go down now. Are you?"

"Yes," she said finally, uncertainly, in barely a whisper.

He came through the wall. Angrily. Where was she? Carlotta felt the onslaught, moved back, crab-like, over the sheets.

"Leave me alone," she whispered.

She moved farther backward, avoiding the sparkling presence in the air. She moved to the far wall, her arm out in front of her body.

"No! No! You'll hurt me!"

He came closer.

She found herself on the floor, jammed between the bed and the wall. She tried to hold the lamp out in front of her, but *he* grabbed it and threw it across the room.

"No! No! Please—"

He reached for her. Searing, hot pain shot up through her. Her legs were held firm. *He* worked hard. The pain inflamed her abdomen.

"Oh, God! No!"

She was burning up inside. She screamed silently, her fingers clawing the air. *His* massive weight pressed her down, flattened her against the wall, while *he* jabbed at her.

"Oh, God, I'll die—" she thought dizzily.

Hot sticky fluid ran out over her thighs. She felt the nightdress soaked through. She smelled blood all over the floor. Where was *he* now? She was in shock, unable to rise out of the corner. She tried to stuff a pillow between her legs. Soon it, too, dampened in hot, sticky waves.

She pulled the telephone cord toward her, reeling in the blackness.

"Operator—oh, God—operator," she whispered hoarsely.

She shook the telephone, feeling the dizziness begin to dominate her brain. She was losing consciousness.

"What number, please?"

"Operator," she tried to shout, falling. "I'm bleeding to death!"

Then she fainted, trying to hold herself together. The ambulance came in fifteen minutes. Billy, his face white and trembling, led them through the house, accompanied by a policeman. They found Carlotta, her nightdress heavy with blood, the pool on the floor no longer spreading out, the pulse extremely weak.

Sneidermann entered Dr. Weber's office, saw the sign on the door which read "Come In," and went into the inner room without even looking at the secretary.

Dr. Weber looked up and seeing the expression on Sneidermann's face, slowly put down the file folder in his hands.

"Yes, Gary?"

"Dr. Weber, you were talking to Dr. Chevalier?"

"About hospitalization. Yes. I wanted to arrange something for Mrs. Moran."

"We'd better hurry."

"What's wrong?"

"I just got word from Jenkins on the fourth floor. She tried to rupture her uterus with a sharp instrument."

Dr. Weber stood up from behind the desk, put a hand on Sneidermann's shoulder, and made sure the door was closed. He spoke quickly but quietly.

"She's in the Emergency Room, taking plasma now?" Dr. Weber asked.

"Yes. She lost quite a lot."

"All right. It happens. Get a hold on yourself, Gary. Let's go see her."

Dr. Weber went back to his desk, picked up the telephone, and told his secretary he would be in the Medical Emergency Room for half an hour. Then he put down the receiver and came back across the floor.

"God, I feel rotten," Sneidermann said. "I never expected that she'd—"

"Perhaps she missed her uterus. You don't know yet."

"I know, sir, but I never thought she needed this symptom so badly she'd—"

"Now you know, Gary. Lesson number one from real life."

Dr. Weber looked at Sneidermann, who set his face noncommittally for the others he would meet, and then they went out into the corridor. The secretary did not miss the ashen pallor on Sneidermann's face.

They walked quickly through the corridors, passing medical personnel on both sides.

"Suppose she won't agree, sir?"

"To what?"

"To hospitalization."

They paused, caught in the milling crowd at the elevators. Dr. Weber looked at Sneidermann, waiting insistently for an answer, then he looked away. "If she snaps

216

back to reality, we can only hold her for a day or two, Gary."

They stepped into the enormous elevator. Beside them an old man, breathing through tubes in his nose, lay in white sheets on a bed. Two nurses stood by him, their faces drawn and anxious. Behind them were two administrators, well-tanned and joking softly to one another.

"But she's harming herself!" Sneidermann insisted, trying not to raise his voice. "We have to protect her! From herself!"

"The legalities are complicated, Gary."

"You mean she can cut herself to ribbons and we can't legally force her into a structured environment?"

"The law is biased toward a patient. Especially after the last Supreme Court decisions. She's got the leverage on her side."

The elevator door opened. They followed the stretcher out into the hall and then walked very quickly up a long ramp leading to the fourth floor.

Sneidermann's head was buzzing with thoughts. It seemed incredible to him that a patient had a legal right to maim herself. Suicide, he knew, was different. If a patient attempted suicide, he had the power to institutionalize her for a specific period of time.

"What if she tried to hurt the children, Dr. Weber? Remember the boy's wrist was almost broken by the candlestick? Isn't that grounds for hospitalizing her?"

Dr. Weber shook his head.

"That would be grounds for removing the children."

He looked at Sneidermann, who was searching so rapidly through his meager knowledge of the law.

"And that is almost impossible to do," Dr. Weber said. "*Try* to get a court to separate a mother from her children. No way."

Since there was no way to force Carlotta into a hospital, a mental hospital, Sneidermann accepted his responsibility. He was going to have to make her see the case as it was. He was going to have to explain to her the

217

danger she was in. Somehow he had to make Carlotta take arms against the diseased part of herself and get her to put herself into the wards. Dimly, he hoped she had recovered a good degree of rational control. But he was pessimistic.

"Let me see Dr. Chevalier," Dr. Weber said.

Dr. Weber ducked into a small office, went straight to the inner office, and opened the door without knocking. Sneidermann stayed out in the hall. A passing resident said hello to him and he raised his head and smiled without paying attention. It suddenly struck him that either Billy or Cindy would be somewhere in the hospital, in a waiting room or lobby somewhere. He would talk to them first. See if they wouldn't help convince Carlotta.

Carlotta, Carlotta, he mused sadly. Why have you done this thing to yourself?

She was so pert, so pretty, so lively, and now this—it was like life attacking itself. What had gone wrong that had made her twist around into herself, creating fantasies more real than real life? How was he going to straighten her out now? Delusion, he had discovered, was more than a mistake in judgment. It was a power, a force, like a tree that slowly splits a rock, and to uproot it was the battle of a lifetime.

"I've got the papers," Dr. Weber said, coming out of the office, holding several administration forms. "You'll be happy to know she's physically okay. No perforation. Just generalized weakness from loss of blood but well enough to be discharged by evening."

They walked quickly to the wards, then slowed down instinctively, avoiding any show of emergency. Patients sat in chairs, wrapped in robes, with nothing to do. Sneidermann stepped over a child, playing with crayons on the floor.

"You didn't say whether there was an alternative," Sneidermann said.

Dr. Weber paused at the door. Through it they saw Billy, his face pale but trying to smile, at the feet of their patient, whose head was hidden from them by the door.

There were four other patients on beds, two of them unconscious, taking transfusion, the other two also taking plasma, but dully watching the blue televisions hung from the ceiling.

"Of course there's an alternative," Dr. Weber said softly. "If she won't sign, you'll continue seeing her as you did before. She will probably come, as though nothing happened."

Sneidermann shook his head wearily.

"I think we've been spotted," Sneidermann said. "That's her son."

"All right. I'm going to let you handle this."

"I—"

"You're going to have to do a lot of this in your career. Now listen—you want to be friendly but persuasive. Don't panic her into blocking up against you."

"All right."

"I'll be in my office. Come and see me when you're finished."

"All right."

Dr. Weber put a strong hand on Sneidermann's shoulder for encouragement, then turned and walked down the crowded corridor. The loudspeakers were paging doctors noisily, mechanically. Sneidermann swallowed, brushed his hair down, and walked into the ward.

Billy sat on a chair beside Carlotta, by her head. Sneidermann saw the resemblance to Carlotta only in the dark eyes. The stocky frame of the youth was inconsistent with the petite build of the mother. He took a good look at Billy, who seemed to remain at the center of Carlotta's struggle at home. Sneidermann looked down at Carlotta, her black hair fanned lightly over the pillow. Then he faced the youngster.

"Billy," he said, offering his hand, "I'm Dr. Sneidermann."

Billy's grip was firm and strong, surprisingly so.

"Dr. Sneidermann," he mumbled.

"Do you mind if I speak with your mother alone?"

"No. I guess not."

219

Billy left the room. Sneidermann turned. He could see Billy watching him from the bench in the corridor. Sneidermann sat down beside Carlotta's head, out of sight of the boy.

Carlotta looked at him, her eyes slightly crossed. Then she focused. She had never looked so beautiful, he thought. Her face was pale, almost ivory white. Fatigue had softened all the features of her face, made her eyes dark and dreamy. The delicate skin, the small features were all suffused with a soft glow, as when a child wakes from sleep.

"Oh, Dr. Sneidermann," he said. "I thought I was dreaming."

Her voice had a lethargic quality, faraway, exceedingly peaceful.

"How are you feeling?" he asked in a voice which betrayed some emotion.

"I feel so tired," she said, smiling vaguely. "So completely tired."

"I was very sorry to hear you had been hurt."

Her lips moved as she struggled for words, ideas, that formulated themselves only incompletely in her mind. She looked away, as though to find the answer somewhere among the bottles that dripped fluid into her arm.

"I don't know," she said finally. "I don't know what happened."

"The tests were negative."

She turned back and smiled. For a while her mind was blank.

"What tests?"

"The pregnancy test."

"That seems so long ago—just a hundred years ago—"

"The results were negative."

"It's too late, Dr. Sneidermann. The baby is gone."

"There was no baby, Carlotta."

"Not now. Of course not."

The attack still lingered in her memory. He saw her

220

white face grow even paler. She tried to say something, but did not. There was horror in her eyes.

"You said you would believe what the test showed, Carlotta. Are you going back on your word?"

"You see, *he* didn't want me to have *his* child. Just like a man. First *he* had me and then *he* didn't want me to have *his* child."

"Is that what happened, Carlotta?" he asked softly.

"Oh, yes, *he* came and took it back. My God—what if *he* hadn't? What would it have been?"

"It would have been the end of an hysterical pregnancy. You know that."

Tears filled her eyes. She turned away from him. Sneidermann waited a moment, then leaned forward slightly, lowering his voice.

"Carlotta," he said. "If I went home with you, if I looked in your house, maybe in your bedroom, I'd find something with blood on it. Something long and sharp. Am I right? I would find something like that, wouldn't I, Carlotta?"

"I don't know what you're talking about," she said, her voice close to breaking.

"Yes, you do," he said.

"I was hemorrhaging. I didn't do it to myself."

"You're retreating from me, Carlotta. You're playing games."

"No. I'm not. I'm not making anything up."

Sneidermann sighed. He drew his chair closer to her. He smiled as best he could and waited. For a long moment neither spoke. He felt that by not pushing her she would come down, relax. It was important that she be relaxed before he could continue.

"Carlotta," he said softly.

She slowly turned.

"Carlotta, we've known each other now for three months. You know that the only reason I'm here is to make you better."

"I know that," she said weakly.

221

"If I don't know the answer to something, I tell you. If I think I know what to do, I tell you that."

"What are you talking about?"

"I want you to remember all the things we discovered together, all the hidden things—about your parents, and about Franklin—things you had repressed, buried away in the darkest corner of your mind, too terrible to bring back and have to think about. I want you to remember how much better you felt when we made those discoveries."

"So?"

"I prescribed tranquilizers, and they helped you to sleep without being afraid. I told you to have someone adult nearby, and when you did, there was no attack. Now I have another prescription. It's one that I want you to take."

"You're frightening me."

"It's not frightening, Carlotta. It doesn't hurt. I want you to sign yourself into the hospital. For an observation period. Two weeks, three weeks. I want the other doctors to look at you. I want you to be safe from another attack like this one."

Carlotta visibly retreated from him, moving back in her bed.

"I don't want to be locked up."

"You won't be locked up. It's for a short period of time. Just to take better care of you."

Her heart was pounding. She looked around the ward with dismay.

"I couldn't live like that," she said. "Like an animal in a cage."

"You wouldn't be in a ward like this. It's much more comfortable. Like living quarters."

"What about my children? Who would take care of them?"

"If they can't stay with your friend or neighbors, then we can arrange a foster parent for three weeks. We do that all the time."

Carlotta sighed. "Then it's come to that, hasn't it?"

Her eyes became moist again. Suddenly Carlotta saw herself dissolving, disappearing altogether into fragments in some white corridor. All the teachings of Bob Garrett flew away, and she was left fighting to hold one tenth of her former self together.

"Couldn't I see you for a longer period of time?"

"I think it's more serious than that. I think you know it, too."

"What if I said no?"

"I'd ask you why not."

"Because I'd disappear. I'd never be seen again. I'd go crazy for ever."

"You won't go crazy for ever, Carlotta."

Carlotta felt for a box of Kleenex next to her. She blew her nose. She was avoiding Sneidermann's gaze. He would not go away. Like a dull, aching heat in her chest, she knew she had to make a decision. She didn't want to sign away her life.

"Can I let you know tomorrow?"

"What is there to think about?"

"I have to talk to my children."

"All right. Are they taking you home today?"

"Cindy is coming. Later."

"Okay. I'll talk to Cindy. If she can't drive you to the clinic tomorrow, I'll come and get you."

"Thank you."

"I know it's difficult, Carlotta. But it's for a very short term, and it's the best thing you can do."

It was a very delicate moment. She wanted to cry. Sneidermann thought he should leave. She probably wanted to be alone.

Sneidermann stepped into the corridor. Billy looked up. He was remarkably well proportioned for a boy of fifteen, Sneidermann thought. Built like a bull. Yet his eyes now were frightened, like a boy's.

"Is she going to be all right, Dr. Sneidermann?" Billy asked.

"I think so, yes."

"But you're going to put her away, aren't you?"

Sneidermann walked over to Billy. Then he sat down on the same bench. The two sat still for a moment. Sneidermann inhaled deeply, fatigued, drained of emotional energy. He could feel the tension in the boy next to him.

"I don't want to put her away, Billy," he said softly.

"But that's what you were talking about, wasn't it?"

"No. We were talking about an observation period. That's a lot different."

Billy folded his arms. He was not sure whether to trust Sneidermann. Sneidermann cast a glance at him. He did not look at all like Carlotta. Probably took after Franklin. A surly look, a determined, stubborn streak in a basically sensitive young man. Billy was the kind who concentrated on one thing at a time, obsessively. A brooder. He occupied a crucial place in the substrata of Carlotta's personality. Sneidermann moistened his lips.

"I have to ask you something serious," he said.

Billy looked at him narrowly.

"What do you think of all this, Billy?"

Billy shrugged, looked down. His foot traced the lines in the tile of the floor.

"I wish it was over," he mumbled.

Sneidermann watched him. Billy was very serious for his age.

"Your mother told me you saw *him*."

"Naw—I felt *him*."

"Really?"

Billy blushed. He looked away.

"You know. Sick people. Mom was screaming. The girls were screaming. We were all excited."

"Could it be that you were trying to help your mother? By pretending?"

"I don't know. Maybe."

Sneidermann nodded. It was as Dr. Weber had said. *Folie à deux.* Only Billy was now aware of it.

"What do you think now?"

"Now? I don't know. I don't know if it was real—or I imagined it. That whole night was weird."

Sneidermann cleared his throat. He leaned forward,

224

elbows on his knees, rubbing his brows with clenched fists. Then he blew on his fists, concentrating.

"Will you help me, Billy?"

Billy looked back at Sneidermann. As far as he could see, the doctor was straight. But even if Sneidermann was trying to manipulate him, it was for his mother's good.

"What is it?"

Sneidermann's eyes held Billy's. He smiled gently.

"Don't pretend. Next time."

Billy leaned back.

"It ain't so easy," he said. "Things change. They get—"

"Of course. I know that, Billy. But you and your sisters have to pull your mother back into health. Do you understand?"

"Yeah. I guess so."

"When she thinks she sees something or hears something, she wants you to corroborate it. And when you do, it becomes that much more difficult to convince her that it's all in her head, it's a delusion."

Billy was silent.

"Your love will pull her back," Sneidermann said softly. "If you don't give in. Do you understand?"

Billy nodded.

"Promise?"

"Promise."

Sneidermann sighed and rose. He glanced over at Carlotta, visible through the open door. Her eyes were shut, but Sneidermann knew she wasn't sleeping. He turned to Billy.

"Why don't you go in? She wants to speak with you."

Billy stood up slowly, then quietly stepped across to his mother's room. Sneidermann heard their soft voices, then Carlotta's gentle crying. He looked away, fighting his own emotion.

11

THE late afternoon sun blended with the leaves, shaking in a flurry over the tract house. Far away was the sound of the children. Far away the sound of Billy's radio filtering in from the garage. Now Cindy was gone back to her apartment. Carlotta looked out the window at the long, golden shafts of sun piercing through the trees. The lawn looked so green, so fresh. The Greenspans were dimly visible drinking coffee in their tiny living room. Julie and Kim scribbled with chalk on the sidewalk. Normalcy was a vision of loveliness, a beautiful afternoon alone with her children. And now she was on the far side of it, a stranger to it now and perhaps forever.

Carlotta sat down on the couch. For three months her life had been hell. Reasons no longer came to her. There was no point in wondering why any more. Sneidermann was right. Of course, she had to be put away. Her house seemed so comfortable, like an old friend. This nondescript, dumpy house like all the rest. It had been her whole life. It was like taking leave of something fine and permanent.

What would it be like in a hospital? Carlotta had no doubt that after two or three weeks they would ask her to stay another week. Then another. She had no illusions about that. And the children? When you lose your mind, don't they take your children from you? A chilling thought came to her: Wouldn't they be sent to her mother? No, it couldn't be. Certainly she'd have some rights.

226

Didn't Sneidermann say something about foster parents? She had to ask him when she saw him next. And what about welfare? They would take care of the children, too. At least there was that. Until they were eighteen.

It was like preparing to die. She saw ahead of herself only the endless corridors of some forgotten ward, forgotten even to herself. So life had triumphed over her. In spite of everything Bob Garrett had taught her. You could be defeated, even before you were dead.

Carlotta felt a peculiar listlessness. She had given herself to her fate. She put her trust in Sneidermann. She had none in herself. She saw herself the final link in a long line of people defeated by life. Franklin Moran, just an empty shell by the age of twenty-five. And the minister, Pastor Dilworth, that prematurely ancient, self-eaten man, who had never found life. Let him lie dead, Carlotta thought. Let the dead stay dead. Even, in his own way, his own gentle way, Jerry, fighting so hard to make something of himself. Now, what if he knew, what if he even suspected, that the mainstay of his life had disintegrated?

The dying day threw an orange glow against the far wall. A great sense of peace grew around her. When you have given up everything, when you no longer fight it, then the pain dies, too. Like some strange and unforgiving God, the future would do with her as it pleased. Without reasons.

She lay down on the couch, wiping her eyes. She felt sorry for her children. If she had once dreamt that this would have happened, that they would be left without her, even for a moment, she would never have— But she tried not to think. She would sleep. She would sleep one more time in this cheap and familiar house, where everything had exploded in her face. Then she would rise in the morning, and—

It would be over. A death-in-life would begin. That's the way it was. That's the way it had turned out. There was nothing she could do about it now. Jerry? Jerry would never see her again. He would never go to a crazy

227

asylum, looking for Carlotta. Wasn't that as good as over? Nor did she blame him. He had a full life to live. Suddenly, a wave of repulsive loathing swept over her. That it had come to this! Such a vile and repugnant defeat!

Slowly it grew dark. The children came in, found her asleep, and made no sound. They ate a quiet dinner from the cans of soup, some bread, and then went out again. They felt sorrowful. In some way their mother was dying. She would be alive, but she would also be dead. None wanted to say anything about it. They went outside, where the twilight had grown duller and duller. Billy went into the garage. The long shadows seemed desolate, empty, and he tried not to cry.

Carlotta drifted into an extraordinarily deep sleep. Her thoughts were blackness mixed with currents of deeper blackness. She did not know anything. She did not know that she existed. Until she began to rise, lazily at first, like a fish up from the ocean floor, becoming more and more conscious that something was wrong.

Her head throbbed. It was filled with pain. The blood vessels were pulsing and with each pulse the pain increased. She tried to sit up. She could only roll to her side, holding her head. Nausea filled her. A peculiar nausea. It seemed to rise and fall like a black wave in the pit of her stomach, violently trying to weaken her, drag her down to sleep again.

Where were the girls? It was getting late. She tried to listen, tried to locate their voices. But the sounds from outside the window were fragmented, disjointed, and did not come together. She was vaguely aware of the leaves rustling outside the window. The window, she saw, was closed and locked. Why was that?

She turned her head. The other window was closed and locked, too. Nothing made sense anymore. It was dark inside. Tiny spots revolved in her vision. Some insane vise was squeezing her head, making it pound away.

She rolled to a sitting position. She held her head. She knew she was going to be sick. Then she saw the door to the kitchen. It, too, was closed. One more thing that made no sense. She tried to stand up, but could not. Her body felt heavy, impossibly heavy. It looked like a mile to the door leading to the hallway. The door to the hallway was closed, too. It looked locked. A throw rug was pushed between it and the floor.

What is happening? she thought. Where am I? She looked again at the other door. It, too, had a rug stuffed underneath. She was sealed inside the living room. Where is everybody? she wondered. What is that noise? Am I going deaf?

A hiss sounded unpleasantly in her ears. She held her hands over them. It would not stop. But she could hear the heater making noises through the hiss. So she wasn't deaf. She looked. The flickering blue light at the base of the heater was not there. It was black as a deep hole. Only the hiss of the gas spread into the room.

A shock spread through her. *Someone was trying to murder her.*

She crawled on the floor toward the heater. Her eyes were blurred. The nausea threatened to overcome her. She tried not to inhale, until her lungs were bursting. She thought she saw the heater evanesce before her. Then she knew it was only her own field of vision, wavering and losing its control.

She stared into the dark hole of the heater. It transfixed her, as she slumped down. All her despair seemed to hiss out of that black orifice that, like a mouth of hell, condemned her now to death.

"Goodbye—Carlotta—goodbye—"

So *he* was mad at her. For giving herself to the doctor instead of him. With a sudden insight into *his* twisted mind, she saw the limitless depths of true depravity.

"No," she whispered. "No, no—never—"

"Shhhhhhhhhh—Carlotta. Now sleep—"

She roused herself, fought herself, felt she was fighting like Jacob with the angel of God, because she had never felt anything so powerful as her own lassitude. Her whole body wanted to surrender, give herself to that fatigue that dissolved her bones, drew a curtain over her eyes and whispered cruelly in her brain.

"Never," she whispered hoarsely. "Never—"

She turned, crawled toward the window. It looked a million miles above her, down the shaft of a long tunnel.

"Carlotta—Carlotta—"

It was a sound so sibilant, so mixed with the hiss of gas, that she was not certain if she only imagined it.

With a shout like a groan she hurled a table lamp suddenly through the glass. The cord dangled after the base and lamp shade, the window pane cracking, falling outward in sheets, and crashing over the ground outside.

She collapsed. Carlotta never saw the glass give way. Never heard the glass crash over the ground below. Never saw arms reaching for her, the children's faces, horrified, illuminated bleakly, looking down at her on the floor.

She slept the night on the couch where Billy lifted her, and they covered her with a blanket. She talked weakly, then slept some more. The stink of gas slowly disappeared. The girls sat on the easy chair, watching her. Billy by the table. All alone, trusting no one, they kept vigil over their mother. They were silhouettes over her. The night was silent. In the morning she would go into the hospital. Maybe for a long time. Until then it was like a death watch.

When Carlotta entered the corridor, flanked by Billy and the girls, she was not carrying an overnight bag.

"What is it, Carlotta?" Sneidermann asked her. "What's wrong?"

"Can we go inside and talk?"

"Yes. Certainly."

They went into the white office. Billy and the girls craned their necks. So this was the room. The room where their mother came every day. It looked nowhere near so frightening as they had imagined.

"Carlotta, you remember my supervisor, Dr. Weber."

"How do you do, Carlotta?"

Carlotta seemed not in the least flustered by the presence of either her children or of Dr. Weber. A peculiar resolve showed itself on her face, in every gesture she made.

"I've decided," she said, "that I cannot let myself be committed."

"Carlotta," Dr. Weber said quickly, smoothly, seeing that Sneidermann was caught by surprise. "I think Dr. Sneidermann explained to you that you aren't being committed. It's a two-week observation period only."

"That's a technicality, Dr. Weber," she said. "It amounts to the same thing."

Dr. Weber glanced at the children, who were afraid, trying to understand what was going on. Their presence disturbed him, yet he was glad for the chance to see them interact with their mother. He felt certain they were supporting her delusions in some way unknown even to themselves.

"Why don't you want to place yourself under observation, Carlotta?" Dr. Weber asked.

"It's rather simple," she said.

"Yes?"

"I fear for my life."

"But Carlotta, there are no dangers here—"

"No. Not that. It's simpler."

"All right. Will you tell us?"

Carlotta looked both doctors in the eyes. For some reason she felt stronger than both of them. She sensed her power in front of them. Perhaps it was her children sitting behind her.

"There was an attempt on my life last night," she said.

"There was?" Sneidermann said, aghast.

Dr. Weber raised a hand to calm Sneidermann down.

"What happened?" Dr. Weber said.

231

"The gas was turned on in my living room. While I slept. The windows and doors were locked tight and sealed with rags."

Dr. Weber examined the faces of the children. He could find no sign to the contrary. He turned back to Carlotta.

"Carlotta," he said, "we can insist you stay here for suicidal attempts."

"It was no suicide attempt, Dr. Weber," she said quickly. "I've never wanted to live more."

"Come now, Carlotta. You know very well that your mind has given you delusions. Of course it was a try at suicide."

"Absolutely not," she insisted. "It was a murder attempt. Say what you will, *he* is going to kill me before *he* lets me go to you."

"It *was* a suicide attempt, Carlotta, and I can have you in here before the day is out."

"There were no witnesses and I won't say a thing."

"You're very clever, Carlotta."

"It's a decision I had to reach on my own, Dr. Weber."

"To stay sick?"

"To stay alive. It doesn't matter about your theories. *He's* stronger than you are and *he* will kill me if *he* has to."

"To keep you from getting well?"

"However you want to call it. Yes."

Dr. Weber leaned over and whispered to Sneidermann. Sneidermann got up and asked the children to follow him outside. Dr. Weber turned to Carlotta.

"Carlotta," he said, "I want you in the hospital."

"That would be my death."

"There are nurses on every floor. If you want, we can give you a special duty nurse."

"It's never enough. You don't understand how strong *he* is! How insidious *he* is. *He'll* come after me. That's the way *he* is."

232

"Don't you think I can have you entered right now? With all you've told me?"

"No. Not as long as I don't harm anyone."

"Who told you that?"

"My friend."

"Carlotta, listen to me. We can help you, if you continue to see Dr. Sneidermann. But that takes a long period of time. And in the meantime you are running the risk of causing harm to your children."

"They won't be harmed."

"Didn't Billy sprain his wrist? And that was two months ago. You've been through a lot since then."

"That's because Billy was trying to separate us. Now he knows better."

"Then you are harming your children psychologically."

That penetrated. Carlotta turned ever so slightly. Her eyes fixed on Dr. Weber's.

"What do you mean?"

"Children are very suggestible to illness. Especially when their mother is involved."

"There's nothing wrong with my children."

"That's not the kind of environment they need. You know that."

Now she was strangely silent. She looked at him defiantly, but she had run out of answers.

"I want your promise, Carlotta," he said, "for you and for your children. All we want is to return your life to normal as soon as possible. That's exactly what you want."

Carlotta felt trapped. She did not like Dr. Weber. He was tough, insistent, and much quicker than she. Sneidermann could bend a little.

"I don't think you understand the danger, Dr. Weber," she said. "I am perfectly prepared to enter the hospital. But I am not prepared to be killed." She looked at him sharply. A savage glint reflected from her eyes. "You think I'm psychotic, don't you?" she said. "But it doesn't matter. Whether you're right or I'm right. Because I'm going to be dead if I enter the hospital. Isn't it clear by now? Whether it's me or something else is beside the point now."

Dr. Weber looked directly into Carlotta's eyes. He wanted to confront her with her own plan.

"Then what do you want to do, Carlotta? Stay home and be victimized? Is that what you are telling me?"

Carlotta shrank back in her chair. She definitely did not like this aggressive man.

"Yes," she said. "I will stay at home. I will see Doctor Sneidermann. Go to secretarial school. When I graduate, look for work. But the one thing I won't do is go into the hospital."

"You're going to be beaten, frightened, and—"

"No. I won't."

"Why not?"

"Because I'll cooperate."

Dr. Weber paused, his eyes becoming less sharp, perhaps even softening.

"Will you see Dr. Sneidermann this afternoon?"

"I—yes—I suppose so. All right."

Dr. Weber looked at the pretty woman. This was the typical blank wall he'd run into in thirty years of practice. There are some patients who will do anything for you except get better. This was one of the most stubborn.

He doubted now that she could be forced into the hospital. Until she hurt the children, he thought. Maybe Dr. Chevalier could figure something out.

"You can have lunch in the cafeteria," he said. "My secretary will give you and your children some guest tickets."

"Well—all right. Thank you, Dr. Weber."

Dr. Weber opened the door, found Sneidermann with the children. Carlotta took the children down the corridor toward the cafeteria. Dr. Weber gestured Sneidermann to come closer.

"How about some coffee, Gary?"

"Yes. I could use some."

"Not that crap," Dr. Weber said, gesturing to the instant coffee in a glass beaker. "Come into my office."

Sneidermann closed the door behind him. In the quiet office, Dr. Weber prepared some drip coffee. He poured two cups and they drank, neither saying a word. Sneidermann watched his supervisor closely.

"What do you think, Dr. Weber?"

"It disturbs me greatly, Gary."

"Yes. Why the hell did she bring the kids?"

"To demonstrate her role as a mother, give her support."

Dr. Weber looked out the window, squinting at a distant airplane. The sky was hazy, neither cloud nor smog but a heavy amalgam of both. The distant towers of the city center were visible only as ghostly gray forms in the haze.

"What did you think of the kids?" Sneidermann asked.

"Julie's sharp. The other girl is average. Billy is the strange one."

"In what way?"

"Very tense. Very moody. I wouldn't be surprised if he walks in here someday," Dr. Weber said, sipping his coffee.

But the great question was unanswered. What were they going to do with her now? Legally, what could they do? Dr. Weber and Sneidermann, each combatting internal debates, were lost in their own thoughts.

"Interesting case," Dr. Weber mused.

Sneidermann looked up sharply. He hated when Dr. Weber talked about human beings as though they were games to be won or lost. Was this some gross insensitivity? Or was it something you picked up after thirty years of attending hysterical and violently ill personalities?

"Do you think she will try again, sir?"

Dr. Weber screwed up his face, thinking.

"You know," he said, slowly, "the only real danger of suicide is going to come if you strip her symptom away too soon. When a patient is deprived of the symptom but has not yet restructured new defenses nor dealt with the underlying problem—that's when the anger, the hate turns on the self—when they can murder themselves. If you see signs of that, be careful."

"Yes, sir. I wish that were the issue. As it is, nothing is going to get this delusion away from her."

"She certainly hangs onto it, doesn't she?" Dr. Weber said.

For a moment they were silent. The sounds of the secretary outside somehow irritated Sneidermann. He realized that the lack of sleep was getting to him. The whole case had put him on edge. Now he tried to control his impatience. He wondered if Dr. Weber would ever come up with a concrete, definitive solution.

"Where does that leave us?" Sneidermann asked finally.

"Stalemated. She'll see you, every day if you want, but no more."

Sneidermann sat wearily in a chair. He stirred his coffee without looking.

"Not getting better, not getting worse," he sighed.

"You saw what happened when we pushed. Suicide. Before that, abortion. Good Lord. These grandstand plays."

"Why does she need this delusion so desperately?" Sneidermann asked. "I don't understand that ferocious tenacity."

Dr. Weber turned. He saw that Sneidermann had the same abstracted look that often crossed his own face.

"Carlotta is in danger of completely regressing," Dr. Weber said. "She's using this Oriental fantasy as an extreme method of plugging the dike."

"Yes," Sneidermann said, a thought beginning to formulate, a thought that made him speak slowly as it crystallized.

"Desire can be a very frightening and powerful sensation."

"I don't follow."

"Oh, I don't know. I just wonder who's hiding behind that Oriental mask."

Dr. Weber leaned forward.

"Easy, man. Watch your step. Don't you go suggesting motives to her. Don't fall into that trap, Gary."

Sneidermann nodded vaguely, his mind churning, and left.

He walked upstairs to the machine vending rooms for a quick lunch. He wanted to avoid the residents in the main cafeteria. He wanted to be alone. He had a lot of thinking to do, and not much time.

These games, these shifting ambiguities, Sneidermann thought, almost bitterly. Dr. Weber could believe twenty different theories at the same time, as though this were some gigantic chess game. Psychiatry had seemed like a concrete discipline several years ago. It was like surgery. You found the malady, went in, and excised it. But now it seemed like a maze, composed of the twisted strands of a thousand uncertain memories and ten thousand unknown variables. Probing Carlotta Moran was like walking into a computer bank where a million wires were unmarked and only one of them, a microscopic flaw, might be the cause of the whole sickness.

Ahead of her Sneidermann saw one of two things. Either she would be permanently institutionalized eventually against her will as soon as she did something grotesquely spectacular. In which case she would vegetate in some forgotten corridor of some understaffed, screaming state hospital. Or else she would find a way to continue these sessions. With him, and then with the next resident, and then with the next. Until she gave up or something worse happened. Sneidermann was afraid of the long, drawn-out years of meetings. He had little faith in them. What happened was that the patient and the doctor formed a compact, a meaningless exchange of trivia, and the patient was forever closed off to any meaningful probe. He knew one case where a man went to a psychiatrist for fifteen years and said nothing. He just needed the security of seeing the doctor. Sneidermann foresaw Carlotta's future—a crippled personality, unable to function in the real world, with the illusion that somehow, in some magical way, the doctor was making her better by listening to her.

Was there no way to get at her now? Before she closed off to the outside world? Before these meetings had solidified into noncommunication? At the moment she was in a volatile state. She listened, she changed, according to what you told her. Now was the time, if there was any time, to strike hard. In four months his residency would be over. He would be leaving, going back to the East Coast. Then it would be too late for him to help her.

Sneidermann drank his coffee like medicine, threw away the cup, and walked resolutely into his office.

What if it *were* against the rules? he thought.

Seeing Carlotta step into the office, afraid of herself, caught in that peculiar nightmare that had imprisoned her life so savagely, he knew he had no choice.

"Good afternoon, Carlotta."

"Good afternoon," she said, rather coldly.

"Are you feeling all right now?" he said. "That must have been a terrifying experience last night."

"I'm all right now, thank you."

"I want you to know, Carlotta, that we are not going to hospitalize you against your will. Perhaps we could, but it would be useless for both of us. We're not going to try to control your life."

She visibly seemed to relax. Nevertheless, she looked suspiciously at him.

"So you can continue to come here, as an out patient," he said. "We can perhaps help you in some way. That's our only interest."

"All right. I believe you."

"You're a very intelligent woman, Carlotta. And I know that you always listen to reason."

"I can only do what makes sense to me, Doctor Sneidermann."

"So now I want to talk to you reasonably. No more questions and answers."

"Whatever you like, Doctor."

"You told me that you asked Mrs. Greenspan if she believed in ghosts. Then she laughed, because, of course, nobody does. But there was a time when people did believe in ghosts. They believed in witches, in demons, in goblins, in—"

"What are you trying to say?"

"These ghosts and witches were only ideas, Carlotta, but people *saw* them. Would you like to see pictures of them?"

He turned, reached to the shelf, and brought down a heavy volume. He opened the pages in front of her. She looked, repulsed yet fascinated.

Steel engravings of bat-winged demons, pointed-ear crones, and dogs with the faces of children turned in front of Carlotta. She looked away, then found herself looking back again. There were men hanging from the gallows while ravens pecked at their eyes, snakes with wings in the air, and a woman dancing in the forest with a bull.

"These demons," he said, "were very strong. They abused people sexually. Sometimes they were said to impregnate women. Do you see how strong these fantasies were?"

"I'm not stupid, Doctor."

"So why did they see these things? Because they were a way of expressing something that frightened them."

Carlotta looked at Sneidermann with a perplexed, mocking expression. She waited for him to continue, and when he did not, she became flustered.

"This means nothing to me, Dr. Sneidermann."

"Well, let's say a man—a man who wanted to be good—he had a desire for a neighbor's wife. It gets worse and worse. He finally invents this creature—she has a hooked nose, warts, and an evil temper. Of course, it's a picture of his own desire, which is hideous to himself. You see what I mean?"

"No."

"All right. Let's get back into the present. My supervisor had a case once in which a woman developed a loathing for the smell of paint. It made her so ill she had to lie in bed, immobilized. Why? Because she had found out about a case of incest. In her own home. Her husband had had intercourse with their daughter. Do you understand, Carlotta? It had happened while the house was being remodeled. Now everything was blocked out except the memory of the paint. It became the symbol for what she had blocked out."

Carlotta laughed nervously.

"You see how ingenious, yet how direct, the subconscious works?"

Carlotta folded and unfolded her hands in her lap. Otherwise she remained the cool, collected person who had walked in that morning.

"I'm just speaking to your reason now, Carlotta. Do you see how these delusions cover up things, but they always go back to the deep roots, the secrets of our lives that we want to hide?"

"Yes, but I—I have no need of inventing monsters, Dr. Sneidermann! There's nothing so terrible in my life that I have to invent something like that!" Her voice had escalated in intensity, her face seemed flushed.

"All right, Carlotta. Calm down. I just want you to—"

"An Oriental! Where would I invent something like that? You know that means nothing to me! We've been over that a hundred times!"

Sneidermann coughed lightly, shifted in his chair, did other things to let time go by. Carlotta was getting very upset. He had certainly made contact. She was a step away from realizing how sick she was. When she did, she might enter the hospital.

"All right," Sneidermann said. "Let's take this Oriental fantasy."

"I—"

"Let's take a good look at *him*. What do we know about *him*?"

"Really, Dr. Sneidermann—"

"He's big. Very big. Muscular. Frightening, how muscular *he* is. *He* shows you things you didn't know about before. Completely powerful. And who helps *him*? Tell me, Carlotta, who does *he* have by *his* side? Two little ones. Isn't that right? Two little ones and one big one."

Carlotta looked at the clock. She looked as though she were going to bolt from the room. Somehow he knew he had made the contact. She was uncertain, and she felt like staying and leaving at the same time. He had to get to it now, he thought, before she closed up again.

"Let's go back to Pasadena. That's where you first learned to fantasize."

"I don't feel up to this, Dr. Sneidermann. I'm very tired today."

"Bear with me, Carlotta. I'm just pointing out something to you. Nothing more."

"All right. But I do have to go soon."

"You know what the times were like then. In California. When you were the most impressionable. The war with the Japanese was just over and the war with the Koreans was just beginning."

"Of course—I know that."

"A lot of Japanese had been sent to detention camps. Atom bombs dropped on them. The Chinese were crossing the Yalu. Terrible casualties. You know, the Orientals were the enemy."

"I was a kid—"

"Precisely. What does a kid know about war? Only that it is something terrible. Something horribly evil. To be feared. You pick it up, vaguely, from your parents."

"I think I remember."

"What else is evil?"

Carlotta laughed, but her laugh was very nervous.

241

It came out like a broken sound. She stopped abruptly, then turned and looked at the clock on the wall.

"What else is evil, Carlotta?"

"All kinds of things are evil."

"We know your family well enough to know what was evil to them. Why you had to keep running away. Why you had to bury your underpants bearing traces of your first menstrual periods to keep them from facing their own fears, their own inadequacies, their own thwarted desires. Even as a child, you knew what was evil to them, Carlotta."

"Sex. They were afraid of it."

"So—Carlotta. Don't you see it now? It's like a dream. Things get mixed together. It's a kind of symbol."

Carlotta looked at him with a sudden, strange force. It took him by surprise.

"For what, Dr. Sneidermann? A symbol for what?"

Now he became nervous. Had he overstepped? He was not certain that she was under control. He spoke softly, choosing his words carefully.

"It could be a number of things, Carlotta. A specific person. A fear of a specific person. All I'm trying to get you to understand is that—"

"There is nobody behind that mask! Nobody! I am not hiding from anybody or anything!"

"But, Carlotta, you know from your past experience that your mind can deceive you. It can put on these masks, as you yourself called it—"

"I don't believe you."

"But, see—you're getting angry. So you *do* believe me."

"It's obscene, Dr. Sneidermann—what you're suggesting!"

"I didn't suggest anything, Carlotta. I merely said—"

Carlotta stood up abruptly. Her mind was turning rapidly on an axis that Sneidermann had undermined. She was confused. She hated him, loathed him. She

242

needed him to bring her up into the daylight again, but now the sight of him repulsed her.

"Obscene, Dr. Sneidermann!"

"Carlotta! Calm down!"

She backed away from him as he stood behind his desk.

"I'll calm down! But not here! I'll not be degraded by your sick mind!"

"All right. Perhaps I stated it badly. Won't you please sit down?"

She looked at him uncertainly. She was afraid she was looking foolish. Suddenly he looked so reasonable again. Where had she gotten the idea of obscene suggestions? She was terribly afraid. She felt dangerously close to spinning off into space. She had to take hold of something.

"I—I'm going to go now, Dr. Sneidermann," she said.

"All right. Of course. If you want. You're free to go now."

"Yes—I'm going—"

She seemed to sway as she stood rooted. Shadows swirled closer and closer, like bats, into her brain, each calling out a filthy name.

"Would you like something before you go?"

"No—no—"

He took her arm, escorted her to the door.

"I'll see you tomorrow, Carlotta," he said.

She said nothing, but walked quickly—almost ran—down the corridors to where the children waited in the lobby.

Sneidermann felt a kind of thrill. He had contacted the demon. Now she fled from him, from lifting the veil. But she was dependent on him. He knew that. She would not run too far. And he had sunk a barb into the fantasy. By bringing it to her conscious level, he was going to diffuse it; they would be able to talk about the real problems. Painful though it would be, she would no longer be dodging behind an illusion.

"You look pale, Gary," said a nurse at the desk. "What happened?"

"What? Oh—nothing. A close call. The lady is very high strung."

"She certainly left in a hurry."

"Yes. Maybe I pushed a bit hard."

Sneidermann felt very tired. In spite of his successful contact with her, he felt some anxiety. He assumed she was tough enough to adjust to it. Still, the niggling doubt remained: had he pushed too hard?

12

A TWISTED face, the eyes smeared into a kind of slant, reflecting in the chrome headlight. Billy stood over the Buick, working on the engine block. His features were monstrously distorted, bending and curving over the chrome.

"What's wrong, Mom?"

"Nothing," Carlotta said, inaudibly.

She watched him work, the muscular forearms bulging as he wrestled the wrench into place.

The lone light bulb swayed over his shoulder, a second light in a wire guard in the engine. Outside, it was night. It was cold. The shadows merged with the reflections, into a suggestion more hideous than the deformed face of her son.

"It isn't true," she murmured.

Carlotta looked around the garage nervously. Suddenly the family, which had always been her one support, her only support, now in her illness, also fell away from her. Now she was completely alone. The isolation terrified her. She felt completely defenseless. She felt she was operating in a dream, where she did not know the rules or where she was going.

"Where are the girls, Billy?"

"They're inside. Playing."

Carlotta watched the demented, twisted reflection crawl along the Buick chrome until she could stand it no longer. She had to get away from the sight of Billy. The worst thought in the world circulated through her mind. It gave her a black chill, a cold shudder, that made her taste something bilious and bitter as death itself. Was that because it was true? She visibly shivered.

Carlotta went inside, closed the door behind her, and saw the girls on the living-room floor. They looked so quiet, playing with puppets, making strange, demented voices, scaring each other.

"Don't do that, Julie—"

"We're only playing," she protested.

"Not now—"

"Mommy!"

"You'd better go to your room, Julie. You, too, Kim —now!"

Perplexed, confused, the girls took their puppets into the bedroom.

It was silent. But a silence buzzing with a thousand possibilities, each worse than the last. Was there no end to all this? Carlotta was sinking rapidly through a quicksand of slime, and this time, she knew, there was no escape.

She got up quickly. She felt she had to do something, anything, or she would disintegrate. Jerry was a million miles away. Her family had fallen from around her, and had become as dangerous as a nest of deadly reptiles.

Carlotta went to the telephone.

"Cindy," she whispered. "I . . . Yes, it's . . . Oh, God, yes, could you? Could you please come over? . . . Yes, I would. Oh, God bless you, Cindy."

She hung up the telephone.

"Billy!" she called.

He poked his head in from the garage.

"I'm going to spend the night with Cindy, Bill," she said, not looking at him. "Nothing's wrong. I thought it would be a good time for us to get our heads together. After all that's happened."

"Sure, Mom."

"Now, when the Greenspans come home, I want

you to take the girls over there. They'll understand—they told us we could do that—anytime."

"Okay, Mom. Just take it easy. I've got everything under control."

The voice, which was still changing, creaked ever so slightly. Now it sounded hideous, like an ancient door moving on rusted hinges. Carlotta had to get out of there. Fast.

Outside, Carlotta saw the girls walk into the garage, while Billy, framed between them, leaned over the hood of the car. Two little ones—and one big one. It was too much for Carlotta. She went to wait at the curb.

After an infinite period of blackness, in which their voices mingled with the crickets and the leaves, the children grew quiet. Cindy's car turned up Kentner Street. Carlotta got in.

"Oh, Cindy! What am I? A monster?"

"Of course not. You're just—"

"If you had only heard him! It was obscene!"

Cindy turned the wheel. They were on Colorado Avenue, heading toward the central city.

"Well," Cindy said, "he has to probe—"

"Probe! I'm not going back! Never!"

Cindy had never seen Carlotta so twisted up inside.

"Now calm down, Carlotta. I don't want George to see you like this. It's going to be hard enough as it is."

Cindy parked in the subterranean garage. They climbed the black iron stairs and came out in front of the apartment door.

"Okay?" Cindy said. "You all pulled together?"

"Yes—I think so—"

Cindy opened the door. Somehow the light inside looked sickly, yellowed. A smell of overcooked vegetables hung in the air. George looked up from the sports pages.

"Well, Jesus—" then he saw Carlotta. "Look who's here."

"Hello, George," Carlotta said meekly.

"Come to visit, have you?" he said ambiguously.

247

Carlotta followed Cindy inside, closing the door behind her. She felt very awkward, standing with nothing to do.

"You know," George said, "we're going shopping tonight. Cindy and me."

"Good, good," Carlotta said, relieved. The idea of spending hours in such a strained atmosphere was too much to endure.

Carlotta went into the kitchen. Cindy was apparently afraid of a scene. Evidently she had not yet told George that Carlotta was spending the night.

"Could I call the kids?" Carlotta whispered.

"Sure, but use the phone in the bedroom."

Carlotta crossed into the bedroom, sat on the edge of the huge king-size bed, and picked up the powder blue telephone. There was no answer. She tried again. Nothing. She tried a different number.

"Hello," she said as cheerily as she could. "Mr. Greenspan . . . Yes, I'm fine. I just needed to rest with my friend for a night . . . No, no, nothing at all . . . I certainly appreciate . . . No, really, I do . . . Could I? Yes, thank you."

She bit her lip. For a moment she held the receiver away from her ear. Then she brought it closer again.

"Hello, Billy?" she said in a strange voice. "How are you? Are you taking good care of things? . . . Now, you make sure the girls are in bed by eight. Don't make a lot of noise, either. The Greenspans . . . What? Dr. Sneidermann? Did you tell him where I was? . . . Good . . . No, I don't want to talk to him now . . . Yes, I have his number. Anything else? . . . Okay, listen. I'll be home tomorrow."

She hung up, feeling hollow. Somehow, she did not like the idea of Sneidermann calling her at home. It made everything inescapable. He had long tentacles, reaching from the clinic now. There was no safe place anymore.

Carlotta emerged from the bedroom. She crossed shyly, sat down in front of the television set, and tried to read a magazine. Cindy came in, avoided George's glances, and sat down. For a moment it was quiet, except for the sound of the TV.

"Sometimes you have to trust the surgeon," Cindy said when they were alone for a moment.

"Yes. I know."

"It doesn't matter if it's painful. You have to go back."

"Christ. It *is* like surgery—without anesthetic."

"Well, you sleep here. Nothing is going to happen to you here."

George entered the room. While Carlotta sat distraught in the chair, he fumbled for his shoes.

"We'll be back in an hour," Cindy whispered. "I'll get a headache."

"What? Oh—don't worry, Cindy. I'm all right."

"You have the clinic's number?"

"Right here."

"All right, then. Goodnight."

"Goodnight, Cindy."

George leaned against the railing, the far western glow surrounding his head with a dark blue aura. He waved in what seemed a friendly way to Carlotta, then resumed the grumpy mask which was his face. He and Cindy disappeared down the stairway.

Carlotta closed the door. She debated whether to lock the door. She decided not to risk being trapped inside. The mantel clock bonged the hour, a heavy, brassy sound. She turned. Eight o'clock.

Then she saw the curtain flow inward, away from the wall, as though being pulled apart by static electricity. She shivered. It was getting cold. She checked the thermostat. It read normal, but she turned it higher.

It occurred to her to leave the apartment. Then she pictured herself on a street, on a sidewalk, in some strange neighborhood. Running in the dark. She sat on a chair with her back to the wall. She had command of the entire living room.

It was the end of the line. There was no room for mistakes anymore. There was no running anymore. Sneidermann had put her back to the wall. He was going to turn her inside out if he had to. Her eyes moved, assaulted by obscene forms, rising up from the moonlight landscape of an alien world.

"Oh, God," she thought. "I'm afraid of myself!"

She wiped the perspiration from her face. She wanted to be in Sneidermann's office. She needed to be with him. In that safe, white office where he would know all the answers.

She had only to call. The telephone across the room beckoned to her, but it wasn't until the clock bonged the hour of nine that her frazzled nerves propelled her to it.

"Dr. Sneidermann? . . . He's not? I see. Thank you."

She hung up and found his private number in her purse. As she started to dial, the telephone receiver flew from her hand. It rolled at the end of its cord across the carpet. Far away, across the living room, she heard the front door lock.

"No—God—no—please—"

The lights went out. At the same instant a shelf of bric-a-brac toppled from the wall. Ceramic animals shattered over the floor.

"Oh, God! No—"

She was spun into the hallway. A blow, sudden and vicious, flung her into the darkest shadows. She felt something grab at her blouse.

"No—"

Her hair was grabbed, causing her head to jerk back painfully. Lights swam furiously in her vision. Her head was seized and banged against the wall.

"Shut up, bitch!"

She felt hands marauding her body, lifting up her breasts, pressing her into the wall. She gritted her teeth. Tried to cry out as her hair was pulled.

She screamed through clenched teeth. *He* fought her in the entrance to the bedroom. *He* pulled the skirt from her waist. She kicked, tears streaming down her cheeks. Another blow sent her against the wall again. It knocked the breath from her.

"Stupid cunt!"

Blue sparks were flying off the wall. Her reflection was fitfully illuminated in the distant living-room windows. She appeared to be wrestling with the shadows themselves. There was a low, metallic roar, and objects crashed in the hallway. Clothes, a mirror, a rack of magazines disintegrated into splinters and shreds, swirling through the intermittently lit rooms like a storm.

"Stay away from the doctor!"

She threw herself into the living room. *He* grabbed her foot, dragged her backward again.

"No—please—don't—"

Through the storm of buttons, coat hangers, and bric-a-brac she heard the cracking of cabinets. There was pounding on the door. The bolt violently bulged over the doorknob.

"Cindy!"

"Bring your friends in!" he hissed. *"Bring them in!"*

Carlotta screamed again, twisted herself loose long enough to crash through into the open part of the hallway. She could see the bolt being slammed, breaking, giving way.

"Stay away!" she shrieked.

But she saw George's hand flounder through the ruined edge of the door, slapping around for the bolt. Then her face was pushed between her knees. She was pushed into the darkness.

"Christ!" George yelled.

He peered into a subsiding storm of household articles, and he saw a shambles of his former life—his furniture, the pictures on the walls, the dishes and clothes—moving like a living cloud into a pile on the floor. With a staggering dismay he saw the cracks along the wall, the carpet torn into strips of destroyed material. Glass and ceramic shards lay along the carpet like flecks of sinister snow.

"Christ!" George shouted. "She's torn the fucking place apart!"

He could not believe his eyes. Stepping into the darkness, he found that the overhead light would not work. He turned on the light in the kitchen. The living room was completely destroyed. Objects rolled to their final resting places and collapsed. Somewhere in the hallway Carlotta was weeping pitifully.

"Cindy!" she wept.

Cindy felt her way painfully through what had been her living room. She found Carlotta sitting on the floor, her torn clothing beside her.

"Oh, baby!" Cindy said, herself in tears.

George remained standing where the living room joined the hallway, staring in dumb amazement. Then, as if in a trance, he went for a wet towel, returned, and offered it to Cindy. Cindy daubed at Carlotta's face, touching gently the bruises and the cuts, wiping away the tears.

"Oh, Cindy!" Carlotta cried. "*He* wanted to kill me! *He* will! Next time!"

"Hush! Hush!"

"*He* will! Oh, I've got to get out of here! *He*'ll kill you, too!"

"No, no. Hush!"

"*He*'ll kill everybody!"

Carlotta wept on Cindy's shoulder. For a moment George swallowed uncomfortably, then he wiped his eyes.

"Maybe she should be in a hospital," he whispered. "Cindy? What do you think? Shouldn't she be in a hospital?"

But Cindy did not answer. Carlotta slowly realized how strange it was that Cindy said nothing. She looked slowly at her friend.

"You saw it too," Carlotta whispered. "Didn't you?"

Cindy turned away.

"Answer me, Cindy."

"It was such a terrible sight, Carly. I—I didn't know what to think."

George leaned forward. His face was red, apoplectic.

"Let's get her to a hospital!" he whispered hoarsely.

"Go away, George," Cindy lashed back at him. "Can't you see she hasn't any clothes on?"

George stared at his wife, bug-eyed. Then he turned around, facing the opposite wall.

Carlotta trembled violently. Her lips suddenly quivered, as though she wanted to cry. But no tears came. She had a peculiar, dazed look on her face, yet her eyes were wide and filled with—hope?

"I never should have sent her to a doctor," Cindy said. "What did I do? I almost killed my own best friend!"

Carlotta looked at Cindy imploringly with eyes that had the wounded quality of a frightened deer.

"What are you talking about?" George growled. He turned around violently. "This isn't a matter for you. This is a matter for doctors and nurses and—"

"This is a matter for a *spiritualist!*" Cindy shouted.

"The hell it is!"

"It is! It is! You saw it! I know you saw it!"

"I did not!"

"You liar! You send her to the hospital and you'll be killing her!"

George was taken aback. His lips trembled, his face contorted in the shadows.

Carlotta now broke into a soft, hopeless crying, a spasm that shook her shoulders.

"They saw it!" she sobbed. "They *saw* it!"

Cindy stood, her fingers to her lips. She tried to fight off the panic.

"Let me think," she said. "I need to think."

"Thank God, Cindy—"

"Don't cry, Carly."

"You saw it—"

"Yes, I saw it! And we're going to get help. We'll—" She turned to George decisively. "George, we're going to try to get some rest now, Carly and me. You sleep in the living room. Be quiet. Tomorrow we are going to face this problem directly. The way it should have been faced three months ago."

George stood akimbo, like a scarecrow, watching

Cindy lead Carlotta to the bedroom. He watched his wife pull the blanket over the woman.

"What's going to happen tomorrow?" he asked.

"We're getting help, that's what—*real* help," she said. Her hand reached out to Carlotta's face and touched it gently. *"Spiritual help!"*

PART THREE

Eugene Kraft &
Joseph Mehan

While yet a boy I sought for ghosts, and sped
Through many a listening chamber, cave and ruin,
And starlight wood, with fearful steps pursuing
Hopes of high talk with the departed dead.

— Shelley

13

As the night deepened, the memories and images of the last two weeks flowed like a river of ice in Carlotta's brain. She had been dropped so far into the abyss of horror that only now could she frame a few thoughts. Panic was the atmosphere she breathed. Carlotta realized that the universe had whirled around on its foundation, and unreality had taken over life itself. There were forces and fears she had never known. Existence was infinite, cold, and dangerous, and somehow she had broken into a different level of experience.

In those two weeks since Cindy and George had witnessed the destruction of their apartment, Carlotta had visited healers and mediums. George had driven them to a psychic on Sunset Boulevard. She was an East European woman with an imposing posture, situated in a plush office across from the Whiskey-A-Go-Go. She found Carlotta interesting. For $30 she advised Carlotta concerning the congruences of the constellations and their relationship to a healthy love life. Carlotta walked out in disgust. The three friends stood in the hot, dusty afternoon, not knowing where to turn next. Carlotta burst into tears.

Cindy suggested a mental diagnostic. The next day they drove to Topanga Canyon, a hot, dry ride through the brown hills north of Los Angeles. From the astrology center there Carlotta obtained the name and address of a retired pipe-fitter who lived in an aluminum mobile home. When they knocked at his door, he invited them in. He was a very thin man, brittle, with thick white eyebrows. He listened intently to them. His fingers twitched nervously on the top of a tile-covered table. Finally he smiled and refunded her money. He suggested she move, preferably out of the southwest area, since she needed a stabler environment. Beyond that, he refused to deal with external apparitions.

That night Carlotta bolted from the bed. She had heard the sound of laughter. She looked around in the darkness. She felt *his* presence in the room. *His* cold hands gently stroked the side of her face, warned her to be quiet. She was pushed softly back onto the mattress. *He* pressed *his* hands down onto her belly, to separate her legs. She did not resist. *He* did not beat her. *He* held himself off, toying with her for a long time before consummating his lustful nature. More than half the night elapsed before he faded from her, grew transparent, and distended *himself* into the wall and was gone. Her teeth chattered, and she shuddered in a miasma of self-loathing.

Cindy found a psychic group in Santa Monica. It met in an abandoned church at the beach. Holy paintings, vermilion and blue, swirled up the windows, symbols and signs of a religion Carlotta had never seen before. The congregation chanted. Bearded men with red dots on their foreheads, and emaciated girls in filthy shirts. Carlotta never returned.

That night *he* awoke her. *He* was so subtle. So delicate, like a red butterfly. *He* tormented her with strange, radiant dreams that flowed behind her vision like a distant cinema, too awful, too lovely to comprehend. Against all the inclinations of her self-respect, her hold on reality,

256

she felt her body grow warm, her breath begin to come in spasmodic gasps.

She felt the strange images fly apart into a quivering, rainbow heat. She moaned softly, against her will. Then *he* rested. It was silent. She felt she was floating in a breeze of a long summer night, weightless and iridescent, gradually recovering her breath. Then, gently, controlled and masterful, *he* began again.

During the day *he* played other games—prankish, mischievous, deadly games. With no warning a glass would suddenly fly from a shelf and smash against a wall, barely missing one of the children. The toaster would rise from the breakfast table, remain suspended in air, defying gravity, before gently, with feathery softness, gradually settling back down again. Julie and Kim would screech with fright while Billy would bawl obscenities at *him*. Always the toilet would flush without human agency, sometimes for hours. On one occasion—it was late one afternoon and the girls were watching television—the tube suddenly began to glow, then pulsate and finally exploded into powdery crystals, but luckily not until Julie and Kim had run screaming from the room.

It became clear that it was dangerous for the children. The girls were moved into the Greenspans' house, where they spent most of their days and all of their nights. Billy spent more and more time at Jed's. But for Carlotta, there was no escape. It made no difference whether she slept in Cindy's apartment or her own house. *He* came in the night for her.

Awakened by her pathetic cries, George and Cindy would feign sleep, for one night George had gone to the door to investigate and was thrown violently into the hallway by a force that was awesome and unnatural. Now, hearing the anguished moans, and the mattress moving rhythmically, and the bed sheets rustling, George and Cindy would stay put, trembling in their own bed, afraid *he* would come through the wall for them.

George, unable to sleep, looked like a wraithe himself. Cindy's hands and face were beginning to tremble from the ordeal. After a week and a half, they had clung together like survivors of a shipwreck.

Then Cindy, unable to bear the terrible pressure, tried to convince herself that she had seen nothing. George, already confused, wondered if he ought to think the same.

"What do you mean, you saw nothing?" Carlotta hissed, open-eyed.

"Well," Cindy stammered, "it was dark—everything was flying—"

"You think I did that myself?"

"No, but—"

"Cindy," Carlotta implored. "Tell me what you saw—"

"It was dark. I don't know. You were shouting. Maybe that's what made me think I saw . . ."

Carlotta looked into her friend's eyes. She knew that Cindy was afraid. Afraid of dealing with the unknown. She was trying to cover up to preserve her own mental balance.

"Maybe I should go back to the doctor," Carlotta said softly.

Cindy said nothing, almost guiltily. But George looked sharply at Carlotta.

"Well," George said, "maybe you're right. Maybe he can help you through this."

Carlotta remained silent. The thought of going back to that tiny, white office, the steady stream of questions, the anxiety, was intolerable to her. Yet Sneidermann was an expert, in his own way, and he knew a lot about her, about the way she needed stability.

The next morning was hot and unpleasantly smoggy, a yellow haze that filled the lungs and obscured the hills only a mile from the campus. Carlotta stepped off the bus at the university clinic. The familiar pink stone rose ominously around her, and with it, all the monstrous anxiety that the doctor had injected into her life, into her very bone marrow.

Carlotta walked up to the doors several times, then

retreated to a bench in front of the fountain. Residents, patients, and physicians went into the clinic. She began to perspire. The massive columns, full of laboratories and clinics, offices and corridors, leaned over her, threatened to crush her. Suddenly she saw a man's figure in a white coat coming up the steps. Thinking it was Sneidermann, she rapidly turned, left the bench, and went down the opposite steps.

It was not until she had walked clear around the complex, in front of a coffee shop and the medical bookstore, that she dared turn back. It was not Sneidermann. Trembling, she went into the coffee shop.

She drank a cup of coffee. The anxiety had gone, but in its place was a peculiar kind of nausea. She wondered if she was going to be sick. She tried to frame her thoughts. How was she going to tell Sneidermann that it had happened when she was with nonfamily people, that they had seen it, too? She forced herself to eat a piece of cherry pie. But the queasiness remained.

She stepped out into the hot, glaring reality of the city. She paused. She could not yet go up to his office. She looked for a park, a bench, where she could sit in the shade. There were none. She turned, saw the university bookstore, its comfortable lounge, the quiet, studious professors browsing through the distinguished volumes. She went hesitantly into the store.

It was cool, slightly air-conditioned. She felt awkward. The men and women who stood at the shelves or who drank green tea at the tables covered with scientific journals—they all looked so intellectual, so well-dressed. Carlotta stole a look at her own simple skirt and blouse. She was afraid a clerk would come to ask her what she wanted, so she stepped quickly into the interior. Gradually the pleasant carpets, the calm, friendly conversations all around her, had a soothing effect. She slowly began to relax.

On a tall shelf were profusely illustrated volumes in which human skeletons stood against improbable landscapes, each bone or muscle clearly outlined. On another, the human brain was shown in photographs, lying cut open on a gleaming ledge. Carlotta shuddered and moved into an inner room. She was in the psychiatry section. Hesitantly, she reached for the texts. They were full of charts and diagrams. Pictures of children with crossed eyes and protruding tongues. Then she saw a book she recognized. It was the same one that Sneidermann had shown her. The pages showed steel engravings of bats with wings. Old dogs with fangs dripping. Will-o'-the-wisps over dank marshes. It suddenly occurred to Carlotta that somewhere, someplace in that library, was a book, even a whole section, that would have pictures of what she saw, or that would have paragraphs, chapters, to explain it all.

But the few picture books that she saw did not vary from the one Sneidermann had shown her. Disappointed, Carlotta put back a volume. In her mind's eye, she saw herself already climbing the stairs into the corridor, embarrassedly facing Sneidermann after all these days.

She was about to leave when Carlotta overheard a conversation behind the shelf, in an alcove where several journals lay on a round coffee table. Hesitantly, she peered through a space in the volumes and saw two young men, both neatly dressed, arguing in low tones about an experiment.

"The relation between the emotional state of the subject and the frequency of events was not established," said the shorter one. "At least, not to my satisfaction."

"On the other hand," said the other, "the probability analyses are faultless. There were reports of cold spots as well."

"I doubt a connection."

"What about the odor? The smell of rotting flesh? That's very well documented here."

"I still don't concede the case that far," the shorter one objected. "They rarely occur at the same time that objects move randomly."

Carlotta watched them, heated in the debate, flipping through the pages of a glossy journal, running their fingers down through the probability charts reproduced there. She cautiously stepped around the bookshelf and confronted them.

"Excuse me," she said, almost in a whisper.

They both turned and immediately saw that they did not know her.

"Excuse me," she said again, trembling. "I . . . what you're talking about . . . It's happening to me."

The subject of our investigation, Mrs. Carlotta Moran, met us for the first time, quite by accident, at the University Bookstore at the corner of La Grange. My colleague, Joe Mehan, and I had been looking at some recent criticism of the Rogers-MacGibbon experiment, when Mrs. Moran apparently overheard us. She appeared somewhat nervous, even frightened, and began to ask us questions. Generally, they concerned rather basic elements of poltergeist activity.

She confessed that her own home was the locus of such events. Since we get hundreds of such claims each month, and most of them are spurious, we remained skeptical. It became apparent, however, that she was genuinely frightened, and so we agreed to visit her that afternoon.

The house itself is a tract home and completely nondescript. There is nothing to distinguish it visibly from the others built from the same model, except that inside, the ceiling, walls, and doors are scarred by a variety of marks caused by objects having been hurled violently at them. For each mark, Mrs. Moran was able to recall the date, object, and manner in which it was caused. Generally, household objects weighed between two and ten pounds, such as the toaster, a candlestick, a radio, and so forth. The trajectories seemed to be erratic and unpredictable, and no corner of the house was free of the marks of collisions.

She seemed particularly nervous about admitting us to her bedroom. She did, however, and we saw that the walls there were completely free of collision marks. The furniture and curtains were marked, but in different pat-

261

terns. The atmosphere appeared to be charged, as our hair had a tendency to separate and straighten.

We spoke with Mrs. Moran for several minutes. It should be noted that she had seen a psychiatrist out of fear of these events. We reassured her as best we could, and she seemed quite eager for us to investigate the house.

We procured several remote, high-sensitivity thermal sensors from our car and measured the areas adjacent to the closet door and the right rear bedroom wall. I had detected several cold spots as I walked through the room, and now I wanted to verify them precisely. According to our measurements, there were four semi-circular areas, the largest of which was three and a half feet in radius and the smallest of which was one and a quarter feet in radius. The temperature variation, which was proportional to the length of the radii, ranged from 8.24 to 12.36 degrees centigrade below room temperature.

Mrs. Moran believed that the cold spots grew in strength and definition at the same rate as the psychokinetic activity became more frequent, and she believed that both were more likely to occur during dry, windy nights. We discussed with Mrs. Moran the possibility of conducting an investigation of the house. She was quite willing to have it done, and immediately signed a consent form.

We tentatively place the environment as an active poltergeist site. The cold spots and charged areas, variables rarely accompanying recurrent spontaneous psychokinetic activity, bode well for a serious and sustained inquiry. Pending departmental approval, we submit the above as an independent study project for the semester of spring, 1977. Details of equipment requisition and budget are included as Appendices I—IV.

Eugene Kraft
Joseph Mehan

The Division of Parapsychology at West Coast University was a provisional adjunct to the Department of Psychology. There was one faculty member, Dr. Elizabeth Cooley, and thirty students. Dr. Cooley's two research assistants, Gene Kraft and Joseph Mehan, were completing their final semesters for the first master's degrees awarded by the Department of Psychology in parapsychology.

Their report having been distributed and read, Kraft and Mehan stood at the front of the class, ready to field questions. Kraft was precise, voluble and quick-acting. Mehan stood nearly half a foot taller, taciturn, his dark eyes set deep into his bony face. The hot afternoon sun flooded through the windows, enveloping them and the entire classroom in a hot glare. Dr. Cooley walked to the blinds and closed them. Instantly the room became darker and cooler.

"Questions?" Dr. Cooley said.

A Ph.D. candidate in Eastern Religion, interested in the relationship between states of altered consciousness and the writings of the Hindu priests in the Vedas, raised his hand.

"It seems a viable location," he said. "But how are you going to initiate the project?"

"Every event," Kraft said, "has to be translated to precise quantifiable data. This means temperature, displacements of mass, velocities, ion concentrations, and secondary electromagnetic radiation or fields, all correlated to a time reference."

"The structure of our experimental design," Mehan added, "is to provide some hard physical data by recording all encounter phenomena through electronic means."

"You have no theories," asked the Ph.D., "about a relationship between the psycho-kinetic activity and the cold areas?"

"Not at present," Kraft said.

"It's the data-gathering phase of the project," Mehan said. "Specific questions could bias our data gathering, and at this point it is better not to frame biasing questions."

A clinical psychology Ph.D. candidate studying the effects of meditation on short and long term memory, raised her hand.

"What technical considerations are involved in controlling environmental influences?" she asked.

"Such control is the most difficult problem," Kraft said, "in any experimental field environment. We may have difficulties in assessing the influences from 60 cycle noise and radio frequency interference, and so forth. Otherwise, the equipment at our disposal is sufficient to measure almost any physical variable under consideration here."

"We're thinking tentatively," Mehan said, "of trying to develop a photographic system capable of serving in data collection."

A student who had received a grant that semester for his work in computerizing ESP probability studies raised his hand.

"You haven't mentioned interviewing the subject," he objected.

"That would be a good idea," Kraft conceded. "In fact, we should interview the whole family."

Dr. Cooley leaned against the window ledge, folded her arms, and addressed the class.

"Poltergeist activity is usually correlated to certain emotional states. Tension, hysteria, covert hostilities, sibling rivalry, for example," she said. "I think you had better find out why she was seeing a psychiatrist."

"Because of the phenomena," Kraft said.

"Still," Dr. Cooley insisted, "there must be a diagnosis on her."

"That's no problem," Mehan said. "She was a patient here."

Dr. Cooley paused. Suddenly the class was silent.

"You mean the university clinic?"

"Yes," Mehan said.

"We had better be careful then," she said.

Dr. Cooley walked slowly to the side of the classroom, thinking. Kraft and Mehan watched her as she turned back to face them.

"Is she still a patient here?" Dr. Cooley asked.

"No," Kraft said. "She discontinued therapy."

"Was she formally terminated as a patient?"

"I'm not certain."

Dr. Cooley stood silent, trying to decide what to tell Kraft and Mehan.

"Find out what her status is," Dr. Cooley said.

The class was cautious but intrigued by the project. Most of the students were restricted to laboratory studies, since the problems of control were too complicated. Kraft, however, had been an electrical engineer and would be able to measure extraneous data and such variables in any environment. There was a tacit understanding that he, Mehan, and Dr. Cooley operated at a higher level of expertise.

"No further questions?" Dr. Cooley asked.

There were none.

"All right," she said. "I think the project can go ahead. Give me the budget and experimental design today. I would also like you to choose a battery of interviews. The Solvene-Daccurso test would be good."

"Right," Kraft said.

The class was dismissed. The students filed out the door, some to the corridors and to other classes, and others into the tiny laboratories adjacent to the single classroom.

Dr. Cooley reached behind the blinds to lock the windows. Down below was the courtyard of the medical complex, the white modern sculpture twisted in the fountains. Residents, physicians, and patients walked briskly over the tile. It had been thirty years since Dr. Cooley had crossed into parapsychology. Since that day she had been progressively isolated, like an unwanted bacteria, into smaller and smaller laboratories, farther and farther from the main corridors of the medical sciences building. Only the faculty who knew her before she was a parapsychologist still talked to her. As a result, the students were close, protective of one another and of her. Their existence as a division within the Department of Psychology was tenuous and they knew it.

14

THE night breeze stirred up the dead twigs from the hedges. Carlotta felt the charged atmosphere, the dry, sticking air, and then there was a noise at the porch.

Through the peephole she saw two forms she had feared would never come.

"Hi," she said. "Come in."

She unbolted the door. Kraft and Mehan came into the kitchen. Mehan carried several more thermal sensors. The moment they stepped into the living room, both stopped and remained rooted.

The air was charged. There was a kind of acrid, dry feeling in the nostrils. They exchanged glances.

"We should have brought an ion detector," Kraft said.

"Next time," Mehan said.

Carlotta stood in the living room, not certain what they wanted to do next. They stood, looking around the kitchen, well-dressed and polite, whispering among themselves.

"Could we go into the bedroom?" Kraft asked.

"Of course."

She turned on the hallway light. The bulb dangled over their heads. Their shadows undulated across the wall, slowly. She opened the door.

"Jesus Christ," Mehan said.

"My God!" Kraft blurted.

266

Carlotta watched them. The stench now rolled out into the hall where she stood. It seemed to hang almost palpably around them, filling their nostrils and lungs. It had that sickening sweetness of a dead cat. Kraft backed into the hallway.

"If we only had an electronic sniffer, we'd know what that smell is," he said.

"It gets worse in the night," she whispered.

"No wonder you were in a hurry to see us," Kraft wondered out loud.

Mehan probed around the room, breathing through his mouth.

"Generalized coolness," he said. "Very even."

"How long has this been going on?" Kraft asked Carlotta.

"Three months."

"The same as everything else?"

"Yes."

In a conversation with Cindy earlier that day, the two friends had agreed that Carlotta should confess only the most rudimentary of her experiences to the two scientists—the smells, the cold spots, the flying objects— but to make no mention of her nocturnal visitor or the sexual attacks.

"We've run into a lot of fakes, lately," Cindy had argued. "If these two are for real, they'll find out soon enough. If not, then you're back where you started and better off without the whole world knowing."

Now Carlotta wondered if she was doing the right thing. Kraft and Mehan certainly seemed knowledgeable. They had experienced the smell. With them she felt she was in reality again, and that together there might be a way to combat this nightmare.

Kraft went back into the bedroom, holding a hand-kerchief to his nose. She heard them whispering quickly. There were words of scientific jargon she could not understand. Mehan set the gauges on the night table, flicked on the switches and waited for a reading. Then he and

Kraft stepped into the hallway again. Kraft closed the door behind him.

"What do you think it is?" she asked, her voice tremulous.

"Could we go back into the living room?" Kraft asked. "We'd like to discuss this with you."

Carlotta sat on the couch, steeled herself for the worst. Kraft was reaching for words, trying not to alarm her. Mehan sat behind him, watching Carlotta.

"These marks on the ceiling," he said slowly. "It's called poltergeist activity."

"Poltergeist—?" Carlotta said, puzzled.

"The word literally translates from the German as 'playful spirit.' It's used to describe mischievous prank-playing acts, like those of a young child."

"Like objects flying around the room," Mehan added, "lights going on and off, that sort of thing."

"Right," Carlotta said hollowly.

"But the cold spots and the odor," Kraft said. "Very rare to get them at the same time."

"What are you saying?" she asked.

"There may be a second kind of phenomenon here," Kraft said.

Mehan was observing Carlotta carefully. "Let me ask you, Mrs. Moran. Have you ever been touched, pushed, grabbed by something you couldn't explain? Have you ever seen anything out of the ordinary?"

"I—I—things have been confused—"

"Of course," Kraft said gently. "I understand."

"It's a little bit more complicated than we thought," Mehan said.

Carlotta's heart raced. Each nerve, each fiber, wanted to scream, to explode at them with the truth. But she stopped herself from doing so, waiting for them to verify it for themselves.

"It's more involved," Kraft said.

They were silent for a moment. The air pricked at their skin, their scalps. They realized what an ordeal it must be to live in this house. They seemed to be waiting for her to say something. Their intelligent, youthful faces looked directly at hers. All around them the house was dark and silent.

"Are you going to investigate it?" she asked fearfully.

"If that's all right with you," Mehan said.

"Yes. Please do."

Kraft smiled. "I'm going outside for a moment."

Carlotta nodded. Kraft took a flashlight from the car and poked the beam into the foundations of the house. Mehan went back into the bedroom. He took a second reading from the gauges there and entered the numbers into a black notebook. Carlotta watched him from the open door.

"What is it really?" she asked.

"No theories. It's just been reported a number of times."

Carlotta watched him move the meter closer to the closet. Evidently the numbers began to change where the cold spot had been. He passed it through the area several times and wrote down several readings.

"Sometimes there are things associated with the smell," Mehan said.

"What kind of things?"

"The literature is contradictory. Most of it is not reliable."

"What kind of things?"

Mehan looked up. The tone in her voice had changed. She was frightened.

"There was a record of an elderly lady in London," he said. "She had the best documented record of the smell."

"What happened?"

"She lived with it for sixteen years."

"Sixteen years," Carlotta whispered.

He went into the closet where the odor was the most intense. He felt with his hands along the wall, tapping for studs, raising and lowering the gauge.

"She actually started going crazy from it," he said. "Of course, she was a very old woman."

"Crazy?"

"She reported it had personality. Something that was after her."

Mehan stepped out of the closet. Carlotta's face was white.

"Are you all right, Mrs. Moran?"

"Yes—I—I'm fine."

"I didn't frighten you, did I? Your case is completely different."

"Yes," she said, without comprehension. "Different—"

Outside Kraft let himself under the timbers. He saw that the foundations were poorly constructed, the boards and plaster above slapped together in rapid fashion. The upper part of the house had been rebuilt. He also noticed that there was an extraordinary amount of metal wire and pipe down below. Through the entrance to the dark places below he looked into the yard, and across that, the alley. Huge transformers rested on steel arms and the wires were densely packed in clusters. Any current leakage, Kraft thought, and the house would become a transmitter. He pounded on the pipes. A grotesque, rattling growl filled the air.

Carlotta jumped.

"That's Gene," Mehan said.

He pitied Carlotta. The poor woman was at her wit's end. He knew the best thing was to keep working, calmly and methodically. That's what normally brought subjects down to reality again.

Kraft came back into the house.

"May I have a glass of water?" he asked.

"Of course," she said.

He went to the kitchen sink and poured a glassful of water. He leaned against the ledge of the sink, thinking about the construction of the house.

Out of the corner of his eyes he saw a movement.

The cabinet drawer was knocked open, a pot revolved in mid-air, spun, twirled, and smashed into the opposite wall. Fragments shot out into the darkness.

"Gene!" Mehan called out. "Are you all right?"

Kraft slowly put down the glass in his hand.

"I'm all right," he said.

Kraft walked to the wall, where the pot was still spinning, slower and slower. He nudged it with his shoe. It became stiller. Then it was motionless.

"Flew out of the cabinet," Kraft said, a note of wonder in his voice.

Mehan had stepped into the kitchen. He stared at the pot, then reached down to pick it up.

"Feel it," he said.

Kraft touched it.

"Freezing."

Carlotta had come into the kitchen. They looked at her now, her face white as alabaster, outlined softly by the living-room light.

"See?" she said softly. "I wasn't lying."

"I know you weren't lying," Kraft said. Then to Mehan, quickly, "Get the cameras."

Mehan hurried out to the car. Kraft turned to Carlotta again. She looked ethereal, the light coming through her hair like an aura.

"Does this happen often?" he asked gently.

"All the time."

Kraft said nothing. He looked around at the kitchen. The utensils, appliances, and the clock on the wall gleamed back at him from the shadows. Mehan came in, carrying a large camera on a tripod and a metal brace. Kraft set up the camera so that it pointed toward the kitchen. He placed a photographic plate into it, removed the film cover.

"We're going to keep the shutter open," Kraft said, "so stay out of the kitchen."

Mehan leaned forward and clicked a tiny silver spring. Carlotta heard a click. It gave her a strange feeling to realize that the camera was taking in light, like an alien eye, silent and mechanical. Kraft and Mehan came back into the living room with her.

"What can you take a picture of?" she asked.

271

"Everything is still," Mehan said. "If anything moves slightly, it shows up as a blur. Sometimes the eye misses the very small movements."

They sat on the couch and talked until midnight. Carlotta told them about the psychiatrist. They were satisfied that she had discontinued therapy. They were curious about Billy and the girls. Kraft wanted to interview the children at the same time they interviewed her, but Carlotta explained that she had sent them to stay with a friend.

Carlotta felt strangely safe that night, even though the atmosphere was dry and brittle and charged with an aura of violence. Stretched across the bed, fully clothed, Carlotta could hear the soft murmurings of Kraft and Mehan in the next room. They had brought in a smaller camera with a motor attachment, and from time to time they tested the motor. Kraft fired automatic bursts of six to ten frames at different speeds. The clicking sound had a soft, metronomic effect on Carlotta, although nothing startling happened.

At about 2:30 A.M. Carlotta realized she had fallen into a light sleep. She realized it because now she was awakening. Why was she awakened? Because two men were whispering at her side. They had moved their cameras into the bedroom.

"Over the door," Mehan whispered.

Several clicks were heard as the 35 mm camera burst forward.

"Are you awake, Mrs. Moran?" Kraft whispered.

She saw their dim figures hovering by the doorway.

"Did you see that?" Mehan whispered.

Carlotta rose from the bed slowly. They had drawn the shades. The blackness revealed nothing. She had a dim premonition that *he* was coming up from some distant, foul pit. Mehan wrestled the large camera and its tripod into a mechanical brace by the window. The lens faced the upper reaches of the wall, the door, and an edge of the closet.

"Do you smell something, Mrs. Moran?" Kraft whispered.

"It's getting stronger," she said, fearfully.

There was silence everywhere in the house. Carlotta edged closer to Kraft. A soft, metallic rumble was heard as the vents expanded. The heater had turned on though the night was warm.

Then over the door, in the opaque darkness, a blue area began to form. It hung, cast a glow over the closet door, and then became transparent and was gone. It happened so quickly, soundlessly, almost before they were aware of it.

"Did you ever see that before, Mrs. Moran?" Kraft whispered.

"I—I'm not sure—I—"

Mehan replaced the photographic plate with a fresh one. Carlotta edged farther and farther into a corner, watching, waiting. She felt *him*, moving hesitantly, on the far side of the wall.

"I'm nearly out of film," Kraft whispered.

Mehan reached into his pocket and tossed a roll of film to Kraft. Kraft crouched at the edge of the bed, reloading.

"Did you say you've seen that before?" Mehan whispered to Carlotta.

"Maybe—I'm not sure—"

Kraft looked at her. Her white face trembled in the night, her black eyes went from Kraft to Mehan and back again. She was terrified.

"Gene!" Mehan hissed.

Kraft turned. On the opposite wall, over the closet door, a shot of blue arched and dissipated into the darkness. Then it was silent.

"Did you get that?"

"No. It happened too fast."

Carlotta watched Mehan replace a film plate. She saw Kraft aim a burst of photographs at the wall.

273

She sensed *him* on the other side, going from side to side, looking in.

"Gene!"

Suddenly a cloud formed, burst, and streamers of a gaseous blue trailed back into the door. They felt a burst of cold stench.

"You get it?"

"I think so."

For an instant it was quiet. Carlotta felt her skin grow clammy. *He* was agitated, pacing faster and faster, wanting them to go away.

A crack of static electricity shot out from the wall and buried itself in the wall just over Kraft's head.

"Gene! Are you all right?"

"Missed me."

A metallic growl sounded below the floor.

Kraft braced the camera against his knee and increased the exposure. Mehan felt Carlotta brush up against him as she pressed back against the wall. For several minutes they were prepared, and nothing happened. Their eyes became more accustomed to the darkness. The room seemed full of pale shadows on the verge of moving.

A kind of sparkle slowly came from the wall, bright specks of iridescent sand that gave off light and grew invisible as it approached them. Suddenly they were engulfed in cold air.

"Christ, that stinks," Mehan muttered.

"What does your skin feel like?" Kraft said.

"Like it's on fire."

"Must pack a charge."

Several streaks of blue embers shot into the room. They sizzled, snapped, and fluttered through the lamp and the night table before they touched the floor and went out. Kraft's camera was heard in a sustained burst. Mehan tossed him his last roll and he reloaded.

"Camera's jammed," he muttered.

He tore off the motor and began pressing single frames.

Carlotta felt *him* roaming the void on the other side. *He* was getting angry.

For a long time, trailers of blue cloud revolved, twisted, and crawled forward along the upper side of the wall and along the céiling. They dropped bright balls of blue that revolved, burning, and extinguished as they fell. Kraft reached out. Intensely cold spots fell through his hands.

"Got it," Kraft said, lowering the camera.

Mehan put the last photographic plate in the big camera.

Then nothing happened for an hour. A blue-gray light appeared over the trees outside. Kraft raised the shade. The pre-dawn coolness and silence was everywhere. Fatigue had invaded Mehan, until he kept shaking his head trying to stay awake.

Carlotta looked out at the neighbor's house, where the Greenspans and her children were sleeping soundly. It seemed that now, for the first time, that normal life was in her reach. Kraft smiled wanly at her.

"That was quite a show," he said gently.

"Jesus," Mehan added, "I've never seen anything like that."

Carlotta looked at them both as though they were saviors from a distant planet.

"You never saw that?" she asked.

Mehan shook his head.

Carlotta wondered if she should now tell them the truth. But the truth was that *he* was afraid to come in. In some way, they were dangerous to *him*.

"I certainly can see why you were frightened," Mehan mumbled tiredly.

Kraft felt strangely exhilarated, from the lack of sleep, from the things he had seen and felt. His mind suddenly raced ahead to equipment he wanted to bring to the house.

Carlotta half sat, half slumped at the edge of the bed.

"But I don't think *he*'ll come back again," she said, looking at both of them.

"It's possible," Kraft said. "These things are very random. We might never see them again."

"What do you mean 'he'?" Mehan asked, coming suddenly alert.

Carlotta looked up sharply. Her lips played with words she dared not utter. Concepts and images formed in her brain she dared not express.

"These things," she said simply.

Mehan understood that many subjects gave a name or even a personality to events they could not understand. It was a normal reaction. Still, he wondered if Carlotta were hiding something.

The light had grown lighter over the roofs and trees.

"I have to develop the film," Kraft said apologetically.

"You don't mind if we leave?" Mehan asked.

"Not at all. He—it—won't come back. I know it."

"All right," Mehan said, unscrewing the metal brace from the tripod. "We'll come back tonight, if that's okay."

"Of course," she said. "And thank you so much."

"It's really we who have to thank you," Mehan said, carrying the tripod, brace, and camera into the living room. "This is quite an opportunity for us."

The bright sunlight came into the living room, burnishing Kraft's hair with a golden lustre. He smiled at Carlotta as she came from the hallway with Mehan.

"It's such a beautiful morning," she whispered.

Her eyes took in the golden glow of the sunlight, the path it made on the carpet, the crisp air, as though it was the first morning of the world itself. All three felt very good. For different reasons. They had been through an extraordinary evening together. Now it had come time to part, and they felt suddenly very close together.

The dull red Volkswagen left the curb. Carlotta watched it until it turned off Kentner Street. Mehan waved and she waved back. When she turned, the house was delineated by the fiery glow of the rising sun. She felt elated, lighter than air, determined to live and find joy again. It was like being born again. In the Greenspans' house a shade went up. The children would be over for breakfast soon. She decided to fix them a massive stack of blueberry pancakes.

15

THE laboratory was dark. Electronic grids, photographic plates, and complicated electronic equipment gleamed in the work area. The shelves were filled with Russian texts and folios bulging with graphs. Dr. Cooley stood between Kraft and Mehan, studying a group of photographs, freshly developed.

Against a black rectangle she saw a blue-green wave, like a curtain of mist, arching into the void. The next photograph showed a tightly bunched cloud, from which long streamers shot out and trailed away, leaving iridescent color streaks. Other pictures showed luminescent auras surrounding a pebbly surface which was, they told her, the wall of the Moran bedroom. Then there were several smaller photographs, in black and white, which showed Carlotta sitting in her bedroom, sometimes dark, sometimes brighter and softer, almost as though wrapped in a gauze veil, in something less substantial than gauze, that softened her features and made the pupils of her eyes large and dark, like pools of blackness.

"Those are the infrared pictures," Kraft said. "We got these on the third night. Whenever Mrs. Moran moved in and out of the cold spots Joe photographed her steadily. When she's out of the cold spot, the picture comes out normal, very difficult to get any kind of exposure. When she moves in, there's enough infrared in the atmosphere to give us an exposure."

Dr. Cooley picked up the photograph. It looked eerie, as though two separate selves had been photographed. One looked nervous, frightened, almost eaten up by the surrounding darkness. The other was luminous, the skin soft and glowing, sensual, even the body looked shaped differently.

"She looks so different," she murmured.

"I can't figure it," Kraft said.

Their eyes grew accustomed to the darkness. The red bulb gleamed over the trays of liquid chemicals and water, sending red-rippled waves of light over the wall, the spigots, and the metal sinks.

"Well, it's certainly electrostatic energy," she said.

"It held together. It was condensed," Kraft said defensively.

"But it gave off trails," she objected.

"More like sparks."

"I don't know," she cautioned. "It takes a long time to get anything reliable. You have to rule out a thousand alternatives before you get valid results."

They watched her wash the photographs in distilled water.

"For example," Dr. Cooley said, "I'd investigate the house. Perhaps there's a current leakage somewhere."

"You think that's all it is?" Kraft asked.

"I'm saying you have to find out for sure."

"What about the smell?" Mehan asked. "We all smelled it."

"Like a horrible dead cat," Kraft said.

"That's probably what it was."

"Impossible," Mehan said. "It gets stronger at night and weaker by day."

"It's probably near the house. The breeze changes direction at night," Dr. Cooley said. "It blows from the ocean, west to east."

Dr. Cooley was skeptical of anything not measured or photographed. The scientific method was based on precision, numbers, and replicability. Even if, in her heart, she wanted to believe things for which there had never been proof, she ruled them out religiously from her work.

She demanded of herself and her students a rigorous analysis of data from any experiment or project.

"You do much better," she said, "if you start in the traditional world and move outward. Otherwise you'll be strung up by the thumbs, scientifically speaking."

Kraft was puzzled.

"I don't believe we jumped to any conclusion," he said hesitantly.

"No, but you didn't first consider and rule out natural causes."

"It really all depends on the kinds of readings we can get on the events in the next few days," Mehan said.

"All right," she said. "But keep in mind what I told you."

Kraft was still puzzled. His experimental design seemed right to him. Dr. Cooley, he realized, had an Achilles' heel. For her, respectability was extremely important. Her career rested on that. She had seen too many of her colleagues refused tenure, dismissed from universities, or kept from receiving grants. That was why she stayed with the more precise and accurate laboratory studies that were harmless to the scientific community. That was why she promoted the ESP probability studies for which her students were becoming known. Safe experiments, controlled, never significantly departing from the scientific laws. In her heart, she probably wanted to be re-admitted some day to the mainstream of scholars. To Kraft, however, membership in the tradition was not important. He had worked with engineers and laboratory assistants for several years, and he considered them unimaginative slaves to their work. Some day, Kraft thought, Dr. Cooley was going to have to face this head on and choose either parapsychology and the future or the laboratory mentality she had left thirty years ago.

And yet, her words of advice clung. "Start in the traditional world and move outward."

Kraft stepped briskly into the city planner's office, sized up the secretary and was told to sit down. She was

280

uncommonly attractive, he thought. But like many women, she found his quick manner amusing. He decided to play the role of young student.

"Eugene Kraft," he said when asked, "from West Coast University."

She notified the assistant city designer through the intercom.

"He'll be with you shortly," she said. "Please take a seat."

Kraft sat on a chair that seemed purposely designed to deny comfort. For a time he watched the secretary, her long, slender legs tapering nicely to the delicate ankles. Then he closed his eyes.

Random thoughts flitted through his brain. Past memories of his life that had only recently ceased being painful. As a child, he remembered life was full of activity and curiosity and the awareness that he was different from his brothers and sisters. There was a feeling inside him that he was different from all people he knew. Neither bookish nor athletic, he preferred the solitude of his small room and the delirious journeyings into the farthest reaches of his imagination, where he would dwell in a world of his own making, often for hours at a time. His friends and schoolmates thought him weird, taunted him and called him "freak," which worried his parents. But Harry and Sadie Kraft were certain of one thing: unlike their other children, Eugene had a mind!—a finely tuned instrument that, bent to the practical, would insure for him a life of security, free of pressures and worry.

Entering the university, and with the full blessings of his parents, Kraft embarked on a career in electrical engineering, the neatly programmed pre-digested nature of which soon dissatisfied his questing brain.

After two years, Kraft felt he had made a terrible mistake. His interest was not the practical, but the theoretical. He returned to the university to study philosophy. It was too abstract. He needed something that involved the real world as well. One evening, he was invited to assist in preparing the circuits for a large experiment in the psychology department. After laboring nearly a night in preparing the complicated system of switches that Dr. Cooley had designed, he stayed to watch the experiment. He was intrigued. Dr. Cooley had set up a system of sensors that were influenced by animal heat or nervous-system rhythms. He talked with Dr. Cooley well past midnight. She invited him to join her as a research assistant. Since that night, Kraft knew where his future lay, and his career had progressed rapidly.

"Mr. Kraft," the voice broke into his thoughts. Looking up, he saw a balding, rotund man, smiling, extending his hand.

When Kraft sat down in front of the desk, he tried to evaluate the person in front of him. Obviously a low man on the organizational totem pole. He could be intimidated. But subtly. Probably defensive. A few indications—filled ashtrays, spots on the carpet, books in disarray—hinted at a lack of perfect organization. Kraft decided to drop the role of humble student and come on as a well-oiled businesslike machine.

"I am in the psychology department of West Coast University," Kraft said quickly, matter-of-factly. "We are conducting research in the relationship between emotional changes and changes in the atmosphere. By this we mean to include ionic concentrations, electronic interference, microwave patterns, and so forth."

"Sounds more like physics than psychology."

"I am an electrical engineer."

The designer raised his eyebrow. He was evidently impressed by the bright young man in front of him. He had expected an inarticulate student in sloppy clothes.

"And what do you want from me, Mr. Kraft?"

"May we have duplicates of your maps for a given sector of the city? We need to know the sources of such patterns—airport control towers, radio transmitters, and so forth—so that we can study a particular case located in the midst of activity."

The man nodded. "I understand."

"Our information must be accurate in every detail,

282

and your maps are the most precise and the most up-to-date."

The designer nodded again. He felt himself falling under the spell of Kraft. He liked Kraft. Liked his energy, his quick forthrightness. It was a pleasurable respite from a dull day.

"I always like to help the university," he said.

"Thank you," Kraft said.

The designer telephoned to the records department. Kraft left the building an hour later with twelve rolled-up maps in tubes under his arm and an invitation to return.

At the same time that Kraft was in the city architect's division, Mehan was in the basement of the courthouse library, opening enormous ledgers of property ownership at a long, dusty table.

A librarian, an elderly man with thick white brows and a suspicious nature, watched his every move.

Mehan stayed four hours. When he left, he had the information on every person who had owned or rented the property on Kentner Street.

He drove back to Kraft's apartment slowly in his ancient Volkswagen. The engine badly needed an overhaul. But money eluded Mehan. It was something he never cared about, found too much trouble to worry about. All he wanted was a little bit to keep himself going. His thoughts concentrated on the psyches that had suffered, slept, and died in the Kentner Street location. He was oblivious to the streams of drivers on all sides, all rushing to their homes, their normal lives, their personal problems.

Mehan pulled out his notebook. He read an entry again, put the notebook back into his shirt pocket, and shifted gears. The Volks went slowly forward.

Mehan had been raised as a Christian Scientist. It was a religion that taught that the powers of the mind overcame those of the body. As a child, he used to test himself. He denied himself food, water, and he subjected

283

himself to intense physical pain. It was true. By concentration, he could eliminate the sensations from his consciousness. By the time he was thirteen, he was remarkably in control of those sensations he decided to admit and those he decided to reject. He developed the habit of studying people to see if his powers of concentration could control the anxiety he felt when he met with strangers or dealt with his family. He found that within a few months he could handle any kind of interchange with a full and complete knowledge of the other person's psychological mechanisms. As a result, he became known for his odd mannerisms, his monumentally slow responses to people, his habitual stares at their eyes, fingers, and faces. He soon was able to know what people were thinking by their gestures alone. And when he was with people he knew well, he could almost answer unspoken thoughts. He realized that communication was an infinitely more complicated maneuver than articulating the mouth, teeth, and tongue.

He became scared. He could distinguish between what people truly meant and what they expressed. He could perceive the hypocrisy that strangers tried to cover up. And so Mehan spent much time in the privacy of his own bedroom, to avoid the agony of communicating with people.

Then he met Eugene Kraft. Kraft had been teaching a course on the philosophy of science. Mehan was his best student. Kraft could see that there was a reason for Mehan's determination besides preparing himself for a Ph.D. in the field of philosophy. After the final examination, Kraft invited him to his apartment. Mehan understood that Kraft was sounding him out, but he suppressed what was in his mind. He had lived too long with a secret buried too deeply.

"You're not in this for the units," Kraft observed.

"I guess not."

"Am I overstepping bounds if I asked you what your real interest is?"

"No—I just—It's difficult to say."

Kraft studied Mehan. Mehan was frightened. Frightened of the world, of himself.

"You seem unsatisfied with science."

"No. But rats running across an electrified grid is not the science I had in mind."

Kraft realized that Mehan wanted to come out of his shell. But he needed a pull, and Kraft took a chance.

"Do you know Dr. Elizabeth Cooley?" Kraft asked.

"I've heard of her."

"Next semester I'll be her assistant. Would you like to meet her?"

Mehan looked carefully into Kraft's eyes.

"Yes," he finally said, very softly. "Very much."

After two more semesters, Mehan switched his major to parapsychology. He was interested in the thought transference projects.

In another semester he became a research assistant. His parents felt he had thrown away his career. They gave him an ultimatum. Either he continue to work for a degree that would enable him to teach, or join his father in the paint manufacturing plant, or leave home.

Mehan spent two weeks in the YMCA before Kraft found out about it and invited him to share his own apartment.

It was when he met Dr. Cooley and Kraft that Joe Mehan finally found himself on firm ground. Here were people who had a different experience of life, who, like himself, were abnormally sensitive to thought. In this positive atmosphere, Mehan was able to expand his abilities, so that by the end of the year, he was known as the most reliable transmitter and receiver of thought pictures on the West Coast. Dr. Cooley advised him, however, to keep that fact quiet except for strictly professional work.

Mehan's parents found out about his specializing in parapsychology. When they learned he was joining Kraft in graduate school in the same department, they removed his name from their will. Mehan tried to be philosophical about it. He understood their fears for him, their intense desire that he work in the traditional world. But he had

285

dedicated his life to something else. Where it would lead, he did not know. All he was certain of was that, without Kraft, he would have been drowned a long time ago in the vicious sea of isolation and social ridicule.

"Okay," Kraft said. "Tell me what you got."

"Three owners, five occupants before the Moran family," Mehan said. "Built in 1923 by the Owens Real Estate and Development Corporation. First owner, a laborer for the railroad. Italian. Worked on the Hollywood-Santa Monica line. Died 1930. Next owner, a shopkeeper in paints and hardware. Sold the house in 1935. Next, a disabled farmer from Oklahoma. Very large family. Moved out 1944. House vacant one year."

Kraft raised an eyebrow.

"Anybody could have moved in," he muttered.

"Derelicts, transients—I thought of that. I don't know what it could mean for us."

"Go on."

"Then came a Japanese widow. Lived there until 1957. Died in the house. Next resident, retired grocer. From Ohio. Moved out 1973."

"That leaves several vacant years before Mrs. Moran moved in."

Mehan nodded. He replaced the notebook into his pocket.

Kraft rubbed his eyes wearily. "Lots of old people," he muttered. "Different psychic patterns. Several deaths. What does it all add up to, Joe?"

Mehan shrugged. "Got me. *Something* gave us those pictures."

There was a long silence as Kraft slipped a Vivaldi record from its jacket and placed it on the stereo. Soon the sweet, spiritual sounds of the Renaissance flooded the apartment.

"Okay," Kraft said. "What do we know from the literature?"

"Some kind of electrostatic activity seems to be the most reasonable answer," Mehan said. "Maybe we should check with the meteorology department. The ionization layers shift during the seasons. It has an effect on people."

"All right. And I'll work on more complete patterns of electromagnetic waves in the house."

Mehan nodded. Suddenly he became deflated. "Christ. This is going to run into money."

Kraft sat down and sighed. "Maybe we should start thinking about applying for grants," Kraft said.

"With what? All we have are—"

"We have some photographs—enough to show what we're on to."

Mehan shrugged. "All right. Maybe. Let's send a few feelers out."

They listened to the Vivaldi. Kraft seemed to feel optimistic now, considering the grants. Their photographs were not perfect, but they were tantalizing. He realized he should outline a detailed budget for the additional equipment they would need.

"Well, let's be optimistic," Kraft said. "What about the paranormal aspect?"

"Take your choice. It could be directed psychokinesis. Caused unconsciously by any one of the people in the house."

"Even the visible events?"

"I think so."

"All right. What else?"

"It could be a projection," Mehan continued.

"Yes," Kraft agreed.

"In which case it could be from a living person in the house or—"

Kraft looked up.

"Or dead."

Kraft leaned back in his chair. The pleasant, refined strains of the Vivaldi cellos always relaxed him, made his thoughts come more easily.

"A third possibility," Kraft muttered. "It's a sort of stored information in the environment that's reconstructed by the presence of certain unique individuals."

"You mean us? *We* act as the heads in a video-tape

recorder or the needle in a phonograph allowing the information to play itself back?"

"But in this case our consciousness is doing the animating."

"Well, what kind of energy could account for this audio-visual display?"

"That, my friend, is what we have to find out."

They were silent for a moment.

"Well, hell, man," Mehan said, his spirits rising. "All we can do is keep pounding away. Sooner or later we'll narrow it down to what the hell it really is."

Kraft leaned back on his couch, thinking.

"Whatever it is," Kraft said, "let's hope it comes back."

Their thoughts soared along with the music—gently settling on the tiny house on Kentner Street.

Kraft and Mehan returned that night. The first thing Kraft did was to test under the house for current leakage. There was a slight electromagnetic indication. He took several sheaths of wire from his car and grounded the house at the key points. Then he interviewed Billy and the girls while Mehan queried Carlotta in the kitchen. Kraft was convinced that Julie was above average in intelligence. But something about Billy was enigmatic. Billy glared at Kraft.

"When you felt it," Kraft asked, "was it like a rush of wind?"

"No," Billy said. "I mean yes. Like a wind."

"You felt a grip?"

"*He* beat Billy up," Julie said.

Billy flashed a look at Julie to keep quiet, which Kraft caught. Kraft was sure that Billy was hiding something. He spoke too deliberately, measuring out his words.

"Well, you know," Billy said, "that's just the way it seems."

"Did you ever see anything? Besides the objects flying?"

"No."

"Mommy does," Kim said.

"Shut up, Kim," Billy said.

"Your mother sees something?" Kraft asked. "You mean, the sparks?"

"Yeah," Billy said. "That's *all*."

"How many times did she see these things?"

Billy shrugged. "Ask her."

"I'm asking you."

"Five, six times. Maybe more."

"Always the same thing?"

"More or less."

"But when you felt it, you saw nothing."

"Right. I didn't see nothing."

"Did your mother see anything that time?"

"I never asked her."

Kraft asked the girls if they had ever seen anything. Julie and Kim shook their heads. Kraft wondered why Billy was hostile. Probably a normal protective reaction, he thought.

"Did you ever hear noises?" Kraft asked Julie.

"Sometimes."

"What does it sound like?"

"Like a broken airplane."

"It's just the pipes under the house," Billy said.

"He called Mommy a—"

"Shut up, Julie," Billy warned. "The man is trying to help Mommy and you're telling him stories."

Kraft scratched his head. He hoped Mehan was having better luck with Carlotta. Kraft had the feeling that the phenomena were much more variable but that Billy, like most lay people, was afraid to talk about it much.

"Okay," Kraft said, smiling. "Maybe we can talk later."

"Sure," Billy said. "Any time."

In the kitchen Carlotta was answering questions that Mehan methodically read to her from a long series of printed sheets. Kraft went into the kitchen. Having the

289

children in the house had changed the atmosphere. It was calm, almost heavy, unlike the charged air of the night before.

At ten o'clock Billy and the girls left the house to spend the night with the Greenspans. Carlotta was ashamed that Kraft and Mehan witnessed the disintegration of normal life. But she wanted to take no chances.

Mehan placed a series of meters around the hallway and the bedroom. He found that the ion concentration was high, but not abnormally high. When he opened the bedroom door, only a faint odor seeped out around him. It was a little after 10:00. It would be another long night.

Kraft and Mehan sat on hard kitchen chairs to discourage comfort. Their cameras were both locked on tripods, poised for action. The windows and electric lights and mirror had all been sealed off with black paper and black electrician's tape to give them long exposures.

At around 3:00 in the morning Kraft jerked awake. Mehan had slumped over, hitting Kraft's shoulder. Kraft shook him awake.

"It's getting cool," Kraft whispered.

"Just the morning breeze."

Carlotta was asleep in the bedroom. Kraft and Mehan waited two more hours and then stood up heavily as the dawn came into the bedroom.

Carlotta stirred enough to watch them go. As they packed up their cameras and took them outside, she put on her robe and went barefoot out to them.

"I'm sorry nothing happened," she said.

"That's all right," Kraft said.

They packed their equipment into the car. Kraft realized that he would have to figure a way to automate the meters. They could not do this night after night.

"My health isn't going to hold out," Kraft muttered, half serious.

Carlotta waved to them as they drove off. It was four nights now. Four nights of blessed peace. Four lovely, dreamless sleeps. When she had awakened to see Kraft carry the small camera out the door, it was like rising from a pleasant, dark void. Now she felt calm and rested. Cindy had agreed to stay out of the house while Kraft and Mehan were investigating. But now she wanted to telephone her, tell her the good news. She looked at her watch. It was 6:30. Soon she would have Billy and the girls over for breakfast. She fastened the red robe around her waist and felt the cool dew underfoot as she walked onto the lawn, admiring the water drops hanging on the stems and leaves of the roses and lilies. This morning, she decided to repeat the blueberry pancakes bit for breakfast. The kids had loved them.

She went inside.

In the cupboard she found the pancake mix, the syrup, the powdered sugar, but no more blueberries. She substituted strawberries, an experiment. Billy loved them with whipped cream. She smelled the whipping cream. It was as fresh as a country morning.

There was a crash. It came from the bedroom.

She sliced a quarter stick of butter into the bowl. She added flour.

A second crash, louder than the first. Something thrown against the wall.

She put down the bowl. Everything was silent, fresh, and crisp in the air. She smelled lilacs. Strong odor of lilacs. She noticed it was coming from the bedroom. She went into the living room. The whole house was filling with the scent of lilacs.

Glass twirled and tinkled merrily in the bedroom, like musical chimes.

She cautiously stepped into the hallway and peered through the partially opened bedroom door.

The glass stopper to her cologne bottle was bouncing delicately at the base of the wall, near the night stand.

She opened the door wide.

A cosmetic bottle lifted from the dresser, twirling lazily, and came apart in mid-air. The pink powder and pad exploded, sending a shower of pleasant-smelling pink over the room.

291

"That will clean up the stink!" she said, laughing.

She took a step into the room. The sunlight was caught in a shaft on the cloud of cosmetic powder. It looked almost iridescent, hanging, slowly drifting down to the floor.

A glass butterfly from the dresser rose, disintegrated, sending a shower of rainbow-colored wings gently through the air.

"More!" she suddenly yelled, clapping her hands, laughing.

The alarm clock rose into the air. As it hung over the bed, the alarm gave off a soft chime, exploded in slow motion, and the pieces of metal flew like feathers, wafting down in the air.

Carlotta stamped her feet. Suddenly she burst into a shrill laughter. She had suffered so much that now this puny show was an admission of *his* impotence and *his* coming defeat. She could not stop laughing.

"You can do better than that!" she yelled, clapping her hands, stamping her feet.

The curtain wavered, separated, and tore loose from the rods. The gaily colored material floated over her like enormous butterflies.

"Is that all you can do?" she cried, wiping the tears from her eyes. "My girls can do better than that!"

All the pieces on the floor, the metal and glass, liquid and powder, undulated in a slow pool, drifting up and then down.

Carlotta stamped her foot on a perfume bottle. It burst into slivers.

She laughed.

She stepped on the curtains, catching her feet. They fluttered to the floor and were still.

"You're dead!" she yelled. "You're dead!"

Shards of glass and bric-a-brac flowed around her like a river. She stepped on them, laughing, dancing, crying.

"Dead!" she yelled. *"Dead! Dead!"*

16

CARLOTTA rode a long wave of euphoria. Sometimes it seemed like a dream. But the girls showed it in their faces, Billy in his behavior, in the way he whistled tunes to himself and joked with her. She could scarcely believe it. But it was true. A full week and there had been no attacks.

Sometimes it became cold. The smell fluctuated, disappeared, and grew again. Sometimes the visible formations frightened her, the wall shaking terrified her, but the presence of the cameras, the automatic shutters, the recording devices in the hallway, and Kraft and Mehan themselves—repulsed *him*, frightened *him*, and *he* never came closer than a few feet away without dissolving into sparks, clouds, and cold waves. *He* seemed angry, furious, but frustrated. Whatever they were doing had diminished *him*. For the first time since October, Carlotta began to enjoy waking up in the morning, seeing the sunlight streaming into her bedroom.

And best of all she no longer felt guilt for not having told them the full truth. What was the point of telling them any more than they had seen and photographed? It was over, gone into the nightmare of the past. Exposure would mean publicity, ridicule—and worse. Welfare would know. They'd subject her to a battery of tests to determine if she were fit to take care of her own children. She'd lose them. And so Carlotta rationalized her silence. She, the children, Cindy and George formed a tight, tacit bond to keep the secret from the cold and dangerous scrutiny of a cynical world.

Only one thing upset her. Suppose Jerry came back before they were through? How was she going to explain all the gear in the house, the cameras, the gauges, all the wires trailing over the windows and doors? She couldn't even tell him she was seeing a psychiatrist. How could she explain this?

But there was the positive side and Carlotta clung to it. The attacks had stopped. *His* power had been sapped, and soon—please, dear God, before Jerry returned—there would be the resumption of a normal life. A normal life! she thought. Like a burst of sunshine it illuminated her thoughts and feelings. San Diego! Jerry! In her mind's eye she could see them romping among the sand dunes by the ocean. Horseback riding. There were ranches north of the city, and long, sandy beaches where there were no housing developments. The cool, bitingly fresh salt air—she could taste it, feel it. She wanted it more than anything in the world. It was so close and so maddeningly far away.

Neither Kraft nor Mehan had to examine their data to discover the obvious: the events had diminished in both intensity and frequency since the day they had first met Carlotta. All they were getting now were slight, jittery movements of dishes and pans in the kitchen, and cold shafts over the hallway door to her bedroom.

Depressed, they tabulated their data and Kraft presented it to the class. The lecture lasted just under five minutes; there was so little to tell.

Kraft sat down while the next project report was delivered. He felt dissatisfied. He knew the class was interested, yet not galvanized the way they had once been. To Kraft and Mehan, it was still the most exciting find in three years of laborious study. What was going wrong? Was it only that the events were decreasing? With a sudden start, Kraft realized that, at this rate, they would not have enough data for statistical reliability. Across the row, he saw Mehan looking at him. Apparently, Mehan felt the same thing. For the first time, there was a pressure on them both to produce, and the project to which they had given themselves was going dry.

Outside, three floors below, Gary Sneidermann stepped down the cool asphalt path into the botanical gardens. Over the tiny hill the foliage was thick with palms from Australia, red flowers in vines from Hawaii, and rough, spiny blue plants from New Zealand. He sat on a bench, heard cold water dripping around him, and listened to the quiet of the park.

Down the distant path a coed walked, her books under her arm, her blonde hair cut neatly at the shoulder. A quaint wooden bridge arched over a pond. In the pond lilies grew, white flowers opening up on pads. Sneidermann began to realize that there were things he could not analyze. The distance from his home, the loneliness and competition of the university filled him with sorrow.

Carlotta had come into his life as much as she had into his profession. Everything he had done had centered around her so quickly, so intensely, that he had been thrown into confusion, even despair, when she hadn't returned. Sneidermann understood that he had thrown himself too far forward. He now tried to find out how to pull himself back, to find that equilibrium he had once started with.

What was the nature of his involvement? She had acquired a kind of aura in his mind, everything she did, everything she said, so that he found himself circling inevitably to images of her. Was that natural, he wondered. Did every psychiatrist find himself embroiled with an intense patient? Was it the result of inexperience? Why did his feelings become involved each time he tried to analyze what to do next? Was it his pride that had suffered? His male ego? Suddenly his own motivations had become suspect, and he found no way out of the confusion.

Perhaps the problem went deeper, Sneidermann

thought. The problem went into the nature of psychiatry itself. It was so fragile, so abstract. Human beings drowning in horror and guilt are thrown lifelines made of sparkling words. Carlotta needed a human being to believe in, to love, to be restored in. She was not a piece of intricate machinery to be repaired. She was far more complicated, and composed of things which were ephemeral, insubstantial, and deadly.

Psychiatry seemed so distant from life. Patients spent whole lives in controlled environments. Cracked psyches and deformed personalities never really were cured. It was all a facade—the smooth talk of the physicians, their glittering theories and their brilliant theoretical constructs. In reality, they floated above life like pale butterflies. Patients like Carlotta lived in hell.

Through the Chinese ginko trees Sneidermann saw a familiar form come down from the medical complex courtyard, pause among the lilies, and see him. The form came slowly forward.

"Gary," Dr. Weber said softly, almost sadly, Sneidermann thought, "do you mind if I join you?"

"Of course not."

Dr. Weber sat beside Sneidermann. The park was nearly empty, the shade dark and cool behind them where the willows trailed their lengthy leaves into the ponds.

"Pleasant breeze," Dr. Weber remarked.

"Very pleasant," Sneidermann agreed.

There was a long silence in which the two men seemed absorbed in the heavy coolness of the area. Above them birds fluttered through the trees.

"Do you come here often?" Dr. Weber asked.

"On occasion."

"I come here whenever I want to be alone. Something about the flowers here."

"Yes. Very lovely."

There was another long silence. Two children ran across the lawn, laughing. Then they were gone.

"You have missed a few seminars," Dr. Weber said gently.

"I haven't been feeling well."

"Have you gotten the notes?"

"Yes."

"Perhaps you should take a vacation."

Sneidermann put his hands in his pockets and leaned back. It was comfortable sitting next to Dr. Weber, saying nothing.

"I suppose you have some advice for me," Sneidermann said.

"Not at all, Gary. It's for you to work out."

"But if you had advice, what would it be?"

Dr. Weber smiled. He loosened the tie at his collar and opened the top button to the spring breeze. Shadows dappled over his forearms.

"It would be to take a vacation."

"I don't understand why she didn't come back, Dr. Weber. I just can't figure it."

"You hit some high-anxiety material. Have you tried to contact her?"

"Three times. Once she was not at home, and the other two times she would not come to the phone. Her son said that she was fine. That she had never felt so fine, and she would not be coming back."

"Then we've lost her."

Sneidermann sank back in a moody silence. The last weeks he had grown less and less communicative, as though pondering thoughts he found difficult to tell even Dr. Weber.

"I've been doing a lot of thinking, Dr. Weber. What am I in psychiatry for? To get rich? To be famous?"

"There's no shame in ambition."

"But that's not all there is to it. Human relationships—I—I just don't understand them. I mean, when I am involved."

Dr. Weber nodded slowly.

"When you stop being the doctor," Dr. Weber said, "you operate under the same rules as everyone else."

"Do you think that's what happened?" Sneidermann said, gently but earnestly.

297

"You lost your perspective, Gary. It happens."

Sneidermann felt emotions rise in his breast, emotions he knew Dr. Weber could analyze. But he did not want analysis now. He needed to share his feelings.

"I've never been in love," Sneidermann said. "I mean, my feelings for women have been—I—I wonder, is that what happened? I just don't know."

Dr. Weber thought for a long time before he said a word.

"You're more than a student to me, Gary," Dr. Weber said softly. "I've always considered you a colleague. If I may say so, a friend."

Sneidermann was deeply moved, unable to say anything.

"And I would speak with you as a friend, not as a supervisor. I suggest that you purchase time for yourself. Time to reconsider what you are going through. Time to disengage yourself from your emotions."

Sneidermann shifted his weight on the bench. He was blushing.

"There are areas of your personality you do not know," Dr. Weber said. "It's time to discover them, get to know them."

"All right."

"As for Carlotta, I predict she will pass into a stormy but forgotten case."

Sneidermann pursed his lips, still confused.

"Are you offended?" Dr. Weber asked.

"No, of course not. Only it's hard to leave her. I mean, as she is."

"There are many patients who do not complete therapy."

"I know. But she's special to me."

Dr. Weber looked at Sneidermann.

"Let her go," Dr. Weber said, gently and sincerely. "You have no choice. Professionally and, if I may say so, personally."

Sneidermann remained silent. Perhaps his words had penetrated, Dr. Weber hoped.

Sneidermann drove toward West Los Angeles in his battered white MG. He found Kentner Street without much difficulty and parked at the dead end. In the daylight, Carlotta's house seemed smaller than he remembered, but much cleaner, brighter, and it had a full blooming rose garden along the side. He stood for a moment, wondering whether to go to the door. Then he noticed several other cars parked in front of the house.

He walked to the door and knocked lightly. He heard voices inside. Billy opened the door. Sneidermann smiled pleasantly, though he was nervous. He saw Billy's face fall, transform itself into a smile, then cloud over with worry. All in a fraction of a second.

"Hello, Billy," he said. "Do you mind if I talk to your mother?"

"I don't think she's—"

From the inside of the house Carlotta's form appeared among the furniture.

"Who is it, Billy?"

Billy turned helplessly.

"Can I come in?" Sneidermann asked.

"Yeah, sure," Billy said.

Sneidermann walked into the house. Carlotta saw him from across the living room. Behind her were two young men manipulating electronic assemblies with tiny pliers and screwdrivers. She seemed to straighten on seeing him; her face indistinctly clouded over as though by a distant memory, then by something awful, and then she set her face ambiguously and came forward. Her body moved lightly, gracefully, and her face had regained most of its fresh vitality.

"Hello, Dr. Sneidermann," she said softly, simply.

She extended her hand, which relieved him. He smiled as best he could. She seemed unaccustomed to seeing him outside the office, as though he had no human reality at all, only a kind of white ghost that flitted from hall to hall.

"Hello, Carlotta," he said gently. "You look very good."

She did not know what to say. She was flustered. He could see a kind of excitement in her eyes. A cheerfulness he had never seen in his office. Somehow she looked more womanly, more self-possessed, more sure of herself in her own home.

"I was worried about you," he said simply.

"That's very sweet of you. As you see, I'm fine."

"Yes, but you stopped coming. I thought—"

"I've never felt better, Dr. Sneidermann."

He felt distinctly unwanted. He could see it in her eyes, how distant she had grown from him. Billy looked at both of them, wondering what was going on underneath the deceptive simplicity of their words.

"Do you mind that I came?" he asked.

"No," she said, hesitantly. "Why should I? Come on in."

She led him inside. The house was very clean, the windows open, and the sun shone in over the carpet. A fresh breeze blew in from the garden carrying with it scents of warm grass and leaves. She seemed embarrassed still at having him in her house, confused to be seeing him in street clothes instead of a white jacket.

"I'd like you to meet some colleagues of yours," she said, "Mr. Kraft and Mr. Mehan. They're from your university."

Sneidermann shook Kraft's hard, warm hand and then Mehan's limber handshake. He felt a pang of jealousy, then stifled it. At least she was not alone, he thought with relief.

"I don't believe I've met you," Sneidermann said.

"We're in the psychology department," Kraft said.

"Clinical psychology? Dr. Morris?"

"No. Another division of psychology."

Sneidermann thought it strange they did not tell him with whom they studied. Suddenly he had a vague apprehension of something he did not like. It occurred to him that, just as he should not have been there, they, too, were certainly under a similar injunction. In any case, there

300

was something strange here. And what were those black meters and tripods doing in her house?

"You're taking photographs?" Sneidermann asked.

"Yes," Kraft said brightly. "We have been photographing the bedroom and hallway at night."

"What for?"

"To get an image, of course."

"It's infrared film," Mehan added, to Sneidermann's confusion.

Carlotta laughed. Evidently she was on excellent terms with the two psychologists.

"They've been doing all kinds of tests," Carlotta said enthusiastically. "Would you like to see?"

"Yes," Sneidermann said. "I would. I would very much."

Sneidermann conditioned himself not to feel any professional jealousy. If they were working to help the patient, he realized it was his business not to interfere.

He followed Kraft into the bedroom, stepping gingerly over networks of wires. The room was a maze of boxes and tubes.

"Gene built the entire console," Mehan said.

"It was really just jimmied together from available equipment," Kraft said modestly.

"It looks very impressive," Sneidermann said, recognizing the artistry it had taken to put together such a complicated arrangement of electronic assemblies. "What does it do?"

"Well," Kraft said, "basically, it's an attempt to integrate a series of readings of various electromagnetic or light readings—with certain changes in the atmosphere. There's an FM tape recorder that stores data for our computer in there, behind that row of switches. In this way, we hope to find some kind of physical changes that are timed to coincide with the arrival of paranormal events."

Sneidermann felt a chill. Suddenly the props of reality had been knocked backward about ten yards. He took a closer look at the young man in front of him, so neatly

301

dressed, the black eyes sparkling with the enthusiasm of a boy scout at his first Indian pow-wow.

"Paranormal?—you mean psychic—?" Sneidermann said slowly.

"Yes, of course. What did you think this was all—"

"This is *Doctor* Sneidermann," Carlotta broke in. "I should have told you that. I used to visit him."

Kraft looked uncertainly at Sneidermann.

"I don't get it," Kraft said.

"I'm a resident in the department of psychiatry," Sneidermann said.

He felt an immediate hostility come forward at him from both Kraft and Mehan. In an instant they clammed up.

"And you?" Sneidermann asked.

"I told you. We're in the department of psychology," Kraft said deliberately.

"Studying what?"

"What difference does it make?"

"It's a friendly question."

"We're studying with Dr. Cooley. Do you know her?"

"No. But I promise you I will when I get back."

There was an ominous silence. Carlotta sensed the sudden coldness that had come between them. Somehow Sneidermann always brought out the hostility in people.

"Would you like some coffee, Dr. Sneidermann?"

He turned to face her. Evidently she was on their side. He knew he had to remain as polite as he could. Internally, he was boiling furious.

"Yes," he said. "Thank you."

She led him into the kitchen and poured some coffee into two cups, then preceded him to the steps of the front porch outside. Mehan and Kraft quietly returned to their work.

Sneidermann sipped his coffee. Carlotta sat on the wooden railing next to him not looking at him. Never had she been as close to him as now. And never had he felt

302

so distant. Never had he known contact with this elusive, maddening patient to be so horribly fragile.

"Why aren't you coming back, Carlotta?" he said gently. "Why won't you talk to me on the telephone?"

She still did not look at him, but watched the honey bees over the garden instead. The sun bathed her forehead, making her eyes bright, almost a silvery hue. Strange, how much the color of her eyes shifted, he thought. They could be as black as coal sometimes.

"You have to understand something, Dr. Sneidermann," she said after a while. "I feel very fine now. There are no more attacks. I have no reason to see you."

Conversation with him evidently displeased her. She was only being polite out of necessity, and wished he would leave.

"It's only because of these two scientists, Dr. Sneidermann, that I've been able to find any peace at all. They've been able to prove—"

"Prove?"

"Yes. They have photographs. They saw it," she said, turning at last to look at him, her eyes bright, almost laughing, mocking him, he thought. "You don't believe me? They did! They saw him! The last part of him!"

She looked at him strangely. As though enjoying his discomfiture. Perhaps it was her revenge for all she had suffered in his office.

"Carlotta," he said, "do you have any idea who they are? What their qualifications are?"

"They're scientists," she said stubbornly.

Sneidermann made a face.

"You make me feel like I'm in the office again," she said. "Here we are, trying to have a cup of coffee, and you put me on the firing line."

"Do you remember that book I showed you? Bats and dragons? That's what these two are looking for. Fantasies. Is that what you've decided is going to help you?"

Carlotta held her temper, sipping her coffee. She looked away, the breeze gently lifted the hair at her temples. He had never seen her so soft, so lovely.

"It's my business, Dr. Sneidermann," she said finally.

"What about Jerry?"

"He won't find out."

"You're sure?"

"Positive. They've all but gotten rid of this thing."

Sneidermann felt angry. Kraft and Mehan could be seen working behind the living-room window. He had a sudden impulse to run in and tear their maps and graphs to shreds.

"What about Billy?"

She stared at him suspiciously.

"What about him?"

"What does he think of all this?"

"He's completely on their side. He's seen what they've done."

At least that was consistent, Sneidermann thought. Everybody was feeding one delusion. He suddenly realized that things were worse than he had anticipated.

He turned to look at her, but she was looking in through the screen door, where Kraft stood, beckoning to her.

"Carlotta," Sneidermann said. "Carlotta, let's make a bargain. You can see me at the same time that these two are helping you."

She turned back, distracted.

"What's the point of that?"

"Sometimes two different kinds of doctors—you know, like a bone specialist and a blood specialist—they work together."

"No—I'd rather not."

"You have nothing to lose, Carlotta."

Kraft was insistent. She clearly wanted to go inside again. She turned one last time to Sneidermann.

"I believed in you," she said. "You know I did. I really wanted to believe in you. But things just got worse and worse and worse. Every time you discovered something new about me, something worse happened. How much longer was that going to go on?"

"Carlotta—"

"I got sick of hearing you say it would all go away when we got to the basic problem. As though it was in *me!*"

Sneidermann stood. He wanted to grab hold of her, shake her, make her listen. He was very uncertain of himself. His contact with her was fragile as a gossamer thread.

From inside the house Kraft approached the screen door. He stopped when he saw that Sneidermann had not left.

"Mrs. Moran," Kraft said, "we need your help."

Carlotta put her hand on the screen door. Then she turned, smiled, but coolly, and extended her hand to Sneidermann.

"I think you'd better go," she said softly.

He smiled unsurely, shook her hand, and watched her go inside. Kraft and Mehan were huddled over bunches of rolled house plans and graphs, some of which Billy was studying, hunched over on his elbows. Sneidermann walked down the sidewalk, got into his MG, and let out the clutch. The MG roared down Kentner Street toward the medical clinic.

Dr. Weber was caught between the door to his office and the secretary's desk before he had a chance to get a word in edgewise.

"You want to know why she isn't coming back?" Sneidermann said quickly, angrily. "She's fallen into the hands of some charlatans who are feeding her delusions! They're watching her visitations! They've got the house wired to look for poltergeists and reincarnated bodies and Jesus Christ, Dr. Weber—she's bought it! She refuses to see me!"

Dr. Weber was stunned for a moment.

"What charlatans, Gary? You're not making sense."

"They say they're from the university! *This* university! Scientists! Hell—it isn't science. It doesn't even smell like science. Not to me—"

"Are they selling cures to her?"

"I assume so. They've got cameras and wires everywhere. It looks like a laboratory in there!"

Dr. Weber maneuvered Sneidermann into his office. He closed the door, shaking his head sadly. Vulnerable patients attract confidence men like honey draws flies.

"From *our* university?" Dr. Weber asked.

"Psychology, they said. Dr. Cooley."

Dr. Weber grinned broadly.

"Elizabeth Cooley," he said grinning more and more. "Bless her heart. So she's behind this. That's not psychology, Gary. That's *para*psychology."

"Well, they sure as hell have Mrs. Moran buffaloed."

Dr. Weber sat down, his mind on something distant and yet familiar.

"I've known her—let's see—thirty years now. She used to be a big shot in the psychology department."

Sneidermann was barely interested, his thoughts fixed on the image of his patient surrounded by wires and ludicrous poltergeist maps.

"Yeah?" he said. "What happened?"

Dr. Weber tapped his forehead with a finger slowly, sadly.

"She started seeing ghosts."

Sneidermann leaned against the ledge of a window, his arms folded.

"So how do we get rid of these assholes?" he asked.

Dr. Weber's reverie faded. He came to, swiveled in the black leather chair, and saw Sneidermann's humorless face over him.

"They aren't snake-oil peddlers, Gary. These are academic brethren."

"They're confirming Carlotta's delusion. They have to go."

"They'll leave. They'll lose interest, drop off the face of the earth in a couple of weeks. They never seem to get what they want. For one reason or another. Then they descend on somebody else."

306

Sneidermann looked out the window, his jaw clenched.

"It was hard enough having Billy seeing this thing," he said. "Now Buck Rogers and his trusty sidekick are in on it, too."

Dr. Weber lit a cigar. Having been accosted by Sneidermann had made him lose his aplomb, and only now did he feel in control of the situation again.

"You talked to Carlotta?"

"She looks great. Full of energy. Eyes bright. No attacks."

"Complete hysteria."

"Absolutely."

"After they leave, she'll come back to you."

"Think so?"

"I do. She needs to readjust. Until then she'll hold onto her symptoms. I'm not sure that's so bad for her."

Sneidermann shook his head.

"No. It's more than that. She's really fixated on this thing now. Those two have got to go."

Dr. Weber shook his head.

"There's nothing you can do. Not legally. Not medically. It's her life, her house, her delusion. Until she crosses that line of legal sanity, nobody can touch her. And I wouldn't try it unless I had to. Remember what happened the last time?"

Sneidermann nodded, but dug his toe ominously into the carpet.

"Look. This Dr. Cooley—is she legitimate?"

"According to the university she is. I wouldn't tangle with her."

Sneidermann looked away in disgust. Dr. Weber began to fear he was going to do something a second time against advice. Sneidermann had gotten very stubborn. And his instincts were not always sound anymore.

"I don't want any grandstand plays out of you, Gary."

Sneidermann said nothing. He felt torn up inside. Angry at himself, at the two jerks he had seen that morning. At Dr. Weber. He suddenly realized that for the first time in their relationship he was strongly at odds with his supervisor.

"You're getting in over your head," Dr. Weber said.

"I have a responsibility."

"Your responsibility is to treat her within the rules of the university. Is that clear?"

"Very clear."

Sneidermann avoided Dr. Weber's glance and then walked out the door. Dr. Weber had the foreboding impression that he was losing his best resident.

17

CARLOTTA gave a party. A barbecue. Cindy and George were invited. She did not have to say what the occasion was. They knew. It had been nearly a month and no attacks. It was as good as over. The cloud had lifted. Carlotta spent the remainder of the welfare check on food and fruit punches, and invited Gene Kraft and Joe Mehan as well. They declined for the moment, working instead to affix black cork boards to the walls and ceiling of her bedroom.

They had arrived early that morning carrying stacks of the boards and huge rolls of white tape.

"What is that for?" Carlotta had asked.

"Remember those photographs we got?" Kraft explained. "Well, we got images, but there was no way to tell where they were situated in space. Or at what velocity they were traveling. In pitch darkness there is no reference. So, by putting these reference crosses in the background, we'll be able to measure the speed and shape of anything moving in a long-exposure photograph."

Carlotta sighed and shook her head slowly. She was sorry for them. Sorry for all the pains they were taking that now seemed so useless.

"Do you mind if we nail the boards to the walls and ceiling?"

"Not at all."

"They'll be hard to pull out," Kraft said, "but they have to be rock-steady and stable."

Carlotta tugged at a board. She laughed lightly. "I hope you can get these off again."

Passing around the plate of chicken, Carlotta sneaked looks at the bedroom window. The walls were partially covered in a strange pattern of fluorescent white crosses on soft, dark cork. Kraft and Mehan were on ladders, working steadily to complete the job.

Cindy selected a crisp wing.

"So you never told them?" she whispered.

"No reason to."

"They never found him?"

"They just saw the tail end of him," Carlotta said. "As he left."

"Are you ever going to tell them?"

"Maybe. Some day," Carlotta said, smiling.

George reached for a third ear of corn.

"All I can say," George said, buttering the corn, "is *that* was a hell of an experience."

In the bedroom, Mehan could see them at the picnic bench and hear their soft laughter. Every now and then, Carlotta could be seen flashing a covert look in their direction.

"Do you think we came too late?" Kraft muttered.

"I don't know," Mehan replied.

Outside the window a neighborhood puppy dog was chasing Kim under the picnic bench.

Mehan smiled. "At least we've made them happy." His expression sobered. "You think they're being honest with us?"

"No. Probably things were more varied than what we saw."

"What are they hiding?"

"I don't know," Kraft said.

"George is their weak link. Get him alone, and he'll talk."

Kraft turned. Out the window, George was reaching for a plum in an earthenware bowl.

"We'll see him tonight," Kraft said.

Billy had begun to play croquet with the girls. They

used old mallets and dented wooden balls. They seemed curiously artificial, as though play was something that had been absent from their lives for a long time.

When Kraft and Mehan found out that Cindy and her husband had witnessed the destruction of their own apartment, they were thrown for a complete loss.

It was late that night in Kraft's apartment. Mehan sat isolated, silent, unable to figure it out. For a moment everything they had done, every design, every wire and tube looked irrelevant, their carefully constructed theory, now a meaningless mass of scientific trivia.

"It could be RSPK in both places," Kraft said.

"George said something about intermittent flashes."

Kraft said nothing. There was simply no way to bring together two completely separate environments and hope to find an explanation based on the wave interference patterns.

"Before we consign our construct to the shredder," Kraft said, "is there any way to save it?"

There was no way. Some other explanation had to be found for the startling congruence of visible phenomena over ten miles apart, made manifest to two very different types of personalities.

Mehan watched his friend. He knew Kraft very well. Kraft's mind was sharply focused. It concentrated on one thing at a time, resolved it, and moved to the next thing. Mehan's mind was more like a series of thoughts, each floating into the bright light of consciousness, developing, and moving away as the next thought came into being. In this way he was able to synthesize many details that a person like Kraft would have had to outline in pencil. But in reality their minds complemented each other. It was a kind of symbiosis. They knew each other so well that they could speak in half sentences, in fragments. Mehan could feel the subtlest change in Kraft's moods and feelings, and often knew what Kraft was going to say before Kraft said it.

311

"Unless," Kraft finally said, "Mrs. Moran might be the poltergeist agent in both cases."

Mehan tried to clear his head. For the first time in a long time he needed a drink. Kraft maintained his calm at the end of the couch, staring out the plate-glass window to the vivid night landscape below.

"Let's cool it for tonight, Joe."

Kraft meandered to the bathroom, where he drew a bath. He lay in the hot water, watching the steam rise, almost invisible, from his body and the water surface into the air. It reminded him of a recent study from Columbia, a cross-cultural comparison of death rites and experiences. In forty-two known cultures, including the British Isles and the United States, witnesses to death claimed they visibly perceived a nonmaterial substance leave the body at the moment of death. Kraft realized that some cultures built religion around that experience and other cultures suppressed it in favor of established, organized religions.

But the universe was composed of experiences for which there are no names, no concepts, except the rudimentary explanations that science provides. And when those explanations are punctured by some supernormal reality, a person suffers terribly in his isolation and fear.

As Kraft lazed in the hot water, relaxing, he thought of Mrs. Moran and what fearful reality had she fallen prey to.

Kraft dried himself with a large, worn towel, blow-dried his hair, and went to bed.

When he awoke in the morning it was as though he had not slept at all. Only that a gentle hand had brushed away his fatigue and left him lying in bed, feeling pleasant. When he stepped into the living room, he discovered that Mehan had already left, and that the telephone was ringing. It was Mehan.

"Listen, Gene," he said. "I'm over here at George's and Cindy's. Billy's here, too. We were talking about

312

cars." His voice lowered. "Gene, this thing happened in her car as well."

Kraft sat down.

"RSPK?" Kraft asked.

"No. Voices. She heard voices."

"What kind of voices?" Kraft heard himself say.

"Billy doesn't know. I think we'd better talk to Mrs. Moran."

"All right. Let me get my mind clear. Jesus—all right. I have a seminar this afternoon. Let me talk to Dr. Cooley before I come down."

"Okay," Mehan said. "I'll be here most of the afternoon."

Kraft hung up the receiver. That made it three separate environments. Including aural manifestations. Kraft could not understand why the Morans were being so secretive. He had to hand it to Mehan, being able to worm it out of Billy. There were now three classes of events—RSPK, visible forms, and sound. Kraft could figure no way to put them into a unified construct. He stepped into the parking stall, got into his car, and drove quickly to the university.

Dr. Cooley raised an eyebrow. She seemed almost tantalized in spite of her ingrained skepticism.

"Two separate environments," she mused. "Close friends. A rare coincidence. Very rare."

"And the same kinds of marks on the ceiling. We saw them."

Dr. Cooley sat down, tapping her finger lightly against her lip.

"Something more," Kraft continued, his eyes flashing.

"What?"

"It happened in her car."

Now Dr. Cooley looked up, disturbed and yet strangely intrigued.

"The RSPK?" she asked.

313

"I'm not sure just what. She heard voices." Kraft paused. "Dr. Cooley," he said hesitantly.

"What?"

"Joe and I discussed the possibility—of asking you to come down—to talk to Mrs. Moran."

Dr. Cooley frowned.

"I don't like to interfere in student projects, Gene. You know that."

"But we don't have any experience as psychologists, Dr. Cooley. If you could talk to her, sound her out, make a judgment on her—"

"I'm not sure—"

"Besides, this would give you a chance to see our set-up. It would be your chance to make sure it looks right."

Dr. Cooley smiled, yet Kraft knew her well enough to know that she was terribly worried.

"All right," she sighed. "This evening."

"Great," Kraft said. "Then we'll talk about Mrs. Moran afterwards."

Jerry Rodriguez shifted his weight uncomfortably in the airplane. His face, once tanned by the Southern California sun, was now pale. The winter in the Midwest had been one of the worst on record. The cars were sliding on the ice, the hotels cold. Jerry rubbed his eyes. The sleeplessness of the last two months had finally caught up with him. Coming home to Carlotta, he let the exhaustion flow through his body.

Life without her was a series of empty rooms, a progression of empty streets, bars and restaurants hemmed in by the bleak isolation. From somewhere she got that energy, that liveliness that made him a man, a whole man, a man who loved life. He sensed her personality now, wherever he went, whatever he did.

Until he had met her—it was nearly a year ago, on a Monday—his had been a life of chance encounters, business colleagues with forced laughter and a cruel light

314

of day that shined with a blank indifference on everything he did and said.

He recalled the night—a night he'd never forget.

He had crossed the wide boulevard leading from the Holiday Inn and had ducked inside a nightclub. Traveling men, like himself, were walking in and out of the lounge. Across from the nightclub, behind the parking lot, the international airport rose, a series of fantastic forms in the night. Depressed, he went into the lounge.

Exotic plants rose from huge, ornate pots. A jazz score floated in the air. In this artificial pleasantry he sat at a table, watching the scantily dressed hostesses. The light made their bodies soft, their smiles almost real. They looked velvety, supple, but undesirable. Jerry felt an ashen taste in his mouth that only whiskey could dissolve. The travel, once so enticing, had suddenly paled. He saw in front of him a long life of moving from city to city, empty inside, chasing something he did not want. He was thirty-eight years old. He wanted something else. He ordered a double whiskey. Soon the jazz sounded better. The girls looked lovelier. Mentally he imagined himself with one, then the other. But only as a pleasant fantasy. He knew well enough the bitter taste in the morning. When the day rises on two strangers in an ugly hotel room.

He ordered cigarettes. He watched the girl approach, her breasts quivering through the sheer blouse as she walked. Her glazed face did not hide the vulnerability she felt. Jerry figured she would be out of a job soon. The girls have to present a happy face to the customers. Men don't like to feel exploitative.

He had a small supper. Then another whiskey. He noticed the cigarette girl, waiting by the bar. She seemed to have no guile. Yet, underneath, Jerry could see that she was not afraid of men. Intrigued, his eyes followed her as she walked down the long line of tables. Suddenly the comments and stares from the men at the next table irritated him.

315

He slept, as usual, in the Holiday Inn across the wide boulevard. The roar of the airport sounded outside the windows. Flashing red lights revolved high in the air, sentries for some incredible civilization that he no longer felt part of. He was suddenly afraid that his entire life would pass by in a series of such nights, without meaning, that he would grow old, decay, and disappear, in just the same way. Without meaning.

The next day he had to call Vancouver. He waited at the nightclub for the operator to return his call. He had spent the whole day making arrangements with Vancouver, only to be told two hours before the flight that he might be going to Sacramento instead. Cursing, he leaned against the bar with nothing to do but wait for the call.

He turned. Hostesses were walking by, toward the lobby. Behind them, alone, was the cigarette girl. She walked past him without seeing him.

Two weeks later, on a layover, Jerry and two salesmen stepped into the nightclub. Killing time was no art. Keeping yourself sane while doing it was. Like all the nightclubs near all the airports, this one was filled with the same kinds of faces, listless, transient faces; and Jerry knew he was part of someone else's depressed view of the traveling life.

The distant jazz score sounded familiar. It reminded him of the cigarette girl. He tried to find her. Then he heard an argument behind the bar. The bartender was speaking in a strident whisper to one of the girls. Then Jerry saw it was the girl he had been looking for. She left, not looking back when the bartender called her back.

"What was that all about?" Jerry asked.

"Ah, nothing. Girls get stuck up, time to time."

"It's hard on them, going around half-naked."

"Nah—they like it."

"What's her name?"

"Carlotta. But forget it."

Jerry laughed.

"Why?"

"Men don't exist for her."

316

Jerry laughed again. He enjoyed the bartender's discomfort. Evidently she had told him off.

He ordered some cigarettes. A different girl came. Jerry asked for the short brunette. Carlotta came. Jerry paid for the cigarettes, stealing glances at her. She was young, perhaps thirty. She was small-boned, her black eyes wide in her small, round face. She watched some point vaguely over his shoulder, avoided his glance, then smiled and walked away.

"See?" the bartender said. "She's a nun in disguise."

Jerry paid for his drink. Somewhere he had lost the two salesmen. Suddenly he felt very depressed. He smiled without meaning it, waved a half-hearted goodbye to the bartender, and walked out into the cold, gray twilight.

Later that week, departing Vancouver, he routed himself to Los Angeles International instead of the Burbank airport. He knew it was the cigarette girl in the back of his mind. He felt like a dope, but there it was. What he was going to do, he was not yet sure.

Upon his return to Los Angeles he sought her out.

"Carlotta," he said softly.

Startled, she turned. She stood in the lobby, her smooth skin soft and brown in the dim lights. She scrutinized his face, to see if she knew him.

"I just guessed," he said.

Her face glazed over again with a protective veil of indifference. Seeing he wanted to buy nothing, she turned and walked away. He watched her go into the main lounge. He wondered how many other men had done the same. No wonder she had to protect herself.

He sat at a table. The musical group was taking a break. He looked at his watch. He had left word at the Holiday Inn to transfer telephone calls to the nightclub. The meaningless babble of guests and dates was far better than the hotel room.

"Mr. Rodriguez," Carlotta called, searching the faces at the bar.

She came forward with a note and seemed slightly startled to find it was he. She handed him the note.

317

"Long distance from Seattle," she said.

"Thanks."

He rose and picked up the telephone in a small lounge. He talked for half an hour, taking notes, not arguing, but fuming inside. Then he slammed down the receiver and went back to his table. Carlotta was standing nearby, separating the change in her tray.

"Christ!" he muttered. "They ship you from Seattle to Vancouver to Portland to Sacramento to San Francisco—like a soccer ball. Give me a break!"

He finished his drink, standing up. Carlotta was not sure if he were talking to her. She smiled vaguely, just in case he was.

"You see, Carlotta?" he said, "it's the same with you. See what they make us do?"

Startled, she did not know how to respond.

"I'll see you in two weeks," he said, resigned, smiling.

"Yes. Goodbye, Mr. Rodriguez."

He chuckled ruefully, left a tip, and walked out. At the glass doors to the street he looked back. She had remembered his name. It had vaguely electrified him. He tried to see her silhouette in the crowd. Was she looking his way? Carlotta, he said to himself, smiling. A lovely name. Who was she?

He moved fast in Seattle, foreclosed an operation, and found himself the deliverer of good news to his firm in Los Angeles. However, the image of Carlotta pricked at his thoughts. He prayed in his mind that when he returned and saw her again, something might happen. What was it about her? Something special. Something serious. He intended to find out.

"Carlotta," he said, "you have no strong cigars."

"I only sell what they put on my tray, sir."

"You don't even remember my name."

She looked at him distrustfully. Then she did, vaguely, recall his features.

"Mr. Gonzalez," she said.

"Rodriguez," he laughed. "It's okay. I've been called much worse."

"Mr. Rodriguez," she apologized, "I'm sorry. Would you like a strong tobacco? I can get it for you from the counter."

"What? Oh, yes—thank you. Please."

Suddenly the sight of her breasts peeking through the filmy fabric infuriated him. They were meant to be concealed. A woman's body is a private thing, a soft thing, not meant for this circus of—Jerry looked around him. The businessmen were laughing, drinking, carrying valises in and out of the lobbies. What was he thinking about? What was going through his head?

"Mr. Rodriguez."

"Yes? Oh—the cigars. I—here—no, keep the change."

She smiled. He thought she mocked him. In fact, he felt like a fool. Suddenly he was flustered. When she had stood so close to him, her breasts pointed, he trying not to look except at her face, her eyes—he had smelled a kind of warmth, had sensed a kind of presence in front of him. It was almost intoxicating.

"It's all right," he said. "I—no—you keep it."

Awkwardly, he left the lobby, went out into the street. The taxis blew their horns. Porters asked him to move. Middle-aged couples argued about their luggage in front of automatic doors. Overhead was the whine of the jets. Suddenly, he turned back and went inside the lounge again. He waited for hours, until the day began to break and the bar closed and she came out of the dressing room. She was the last to emerge.

"Well," she said. "Mr. Rodriguez. We're closed."

"Yes—I know. Carlotta—it's raining outside. A terrible storm. You'll need an umbrella. I have one—"

"It's not raining," she said, laughing.

Her eyes regarded him with a sparkling mockery. He felt everyone in the lounge was watching him make a fool of himself. Doggedly, he stood beside the door. His pretend-smile faded, and a natural one emerged. A delicate breeding, he thought. So delicate. Where did she get those manners? Suddenly he felt elevated himself, removed from the tawdry facade that crippled his real self. He held up his empty hands.

"No," he said, "you're right. It's not. I don't have an umbrella, either."

She laughed in a beautiful way. She covered her small, even white teeth with her hand. Dressed now in a short black skirt and a red blouse, she looked far more alluring than she had inside. Now there was charm in her every movement. He was not afraid of making a fool of himself anymore.

"It could, though," he said. "It could rain any time. Weather's like that."

"Not in this part of the world."

The bartender was locking the doors to the lounge. Outside the light had turned gray. It was too early to see if the sun would rise cleanly or diffuse itself through a bank of clouds. She was in an impasse, too. He didn't know what to do. For an instant it was as though they were a couple. The thought made him almost delirious. He felt he had to say something, show her he knew what he was doing. And yet, she was in charge, too.

Outside, they stood awkwardly, neither knowing precisely who the other one was. He did not know what to make of her. She seemed afraid of giving herself, yet needed people. As he did. In some way, life had broken her down, too, to a more supple, stronger substance. It had softened her on the inside, made her grow a shell on the outside. As it had with him.

The taxi drove up. The driver opened the door to the passenger side. He waited, not knowing who was first.

"No," Jerry said. "You take it. I'll take the next one."

"They come every ten minutes."

"No. It's yours."

"All right. Thank you."

320

She got into the seat. The driver turned the ignition key. Before the door closed, Jerry sat down beside her, and the taxi drove off.

His heart was pounding. The gesture was in the open. He knew each moment she said nothing, she was compromised. Gradually she relaxed. Jerry looked at her from time to time. She looked down, or out the window, blushing faintly.

"Up this way, please," Jerry said.

The driver let them off at a Mexican-style hacienda, a motel in the hills, embedded in a grove of palms. Just before he shut the door of the taxi, she placed her hand on his arm a moment and looked directly into his eyes. Her voice was soft and seemed to tremble.

"I haven't done this—ever," she whispered.

"I know," Jerry said, believing her, knowing that this time it would not turn out the way it always did. Not this time.

In the airplane, Jerry smiled. And she had been so open, so honest, he thought. There was no hard edge at all. For the first time in his life, the hard shell fell from him, too. He was afraid it was an illusion—this girl he did not know, who seemed so distant, yet so direct at the same time. But no, she was for real. And she made him feel real.

Jerry coughed slightly and picked up a magazine. He didn't want to start thinking about Carlotta in bed. That sort of thought had maddened him in lonely hotels for the last eight weeks. Deprived of her, he felt deprived of life itself.

She took him to her house once. They slept together in that crazy European bed, bequeathed by some unknown tenant from years gone by. When the sun rose and the voices of the children were heard, he felt suddenly as though this were his house, his wife, his children. It was a fantasy that made him almost dizzy.

Carlotta felt it, too. After six months, they both

knew it. It was a strange thing. Neither could live now without the other. They had wanted their independence, but, Jerry reflected, wasn't that out of the question now?

The tension continued to rise in him. Marriage was a completely different proposition. Especially with Billy part of the deal. Two angels and Billy. Jerry leaned back, trying not to think of Billy. The stocky youngster, as strong, as bull-headed as they come. For four months, ever since he first stayed over, Billy had dogged him, ridiculed him, egged him on.

Jerry wanted to move someplace else, set up his own apartment, maybe at a good hotel. But waking up with Carlotta—the sunshine over her soft shoulder, the girls giggling in the other bedroom, the birds outside the window—it was that which made him fill up inside with a peace he never before knew existed. Everything he wanted, had ever secretly wanted, was there. He would be a good father, an excellent husband—whatever she wanted, he could do—but there was Billy.

He barged in on them if they slept late, made a lot of noise, made sarcastic remarks at breakfast, until even the girls were embarrassed. Jerry could do nothing without Billy on him. Finally he pointed his finger at Billy across the table.

"Now you keep your mouth shut, young man," Jerry said. "I've done nothing to deserve this sort of thing and you know it."

Billy, flustered, looked to his mother. For the first time in his life she gave him no support. She looked away. His eyes moist, he stood up abruptly, knocking over a bowl.

"Point your fingers at yourself, you creep!"

Then, feeling foolish, childish, unable to bear Carlotta's suppressed anger, Billy threw himself out of the house.

"I'm sorry, honey, he just—"

"I know," Jerry said for the hundredth time. "He's just a kid."

One night Jerry came out of the bathroom, wrapping

his bathrobe tighter around him. In the hallway Billy stood, barring the way to his mother's bedroom door.

"You know, you got a lot of nerve coming around here. Like you owned the place."

"Your mother invited me."

"You made her invite you."

"It was her idea, kid."

"Don't call me kid."

"Billy."

"You know, you never asked *us*. You never asked *us* if we wanted you here!"

"It was never up to you."

"It's *our* house, and you're not wanted."

"All right," Jerry said. "I'm sorry you feel that way. Now, if you'll just move aside, I'll go where I *am* wanted."

"She don't want you, neither."

Carlotta's voice came from behind the door, sleepily.

"What is it, Jerry? What's going on?"

"It's nothing, honey. I—"

"And she ain't your honey!" Billy suddenly said, pushing Jerry against the wall.

Jerry found himself humiliated, off-balance against the wall. His face flushed.

"Why, you little twerp!"

Jerry suddenly leaned forward, grabbed Billy by the shirt collar, and struck him across the cheek. The slap resounded through the house. Carlotta screamed. Jerry turned. To his dismay, she had seen the whole thing. She stood at the open door in her nightgown.

"You bastard!" Billy screamed. "You son of a bitch!"

Billy fell forward onto Jerry, pummeling him the way a boy fights, the fists flying blindly. Jerry, embarrassed at losing his temper, covered his face and let Billy hit him. Carlotta tried in vain to pull Billy off.

"Billy!" she screamed. "Goddam it! Billy!"

Finally, weeping, Billy threw himself off, gazed at both of them, and shouted, "Both of you! Go to hell! I don't care!"

He ran from the hallway, tripping over chairs in the living room. Then he slammed the door on his way out.

"Jesus, honey," Jerry said. "I'm sorry! I'm sorry! I don't know what happened! I lost my—"

"It's all right, Jerry. It's all right—"

"I could cut off my hand!"

"It's okay, it's okay."

That night Jerry and Carlotta slept in the large bed. Jerry's dreams were troubled and violent. Carlotta tried to soothe him. But they both knew that the pressure was rising and that the moment had come to make their decision.

And now, at last, the decision was made. It was, finally, quite simple. Life without Carlotta would be dying inside, being reborn as half a man, an empty shell.

The pilot turned on the "no smoking" sign. "Please fasten your seat belts," said the stewardess.

Jerry looked down at Los Angeles speeding up, closer and closer below him: the endless straight roads; the million flat-roofed houses spread out like a vast and indifferent quilt; the homes of the wealthy in the hills; the barrios in the center, gray, regular, and dull; and the ocean like a blue sky, with tiny humans standing sentry on the sandy fringe—

—and Carlotta. His Carlotta. Soon to be his wife.

18

DR. COOLEY felt misgivings, knocking on the door. Seeing the cars parked outside on Kentner Street gave her an uneasy feeling. It reminded her of meetings she had attended, so-called conferences where all manner of people came from miles around to witness something or to examine something. Dr. Cooley had met with scores of eccentrics, with the gullible, the frightened, and the suggestible. She realized that the project was in need of scientific control if Kraft and Mehan were seriously considering the exotic, the story-book branches of parapsychology. She suddenly knew that, if she had to, she would terminate the project.

Billy opened the door and stood there, blinking.

"Hello," Dr. Cooley said pleasantly. "My name is Dr. Cooley. From the university—"

"Who is it?" called Carlotta.

"It's a lady," Billy answered.

Carlotta came to the door. She was younger than Dr. Cooley had guessed, much prettier, petite and black-haired. Carlotta smiled graciously and held out her hand.

"Dr. Cooley," Carlotta said. "Come in."

"Thank you," Dr. Cooley said, stepping inside.

Several undergraduates from the parapsychology division looked up, startled, smiling. In front of them, on the kitchen table, were oversized maps of the house plans on which had been traced trajectories of the psychokinetic events.

"Good evening, Dr. Cooley," one of the undergraduates said.

"I'm not checking up," Dr. Cooley said. "I just wanted to talk to Gene and Joe."

"They're in the bedroom," Carlotta said.

Dr. Cooley followed Carlotta through the living room. She observed that Carlotta moved with the light grace of a well-bred person, a kind of grace out of keeping with the tiny tract home.

In the bedroom, Kraft and Mehan looked up. Wires were in their hands and they were snipping off the insulation at the tips.

"Good evening, Dr. Cooley," Kraft said. "Have you met Mrs. Moran?"

"Only briefly," Dr. Cooley said. "I'd like to speak with you before I do."

Carlotta understood that they had scientific things to discuss. She smiled, remained awkwardly at the door for a moment, then excused herself to answer some questions that the undergraduates had for her in the kitchen.

"I've thought it over," Dr. Cooley said in a low voice. "The whole matter of apparitions and what not. And it doesn't feel right for me."

"It's nothing we made up," Kraft said.

"I think that caution is the password. In the long run, no one here can afford to get involved with bizarre behavior."

"Dr. Cooley," Mehan said, "there's something else on your mind."

"It's this, Joe," she said. "If it comes to it, I'll cancel the project. I want you to understand that."

Kraft and Mehan exchanged glances.

"It's for the good of the department, and for your own good, too," she said.

"But—"

"I'm not saying I will, only that it could happen. I want to be up-front with you. It depends on what happens with Mrs. Moran."

326

"You mean, if she's hysteric—"

"Exactly. I don't want this house to start looking like some of those seances I used to attend when I started out in parapsychology. A lot of people wandering in and out—"

"Everything here is controlled," Kraft objected.

"I can see that—but—I'll go talk to Mrs. Moran. I'll meet with you afterward."

Dr. Cooley walked into the living room. Carlotta was correcting the dates on several charts that undergraduate students held before her. Dr. Cooley indicated, by a nearly imperceptible gesture, that she wished to speak alone with Carlotta. After the students left for the kitchen area, Dr. Cooley sat down in the easy chair, facing Carlotta on the couch. Dr. Cooley studied Carlotta's eyes, hands, and manner of speech with the objective demeanor of a trained psychologist.

"Did Mr. Kraft or Mr. Mehan tell you I am a trained psychologist?" Dr. Cooley asked.

"No."

"There are many times the two disciplines become connected."

"I see," Carlotta said, uncertain what the distinguished-looking woman was driving at.

"What I have to ask you, Mrs. Moran, is whether the events which you have experienced are the kind of things that you felt or saw, or the kind of things which are more like a dream."

Carlotta laughed.

"That's what the psychiatrist asked me."

"Well, it's very important."

Carlotta's face clouded over.

"I can tell you," Carlotta said, "that the objects flying, the smell, the cold—that's all real. Your people discovered them, too."

"I know that. But your son has been telling Mr. Mehan that other things have happened."

"What do you mean?" Carlotta said, evasively.

"For example, in your car."

327

Carlotta laughed. Dr. Cooley noticed the change in her dark eyes, something mysterious had clouded them.

"I smashed into a telephone pole."

"Billy told him why."

Carlotta was silent. She reached for a cigarette. She felt the first twinges of nervousness since she had been to Sneidermann. Wasn't a psychologist the same thing as a psychiatrist, she wondered. She examined the handsome woman in the tweed skirt and jacket.

"All right," Carlotta said. "I heard voices."

"Have you ever heard them in the house?"

"Sometimes. I wasn't sure."

"Has anyone else heard them?"

"Billy has."

"And the girls?"

"No. I don't think so."

Dr. Cooley watched how nervously Carlotta smoked. The abrupt change of behavior was significant, she knew.

"May I ask you, Mrs. Moran—Why do your children sleep at the neighbor's house?"

"It's too dangerous in here."

"Because of the poltergeist activity?"

"Exactly."

"There's no other reason?"

"No."

Carlotta smiled, a thin, nervous smile. Dr. Cooley recognized the mannerisms of anxiety.

"And what about your friends?" Dr. Cooley asked.

"What about them?"

"Mr. Mehan spoke to them in their apartment."

Carlotta said nothing. She made a show of looking for an ashtray.

"What happened to their apartment, Mrs. Moran?"

Carlotta shrugged.

"I don't know," she said. "I can't explain what happened."

"But you all saw something?"

328

"It was terrible. The place just came apart. We were scared to death."

Dr. Cooley knew that Carlotta was hiding something. What it was, she could not fathom. She pressed on, her voice becoming sterner.

"What did you see, Mrs. Moran?"

"See?"

"You and your friends."

Carlotta groped for words.

"It was—so dark—"

"Yes?"

"Then *he* came—without warning—"

"Who did?"

Carlotta looked up, startled. Billy was calling.

"Who did?" Dr. Cooley repeated.

"Mom!" Billy yelled. "There's somebody here!"

"Let him in."

"No. Come here!"

Mystified, Carlotta rose from the couch. She looked out the window. A familiar form stepped from a taxi.

Jerry stood immobile in front of the door. He watched Billy carefully. The teenager was not certain what to do. He licked his lips, looked back inside at a crowd dimly visible in the interior of the house. Jerry moved past him and stepped inside.

Carlotta stood in the entrance to the living room. Her hand was raised involuntarily to her mouth. Dimly stirring, babbling in low voices, several men and women sat on the couch, on chairs, looking at photographs and maps on the floor.

"Jerry!" she tried to say. But the word did not come. Only her lips moved.

Jerry grinned, held out his hands to her. But he knew something was dreadfully wrong.

"Baby!" He felt her limp in his arms. He laughed nervously and raised her face gently by the chin, looking into her eyes.

"Why didn't you call?" she said weakly.

"I did. Every time I got a different voice on the line. What's going on here?"

She looked at him with the wild eyes of a trapped animal.

"Oh, Jerry!"

"What is it? Aren't you glad to see me?"

"Yes, but I—I—"

A short young man poked his head around the corner.

"Mrs. Moran," he said brightly. "Oh, excuse me!"

Jerry wondered who the kid was. Now the babble of voices became more and more distinct. He looked at Carlotta with a puzzled expression.

"They're doctors," she said weakly.

"Doctors?"

Kraft came forward, his oversized sweater bulging, his hand extended.

"Good afternoon," he said. "I'm Gene Kraft. Department of parapsychology. Are you from Sonoma State?"

"No. I'm not."

"I'm sorry. Please make yourself at home."

Jerry whispered in Carlotta's ear.

"Who the hell was that?"

Now Carlotta began to look pale, as though she would faint. She felt herself waking up from the long high of the hysteria that had sustained her for nearly a month. She began to fall down into a depression. She tried to catch herself, suspend herself over the void that opened up underneath her. But Jerry had seen it all. The doctors, the students, the devices, the photographic grids. Certainly now her last prop was kicked out from under her. Now she was going to watch as the world caved in.

"I'm Dr. Cooley," said a tall, formally dressed woman. "Director of the Division of Parapsychology at West Coast University. I hope this isn't an intrusion for you. We are only here at the invitation of Mrs. Moran."

Jerry shook her extended hand.

"Not at all. You go ahead and do what you want, Dr. Cooley."

Maintaining a semblance of a smile, he turned to Carlotta and said in a low whisper, "Get a sweater, Carlotta. We're getting out of this monkey cage."

"Jerry, I can't—"

"Now!"

Carlotta went to the closet, spoke several minutes with Kraft, who expostulated about something and looked very upset. But she saw Jerry fuming at the door, and she carried her sweater in her arm, and together they went outside to the car.

The roar of Carlotta's just-repaired Buick taking off thundered over the babble of voices inside the house.

The Buick made its way toward the ocean. Jerry said nothing. He could find nothing to say, no way to say it. He wasn't sure if he was angry or frightened. He looked at Carlotta from time to time. Sometimes she looked all right. Sometimes she had a sick, pasty look that made him queasy.

She tried to avoid his glance. She kept her head turned away, looking at the houses speeding away.

Jerry maneuvered the Buick onto the cliffs overlooking the pier and stepped out. They went into a seafood restaurant. Still, they did not speak to one another.

Inside, sea nets were hung from the walls, candles cast a soft orange glow over the tables, and starfish were spread out in glass cases by the counter. Jerry ordered for them both, lit a cigarette, looked around him as though he were afraid he might have been followed by the horrendous mob that had filled up their house, and then leaned forward gently.

"What was all that?" he said softly.

Tears came to her eyes.

"Come on. Come on," he said.

"They're trying to help," she said hoarsely.

"Help? Help who?"

"Me."

331

He looked around, scarcely believing his ears.

"I don't get it," he said.

Carlotta looked at him. She saw him fading away from her. Somehow, she had known it would come to this. She hadn't pictured it happening in a seafood restaurant, but it had to come out this way. She would tell him, he would blow up, and that would be it.

"I've been sick, Jerry."

"Sick? What kind of sick?"

"I can't sleep. I've been seeing a doctor."

"Go on."

"Things have come to me. In the night."

Jerry paled. Talk like this made him ill.

"Nightmares, you mean."

"Like nightmares."

"And you've been seeing a shrink?"

Carlotta knew there was no point to evasion anymore.

"Yes. A psychiatrist."

"So?"

"So I'm not seeing him anymore."

Jerry raised an eyebrow. He seemed relieved.

"That's good. Anyway, what's that got to do with all those people in your house?"

The waiter came with lobster and salads, set them down on the table, and went away again. The twilight was casting a turquoise glow through the enormous plate-glass window that looked onto the Pacific.

"Answer me, Carlotta."

"The psychiatrist couldn't make it go away. So these people are trying to help me."

Jerry seemed to think it over. He seemed to be wrestling with all kinds of thoughts. Suddenly, ravenously, he stuck a fork into his salad and began eating.

"Hmmmm," he murmured, chewing. "I remember that lady said she was a psychologist or something."

"You're not mad?"

Jerry did not answer for a while.

332

"Why the hell should I be mad? You can't sleep at night, you can't sleep."

Carlotta was amazed. She had expected him to storm off. Still, she wondered what he was really thinking.

"It's only been recent. Since you went away."

Jerry laughed.

"I know why you can't sleep," he said, winking.

Carlotta had no appetite, but she hesitantly sipped some wine. Being with Jerry, she began to slide into their old relationship again. She felt comfortable, even charming. She wanted to go somewhere with him.

"By the way," he said, "what was all that gear doing there? They had enough wires to make a computer."

"They were measuring."

Jerry looked up. His eyes sparkled. She could not tell if it was with amusement or anger.

"What were they measuring?"

"The house."

"You know, Carlotta, I ask you a question and you don't tell me anything. Ever since I came home. You want me home or not?"

"Of course, I want you home," she said, leaning forward, putting a hand on his arm.

The touch sobered them both.

"Then tell me what they are measuring," he said simply.

"They have a theory," she said, "that something in the house keeps me from sleeping."

He drank another glass of wine and poured them both some more.

"Sounds reasonable, I suppose."

Jerry chewed and swallowed. For a long time neither spoke. She found her appetite returning. She felt once again that she was part of the world the other guests belonged to. She was a woman, having supper with her lover, and they listened to the soft music and watched the sun slide far away into the horizon of the earth. She was no longer the freak. The circus was over. She tried not to even think about her own house.

"Some crazy hello, wasn't it?" he said, smiling.

"I should have told you, Jerry. Please forgive me."

Jerry finished his dinner. He gestured for her to finish hers. Slowly, her appetite grew. She felt as though she had regained an appetite for life itself. Jerry stroked the soft skin of her forearm as the bracelet dangled lightly over the white tablecloth.

"I've always thought," he said, "that there is only one cure for not feeling well. I mean, not feeling well in here. In your heart. It's when you care for somebody and that person cares for you. Then you can face anything that comes your way. Without somebody else, you could be a millionaire and still be miserable." Jerry blushed. "You know what I mean? I don't believe in those kinds of doctors. Don't get me wrong. If you can't sleep at night and you want to go see them, that's okay with me. But I believe it's what takes place between two people that's more important."

Carlotta smiled. She put his hand against her cheek.

"Let's go home," he said gently.

She froze.

"What's the matter?"

"It's so full of people—"

"Well, they must be gone by now."

"Sometimes they leave their things in the house."

"What difference does that make?"

"It's not very romantic. Why don't we go back to the motel. Over the ocean?"

"Because I want to wake up in *our* bed with you."

She smiled uncertainly.

"Something *is* wrong," he muttered.

"No. I'll go telephone the house and make sure they've gone."

They got up to leave. Carlotta telephoned home. Jerry found himself getting angry again. But he didn't know who to blame. He thought of the young people perched everywhere in the house. Why did they give him cause for alarm? Why did he feel, even now, that Carlotta was hiding something from him? Why this telephone call? Suddenly their relationship was full of tensions and mysteries. Some homecoming, he thought bitterly. He finished the wine in a single gulp.

19

CARLOTTA held onto Jerry's arm. She was afraid of the house with its strange emptiness now that the people were gone. Where was her army now? The night was dark, moonless. Billy was in the garage. She heard his radio. The girls were next door preparing for sleep. It all seemed so familiar and so hideous.

"It would be so much nicer," she said softly, "far away."

Jerry nuzzled the back of her neck, kissed her softly on the lips.

"I brought you something from back east," he whispered.

She seemed almost distracted, her mind fixed elsewhere. He could not figure it out. She was not responding.

"What is it?" she asked.

"You'll see," he said, smiling.

Inside the house Jerry turned on the lights. It looked unsettled; bits of paper and notebooks, ends of wires, and occasional screws littered the floor. Jerry opened the window and was grateful for the night breeze that separated the curtains and blew into his face. The neighborhood out there looked so peaceful, several rectangular yellow lights scattered here and there through the veil of darkening shrubbery. He wondered, vaguely, why the girls were spending the night with the neighbors. He was distracted by a distant dog barking, and now the street lamps flared

336

oddly, diminished, and then grew brighter again. What was wrong? he thought.

"Oh, Jerry!" she whispered. "It's beautiful!"

She held in front of her a silk nightgown. There were black ribbons interlaced along the front, and thin white lace down the sides.

"Well," he said, "I hoped it was your size."

She smiled at him, kissed him on the lips. But her eyes were vacant, or rather, they were looking for something else. Not him at all. Jealousy began to grow in him like a black cloud. He watched her as she pressed the silk against the side of her face, feeling its smoothness. She looked suddenly like some kind of marionette, empty and devoid of feeling. Who was pulling the strings? he thought.

"Maybe it's a little elaborate," he said.

"No," she said, laughing. "I'm going to feel so fine in this."

"You can return it if it's the wrong size. They have branch stores—"

"It's perfect, honey," she said.

He sat on the couch with her, staring into her eyes. Whatever he had seen in them, like some distant storm cloud so many months ago, had grown. It dominated her now, he knew. It had taken her over. That strangeness that can come over two lovers when they have been separated—it was not going to go away, he thought. He began to feel angry, humiliated, and the loneliness grew around him as thick and endless as the night that had fallen on the earth.

"Carlotta," he whispered, leaning forward.

His lips found hers, soft but not yet warm, and they pressed against his. Only when he touched his hand lightly along the back of her neck, firmer and firmer, did she catch her breath, hold him tighter.

"It's so good to have you back," she whispered.

He felt her trembling in his arms.

"It's the last time," he said. "I have a firm offer."

She said nothing. He could not see her face. He wondered what thoughts were circulating through her mind. He felt awkward. He had not realized that he would feel unsure of her once again when he came back.

"I wanted to find a place for us in San Diego," he said, "but there was no time."

She murmured inaudibly, kissing his neck over and over again. He felt tears come to his eyes. He had been too lonely. Now he could not believe she was in his arms again.

"We can pick out a place together," he said hoarsely. "It's better that way."

She only whispered softly, in a trembling voice, "I want to, Jerry. Yes. As soon as we can."

Now, like a sudden warmth between them, the strangeness was gone. He felt the warmth of her body rising toward him. For an instant he felt almost dizzy.

"Jerry, Jerry," she said softly.

From far away a man called his dog. Distant traffic echoed far from Kentner Street. He closed his eyes. There was only Carlotta. He smelled the soft scent of her skin, felt her delicate hands on his, and he wanted her then and there.

"I have some wine," she offered, smiling.

Jerry held her face in front of him. The fear was gone from her eyes. He saw only Carlotta in there. The pupils were large and deep in the dark room, her face slightly flushed. Her hair fell delicately from her forehead and temples. Her nostrils flared slightly as she breathed, smiling at him.

"I don't need any."

"No. Let's," she said playfully. "It's for you. To celebrate your homecoming."

She got up and went to the refrigerator. He watched her from the doorway to the kitchen, her lithe, lovely movements. Neither turned on the lights. She wrestled with the cork.

"That was quite a homecoming," he said lightly.

Her face fell an instant and then she laughed. A

forced laugh. She gave him a glass, sparkling with transparent liquid. They toasted each other and drank.

Jerry had never seen her so beautiful. It was a new quality. She looked as though she needed someone to protect her. From what, he didn't know. But it made him see her in a different way. She looked softer, almost smaller, darker. Perhaps it was the shadows, the wine. But he wanted her now, and he saw the same in her eyes.

"One more glass," she whispered.

A tiny bracelet dangled from her wrist as she poured. Jerry raised his glass. His lips met hers again, cold and wet from the liquid. It sent a shiver through him. The darkness had become maddeningly seductive, a soft presence folding them both into its infinite secrets.

She took him by the arm. They walked through the living room, past the temperature meters protruding from the linen closet. She stopped, put her fingers to her lips, and then turned to him.

"Let me try this on," she said, holding her nightgown to her chest. "Then you come in."

"All right," he said.

She opened the door to the bedroom. A moment later her hand came out, holding his bathrobe.

"I wonder whose that is?" he said, grinning.

Carlotta gaily winked at him and disappeared into the bedroom.

He was in the bathroom when he heard a voice outside, mingling with the radio. It was Billy, leaning against the work bench, repeating the words to a song. Jerry could see Billy's shadow as it bent again over the vise. Frowning, Jerry softly closed the window. He wanted nothing to go wrong tonight. Billy's voice faded away and disappeared.

Carlotta made a soft moan. It sounded like a child making fun, a kind of extended moan. Jerry slipped into his bathrobe and laughed lightly.

She moaned again.

"Carlotta, Carlotta," he gently chided.

He smoothed down his hair, examined his face in

the mirror, and rinsed his mouth. He stepped into the hallway. He turned off the bathroom light. It was chilly, and he wrapped the robe closer around his shoulders.

She moaned again.

Jerry growled, a mock tiger's growl. He laughed, stumbling, trying to find his way through the hallway. He burst out laughing as he accidentally stuck his hand into the linen closet, and found a mess of wires in a tangle.

When he got to her door, she moaned again. It did not sound funny.

"Carlotta?" he whispered.

The door was stuck. He leaned against it. It did not move. He pushed against it. She moaned a long, soft, despairing moan.

"Carlotta!"

He bashed the door open. It banged against the wall and bounced back, hitting him on the arm. In the darkness he saw Carlotta in the shadows. Her body was arched. He saw the pale glimmer of the sheets separate from her back, as the soft skin rose and she moaned.

"What is it, honey?" he said. "Are you sick?"

Suddenly she thrashed, was rigid, and then her hips slowly undulated, revolving, her naked thighs separated.

"Ooooooooohhhhhhh!"

Now in the darkness he could make out the outline of her soft body, the breasts flattened as though pressed down, spread out until they were distended along the chest wall.

"Carlotta!"

"Oh, God!"

With a great pelvic heave she groaned. Yet there was nothing there. His brain shot with a thousand wild sparks, each a thought that led to nowhere. Now he thought he saw clouds form over the closet. It was a kind of reflection from the window, he decided. His mind was playing tricks with him. He knew now, with a sickening feeling, that he had to get her out of there. She was sick. Whatever else he would do, he had to get her out of there.

He stumbled forward, took hold of her arm. She pulled violently away from him.

"Oh! Oh! Oh!" she suddenly shouted.

He backed away, rubbing his eyes. She was having a fit! That's what it was! He had never seen it before. The rolling of her abdomen made him ill. Her thighs were grasping, pulling something forward, widening. Did she even see him? She gasped for air, fought, pulled, pushed something away, rolled. And then the bed dipped under her weight. Dipped far down under a weight that was greater than hers alone, as the springs squealed rhythmically.

"Oh Jesus!" she moaned. "Jesus! Oh!"

Jerry's brain was on fire. He realized he was panicking. He was frozen in the shadows.

He thought he saw her skin glow. The light from the window seemed to coalesce along her sides and abdomen, growing into a green-blue flame.

"Stop it!" he shouted foolishly, absurdly.

He wrestled himself onto her thrashing limbs, tried to pin her legs down, her arms; then he saw a bright flash of red and yellow and fell back, flung back by an awful blow. Blood was flowing in lines from his face. His right eye was dizzy with the impact of her fingernails.

"Stop it!!" he shouted.

Now the green-blue glow began to ball up, rolling subtly over her, growing deeper and deeper in color, until he saw her body illuminated by its foul light. Through his one good eye, he thought he saw the buttocks thrusting, tightening, thrusting, tightening.

Jerry reached blindly around in the dark, found a spindly wooden chair and raised it above his head. He brought it crashing down on the cloud that held her head back against the pillow, that had separated her and entered her until the bed rocked.

The wooden spokes shot apart. Carlotta screamed.

Jerry saw blood. Blood coming down, like an explosion from that delicate head. She was huddled on the

341

bed. The sheets were bright red. They blinded his eyes. Why was he blinded? Nothing made sense anymore. He held the remnants of the chair in his hand. He realized that the light was on.

"You bastard!!"

Turning, Jerry saw Billy standing at the door. Billy's eyes were slits of anger. Transfixed at first by the sight of his mother, moaning in pain on the reddening sheets, he then looked at Jerry, standing with spots of her blood on his clothes, and on the broken chair in his hand.

"You dirty bastard!!" he screamed in a high-pitched wail, and threw himself forward.

"Wait," Jerry mumbled, blinking, confused. "I didn't—"

But Billy's weight hit him full on the chest. Jerry felt the air go out of him. He had a dim sensation of warm sheets cascading up around his head. He realized that the sounds from far away were Billy's fists thudding into his chest, his face, his groin, and that Carlotta, rolling clumsily, had slipped slowly from the far edge of the bed. And her moaning had stopped. She sat, holding her head, drifting farther and farther toward the floor, growing more and more silent.

"For Christ's—Billy!"

But his face was battered, nose flowing with blood onto his robe. Blindly, he lashed out with his huge fist and heard something crack in Billy's face. Billy crashed backward against the night table, and the ashtray and clock flew back and shattered into the wall.

Jerry turned, crawled forward, crying. Carlotta was sinking into a pool of her own blood.

"Killer!" Billy cried, and brought the lamp down as hard as he could. It missed Jerry's head, struck the left shoulder instead. Jerry covered his head, wanted to get up, flee, bring Carlotta back to life. He wanted to be dead, wanted to wake from this nightmare. But his feet were entangled in the sheets. And the lamp crashed again on his shoulder, the base cracked, and bits of enamel showered onto the bed.

Suddenly there was a sharp slap.

"Jesus!" Jerry said, tears and blood both streaming from his face. The fractured chair had somehow fallen behind the night table. Billy was trying to cover his face from a blow. A policeman was at the door. Who was screaming? Jerry fought to stave off unconsciousness. The girls—her daughters—in pajamas—and an old lady—

"Carlotta!" Jerry yelled.

A policeman was feeling her pulse. Someone had grabbed his arm. He felt the pain as it was pressed upward, immobilizing him.

"No, no," he stammered. "Leave me alone! You don't under—"

He felt handcuffs clicked onto his wrist. He was made to sit at the edge of the bed. He saw Billy disappear with a policeman. Heard the words, "murder," and "kill," and tried to rise from the bed, but a police baton struck him in the ribs and he fell more than sat back again.

"You'll get up when I tell you to get up."

The harsh voice, the harsh light everywhere sobered Jerry. Where was Carlotta? She was gone. Only the blood remained.

"Where?"

"She's on her way to the hospital. Nice try, buddy."

"I didn't—"

"Somebody did. Now shut up. For your own good."

The second policeman read off a statement of his rights. They asked if he understood. He said, "Where's Carlotta? Is she all right?"

Finally they jerked him to his feet. They pushed him, escorted him, through the living room. Jerry could see the smashed front door. Red lights revolving outside, a crowd—

A shriveled old man in shorts and a housecoat pointed at him.

"That's the one! That's her boyfriend!"

A policeman quieted him with an outstretched hand.

"Okay, okay, we'll give you a call. Now go back home and go to bed."

Into the police car Jerry stumbled blindly, shaking off the confusion that swarmed like smoke behind his eyes. He had a dim vision of eyes peering into the window glass, looking at him like he was some kind of rare snake. Then he passed out. He thought he heard someone say that Carlotta was dead.

Dr. Weber awakened from his thoughts. He padded softly to the door in his slippers. He opened the peephole of the door and saw a face in the darkness, outlined strangely in the yellow night light. The crickets screamed, a doleful, weird sound that made the night even more ominous. Without a word, he opened the door.

"I'm sorry," Gary Sneidermann said, "but—"

Dr. Weber put a finger to his lips, gesturing that someone was asleep elsewhere in the house. They walked quickly to the study. Dr. Weber closed the huge wooden doors behind them. Sneidermann looked confused, angry, intense. His hair was uncombed, perspiration dripped from his forehead, and his eyes had a wild, direct look. Now, it was quiet, except for the flickering hiss of the fireplace. Sneidermann's face alternately glowed yellow and orange.

"What is it, Gary?"

"It's the Moran woman."

Dr. Weber gestured to a large leather chair. Sneidermann sat down awkwardly. Dr. Weber sat opposite him, feeling terribly depressed. He had lost his best resident, he thought. It was as simple as that.

"What about the Moran woman?"

"She's in the emergency ward. Unconscious."

Dr. Weber raised an eyebrow.

"What happened?"

Sneidermann looked up with a terrible, anguished expression. His eyes looked red, sleepless, and moist. "Her boyfriend came back. He cracked a chair over her head. He's booked. Attempted murder."

Dr. Weber fortified himself with a shot of brandy.

344

"That doesn't sound like the Jerry we know about."

Sneidermann swallowed. "He gave a statement to the police. Claims he saw it."

"Saw what?"

Sneidermann looked away. The flickering firelight reflected in his frightened eyes.

"I don't know—saw the same thing Carlotta always sees. He tried to knock it off and hit her instead."

Sneidermann looked back at Dr. Weber.

"How could this happen, Dr. Weber? Jerry's a stable person."

Dr. Weber shook his head sadly.

"He's suggestible, Gary. Like Billy and the girls. He picked it up from Carlotta."

Sneidermann sank back in the chair, moodily. He put his head against the back of the chair.

"I don't know if she's alive or dead," Sneidermann said, wearily.

Dr. Weber picked up the telephone and dialed a number. "Emergency? This is Dr. Weber . . . Right . . . Fred, this is Henry. When you have a diagnosis on Carlotta Moran, M-O-R-A-N, give me a call, will you? A personal friend. I'd appreciate that."

He put down the receiver. Sneidermann nodded thanks, mumbled something inaudibly. He did not know what to say now.

"He was the only contact she had with reality," Sneidermann said softly, hopelessly.

Dr. Weber looked for a cigar, found none, and poured himself another brandy. Sneidermann was wrestling with something internally. And he was losing.

"He was her only future," Sneidermann said, oblivious of Dr. Weber.

Sneidermann sat up abruptly, staring into the fireplace. For an instant the only sound was the logs spitting and hissing in the andirons.

"First thing to do, Dr. Weber, is to castrate those two."

"I told you not to get involved."

"It's life and death now. If it's not too late."

"Stay out of it."

Sneidermann turned slowly. Suddenly the cool, objective mind of his supervisor seemed abhorrent, inhuman. How was it possible to be a doctor with no feelings?

"I'm not going to stay out of it, Dr. Weber. I want those two guys out of her life."

Dr. Weber paused, the brandy glass halfway to his lips. He studied Sneidermann. Then he drained his glass quickly.

"I don't see what the hell we can do."

"Let's go to the dean," Sneidermann said, strongly.

Dr. Weber replaced the glass slowly to the oak table at his side.

"Christ, Gary—what you're suggesting is a whole month of debate. You have no idea how complicated that can get."

Sneidermann leaned forward and jabbed his finger with each word at the table, shaking the brandy in the decanter.

"You have to get through to the psychology department. Make them pull those creeps back."

Dr. Weber was angry at Sneidermann. He did not like being pushed. Least of all by a resident.

"All for this Moran woman?"

"Somebody has to look after her."

"Doesn't have to be you."

"Well, it is."

Dr. Weber finally found a cigar and lit it with a trembling hand. He snapped the lighter shut and put it back in his pocket. Sneidermann was looking at him steadily.

"All right," Dr. Weber said. "I'll take it to the dean. He owes me a favor."

Sneidermann leaned back again in the chair. He felt a flush of victory. In the warm, comfortable study, however, he began to realize how much their relationship had deteriorated. He looked at Dr. Weber. There was an im-

346

passe. They were both filled with emotion. Each strangely unable to say what he felt.

"I'm sorry it's come to this, Dr. Weber."

Dr. Weber made a vague gesture.

"Let's have a brandy, Gary. Let's not be enemies."

Dr. Weber poured from the decanter. The brandy glowed as it went down, smoothing things over. Neither spoke. The silence was complete, with only the great clock marking the passing seconds.

So Sneidermann was caught, Dr. Weber thought. So human, so utterly human. He was no machine. He studied the handsome face of his resident. Life was only beginning for him and already it had caught him.

Images rose to Dr. Weber's mind, images from the past. A fireplace, but not like this, and a room filled with strangers. It was the lobby of an international hotel in Chicago. Distinguished delegates and psychiatrists crossed over the plush carpeting, answering summonses from bell boys, and guests from Austria came through the door, shaking the snow from their shoulders. And he, not yet a doctor, but a graduate student, sitting silently, moodily, with his advisor, Dr. Bascom.

Dr. Bascom was an old man, the director of the psychiatric department at the University of Chicago. Weber was the only student permitted to attend the conference. But he had not been invited to discuss the latest news and reports of the psychiatric world. Bascom had other words for him.

Dr. Weber looked past Sneidermann, remembering that painful, half-forgotten day. Dr. Bascom had talked for several minutes before Weber had caught the drift of it. Then, understanding, he was confused. Then offended. Then ashamed. Dr. Bascom was advising him to leave school. To take a vacation. To Europe, if need be. And Weber had stared moodily into the fire, much as Sneidermann was preoccupied now, the fire glow reflecting off his face.

Thinking back, Dr. Weber's eyes grew moist. Blum-

347

berg. Bloomfeld. No. Simply Bloom. A Jewish girl. High cheekbones, like alabaster, like delicate white sculpture. The long afternoons with the girl with the translucent skin, the deep, deep black eyes, the brilliant mind so close to schizophrenia. Dr. Weber swallowed, raised his brandy to his lips.

Dr. Bascom was correct. Henry Weber was involved. Stranger than fiction. Not love, not the sentimental nothing you read about in novels. It was a fixation, a consciousness of existence in which she burned like a star and he, helpless, had become a revolving planet, circling endlessly around her. Yet he had never touched her. For nearly a year his career had slid into the bright circle of anxiety and terror with the deep black eyes, imploring him for help, closer and closer, like a moth to a flame, until the old man had discovered what had happened.

Dr. Weber blew his nose gently into his handkerchief. So beautiful a girl he had never seen, before or since. He could gladly have spent the rest of his life with her. A psychiatric patient, he mused, is a human being, but of a different order. Dr. Bascom had outlined a clear choice. Either a career in psychiatry or a lifetime with the patient. Of course, there was no choice. Two weeks later, Dr. Weber left for Europe. He stayed six months, and when he returned, discovered that she had been committed to the asylum in Wingdale, New York. Many years later, he was tempted to go see her, but—

"Rachel," Dr. Weber whispered. "That was her name."

"Excuse me, sir?" Sneidermann said.

"Pardon? Oh—nothing—a case reminded me of Carlotta."

The telephone rang.

"Yes? . . . Right. I see . . . No—I trust you. I'm sure you're right. Of course. Thank you, Fred. Very kind of you."

He hung up.

"Hairline fracture. Some splinters from the chair

embedded into the scalp. Concussion. No brain damage, no clots. Condition stable."

Sneidermann found himself unable to speak. His eyes had grown unexpectedly moist. Perhaps it was the late hour, the brandy, the fatigue of waiting for some kind of word, or just the turbulence of the night.

"Well," Sneidermann said thickly, "she's lucky."

Dr. Weber finished his brandy. He offered Sneidermann a refill, but Sneidermann shook his head.

"Thank you very much, Dr. Weber. Sincerely."

"But you won't take my advice?"

"No."

Dr. Weber saw the dark fire in Sneidermann's eyes. How very human, he thought sadly. Trapped by the heart instead of the head. A wave of sympathy flowed through his feelings for Sneidermann.

"Well, who knows," Dr. Weber said, rising. "It might be interesting. I used to be a real radical thirty years ago. It's going to be just like old times, raising hell with the deans."

20

In the hospital Carlotta opened her eyes. The white ceiling over her head wavered. Voices floated through the air. Strange lights went on and off. She thought she saw Joe Mehan leaning forward.

"Mrs. Moran," he whispered.

She moved her lips, but no words came. Mehan stepped closer, then hesitantly pulled up a chair and sat down.

"They'll only let me stay five minutes," he said softly.

Carlotta looked at him carefully. Mehan stopped wavering in front of her. He was so neatly dressed, so compact, so smart. She tried to speak, but found her tongue swollen and feeling like wool.

"Jerry," she whispered.

Mehan swallowed.

"He's at the jail," he said.

"Jerry," she said again.

Dim images, shattered memories grew sharper. Jerry floated in a green haze, raising the chair.

"Where's Jerry?"

"He's been booked," Mehan said. "Attempted murder."

Carlotta sank back on the pillow. Mehan looked deeply into her eyes. He had never seen her eyes so black, so widened in the horror of something he could only guess at.

"Mrs. Moran," he whispered. "What happened?"

Carlotta turned, looked at him with misty, black eyes.

"I need to know what happened," he softly insisted. "If it has anything to do with—"

Carlotta turned away, drifting, falling away, into sleep.

"Mrs. Moran?"

Mehan leaned forward. Carlotta's face seemed whiter than the bed sheet, whiter than the distant lights that gleamed from the consoles.

"Jerry—" She mumbled something unintelligible.

"What?" Mehan demanded.

"G—get *him* off! Help me, Jerry! Help me!"

She was sinking, sinking into sleep, into disconnected images, flashes, and imagined shouts of fright.

"Get *him* off, Jerry," she cried in a choked sob. *"He*'ll kill me."

Mehan leaned forward until he could feel the warmth of her face, see the beaded perspiration on her lip. Her eyes had that distant, vague look that meant she was slipping under.

"Who?" Mehan whispered, hesitantly, frightened. "Get who off?"

"He'll kill me. *He*'ll kill—kill—"

She was under. Her eyes remained open, staring unconsciously into a fixed image of horror. Then Mehan saw her lids flutter down, her pupils roam inward, together, until she was asleep. He stared at her, afraid to touch her, wanting to awaken her.

Mehan turned. A nurse was standing at the door.

"She's sleeping, Mr. Mehan," the nurse said. "I think we should let her."

"What? Oh, yes. Of course."

Mehan stood at the entrance to the emergency ward. She slept so deeply, so motionlessly, that her face looked like soft wax, a gentle white sculpture.

"Is there a telephone on the floor?" he asked.

"At the end of the hall."

351

Down the hall Mehan recognized a tall, quickly moving figure with a white physician's jacket. It was Sneidermann.

"There he is," Sneidermann said, to no one in particular.

Mehan did not like the way Sneidermann approached. Much too rapidly, with a strange expression on his face. Mehan fumbled for change in his pocket and hurried toward an alcove near the elevators.

"Just a second, friend," Sneidermann said.

Mehan felt his arm grabbed. He was whirled around to face two malevolent eyes.

"What the hell are you doing here?" Sneidermann said.

"I'm here to see my friend."

Sneidermann twisted Mehan's collar until it tightened. There was no one else in the alcove.

"You come here to finish the job?" Sneidermann hissed. "Is that it?"

"You're insane," Mehan whispered as best he could. "You want me to call for help?"

Sneidermann slowly relaxed his grip, staring into Mehan's eyes.

"You know you damn near killed her?" Sneidermann said hoarsely. "You and your magic boxes, your levers and wires. You confirmed a psychotic delusion!"

"I did no such thing," Mehan protested, trying to shake himself free.

"Listen, you idiot!" Sneidermann said angrily. "When a patient is suggestible you can't go feeding her anything! She'll believe you! And she'll make everybody around her believe it, too. She made her boyfriend believe it. You with your goddamn apparitions, spectral rapists—"

"Spectral what?" Mehan said, open-mouthed.

"Life is real, punk!" Sneidermann shouted, leaning so close that Mehan felt the warmth of his breath. "I'm not going to let you—"

"Spectral *what?*" Mehan whispered again, wrenching himself free and moving backward. He could see it was no use talking to the resident. The man was hysterical. Mehan had to get to the phone.

Several physicians came out of the elevator, and he took the opportunity to walk with them into the main corridor. Sneidermann, frustrated, dogged his steps.

"I'll take you to court for this," Sneidermann said.

"Go ahead."

"Your partner, too."

"Be my guest."

"And that woman witch doctor of yours."

Two nurses walked in between them. Sneidermann had to double-step to catch up to Mehan again.

"Whatever I have to do to keep you out of her life, I'll do," Sneidermann shouted.

Unaccustomed to angry confrontations, Mehan trembled slightly and hurried toward the telephone booth at the end of the corridor. He felt an odd elation, as if he were at the precipice of some startling new discovery.

Sneidermann paused as Mehan entered the booth and shut the door.

Mehan leaned over the receiver, so that his face was hidden from Sneidermann, who stood awkwardly, angrily glaring at him from the corridor entrance.

"Gene," Mehan whispered. "I'm at the hospital. She's okay, but listen—"

Mehan turned and saw Sneidermann ambling sulkily down the corridor. Then, breathless with excitement, he blurted to Kraft:

"Would you believe a spectral rapist?"

Kraft walked briskly through the hallways of the Criminal Courts Building. The sounds echoed more strangely, the farther into the massive building he walked. Then he stepped onto a huge wooden staircase and bounded up the stairs. He came out on a floor where several stocky men in suits eyed him suspiciously as he came across the tiles. It was quiet up here, dark, and an ominous sense of danger, of tension, hung palpably along the cracked walls and dingy ceiling.

353

He had been directed by the desk sergeant to Room 135 and knocked hesitantly.

"Come in," said a gruff, weary voice.

Kraft suddenly realized he would have to steel himself for this contact. He found himself surprisingly fatigued, nervous. He shook himself clear of anxieties, read the name on the door as he pushed it open—Matthew Hampton, Public Defender—and sized up the man sitting behind the desk.

Hampton was lighting a crumpled cigar. He was prematurely bald, a bit round in the stomach, and his face flat and oddly pleasant, a highly disciplined, cynical face. He eyed Kraft coolly.

"Yes?" he said softly, almost ironically.

Kraft realized he was standing in the doorway, absurdly, his hand on the knob. He closed the door behind him.

"My name is Eugene Kraft," he said, "and I—"

"Sit down, Mr. Kraft. What can I do for you?"

Hampton spoke in the detached, sympathetic tone of a man who had seen misery and violence for most of his professional life. Kraft decided to trust him, to approach Hampton briskly and precisely, the way a legal mind must work.

"You are in charge of the case of a certain party," Kraft said. "I would like to visit him tonight."

"Could be arranged," Hampton said. "Who is it?"

"Rodriguez."

"The assault?"

"Yes, sir."

"He was booked on attempted murder, Mr. Kraft. No one except family can see him. Are you family?"

Kraft crossed his legs, felt energetic, determined to crack the opposition in front of him.

"No, but it's quite important that I talk to him," Kraft said.

Hampton only raised an ironic eyebrow slightly.

"I have information that he needs," Kraft tried again. "He has information that I need."

354

Hampton reached for his lighter a second time. In the flare of the flame, his face looked old, heavy, though Hampton could not have been more than fifty. Kraft wondered whether the man had once entertained dreams of office suites on Wilshire, leather-bound chairs and legal secretaries.

"Everything has to go through me," Hampton said, puffing a cloud of dense smoke into the dark air over his lamp. "You have a message, I'll give it to him."

Disconcerted, Kraft found it difficult to bring up his purpose in coming down to the station.

"Let me introduce myself more formally," Kraft said, opening his wallet. "I am a research assistant at West Coast University."

Hampton cast an eye at a personal identity card that Kraft held out for him.

"Psychology," Hampton read.

"I have been investigating the home in which the assault occurred," Kraft began nervously.

"Investigating?" Hampton said darkly.

"Not in the police sense," Kraft said quickly. "Other events have occurred."

"Such as what?"

"Are you familiar with poltergeists?"

"No. What's that, a disease?"

Kraft shifted his weight. He realized that Hampton was waiting for him to come quickly to the point, that the lawyer had a dozen cases, that the man was working long hours into the night with minimal pay.

"Objects have been moving within the house," Kraft said. "Without a human agent. Also smells. And certain clouds have been discovered, mostly at night, that dissolve and give off cold trailers of light."

"You don't say," Hampton said, studying Kraft more closely.

"Certain indications have led us to the thesis that there was more than that. On the basis of various eyewitness accounts, we were led to believe that Mrs. Moran was terrorized by something else."

355

Hampton leaned back. Darkness fell over the top half of his face, so that his eyes gleamed like two bright points of light. He was watching Kraft carefully, as if he were evaluating his stability.

"Terrorized by what?"

"That is what I need to speak to Mr. Rodriguez about."

Hampton shook his head slowly, still watching Kraft.

"Not possible."

"I need to verify—"

"Your needs are not significant, Mr. Kraft. Not here."

Kraft rested somewhat in the chair. He tried to map out a strategy, but found himself against a brick wall.

"I'm trying to *help* Mr. Rodriguez," Kraft pleaded.

Hampton gestured to a folder at the corner of his desk. On the top edge the name Rodriguez was spelled out in heavy black ink.

"Don't worry about Rodriguez. No jury in the world would put a man like that behind bars," Hampton said. "Not when his affidavit is read into the court record."

Kraft suddenly felt his mouth grow dry and his face became hot.

"Is that what that is?" Kraft said, looking at the folder on the desk top.

Hampton picked it up, opened it, and brought it around to the light. Kraft saw a blur of typewritten pages, a rough carbon with heavy dots and numbers along the sides of the page. Hampton was reading down through the copy.

"It's a clear case of insanity, Mr. Kraft," Hampton mumbled, tossing the pages across the desk.

Kraft's eyes flitted down the print and for an instant he was filled with anxiety. Rodriguez' statement read like the confused rambling of any man picked up at 3:00 A.M. with blood on his hands and shirt. Then Kraft spotted those excerpts that made his smile spread and his confidence return.

. . . and I see that . . . that her breasts, they're being pressed and squeezed, by fingers . . . only I can't see the fingers . . .

. . . Then I see her legs, ripped open, pushed open, they're pulled apart, and she starts screaming, but all the while she's holding . . . holding . . . someone . . . or something . . .

. . . suddenly I find myself standing over her with the . . . the . . . I went over there with this wooden chair and I smashed it . . . I had to get this thing off her, I had to save her.

. . . I didn't want to hurt Carlotta, but it's that thing, that thing that was on her, that was pressing her, okay, that was screwing her, fucking her.

. . . I saw something. At least I saw something that she was feeling. Something on top of her. I couldn't see it with my eyes, but there was something there, you gotta believe me, there was something there.

Kraft's head was swimming.

"Might I have a copy of this affidavit?"

Hampton retrieved the pages and shook his head slowly. "Classified until the trial."

"After that?"

"Public."

"Thank you, Mr. Hampton," Kraft said, rising. "I'm very glad that my friend's case is in your hands."

"I'll do the best I can, Mr. Kraft," Hampton said, shaking Kraft's hand in an easy, practiced manner.

Kraft stepped to the door. Beads of perspiration glistened on his forehead. He nodded awkwardly and left. Hampton stared at the door closing. Something about the young man disturbed him. Probably as crazy as Rodriguez.

Kraft mopped his brow, walking down the long corridor. The lawyer had confirmed what Mehan had whispered, frightened, over the telephone. The dimensions of the project had suddenly expanded, like walls falling

357

away, into an infinity of dangerous concepts. Worse than that, human lives were at stake.

"Spectral rape," Kraft whispered.

The blue-gray of the night had broken into long magenta streaks. Dr. Cooley served Kraft and Mehan coffee from earthenware mugs. Kraft stared out the window of Dr. Cooley's small apartment, as though in the changing of the atmosphere he could divine some sort of clue as to where to go next.

"Five different people have reported it, Dr. Cooley," Mehan said, reaching for a pastry on a plate. "We'd be closing our eyes and pretending if we just sat back, trying to get instrumented readings of the RSPK activity."

Kraft and Mehan waited for Dr. Cooley. Even for her, the silence was long. She seemed irritated, perhaps for being put on the spot. They wondered if there were external considerations she was mulling over. She stirred the cream in her coffee, looked past Kraft out the window.

"I've had cases," Dr. Cooley said, "in which women were tweaked and poked in a mischievous fashion. But nothing like this. Oh, there are cases in the literature about women as well as men being raped by spirits. The terms *incubus* and *succubus* date back a long way. But none of this, unfortunately, has been documented."

Kraft's eyes were shining again. But he modulated his voice. Dr. Cooley preferred dignity, calculation, and skepticism to unbridled excitement. Nevertheless, his voice had a quality in it, a quality of sheer exuberance.

"Spectral rape," he repeated.

The room quieted, became silent as a tomb. Dr. Cooley sighed. How much should she restrict the imagination of her students? How much did they need to find things out freely? It was a dilemma that no teacher ever escaped. Especially in a new science. Where the parameters are broken down on all sides and the frontier stretches out like an infinite landscape everywhere.

"Do either of you seriously understand what you're getting into?" she asked.

358

Kraft and Mehan looked at each other. It was a question they had not considered.

"You don't need ghosts," she said, almost absent-mindedly. "Your careers will function just as well without them."

"It's not a matter of our careers," Mehan objected.

Another long silence surrounded them. Kraft took in Dr. Cooley's small but well-appointed living room. It was the first time he had been invited. To his surprise, he saw many volumes on theater and the fine arts.

"It will be," she said, "before this is through."

Mehan shrugged.

"I just don't think that's the most important thing right now. We're on to something staggering here—something earth-shaking . . ."

"Don't be romantic," Dr. Cooley advised. "You're not invulnerable. No one else has been."

"We're very determined about this, Dr. Cooley," Kraft said. "So I think the thing is to outline how to proceed to the next point."

But Dr. Cooley was already thinking of something else. If the project expanded into areas considered outrageous by the financial and political powers of the university, her own department would attract abuse the way a lightning rod attracts lightning.

"We could do this outside the department," Mehan said softly, anticipating her thoughts.

"Maybe," Dr. Cooley said. "Maybe we could probably work out something. A post-graduate, independent study. Some technicality to keep it out of the university if we have to."

Kraft watched the morning sky turn to orange. There was something fresh about it, cool, awesome, even dangerous, as though he had arisen to watch the first primitive morning on a strange planet not yet even named.

"An external intelligence," Dr. Cooley said measuredly, firmly thrusting aside her skepticism and facing the problem squarely. "A discarnate entity."

For the next four hours, their conversation focused upon the phenomenon which abused Carlotta and which exhibited a rudimentary personality. It seemed to exist as a table or chair existed, but in a different way, the way that a thought existed, noncorporeal. What made this psychic being unique, besides its vividness, was the extraordinary energy that accompanied it. According to Jerry Rodriguez' affidavit its reality was suffused with the strength of an angry tornado.

Its source lay in two possible regions. It might lie in the intense, incredibly repressed areas of the human unconscious. That unconscious, twisted and darkened by the emotional pressures of life, could become a violent generator of dreams, hallucinations, delusions, and also project psychic entities. Dr. Cooley wrestled with the thought that, in some manner, Carlotta, possibly with psychic collusion from another, unconsciously and inadvertently projected the self-destructive, violent being that humiliated her against her conscious will.

But in the late hours, after innumerable cups of coffee, after reviewing letters and bulletins from the parapsychological centers of the United States, Canada, and West Europe, she leaned farther and farther away from that theory.

"My belief has always been," she told Kraft and Mehan several hours before dawn, "that there is a plane of existence, perhaps several planes, distinct and separate, and only one of which we, as human beings, inhabit."

"The entity, then, is independent of Mrs. Moran," Kraft said.

"It's possible."

"Then where does he come from?"

"Where do the stars come from? Where does life come from? Sooner or later, the problem of origin ends in mystery."

Mehan rubbed his bloodshot eyes. He smiled wearily and sighed.

"They've been called many things—demons, ghosts, apparitions—"

360

Dr. Cooley smiled.

"Shall we agree on a correct term?" she asked.

"Discarnate entity. I believe your definition is the most suitable. An existence—without a body—"

The sun began to clear up the eastern sky outside the windows.

"Discarnate entity," Kraft repeated softly.

It was almost as though he were speaking to it, imploring it to show itself, to entangle itself one fatal time in the hard light of scientific reality.

"How do we get at it?" Dr. Cooley said quietly.

An ominous silence now would not leave them alone. Dr. Cooley turned on the flame to heat more coffee. Kraft rubbed his eyes in confusion.

"Draw it in, somehow," he speculated. "Find a way to bring it into a controlled situation. Then examine it."

"You'll need more controls than you have at the Moran home," Dr. Cooley objected. "You'll need to control the environment—every known physical variable."

Kraft drummed his fingers on the table.

"The thing is," Dr. Cooley said, sitting down, "there is nothing in the literature to prepare you. No one has tried this before."

Mehan closed his eyes. He looked asleep. Then he spoke.

"Gene," he said, "what we have to do is design a way to control the environment of the Moran home, around Mrs. Moran, such that we can draw in the entity."

"Do you realize how much money you would need?" Dr. Cooley said softly.

Thinking about how to bring together the right kinds of equipment, the expense of such an operation brought them all simultaneously to the same brick wall.

"Well," Dr. Cooley said hesitantly, "there is the Roger Banham Foundation. We'll apply for a grant."

Kraft and Mehan stared at their professor. She would put her own neck on the block for them. Their respect for her shined from their eyes.

Kraft, Mehan, and Dr. Cooley met a second time that morning. They clustered in her office two hours before they were to meet with Dean Osborne of the graduate school. His memo had stated only that an emergency meeting with the medical school had been called to settle an administrative problem. But Dr. Cooley knew well that no meetings were scheduled for the same day that a memo was issued unless a crucial matter was at stake.

"They're going to come down very hard on us," Dr. Cooley said.

"It's that damned resident," Mehan groused. "He's behind this."

"What are we going to do?" Kraft asked.

"We'll accept as little as we have to. But it depends on them."

"What do you mean?"

"They're going to make an investigation to determine if we have done anything unprofessional. At least, that's what they should do if they want to be fair. At the worst, they will simply cancel the project."

"They can't cancel a project," Kraft said. "That's your jurisdiction."

"There would be an implied threat," Dr. Cooley said. "Either you cancel the project, or we'll cancel your whole support."

A distant bell rang. They looked at the clock. It was 10:30. They had fifteen minutes before the dean's meeting.

21

KRAFT and Mehan, both nervous, brought along with them their photographs, their charts, and their manuscripts of articles they hoped to publish in scientific journals. They tried to hone down their arguments, to be able to explain to the dean and to the Medical School the nature of their project and particularly the meaning of a discarnate entity. Instead of being on the defensive, they came around to the view that they had the best chance if they attacked.

At a round table sat Morris Halpern, M.D., dean of the medical school, Dr. Henry Weber, and Gary Sneidermann, nervously tapping his fingers on a pile of folders in front of him. Suddenly Kraft realized that Sneidermann had also prepared his case. Mehan caught it, too. This was going to be no simple presentation. Dr. Cooley had advised them to be calm, collected, and not aggressive. She did not trust the graduate school, which normally should have been on her side.

Dean Osborne was a slightly obese man who hated conflicts. He wished he were someplace else. Also, he knew Dean Halpern well. The fellow was a tough competitor, with none of the niceties one could expect in the humanities. Halpern was a power broker by comparison to Osborne. Osborne's career was based on his ability to please. Already his palms were perspiring.

"I'm sorry the chairman of the psychology department could not be here today," Osborne began. "Dr.

Gordon left word with my office that he was tied up with an inter-campus conference, and sends his apologies."

Dr. Weber figured the real reason was to avoid being plunged into an internecine battle like this one. Which left Cooley sitting all by herself, without her life raft. But Dean Osborne, he knew, was a professional pacifist, a fence-mender who had to be watched.

"We have a small matter to contend with today," Osborne said. "It involves an overlap between two departments, represented by Dr. Weber on the one hand and Dr. Cooley on the other. I suppose we should get right to the point."

He turned in the direction of Dr. Weber, who spoke in a subdued tone.

"There is a case under our jurisdiction of a woman who is suffering from hallucinations and severe anxiety. We diagnosed her as an hysterical neurotic until we observed a rapid deterioration of her defenses, and now we are agreed that the diagnosis of schizophrenia is indicated. She suffers not only from visual and auditory delusions, but her body is marked by lacerations and bruises which resulted from severe psychotic behavior. It was our strongest recommendation that she be hospitalized, when she abruptly terminated therapy."

Dr. Weber paused. He noticed that the two students opposite him, whom he had not really looked at until now, were squirming restlessly in their seats.

"The resident in charge of the case visited her at her home, and he found that the two students, indicated in your brief, Dean Osborne, had set themselves up in her home with a wide variety of devices and graphs, the purpose of which was to obtain physical measurements of the hallucinations."

Dean Halpern looked away, trying to hide his smile.

"Now, Dean Osborne," Dr. Weber said persistently, "understand precisely what we are saying. The validity of their experiment, their right to study under the supervision of their department—that is not being questioned.

364

But what happened, and this is a point on which the university must make its decision quickly, is that by feeding her delusion in this manner they have buttressed her convictions in a way that is harmful to her."

"Worse than that," Sneidermann said.

"Just a minute, Gary," Dr. Weber said.

Dr. Weber leaned forward, speaking with the authority of his medical experience, looking Osborne directly in the eyes. Osborne wavered.

"Because of these two experimenters," Dr. Weber said, "the delusion became so fixed in Mrs. Moran's mind, that it spread to her boyfriend. Last Friday he cracked her over the head, thinking he was hitting this hallucination in the dark."

Osborne swallowed.

"The university is not liable for that," Osborne said.

"That's not the point, Dean Osborne," Dr. Weber said. "She was almost killed. I don't want my patients brutalized!"

Dr. Weber leaned forward, speaking directly to Osborne.

"Fantasies *have* been supported," he stated, "by two students with no expertise whatsoever in psychiatry or even clinical psychology. I simply have to demand that some constraints be put on them."

Osborne realized that Dr. Weber was through. He stirred uncomfortably.

"Dean Halpern," he said, "anything else?"

"When a doctor has a medical responsibility for a patient, Frank, it's his responsibility to act as other doctors with similar training would do for that patient. Otherwise, he's liable for malpractice. Now, if research is being done on a patient, there must be stringent constraints. The patient has to be told, there has to be a consent form, there has to be a very specific hypothesis, there has to be a review committee—in other words, these two are not medical scientists conducting an approved experiment."

"I see," Osborne said.

"Without meaning harm, I'm sure," Halpern added for the benefit of Dr. Cooley. There was a trace of sarcasm in his voice.

"Well," Osborne said, turning to Dr. Cooley, "it's rather serious, Elizabeth. I don't see any alternatives, do you?"

Dr. Cooley felt totally trapped. Anonymity had been her shield through thirty years of psychic research. On the other hand, it was clear that they were going to be squeezed out if she did not take a stand. The undercurrent through the whole meeting was that her small division was anti-therapeutic, harmful, and now she had to defend it. She would accept the constraints on Kraft and Mehan, but she had to make sure nothing further happened to the embryonic division of parapsychology.

"It's a ticklish position, certainly, Frank," she said in a moderate voice. "But we have to understand things a little bit better. In the first place, we *do* have a consent form. We *always* obtain written permission from our subjects. In the second place, the patient had disengaged herself from therapy prior to her contact with us. We in no way stepped into an on-going doctor-patient relationship."

"She signed your form because she was sick," Sneidermann objected. "And just because she hadn't come to the clinic for a few days doesn't mean—"

"Excuse me," Dr. Cooley said. "We were told by the subject that she was all through with the doctor. She wasn't even answering the telephone when you tried to call. Isn't that correct?"

Sneidermann flushed.

"It is her legal and medical right to speak with anyone, invite anyone into her home. That was our only position. We did not offer medical advice or treatment. The form which she signed carefully defines what we were investigating. As far as we're concerned, it ought to have no impact whatever on any psychiatric treatment she was undergoing."

"But the presence of your personnel, Elizabeth,"

said Osborne, "seems to have confirmed the hallucinations from which she suffers."

Dr. Cooley hesitated. She wanted to avoid trying to defend her discipline. That was always the hole they tried to bury her in. She spoke very carefully, hoping to step around it.

"The presence of our students comforted her," she said. "She was grateful that we were interested in her problem. I might point out that the worst of the seizures, which we now understand were terrible sexual nightmares, completely stopped during that period in which we began to set up some of our equipment and investigatory grids. So I don't believe it is accurate to contend that we have aggravated the case. Certainly she seemed more self-reliant, more cheerful, even confident now in her eventual cure."

Osborne turned to Dean Halpern and Dr. Weber, both of whom looked at Dr. Cooley with respect, but with an undercurrent of distaste.

"I wonder if you could respond to that, Dr. Weber," Osborne said.

"Certainly," Dr. Weber said. "The most crucial phase for any patient is when he is faced with the loss of his symptoms. It's a very dangerous phase. Very vulnerable. No defenses. Just as we got the patient to that point, these two came along and claimed to prove that all her illusions were the real McCoy. Of course she's happy. She's hysterical. And she doesn't have to face the basic problems. At this rate, she probably never will."

Osborne turned back to Dr. Cooley. Tempers were beginning to rise. Osborne hated the prospect of violent confrontation. It was unseemly. Nasty. He hated the stirrings of emotion. He hated controversy. He was trying to keep himself out of this one.

"Aren't we side-stepping the real issue?" Kraft suddenly broke in. "Isn't it really a matter of whether or not there is more than one valid point of view?"

"What exactly do you mean?" Osborne said, blinking rapidly.

"What he means," Dr. Cooley broke in quickly, "is that if she is disintegrating from a psychiatric point of view, then she is moving toward a possible suicide or permanent psychotic breakdown. From that frame of reference, it is better for her to have her symptoms supported. Until she can gain strength. Therefore, we are helping her in the psychiatric sense."

Very clever, Sneidermann thought. Dr. Cooley was no stranger to psychiatry. Who was she? Why was an intelligent woman like that supporting such idiots?

"Frank," Dean Halpern said, "the rules of the university are very clear. If you're not a doctor or supervised resident, you can't go messing with patients. I'm all for experimentation. But it has to be confined. And the liability of the university is very well defined."

"I see," Osborne said.

"Next to the medical well-being of the patient," Dr. Weber added, "all other issues are secondary."

Osborne was convinced. It was time for him to display some leadership. He cleared his throat.

"I believe that a compromise might be worked out on the following lines, Elizabeth," Osborne said in a definitive manner. "Continue your experiments, but not with the patient in question. Certainly her medical and psychiatric therapy take priority over other considerations."

Dr. Cooley figured she had come off as well as possible, under the circumstances. She nodded.

"I accept your directive, Dean Osborne."

"Excuse me," Kraft interrupted.

Dean Osborne found himself turning in the direction of the two students at the far end of the table. It was unbecoming. The meeting was supposed to be over.

"What is it?" Osborne said impatiently.

"We are still ignoring the true issue at stake," Kraft said.

"Let us accept the recommendation," Dr. Cooley said, gathering her papers. "Dean Osborne has been very fair with us."

368

"Just a minute," Kraft said. "They're trying to sink us."

Osborne turned back to Kraft with irritation visible on his face.

"Do you feel you've been treated unfairly?" Osborne said roughly. "Are you dissatisfied with the ruling of the dean of the graduate school?"

Kraft stood up. He separated several files in front of him. He opened them slowly, one by one. Gorgeous photographs, iridescent colors exploding in the void, appeared on the table. In the silence of the group, Kraft showed one, then the other, until the visible records of indecipherable phenomena intrigued Osborne in spite of himself.

"Look! Are these *medical* phenomena?" Kraft asked.

He held up a large picture of a yellow shower of iridescent sparks.

"Is this a *psychiatric* phenomenon?" he demanded.

"What is this, show-and-tell?" Dr. Weber growled.

Kraft held up twin photographs of Carlotta. In one photograph she looked normal, nervous, and somewhat lost in the shadows by her bed. In the other a vague, luminous glow emanated from her body, softened the contours of the wall, and dissolved the edge of the bed into shimmering patterns of light.

"Delusions cannot be photographed, Dean Osborne," Kraft shouted.

Osborne felt distinctly uncomfortable. It was too late to throw them out of the conference room. Already he had lost considerable face. Now he was expected to answer the short kid with the photographs. And he was speechless.

"What the hell is this crap?" Sneidermann exploded.

Kraft thrust the photographs in front of Osborne.

"You see what we're up against, Dean Osborne?" he said. "You can show them photographs, precise measurements, instrumented recordings—nothing makes a difference! You are our only hope."

369

Osborne, flustered, extended his wrist to look at his watch. He felt hot all over.

"I really don't see——"

"Would you like to see our reliability studies?" Kraft said.

He opened a file folder and carefully extracted a massive compilation of documents. Visible among them were excellently penned graphs and charts in a meticulous handwriting and precise notational system.

"Would you like to see our documentation?" Kraft said.

Mehan pushed another fat, clean folder across the table. Kraft opened it and carefully extended a thick pile of graphs and neatly typed affidavits, each signed at the bottom with a different name, toward Osborne, who stared dumbfounded at the two students.

"Read them, Dean Osborne! First hand descriptions of the phenomena——all from reliable eye-witnesses!"

Dr. Cooley was amazed. Kraft evidently had Osborne in the palm of his hand. At least for a while. Everything was in the open now. The fat was in the fire. There was no turning back. Either they would smash her division, her career, or they would never touch her again. Then she could operate normally for the first time in fifteen years.

Kraft stood up straight, his neatly pressed shirt, tie, and jacket conformed precisely to his small but well-proportioned figure. He spoke directly at Dean Osborne, sensing there the fulcrum of the matter.

"The Moran case happens to be the most exciting state of psychic phenomena that has ever been recorded," Kraft said. "There is no wonder that conventional psychiatry has been able to do nothing for her. I repeat——absolutely nothing. If anything, *they* have interfered with *our* attempts by convincing her that these phenomena—which you can see for yourself, Dean Osborne—were really products of her imagination." Kraft swung around to Dr. Weber. "It is *you* who are creating her psychosis by making her believe she has broken from reality! By

370

telling her she is crazy when in fact she just may be experiencing aspects of reality we know very little about!"

"Thank you, Einstein," Dr. Weber snorted.

"What are you afraid of?" Kraft said, angrily.

"Me? I'm afraid you're going to have a nervous breakdown."

"No. You're afraid that you're obsolete. Admit it. Psychiatry is in a cul-de-sac. Categories of cobwebbed ideas left over from the nineteenth century. Interdisciplinary disputes. Flashy grants and pretty magazines. But nothing substantial. Not anymore. The great day of psychiatry is over. Why don't people believe in you any more? Why are there a thousand confused branches of psychiatry, all scrambling for some way to deal with the changes in the universe?"

Osborne rapped angrily on the table. But Kraft was through anyway. He was convinced he had done his best. Mehan patted him on the shoulder. Sneidermann wondered how badly they had infected Carlotta. He knew she was susceptible to scientific jargon. Ignorant of science, she had no critical weapons to combat their sophistry.

Osborne pushed back his chair, ready to get up.

"The recommendation stands, Dr. Cooley. You will receive a written memo this afternoon. I remind you it is binding."

"Thank you, Dean Osborne," Dr. Cooley said. "You have been very fair. We accept the recommendation."

Kraft was furious. There was no way to influence a mind like Osborne's. He was a slave to the university, under the thumb of Halpern and Dr. Weber.

As they left, Dr. Weber loosened his tie.

"Christ, what a bunch of flaming bananas," he muttered.

Jerry Rodriguez held his head. In the confused, predawn shadows of the cell he did not know if he were sane or insane. His arms were sore, his chest ached, and his brain was buzzing. Each time he called out silently to

371

Carlotta, he saw something monstrous, glowing. Jerry moaned and turned his head to the wall.

He loved her. But what was she? What was this power she had to make him see things? This power that made her convulse as though—Jerry shuddered. Jealousy shot through his side like a wall of fire. What was this power that made her moan? The way he had never been able to make her moan?

"Oh, Christ, oh, sweet Christ," he murmured.

The sounds of the cells made him start. Where was he? What kind of animal had he turned into that he was in a cage? He ran to the bars, rattled them, and yelled. He saw a sergeant poke his head around the corner. Frightened, Jerry retreated back to the cot.

He felt as though his mind had been violated. It was on fire. It had been assaulted by a spectral nightmare, playing footloose with his sanity. He could not shake it. He knew his mind would never be the same. How could Carlotta have done this to him?

He tried to close his eyes. A thousand angry moans echoed in the chamber. He saw her, thrashing in the ecstasy of the invisible—*in the invisible!* He opened his eyes. Perspiration dampened his hair. He ran his hands down his face, trying to squeeze wakefulness into it. It was no use. What had he seen? What had he seen?

He must have picked it up from her. Those things happened. You became suggestible. Vulnerable. Defenseless. Love did that to you. And the insanity passed into you, too. And there was nothing, Jerry knew, worse than that.

Many years ago, he had felt it pass into him. Here, in Los Angeles, behind the bakery where his father worked.

In his memory, Jerry walked down the tough streets of his youth, through the vacant lot with the cars hoisted on blocks, past the liquor oozing from smashed bottles in the alleys, into the darkness that always filled the small wooden house where they lived. The smell of olive oil, old newspapers, beans and tortillas, the dishes that lay dirty and cracked in the sink. His sisters and their rag dolls on

372

the steps. But farther in the house was the real darkness.

Even then, Jerry knew that there were two ways to be sick. One way was to be sick like his grandfather. You coughed, shivered, threw up, and finally died. That was a very terrible thing. But there was even a worse way to be sick. And that was a shameful way. From the threshold of the bedroom, dank, smelling of CN and dust, Jerry watched his mother lie on the bed, covered in an old chenille robe, her head swathed in bandages from imaginary wounds.

His mother prayed to Jesus. To deliver them from the border guards. But the border guards were over a hundred miles to the south. And they had their papers. She spoke to her aunt. But her aunt was dead, buried in Ensenada. Jerry watched her speak. She was so animated, so friendly. She sounded so natural. So normal. Except that she was alone.

Then Jerry discovered he was vulnerable to the insanity. He knew that there were no border guards in the neighborhood. But he carefully peered out the window each day before he went to school. He knew better, but he felt a necessity, an obligation, as though the madness of his mother had transferred itself into his own brain and he *had* to do it.

And when his mother spoke to her aunt, he could almost sense her presence. Though she had died before he was born. Jerry closed the door to his mother's room and stayed outside. Even when she called him, he remained outside.

With a sudden shriek she screamed. Jerry covered his ears and remained in the yard. Even when his father ran back from the bakery next door, his hands covered with flour, Jerry stayed near the alley, afraid to enter the house. He knew that she was seeing something. Snakes. Lice. Scorpions. He didn't want to see them.

But she did not stop screaming. His father ran out of the house for help, his eyes bulging, unaware of what he was doing. He jumped into the bakery truck and drove in a panic to his friend's home. And still she screamed.

Inside the house, Jerry wandered, drawn as though by a magnet. On the kitchen table was a half-empty bottle of lye. Jerry knew it was too late. She was breathing spasmodically. The lining of her stomach was eaten through. She began to tremble the way a dog does after it accidentally eats rat poison. Stiffly, Jerry watched his mother trembling.

Jerry mopped her brow with his hand. He begged her forgiveness. But he was still afraid of her. She was the center of his existence, but she was throwing curses with her dying breath. Were they against him? Against nameless monsters of her imagination?

"Oh, Carlotta," he sighed.

He had seen her buck and heave alone in bed. Jerry was amazed at the coincidence. Two women, both the center of his existence. Both insane. Did he have some inner compulsion to be pulled into this hallucinatory state?

Jerry slumped down on the bench. The moon had gone behind the city hall. It was dark in the cell. He knew his existence was at stake. He wondered where he was going to find the strength to cut himself loose from Carlotta. Yet he knew, for the sake of his own sanity, he had to do it.

Eight days after she had been admitted into the hospital, Carlotta was discharged. She was driven to the house on Kentner Street by Billy. It was a slow, silent, funereal ride, punctuated by occasional stops to add water to the radiator, which still leaked. For both of them it was a journey back to hopelessness.

Entering the living room, Carlotta was shocked to find that Kraft and Mehan were not there. No students were there. And no equipment. Everything had been dismantled and taken away.

Carlotta looked at Billy. His eyes were downcast, sheepish. He had not been able to prepare her. Now he said, simply: "They're gone, Mom."

Carlotta shook her head vaguely. She could not

figure it out. She was frightened. They had promised to help. Why had they deserted her? If they ran out of money, they should have told her. She would have understood.

Her hair, shaved in a few patches, was covered with a bandana. A dull pain still throbbed behind her temples.

"You look white," Billy said.

"I feel dizzy."

Carlotta sat down on the couch.

"You better lie down," Billy advised.

"Let me go to bed," she said softly.

Carlotta undressed and slipped under the covers. The dizzy spells came back, as they did from time to time, ever since she had been struck over the right side of the head. Nausea rolled up like a wave and then disappeared again.

"Don't go away, Bill."

"I won't, Mom. I'll never go away."

Gradually the room stopped spinning and things seemed to settle down onto the ground again.

She drifted in and out of sleep. Occasionally she would open her eyes. Once she saw the girls looking down at her. Then they went away. It grew darker. She felt herself falling. In a panic she reached out. She felt a hand hold hers. A warm hand.

"I'm here, Mom," Billy said.

She nodded, her face drenched in perspiration. Billy gently dabbed at her face with a soft cloth. She held his hand against her cheek for a while, then drifted again into sleep.

The house darkened. The crickets chirped. A melodious sound. A dull ache filled the world. Jerry was gone. The darkness was everywhere, infinite and cold. Jerry was gone. She felt cut in half, on the bottom of a huge, frozen ocean. Nothing was normal anymore. Or ever would be.

Carlotta moaned softly in her sleep. Visions of Jerry came and went. She saw him lying beside her, champagne in his hand. Then he bent over her, kissed her, his lips

375

cold and wet. She remembered pulling his bathrobe from the closet. She opened her eyes and wiped the tears from her face. In the darkness she saw that the walls and ceiling looked strange. They were covered with the peculiar cork boards. They had left them intact.

Then with a hideous chill she remembered why the cork boards were plotted all over with white crosses. It was a photographic grid to map the monster who—

There was a crackling sound.

She looked. Nothing. It was cold. The night had turned to a vacuum, a cold vacuum like outer space. It caught at her throat, turned her skin to fiery pricks of pins and needles. She dimly heard Billy in the kitchen humming softly.

Another crack.

She sat up. It sounded as though the walls were shifting.

Then a piece of corkboard ripped from the wall. A nail, suddenly released, sprang to the floor, rolled over and over, and the sound died slowly in the darkness. The corkboard bounced slowly on the edge of the bed, then slipped down to the floor, fell once or twice, and was still.

Two cracks.

She turned. A rip shot up through the corkboard on the opposite wall. Nails sprang in a cluster through the air. Fragments of cork spit out at her. The segment of wall became visible as the cork was pried away, torn away, until it bounced through the room and fell against the door.

"Ha ha ha ha ha ha!" She was enveloped by the soft, vicious laughter.

Cracks shot all over the walls. Cork disintegrated. Planes of the cork revolved like spinning constellations across the room. Nails showered down upon the floor. Bits of plaster added snow to the maelstrom. Everything floated, swam dizzily, around and around the room, settling slowly, iridescently, as the cork began to glow blue and green.

376

"Ha ha ha ha ha ha ha ha!"

They flew faster and faster, colder and colder. Carlotta lost sight of the bare plaster walls, the air was so full of soundless, flying bits of cork, nails, white tape, and pieces off her dresser. They grew more and more iridescent, until she saw swarming jewel-like pieces coagulate into a whirlpool over the bed.

"Welcome home, cunt!"

22

ON the fourth of April, Dr. Shelby Gordon, the chairman of the department of psychology, acting on a memo from Dean Osborne, removed two rooms from the division of parapsychology and transferred them to the behavioral psychology division.

"They need the space," he told Dr. Cooley. "It's the same equipment, the sinks, the outlets, the—"

Dr. Cooley was livid.

"So my laboratory has become the domain of the rat psychologists," she fumed. "Where does that leave me?"

"You can put all your equipment in your office," the chairman said. "And utilize the classrooms on a revolving basis. With other lecture classes."

"I need a lab," she said angrily.

Dr. Gordon was unusually evasive. Her old-time friend seemed embarrassed. He avoided her glance.

"This is Dean Osborne's doing, isn't it?" she asked.

He said nothing.

"After all these years, Shel, you can tell me something," she said. "It's his idea to squeeze us out, isn't it?"

"I suppose he has you on a low priority, sure."

"But I only *had* three rooms and an office."

"Well, what can I say, Elizabeth? This isn't my decision. It's the dean's cafeteria. We have to eat what he serves."

Dr. Cooley nervously lit a cigarette.

"You expect me to roll over and play dead?" she said.

"I'm not sure what you can do, Elizabeth."

"I'll go over his head."

"I advise you not to."

"Why not? I can't conduct my research the way I need to. I have a right to be heard."

The chairman turned in his swivel chair. He saw that she was dead serious.

"Elizabeth. Don't go to the academic senate. Why do you want to get involved in a circus like that?"

She paced the floor, smoking rapidly.

"Because that's what it is, a matter of academic freedom," she said. "Hell, we could be a hundred percent wrong about that house in West Los Angeles, but they didn't simply curtail the project. They went ahead and took our space away. You know as well as I do what's next."

"Get off your high horse. It's a legitimate transfer of space."

"Crap. Do you realize I'm in one of the last parapsychology divisions left in a major university? Do you know why? Because I've been very careful. I avoid frauds like the plague. I keep out of everybody's way, I make no noise. My standards for reliability would make Freud blush for shame. Well, I'm not going to be swept into the dustbin like a piece of crap, because that's what they're doing. They hate parapsychology and everything it stands for."

"Elizabeth—"

"When's the next meeting?"

"You're going to alienate the dean. That's a fatal mistake."

"I have no choice."

The chairman threw down a file folder. Papers cascaded from a neat pile onto the floor.

"Well," he said finally, "good luck. But I don't think you'll win."

379

She smiled.

"I'll win. Academic freedom is the ultimate weapon."

In a large room, bathed in the sunlight filtering through palms set in wooden boxes near the windows, the academic senate congregated. More than three hundred men and women of varying ages and racial antecedents, sporting a wide variety of dress and hair styles. The women, in the main, were carefully dressed and coiffed in the conservative mode. Some of the men sprouted a wide fringe of beard around small chins, some affected bushy outgrowths to their ears, some grew their hair down to their shoulders, and others clipped it back until the scalp was visible through the crew cut. But otherwise their manners were identical: polite, reserved, formal. A great sense of frustration and tension was masked by their restraint, and only the twitching legs, the nervous gesture at the eyebrows, the crumpled agenda bulletin in their hands revealed their inner agitation. These meetings were not looked-forward-to events in their busy university lives.

A thin, prematurely balding man stepped to the podium.

"The next speaker on the agenda, Department of Psychology, Dr. Elizabeth Cooley."

He stepped away. Several faculty members, coming in late, tried to sneak into the back row, but one of them caught his foot in a chair and made a loud noise extricating himself.

Dr. Cooley, wearing a small corsage, stepped forthrightly to the platform. Before her were elected representatives of the English Department, the Fine Arts Department, the History Department—every department in the university. Here, everyone was equal. Anyone could speak his mind. The group before her represented the last chance for her division. The regents and the chancellor would never waste a minute on her case. With dismay, she saw Kraft and Mehan enter the senate room. She hoped they would have the astuteness to remain out of this.

"Mr. President, fellow members of the senate. The issue which I wish to present before you today would not have been necessary but that it involves the most fundamental principle of our institution, and that is the right to free and independent research."

The faculty members became quiet. It was an issue which inflamed almost all of them. Some for ideological reasons. Others, because they knew that a threat to one of them was a threat to all. They had learned years ago to band together to resist attempts at dividing them, cutting them apart, and misusing the university for a thousand political or economic reasons.

"I am the director of a rather small and experimental division within the Department of Psychology," she continued. "We have been granted the right to autonomous research and publication for over ten years, and for that privilege we have been extremely grateful."

She spoke well, in a moderate, dignified fashion. She had to. Her survival was at stake.

"However," she said, "changes are being implemented which will effectively terminate our existence as an independent unit. That decision was not reached by the chairman of the department, as the rules of the university stipulate. Nor was it reached by a curriculum committee operating under its responsibilities as set forth by the graduate school. Instead, that decision was unilaterally imposed upon us by Dean Osborne of the graduate school in a memo of April fourth."

Many of the faculty did not like Dean Osborne. He did not have a Ph.D. but an Ed.D., a degree in education, which many felt was beneath the dignity of an administrator. Already Dr. Cooley could feel support swinging sympathetically to her side.

"Had there been a consensus of the department, had even the reason been explained to us, we might have accepted it. But this was not what happened. Without

381

any prior warning two of our three laboratories have been taken from us in mid-semester. We have permanently lost our classroom facilities. And there is no doubt that ultimately we are going to be eliminated as a functioning division."

Dr. Cooley paused, looked up from her notes, and saw Dr. Weber in the third row. The faculty members listened with rapt attention.

"What I am asking of the senate is a vote to request the dean of the graduate school to rescind his memo of April fourth, and return to us our facilities until the matter can be fairly heard by an impartial board of review, or until he drops the action."

There was a sympathetic murmur through the crowd.

She turned to the sea of faces ranged before her.

"I would welcome discussion at this point," she said.

A thin man from the Latin-American studies program stood up. He seemed to tremble in his right hand.

"Perhaps we should know the nature of the dispute," he said, "before we unilaterally accept Dr. Cooley's proposition. It seems to me you have to prove that it causes an ideological dispute. Otherwise, it's simply a matter of relocation of space and classrooms. We all have to contend with that."

Dr. Cooley silently cursed him. But certainly, it would have come up anyway. She took a deep breath and hoped she would be both articulate and sympathetic to the intellectual assembly.

"The area that we study is unique in all the psychological sciences in one aspect only. All branches of psychology, as you probably know, are rooted in behavioral or social sciences, which rely on physical or statistical data. The precise nature of our investigation involves psychic research," she said directly. "It is an area of study systematically excluded from the traditional areas of psychology. You will not find it in the textbooks, in

382

seminars, in government grant projects, or in any experimental program except ours."

The thin man sat down. But the damage was done. Some whispered conversations went back and forth through the rows of cafeteria chairs assembled for the occasion.

A tall woman with red hair piled high on her head stood up. She held what seemed to be a typewritten report in her hand. Dr. Cooley realized that it was the transcript of a lecture by Kraft and Mehan. How had she gotten it? Someone had orchestrated this afternoon against her. She looked at Dr. Weber, who pretended to be lighting an already-lit pipe.

"I have here a paper from the parapsychology division," the woman said. "It will give you an insight, I think, into the reasoning behind the dean's directive."

The woman raised her spectacles from a lanyard around her neck. At last Dr. Cooley recognized the woman. Her name was Henderson. She was chairman of the behavioral psychology division. Rat psychology. Of course—she wanted those two rooms. Besides, rat psychology was the most absurdly narrow discipline since science was born. Everything they did was measured, dissected, weighed, analyzed, charted, graphed, until their students resembled trained robots weighing dead mice. The woman began to read from the paper, in a low, controlled voice, pausing only slightly to let her sarcasm be recognized without being too overt about it.

"The first of the authors," the woman began, reading from the title page, "who is described as the most advanced student within the division of parapsychology, is a former electrical engineer. The second author has a degree in philosophy and is a sensitive."

"A sensitive what?" someone asked.

"A sensitive. He is, according to the article, receptive to thought transference from human agents."

"You mean a mind-reader?"

"Yes."

383

The faculty seemed restless, anxious to get on with it. From a case of academic freedom, which had stirred them to the prospect of a dignified, even heroic fight against the forces of the materialist world, the whole affair had degenerated into a fight over another of the questionable programs established as a sop to the students' mania for the occult and the exotic.

"Both authors have no degree in clinical psychology or training in any other related scientific discipline. In fact they were admitted to the graduate program simply on the basis of demonstrated interest in the subject of parapsychology."

"Hypnotized the dean," someone murmured.

The woman lowered the journal.

"Now the problem is not what Dr. Cooley has led us to believe. The controversy does not center around an ideological battle, but it centers around an experiment these two students have conducted. An experiment in which a woman suffered, as a direct result, a severe concussion and lacerations, and was treated for a possible skull fracture right here in the university clinic. Now, this woman was a registered patient of the psychiatric clinic, she was under their jurisdiction, and Dean Osborne simply exercised his option and cut the program. Dr. Cooley is raising a smoke screen. It has nothing to do with academic freedom."

Dr. Cooley stepped to the podium. This time she faced a hostile audience.

"The problem is not so simplistic as is suggested by Dr. Henderson, who by the way, will take over our laboratories once we are moved out."

Dr. Cooley cleared her throat lightly. She saw Kraft and Mehan in the back row, humiliated, depending on her as they never had before.

"If it were a matter of terminating a program, why did the dean cut out not only the funds and availability of equipment used in that particular project, but remove, in effect, *every* on-going experiment in our division, reducing us to a series of theory classes?"

384

She let the question circulate among their minds. She felt them growing more attentive once again.

"If the physical education department teaches Yoga—which it does—and someone breaks his toe during class, does the whole division get cut down to ten percent capacity? If the political science department raises the hackles of some local politician because of an experimental class in the ghetto—is the whole department shut down? Of course not. The experimental wing of any discipline is its life-blood, its youth, and its future. Whatever may happen with those experimental programs may be catastrophic, neutral, or even spectacularly successful. But the right to experiment, to conduct free and open inquiry, no matter how bizarre it may seem to the established powers of the discipline—and let me remind you, Dean Osborne's background is in education, not psychology—is the single most fundamental right we share. Without it, we are thrown into the jungle of interference, politics, pressures from economic groups. I need not tell you what that implies for the university as a whole. It is the principle that we must defend. Tomorrow some dean will unilaterally declare your course unfit and, without procedural review or explanation, cancel it. It's that simple."

Dr. Cooley paused. She had won them back. Now she needed a vote out of them before something else happened.

But Dean Halpern stood up. He held in his hand several photocopies, holding them up before the assembly.

"Before we take a vote," he said, "the senate should be aware of precisely what will happen if it approves the continuation of the program in question."

The authority of his voice had an immediate effect on the group. Most of the faculty did not recognize the dean of the medical school at first, but his name quickly circulated by whisper.

"You must judge for yourselves," he said, "whether the matter of competence is as irrelevant as Dr. Cooley is trying to persuade you. This is the proposed project plans for the remainder of the semester, entitled, 'Case 142, Discarnate Entity—Recipient of Roger Banham Foundation Grant, 1977.' "

Dr. Cooley stepped angrily to the podium.

"May I ask how you got a copy of that proposal? That was private research material, unpublished and unannounced."

"It doesn't matter how I got this," Halpern said.

"Let the senate decide if this is a fair way to treat a subdepartment," Dr. Cooley snapped back. "Let the senate think of the sanctity of private research."

Kraft and Mehan stormed in protest from the room, slamming the door loudly behind them.

"The project, funded by a private foundation associated with Wake University Department of Parapsychology," Halpern read, "will bring to the house in question holographic laser cameras designed to pick up and transfer a three-dimensional image of the discarnate entity that attacks Mrs. Moran—"

The thin, prematurely balding man, responding to Dr. Cooley's private conversation with him, stepped forward.

"Really, Dean Halpern, with all respect, there seems to be some question of propriety here. Apparently that is classified material."

Halpern turned to face the assembly.

"Why are we hiding what this project is going to do?" he asked rhetorically. "Could it be that something is involved here a little less exalted than the foundation of Western science? I assure you, what is in here will boggle your minds."

"The senate is not qualified to judge the competency of a given experimental project," Dr. Cooley retorted. "It would take hours of patient explanation, particularly to the humanities and fine arts faculty members, just to know what is involved. All that is required is a vote to Dean Osborne to refrain from any action on the division until a proper board of review convenes at the beginning of the next semester."

Dr. Weber rose slowly. He took the pipe from his mouth and addressed the assembly.

"I am in charge of the case in question," he said, "I am Dr. Henry Weber, the chairman of the resident psychiatry program. I believe that the patient is directly threatened by the presence, even one more day, of this project. Never in my life have I seen such an ill-conceived, potentially disastrous project. How can you go about measuring psychic entities in a house where there is a psychotic person? You're going to fixate her permanently. Frankly, I'd sue if I were she, and don't be surprised if someone does sue in her behalf."

An ominous silence settled on everyone. There were no holds barred any more.

"There are times," Dr. Weber continued, "when secrecy hides a multitude of evils. This is such a time. I'd like you to hear this proposal. I'd like you to listen carefully, and decide if this is the kind of research that deserves even the minutest protection of the university. Unless, of course, my dear friend, Elizabeth Cooley, objects."

He turned to face her. Of course, she was trapped.

"Let us listen with an open mind," she said. "Let us remember the advances in science which, had you mentioned them one hundred years ago, would have gotten you dismissed from academies. Let us not make the same mistake. Space travel, electromagnetic waves, nuclear energy—they were figments of diseased imaginations years ago. Faculty in the humanities do not understand how fast things happen in experimental science, nor how heavy is the resistance from established administrations. We are fighting not only the accumulated bureaucratic mentalities of government boards, university politics, and the public media. We are fighting antediluvian concepts of our disciplines, and we have only the energy and fair-mindedness of *your* active support to help us! We only want a fair chance. Let us keep our 1.4 percent of the psychology department budget, our 2.3 percent of its allotted space. Is that too much to demand? Let us keep the

387

right to inquire, to make mistakes, to fail miserably if it happens. But give us the right to exist."

She sat down in a folding chair. Someone applauded, then a few more hands joined in.

Halpern, flushed, held the paper higher.

"Thank you, Dr. Cooley. Let us hear what rights we are really talking about."

He found his place in the paper once again. He spoke loudly, clearly, maintaining eye contact with everyone, particularly those in the humanities, who, he knew, held the majority and yet shied away from the intricacies of the sciences.

"In addition to the holographic laser project," he read, "which will cost an estimated $250,000, from the private grant—the donor of the grant, by the way, is a retired tobacco grower who has maintained regular contact with his wife since 1962. Not so strange, perhaps, except that that was when she died."

Halpern tried to find his place again.

"Oh, yes. In addition to the holographic laser project, the proposal calls for a super-cooling helium apparatus, which will cost $50,000. This cooling device, utilizing suction pumps and liquid helium, is designed to freeze the psychic entity to a jellied form so that it can be preserved and studied. How it is to be moved, it doesn't say, probably in a refrigerator."

Dr. Weber guffawed.

"In addition to that," Halpern continued, "the entire house is to be shielded in a blanket of superconducting niobium and Mu-metal, I swear, I don't know what that is, so as to ward off all external electromagnetic fields and radiation which may interfere with the experiment. Let me remind you once again, ladies and gentlemen of the senate, that the patient is psychotic. In addition to all that, the proposal calls for the presence of sensitives to assist in drawing the entity through various rooms and toward the liquid helium freezing apparatus."

There was no laughter. Several members of the facul-

388

ty paled. Many were horrified. Whispers floated back and forth, and the jokes were more nervous than before.

Halpern had them in his palm.

"What would you do if someone came to you with a proposal like this," he said angrily. "You'd do the same thing Dean Osborne did. *Cut it—*"

He snapped his fingers.

"—like that."

He sat down.

The faculty was restless. They wanted to get rid of the parapsychology division. The whole thing smacked of bizarreness, of exoticism. The vote to sustain the dean's memo would be unanimous, and Dr. Cooley knew it.

A pretty young woman stood up. She was much younger than the rest. She was the student representative.

"But there is still the question of why the dean cut back the entire division. Can this be clarified?" she asked.

"Because," Halpern said, remaining seated, "this experiment is typical of the division. Who knows what else they are doing behind that wall of secrecy?"

But the student representative was not satisfied.

"I think that a compromise can be formed," she said.

Dr. Cooley looked out at the young woman. The faculty had become silent again. Compromise was a magic word. Anything to avoid hurt feelings. Besides, some members had the unpleasant idea that Dr. Cooley was not above going outside the university. This thing had to be contained.

"It seems to be the consensus," the student representative continued, "that, theoretically, experimentation ought to continue. At the same time, everyone seems to feel that the experiment, as presently constituted, is so poorly defined, so potentially dangerous to the patient, as to warrant its dismissal. Why can't the experiment be conducted under the auspices of the university?"

Halpern paled. Dr. Weber was caught, pipe suspended halfway to his mouth. He could not believe his ears.

"I don't understand," Halpern stammered.

"Set up the experiment within the confines of the medical institute, or in the Department of Psychology. That way she can be tested for *psi* powers or, whatever, and at the same time her physical and mental safety can be supervised by authorized personnel."

Dr. Cooley stepped quickly to the platform. She silently thanked the young woman. Youth had been so often her only ally.

"It would be a reasonable way to conduct inquiry," Dr. Cooley said, "and at the same time satisfy the legitimate interests of the residency program of Dr. Weber."

"I will not consent to any such experiments," Dr. Weber said, rising.

Several voices tried to persuade him otherwise.

A man with a thick black moustache stood up. His yellow tie contrasted glaringly with his white shirt.

"It is not Dr. Weber *per se* who is required to give his approval," he said. "His jurisdiction is only with the patient as she relates to the residency program. Perhaps there is another member of the psychiatry department who would be willing to vouch for the patient's safety and perhaps also for the validity of the tests."

"Not if he wants to keep his license," Dr. Weber growled.

A short man with pointed ears stood up. He was relatively young, nervous, and unaccustomed to speaking before groups.

"I might be willing to take a look at the proposal," he said. "I'm Dr. Balczynski, clinical psychiatry. I'm rather intrigued by the whole proposition."

"Balczynski," Dr. Weber groaned into Halpern's ear. "He isn't competent to tie his shoelaces."

"Then you would be willing to accept medical responsibility?"

"I believe so. I'd like to see the proposal, of course."

Dr. Cooley stepped forward.

"Certainly we can modify the experiment," she said,

"to meet any limitations which Dr. Balczynski places on it."

A relieved sensation swept through the chamber. At last they were free of the controversy.

"I move for a vote," said a voice.

"Seconded."

The thin man at the podium spoke clearly, precisely.

"The motion before us," he said, "is to issue Dean Osborne of the graduate school a binding recommendation to rescind his memo of April fourth, to the Department of Psychology, in which said department was instructed to reduce the experimental division directed by Dr. Cooley to one laboratory, and which terminated said division as a permanent class-room unit. This recommendation to remain in effect until such departmental review is held as prescribed by the rules and regulations of the graduate school."

The motion carried, 254 to 46, no abstentions.

Dr. Cooley stepped to the lectern one last time. Her face was beaming, almost illuminated from within.

"Thank you so very much," she said. "I cannot tell you the pressures we labor under. Whether or not our investigations will be fruitful is not for me to say right now. Perhaps not. But the right to continue—which you have affirmed here today—is a victory not only for us but for everyone here. Thank you all again."

She sat down again. Peace filled her mind, her heart, warming her. A victory after all these years! Now there was a precedent. Never before had she had such a rock to stand on. It was almost a dream.

Papers shuffled as the faculty turned to the next item on the agenda—a proposed strike in the cafeterias.

Dr. Weber stood and made an ostentatious exit.

"Sheep!" he muttered loudly. "Sheep! That's what you are! Sheep! Don't you realize there's reality out there?"

He stormed out the door, printed bulletins flying in a cascade from the card table near the exit.

Dr. Cooley could not concentrate on the rest of the senate meeting. She wished Kraft and Mehan were there to discuss precisely the meaning of the senate resolution. What exactly did the resolution mean, "confines of the university?" The only way to bring the experiment into the confines of the university would be to physically relocate the woman. That would not be so difficult. She would certainly be willing. But there were so many variables related to the house. Variables that influenced her psychic moods, that changed with the atmosphere, the earth's rotation, the presence of other people, especially her children. Dr. Cooley tried to map it out in her head. They had grant money. They had authorization. How, exactly, were they going to implement them?

PART FOUR
The Entity

. . . A dungeon horrible, on all sides round
As one great furnace flam'd; yet from those flames
No light, but rather darkness visible
Serv'd only to discover sights of woe,
Regions of sorrow, doleful shades, where peace
And rest can never dwell, hope never comes
That comes to all.

—Milton

23

UNDER the terms of the Roger Banham Foundation Grant, Kraft and Mehan were entitled to introduce any means of technology, so long as it met scientific standards of reliability. Under the terms of the academic senate resolution, however, no experiment was allowed within the Moran house. Therefore, the house—or those elements that were transportable—were moved into the laboratory.

The fourth floor of the psychology sciences building was earmarked for the experiment. With Dean Osborne's approval, and the university comptroller's grudging permission, the walls of what had been four separate laboratories, the divisions between individual rooms, were removed, leaving Dr. Cooley's staff with an enormous shell equipped with a plentiful supply of electric current outlets, ventilation ducts, and piping for gas, water, or oxygen. Undergraduates removed old desks, spigots, shelves, and equipment lockers, until only a hollow space remained, large enough to house several tennis courts.

Workmen climbed on ladders, supported themselves under the unusually high ceilings, and began to soundproof the entire chamber. The walls were lined with double-walled Faraday screening in conjunction with superconducting niobium shielding and Mu-metal to prevent stray electromagnetic radiation from entering the huge space.

A wide catwalk was then built overlooking the central area around all the sides, so that Kraft, Mehan, Dr. Cooley, or anyone else could walk completely around and look down at the interior, twenty feet below.

On May 6, a facsimile of the house on Kentner Street, without a roof, was erected. Kitchen, living room, bedrooms, and hallway were connected in the exact spatial relationships as before. Then Carlotta's furniture was brought in. Carpets were placed over the old floor, the furniture sagged in its accustomed places. Shoes and a few magazines lay on the floor, as though the occupants had lived there for years. It looked like a theatrical set, except that the walls were more solid.

When, on the morning of May 10, initial work was completed, and the curtain set to rise on "Case 142—Discarnate Entity," nearly a quarter of the million-dollar Roger Banham Foundation Grant had already been spent.

The final item to be installed from the house on Kentner Street was Carlotta Moran.

The night before Carlotta was to leave for her two-week stay in the prepared environment—the term mutually agreed upon by Dean Osborne and Dr. Cooley—she was paid a final visit. *He* came to her in the small motel room which the university had supplied.

She had retired early, moody and heavy-hearted. Jerry's absence hung over her like a cloud that would not go away. Still in jail, he refused to see her, refused to accept any message from her. Carlotta had written to the lawyer, explaining that she had tripped, struck her head against the chair accidentally. So far, no word from either the lawyer or Jerry. Carlotta came close to believing that

394

she did not matter to Jerry any more. And with that thought in her mind, *he* came.

No noise, only the cold. One moment the room was empty and the next *he* was there. *He* tried to activate her, stimulate her, rouse her flesh against her will to a full-blooded response. *His* odor wrapped around her like a protective sheath, an envelope of noxious, freezing cold. The mattress moved rhythmically under their combined weight. *He* became rougher, harder, trying to control her.

"Give me more."

He forced her to undulate, to buck herself back and forth, and did not care that nausea, like a mental blackness, inundated her senses. He held her doubled over, in an odd position, and fed her his lust.

"Give this to your friends."

Carlotta arrived at the university at 10:30 A.M., accompanied by Kraft, Mehan, and Dr. Cooley. At 11:15 A.M. she was ensconsed in her "home" and the vigil formally began.

Carlotta's first reaction was a dizzying sense of *déjà vu*. It *was* her home. Except, it wasn't. What seemed to be sunlight filtered through what appeared to be normal windows. The dust floated in the air. It smelled like a normal carpet, slightly worn, a presence of mildew somewhere. The doors led to all the right rooms. Billy's broken radio lay in a corner near his bed. Even Kim's rubber toy languished in the stained bathtub. Like her nightmares, it was and it wasn't.

But instead of lights peering down from the catwalks above, video monitors silently observed in the darkness. Carlotta could not see them. No one could see them, even if they knew where to look.

High above, in the darkness of a cubicle, Dr. Cooley and her team watched through a sophisticated battery of television monitors.

As much as possible, the surveillance equipment had been made automated for continuous monitoring.

Electromagnetic field detectors continuously recorded the presence of electrical, magnetic, and electrostatic fields of both AC and DC nature, throughout the structure below. Ionization monitors of a more specialized nature than those used at the Kentner Street site were installed. Electronic sensors recorded the changes in the rate of resistance of the atmosphere to the passage of electrical energy, and they analyzed the changes with respect to various ranges of frequencies.

Dr. Balczynski, as was his explicit mandate, supervised the proceedings in a delirium of wonderment and confusion.

"The last few months," Kraft explained, "we have made extraordinary detailed observations on Mrs. Moran, her children, and the house. Now that we've duplicated that site to the most minute detail, we hope to draw in the phenomenon by using Mrs. Moran."

"Exactly what is she supposed to do?" Dr. Balczynski asked suspiciously.

"Just live here," Kraft said simply.

"You mean sleep here? Everything?"

"Yes."

Dr. Balczynski's face fell. "That means I shall have to spend my nights here, too."

Kraft smiled. "I hope you will observe every night. In fact, we want you to sign an affidavit attesting to her sound mental health. For our final report."

Dr. Balczynski sighed, which seemed to indicate that he had no objections.

"I doubt you will ever prove this to anyone," he murmured, gazing up at the TV monitors.

"Why not?"

"It's so—so—if I may speak frankly—so juvenile."

Kraft's smile did not change, but his eyes instantly seemed to darken, so that Dr. Balczynski found himself staring at an almost menacing grimace.

"It would be juvenile, Dr. Balczynski, not to believe what is proved."

Dr. Balczynski smiled ambiguously. Hope seemed to wrestle with training in the physician's eyes.

"She must know she's being watched?" he said.

"Of course. We told her. But she slips into an easy familiarity with the rooms and she forgets about us. Which is exactly what we want."

"But all those cameras—such knowledge of being under continuous observation," he told Kraft, "is apt to make anyone jittery. In this case, she's liable to feel a quite justified paranoia."

"But she can't see the cameras," Kraft said. "Come, let me show them to you."

They climbed a steep metal stairway through the darkness. Dr. Balczynski found himself on a parapet, twenty feet above Carlotta, who sat reading on the overstuffed chair below.

"You see?" Kraft whispered. "She is completely unaware of us."

Dr. Balczynski waved his arms furiously. Carlotta did not look up. It was an eerie sensation, being able to observe another human being like that.

In front of a bank of cameras, Kraft faced Dr. Balczynski, smiling.

"This," Kraft said, "is a thermovision video system. It operates by way of infrared radiation. It shows the heat gradients and distribution of any object in the rooms."

Kraft adjusted several knobs. On a screen a green rectangle became visible.

"What's that?" Dr. Balczynski asked suspiciously.

"That's the refrigerator. It's cold, it gives off relatively little heat. Therefore, it looks green."

"What's that orange glow on the bottom?"

"That's where the motor is. It's warmer than the rest of the refrigerator. Therefore the color response is different."

Dr. Balczynski turned to look down. Carlotta was munching on an apple. She looked utterly composed, utterly unaware that two men were standing twenty feet over her head discussing her.

Kraft turned the camera to Carlotta. A multi-hued variation of light covering the entire spectrum flared on the screen. A ghostly, radiated image, streaked and uncertain, giving off its own light in the darkness.

"See that blue object?" Kraft said. "That's the apple."

"My God," Dr. Balczynski said. "You can see her swallow it!"

Fascinated, he watched a blue object slide into the glowing rainbow mass that was vaguely humanoid in shape. The object slowly diminished, and began to grow lighter, until it was indistinguishable from the rest of the image.

"Amazing, isn't it?" Kraft said. "Let me show you the other two cameras."

Walking further, ducking their heads under several support beams, Kraft and Dr. Balczynski reached an area in which a second battery of cameras had been installed.

"This is a low-light level color transmission," Kraft said. "Rather similar to an ordinary expensive television system, except for the electronic light amplification systems. We can use this to photograph in almost total darkness."

"That must be quite expensive," Dr. Balczynski reflected.

"Seventy-eight thousand dollars."

Kraft, pleased, pointed to the other bank of controls, from which a surprisingly small camera lens protruded.

"This is an ordinary color television camera," Kraft said, "the difference being, perhaps, that it is fully automated. Computerized, actually, providing us with miles of tape by the time this is over."

Kraft smiled pleasantly. Somehow the smile disturbed Dr. Balczynski. He wondered if he were being duped. Already, he had allowed them to go far beyond what he originally imagined. That was before he realized how much money they had to work with. There was nothing genuinely dangerous in what they had engineered. Nevertheless, Dr. Balczynski felt they had manipulated him.

"Understand, I am going to monitor you all very closely," Dr. Balczynski warned. "And I'll stop it if I have to."

"I don't think you'll have anything to worry about," Kraft said gently.

Dr. Balczynski looked down. Carlotta had stretched out on the chair for a nap. She wore a tweed skirt and a soft white blouse. Dr. Balczynski could not help but notice that she was alluring in some strange, soft way. The way her whole body seemed to invite harm, the vulnerable way she lay, exhausted and helpless. Dr. Balczynski suddenly realized she had become a kind of bait for this being—but then, since he didn't believe in its existence, he could hardly protest. He would make an ass of himself in the school of psychiatry if he did.

"Is something wrong?" Kraft asked.

"No. Nothing. Only I wish this were all over with."

That night Carlotta undressed in her "bedroom" and slipped under the sheets. The soft light of the lamp bathed her skin in a milky glow. It was deathly quiet. Dr. Balczynski had left a tranquilizer and a white cup of water on a tray. She did not need it. The next thing she knew, it was morning, the simulated sun was shining, recorded birds were chirping, and Dr. Cooley was tapping politely at the door.

"Come in," Carlotta said brightly.

"Did you sleep well?"

"Perfectly."

"No trouble?"

"I dreamed I was an infant. In a meadow of daisies. All around me the sky was blue and the rivers were singing."

"What a beautiful dream," Dr. Cooley said wistfully.

An hour later Kraft and Mehan entered the chamber.

"We would like you to keep a log of your thoughts

and impressions while you're here," Kraft said. "We've installed a digital clock in your bedroom so you can jot down the time. It's quite important to us to know all your subjective experiences."

"And your dreams," Mehan added. "That's especially important."

"It will all be confidential," Kraft said. "The log will be returned to you after the experiment. And if we publish excerpts, your name will not be used."

Mehan handed her a thick, heavy vinyl notebook. He also gave her a box of pens.

"No matter how crazy your thoughts seem, no matter how detached, even incoherent," Kraft said, "they are all of great interest to us."

"If it will help you," she said soberly.

Three days passed uneventfully.

It was arranged that Billy and his sisters stay with Cindy. They could visit Carlotta during the day, after school, but Kraft preferred to keep her as isolated as possible. He wanted her to relax, to forget where she was, to return to as normal a psychic state—for her—as possible. Nevertheless, seeing the children was Carlotta's only respite in what soon became long and tedious days, and she looked forward eagerly to their coming.

She was beginning to adjust. The place was beginning to feel like her old house. But not quite. Too new and clean, different smells and different sounds. Carlotta stretched out on the bed. She was sleepy. A peaceful, relaxed kind of drowsiness. She started to drift away. Pictures of bright flowers flooded the room.

She opened her eyes, picked up the notebook, jotted down the time. "2:34," she wrote.

Very quiet. Peaceful. Feels good. Almost like being at home before all this happened. At last, real peace. Dreamt of flowers—yellow flowers in a meadow again. Sleep will feel good.

She looked at what she had written. Garrett would have known how to put such light thoughts into words, the honey–laden words, the feeling of dropping toward a soft, wonderful future, the sensuous atmosphere of warmth and delight, the quiet mood of being alone and being protected. But she was not a poet, and the fragments of words she wrote seemed poor representatives of the mellow warmth she experienced all through her.

When Cindy came with Billy and the girls, she was asleep.

24

On the eighth day, Carlotta became extremely sensitized to sounds, as though fearful that *he* would approach. Otherwise, there was not the slightest indication of anything abnormal.

Late that morning, Joe Mehan entered the simulated environment carrying a large notebook in which he had assembled many visualizations from studies of psychic phenomena. Some were sketches by artists, others by victims, based on verbal descriptions. His aim was to pinpoint the size, shape, and general appearance of Carlotta's spectral visitor.

Mehan opened the notebook, pulled out the colorful renderings one by one.

"Do any of these look familiar?" he asked gently.

"No," Carlotta said.

"How about this one? It was a visitation reported in France. A brutal character."

"No—he's more—he's taller."

"Perhaps this one? It was reported in Patagonia."

"A little bit—yes. But not so round-faced."

Mehan pondered. He produced several more sketches. Demonic apparitions stared back at Carlotta, frightening, mad, all of them viciously demented.

"No," she said, hesitantly. "Maybe this one—no—much coarser. And the eyes are slanted."

Mehan closed the book.

"None of these resemble what you see?"

"No. None."

"Then do you mind if I make a sketch? Based upon your description."

"Of course not."

Mehan procured several sticks of charcoal and colored chalks, and also a large pad of drawing paper. He worked several hours, his wrist and arm moving nimbly over the paper.

"Like this?" he asked.

Carlotta peered behind the pad, almost against her will. She could see the image taking form. She gasped.

"That's him," she whispered. "But the eyes—are crueler."

"Like this?" Mehan asked, making a few sharp, violent lines on the page.

"Yes. And the face is more—solid—more"

"Muscular?"

Mehan raised the cheekbones with a few deft strokes of pale-blue and white chalk.

"Yes," she said, backing away from the hideous face. "That's what he looks like."

Mehan put the final sketch into his collection. He also transcribed Carlotta's verbal description. He gave his photocopies to Dr. Cooley, to Kraft, and one to Dr. Balczynski.

Dr. Balczynski sent his sketch to Dr. Weber, with a memo that nine days of the experiment were over, and that if he, Dr. Weber, saw anything that looked like the enclosed picture, he should be so kind as to telephone the parapsychology department.

Dr. Weber burst out laughing.

"Put this in Sneidermann's mail box," he told his secretary.

Sneidermann picked it up that afternoon. He unfolded the sketch, embellished with several epithets from Dr. Weber. Sneidermann found humor in neither the picture nor the comments scrawled over it. It was a frightening face. It made him almost ill, the whole idea of their "research."

403

He knocked on Dr. Weber's door.

Dr. Weber was shuffling through his afternoon mail. He had been offered the responsibility of organizing a residency program in Guatemala, and he was trying to organize the affairs at the clinic before the summer began.

"Come in, Gary," he said. "Did you get my memo?"

"Yes," Sneidermann said, soberly brandishing the sketch. "Looks like Balczynski."

Dr. Weber chuckled, signed a memorandum, and reached for a letter opener.

"You think all this—experiment stuff—is doing her harm?" Sneidermann asked.

"You really want my opinion?"

Sneidermann sat gingerly on a large black leather chair.

"Our biggest asset is that they will fail," Dr. Weber said. "When they do fail—and believe me, they always do —she will have exhausted her last refuge from reality. She will have to return to us and face the anxiety. It's as simple as that."

Sneidermann crumpled an envelope and flipped it into the wastebasket. For a while he watched the nurses go by in the courtyard outside the window. Dr. Weber finished typing a memo to the chief of the drug addiction program.

"When will that be?" Sneidermann asked.

Dr. Weber shrugged.

"There's five days left to the experiment. Add on a few days for Carlotta to realize she has no place to turn."

"Five days," Sneidermann sighed. "I get queasy at the thought of it."

"Relax."

"Suppose I went up there and looked around?"

"What did the senate resolution say?"

"It didn't prohibit anyone from visiting."

Dr. Weber gazed earnestly at Sneidermann.

"Then go up and take a look. But I don't want to hear about any trouble from you."

Sneidermann left Dr. Weber's office, crossed quickly through the courtyard, and entered the psychology wing of the complex. He took the elevator to the fifth floor.

Sneidermann bent down for a cool drink at the fountain in the corridor. He realized he was jealous. He had been jealous now for over two months. They had Carlotta and he did not. These juvenile emotions were a plague on him. He was not proud of his feelings but there they were, and he could not pretend he did not have them.

He tapped lightly at Dr. Cooley's office. A student informed him that she was on the fourth floor. Sneidermann wandered slowly, hands in his pockets, through the tiny laboratories. He observed hamsters, their backs and sides stuck with electrodes. He wondered what experiments were being conducted on the poor animals, under the guise of some "theory." He heard a bizarre bubbling sound. He turned. A fish was staring at him from a green tank. It was an exotic, ugly fish, its gills flapping streams of water over the pebbles at the bottom of the tank.

In the next room, he saw several students applying magnetic fields to their own hands. He coughed gently. They turned, surprised, cautious in the presence of an outsider.

"Where's Kraft?"

"He's on the fourth floor."

Sneidermann strolled back through the first laboratory toward the corridors. He stopped to peer at a chart, superimposed over a city map.

"Active Sites, Semi-Active Sites, Dormant Sites," read the legend. On Kentner Street was an Active Site, with Kraft's and Mehan's names penciled in by the side. Sneidermann noted that there were very few active sites anywhere on the map. No wonder they were so charged up about this one. He shook his head sadly, figuring that for every active site there must be a potential schizophrenic being denied proper psychiatric treatment.

On the fourth floor it was peculiarly dark. The overhead lights in the lobby had been replaced with dim yellow bulbs. A student looked up pleasantly from a desk which blocked access to the corridor.

"May I help you?"

"What are you? A guard?"

"We like to screen the observers."

"Well, tell them that Gary Sneidermann is here."

After a while the student returned from the inner recesses, lost in darkness, of the interior.

"Dr. Cooley would like to know the exact nature of your visit."

"Friendly observer," Sneidermann said, trying to stay unruffled.

"All right. In that case, follow me."

Sneidermann followed the student down the corridor. The light became dimmer and dimmer. Soon it was positively dark. Then Sneidermann realized how quiet it was. They turned a corner, and continued walking. The air was stuffy, as though the halls had been sealed off somewhere.

"It's like the goddam pyramids in here," Sneidermann mumbled.

The student, ignoring the remark, opened the door to the observation room. Inside were a wide variety of screens, on some of which appeared the image of Carlotta in what appeared to be her own house.

"Good afternoon, Dr. Sneidermann," Dr. Cooley said warily, extending her hand.

They shook hands.

"I'm just here on my own," he said. "Nothing official."

"I understand that. If you have any questions, please come to me. The others are very busy."

Sneidermann folded his arms. He looked around. The video monitors were on the wall, installed rather high, so that he had to look up to see them all. They were in color, probably very expensive. Then he saw Carlotta on the screens, entering the bedroom. She sat on the edge of the enormous, carved wooden bed and began to make notes in a large vinyl book. Now Mehan stepped into

406

view. Sneidermann's heart skipped a beat. His gaze shifted to another monitor focused on an area which was essentially empty, only boxes of electronic equipment. Kraft appeared in the screen, scratched his head, unaware he was being watched, and pulled several small instruments from the box. In the screen to the left, Carlotta laughed gently at something Mehan had said.

"She seems very relaxed," Sneidermann said.

"She is. She sleeps very well. No tranquilizers."

Sneidermann thought he detected a note of disappointment in Dr. Cooley's voice. He shot a glance at her, unable to read her thoughts. Then he saw, through the open door, the door to the experimental chamber, with its shining new lock. It infuriated him, somehow, and yet he had no real grounds to protest.

"What's all this?" he asked.

"Mr. Kraft engineered that assembly. We are going to install it on the rampart over the experimental quarters. It insures a level of ionization identical to what was measured at her real house."

"You're bombarding her with radiation?"

"This is science, Dr. Sneidermann, not science-fiction. Every organic cell on earth is constantly bombarded by ultraviolet rays, cosmic rays, and many other forms of energy. What we are trying to do is to shape her environment here so that it exactly matches that of her house on Kentner Street."

Sneidermann figured it made no more sense than anything else they did. Nevertheless, he had a vague impression that Dr. Cooley was hiding something.

"Why?" he asked.

"To induce the entity to appear."

Sneidermann looked at Dr. Cooley. He wondered whether the woman had ever suffered a mental collapse of her own.

"You're going to catch it?" he asked incredulously.

"To observe it. If we can."

"Suppose—to take an extreme possibility—it doesn't come?"

407

"Then it doesn't come," she said, ignoring his sarcasm. "I told you, Dr. Sneidermann. We don't invent anything here."

"I would like to speak with Carlotta," he said.

Dr. Cooley paused, sizing up the resident.

"No. We'd rather keep her in isolation."

"Only for a moment."

"I will have to be firm on this, Dr. Sneidermann."

Sneidermann looked from Dr. Cooley to the monitor screens. Carlotta was explaining something to Mehan, her arms gesturing expansively; then she smiled.

"You see?" Dr. Cooley said. "She's in excellent spirits."

Sneidermann stumbled into the dark corridor. For an instant his sense of direction was confused. Then he saw the door to the experimental chambers. He stepped up to the door. He had to confront her, to remain in contact with his feelings as he did so, to learn why she had begun to obsess him. He had to take charge of his life again.

He suddenly leaned against the door. To his surprise, it yielded. Undoubtedly, no one expected him to try to enter. No—it opened because Carlotta had opened it from the inside. She was now stepping into the corridor. It caught Sneidermann by complete surprise.

"Carlotta," he said hesitantly.

For an instant she was startled, not expecting anyone in the darkness. As her eyes adjusted, she recognized the figure before her. Then she said shyly, "Hello, Dr. Sneidermann."

Sneidermann caught a glimpse of the quarters behind her, a perfect duplication of the house he had visited once before.

"They've made a natural environment," she said, almost proudly. "To trap *him*."

"Is that what they're telling you?"

"That's what they're doing."

"Is that what you believe?"

"I want to believe it."

Her eyes sparkled in the deep shadows of the corridor. Sneidermann wanted to grab her, to force her to listen, to penetrate those walls she had let them erect around her.

"Come back to—therapy." He almost said, " . . . to me."

She smiled ruefully.

"You're like a little boy, Dr. Sneidermann. Always wanting something you can't have."

"Carlotta," he said huskily, "deep in your heart you know the difference between reality and fantasy."

"I don't know what you're talking about."

"They're frauds."

Carlotta turned angrily from him.

"You keep saying the same thing over and over," she said. "I don't even know why you bother."

"Don't you know?"

"No."

"It's because I care for you."

She laughed, crudely, surprised, but without malice.

"I care very much for you, Carlotta."

She seemed unnerved. She stepped back, tucked her blouse into her skirt more tightly, then looked at him again, confused.

"Well, you're a very strange man, Dr. Sneidermann," she said.

"I just don't want you to close yourself off," he said. "Sometimes you have to make contact, even with just one person, or else you lose touch with reality."

"I tried," she said bitterly. "And what happened? Jerry won't answer. He's as good as dead to me now."

"But not everyone is like Jerry. Sometimes you have to reach out, right through the pain, the misery—"

"What are you trying to say, Dr. Sneidermann?"

"I'm trying to say," he said, mustering the vestiges of his dignity, "that you and I can make that contact."

Carlotta was silent. Her dark eyes glistened, animallike, in the dark corridor.

"I don't want to make contact," she said.

"Do you understand what I'm saying?"

There was an impasse. Sneidermann could no longer read her face. He had lost his distance from his feelings. All he knew was that they had overmastered him in Carlotta's presence. Sneidermann had never felt so alone. In a flash he understood why Dr. Weber had learned to harden himself against human feelings in dealing with patients. The pain, the isolation of it, was unendurable.

"I appreciate your concern," she said, with a strange finality.

"All right," he said, confused. "I guess that's why I really stopped by. To make sure you knew that."

Without another word, Carlotta opened the door and entered the chamber. The heavy door swung shut, automatically locked after her. But he had caught a vision of her before it closed, a vision that was to torment him in his sleep. The outline of her figure, in the pretty blouse and skirt, alone in her make-believe world. The eyes penetrating, as helpless as they were demonic, destroying every vestige of his own independence. He knew now that, whatever happened, their destinies had mingled. He stepped stupidly, clumsily, backward, trying to find his way out of the corridor.

An hour later Sneidermann listened patiently as an overweight man explained that he could not keep himself from ordering the largest size of dessert in a restaurant. But in Sneidermann's inner eye he saw Carlotta, her figure nearly visible beneath the blouse, and her eyes, burning and black.

As he listened to the drone of the obese man's monologue, Sneidermann discovered a truth of psychiatry, one that only comes with experience. Some patients, in spite of every last bit of your discipline, will bore you, anger you, or seem downright obnoxious. Disturbed by this revelation, Sneidermann redoubled his efforts to help the man in front of him.

In his dormitory room, smoking, thinking, late at night, Sneidermann reflected that only a few months ago there had been no such thing as feelings. Psychiatry was a cool, precise discipline, a surgery of the mind. But now, he understood that no man was immune from his feelings. He realized that he had to confront the Moran case and everything it meant to him, or forever lose his own psychological independence.

Scrubbing his mind of all thought save Carlotta Moran, he tried to view her clinically and in as objective a light as possible: a not-so-young, somewhat pretty woman with three children, one nearly a man; a sick, deluded victim of her own deeply repressed transgressions and guilts, struggling to survive in a hideous nightmare of her own construction. That much was clearly evident. That much he could see and understand. But the element that constantly baffled, that resisted analysis and understanding, was himself. What the hell was he doing in the center of her distorted landscape? What weakness in him had caused him to succumb to this schizoid temptress? Among psychiatric circles it was considered a cliché. If it weren't so fraught with all the elements of a steadily building tragedy, it would be truly laughable—a black comedy with him, Sneidermann, the star performer.

A smile came to his lips as he suddenly visualized his mother's stunned face upon hearing the good news. "Hey, Ma, I'm in love with a crazy lady. No, she isn't Jewish." The smile on his face grew and grew, and soon he found himself laughing—on the edge of tears—uncontrollably.

That same afternoon, Carlotta received a call from Jerry's lawyer. She was informed that, since neither she nor Billy had pressed charges, the state had accepted her letter and ruled her injury an accident.

"Then he's free?" she whispered, biting her lip.

"Well, yes, you could say that."

"What does that mean?"

"He's been released. He's legally free. But I don't know where he is."

Carlotta held the receiver tightly. She felt she was in the middle of the worst disaster yet.

"When was he released?"

"About five days ago."

Carlotta hung up. She called his business in San Diego. She was not given any information about him, not even whether he was still working for them. Nor would they accept a message. But Carlotta knew what it meant. Jerry was afraid. He had panicked, flown, and he was gone. She could not blame him. But with his absence, now made permanent, something snapped inside of her.

She no longer believed she would get better, or that they would get rid of the brutal visitor.

Raped by psychic entity
Haunted woman studied

Exclusive — A woman was reported as having been sexually assaulted by what was described as a "green cloud" with the muscles and voice of a man.

Mrs. Carlotta Moran, an unemployed night club hostess, is said to have been frequently visited in her home by strange occurrences. On one occasion her bedroom was reportedly torn apart by an unknown force or forces looking for her. Mrs. Moran sought refuge in a friend's apartment, but was assaulted there by the same "green cloud," who was said to bear a striking resemblance to Dr. Fu Manchu. Later, when her friend returned, she found Mrs. Moran partially clad, screaming, and the apartment torn to a shambles.

West Coast University Medical Clinic confirms that Mrs. Moran has been treated for bruises, lesions, and such injuries as normally accompany rape.

Further investigation revealed that the trouble began in October, when Mrs. Moran had returned home late at night. Slipping off her clothes in the bedroom, she noticed a strange odor, then was grabbed from behind and forcibly raped. She saw no assailant, nor was there anyone in the room when she freed herself from his grasp. The windows were locked from the inside.

This scenario was repeated during the months of November, December and January, while Mrs. Moran was under psychiatric care.

Mrs. Moran is currently being investigated by the Department of Parapsychology at West Coast University, which hopes to use Mrs. Moran in order to lure the psychic assailant into their laboratory. The Department of Parapsychology, headed by national authority Dr. Elizabeth Cooley, is currently working out details of the dangerous hunt. The project is expected to take several weeks.

Remember! — This is an AMERICAN INQUIRER, EXCLUSIVE!!!

To be continued —

In Pursuit of Higher Learning

25

Dr. Cooley let the newspaper slide into the trash.

"Oh, God in heaven," she murmured.

For the rest of the day, Kraft and Mehan looked like beaten dogs. Their anger began to mount slowly, though neither was certain exactly who had leaked the story. Dr. Balczynski denied everything.

"It was Weber," Mehan said.

Dr. Weber found Dean Osborne at the buffet lunch table in the faculty club. They stood serenely, holding their plates in hand, as the line moved slowly forward, aproned waiters dipping ladles into soups, all the sounds muffled and quiet. The palms arched over the white-covered tables, and a steady whispered conversation was heard over the soft carpets.

Dr. Weber leaned forward, smiling ironically.

"I see you made the front page today," Dr. Weber said.

"What? Oh, the *American Inquirer*."

"How's the reaction been?"

"Hectic," Osborne admitted, his face showing weariness. "Very hectic."

Dr. Weber chuckled and picked out several pieces of garnished salmon. The salad was robust, dietetic.

"Nice picture," Dr. Weber murmured.

"What? Oh, the—er—"

414

"Entity, Frank. It's called an entity."

Osborne said nothing, started to walk to a table by the window. Dr. Weber sat down opposite him, setting his tray on a nearby rack. They began sipping their soup in silence. Osborne looked disgruntled. He knew Dr. Weber was needling him.

"What about it, Frank? Doesn't this whole thing start to smell to you?"

"Oh, hell Henry. A lot of things smell to me. I can't close them all down."

"But this is—"

"You know what they were doing in the fine arts building? Growing mold on an acre of bread! Is that art, Henry? What am I supposed to do, close down the Art Department?"

Dr. Weber chuckled.

"You know what the Theater Arts Department tried last semester?" Osborne asked, vigorously buttering his bread. "They were fucking on stage. That's right. Fucking. Hell, if I'd known you could have gotten credit for that—"

Osborne drank his tea. His Adam's apple bobbed. He still looked agitated.

"Frank," Dr. Weber said gently. "This is a farce and it's a dangerous farce. You have got to show some leadership. Stop it."

"I have to follow the senate resolution."

"I simply cannot understand your obstinance, Frank."

Osborne looked back sharply, then looked down, slicing his salmon.

"Because I don't like to be pushed, Henry."

"Oh, come now."

"You've been leaning on me for three weeks now and I've had it. The kids have a right to conduct an experiment. It's no crazier than half the things that go on around here."

"But the publicity, Frank—"

"That's what I meant about being pushed, Henry. I know who leaked that to the press. Well, you hurt yourself on that one. Because I don't like these cheap shots."

Osborne began brushing crumbs from his lap.

"I don't know how that happened," Dr. Weber said with sincerity. "In any case, I see I'm licked."

"Let's not talk about it."

Dr. Weber ate, without tasting his food. He wondered where to go next. There was no place to go now.

Two days slipped by. Kraft and Mehan regularly checked the apparatus on the catwalk, from which they could see, twenty feet below, Carlotta in her duplicate house.

She seemed not to hear them working, though she was aware that monitors and scanning devices of various sorts observed her from the darkness overhead.

Kraft's supreme interest was the double-pulse holography, a laser system that could produce a three-dimensional image and, once developed, transmit it to the observation deck in the darkness. That meant that any apparition, any event, could be played over and over in its full shape and color, but miniaturized, in a tiny three-foot square area. More importantly, the double-pulsing was extremely sensitive to changes in the object being photographed, and it included not only the visible light spectrum, but reached into the ultraviolet region and the infrared region as well.

There was, however, not the slightest indication on any of the recordings being made on a 24-hour basis that there was anything in the living quarters except a woman whose patience was growing thin, and whose thoughts had begun to stray, according to her log book, and grow dark with apprehension.

In the night she woke up, saw it was dark. She mumbled, half asleep, not realizing she was at the university.

The room was so strange. It was hers and it wasn't

hers. It was a dislocated reality. She felt like she was in a dream when she was awake, and awake when she dreamt. It was a giddy sensation, like being perpetually at the top of a roller coaster, and she did not like it.

It was very quiet. The air conditioner hummed from deep inside the bowels of the building. The strange shapes and shadows of her bedroom made bizarre sculptures out of darkness. Carlotta lay on the wide, soft bed, unable to sleep.

She got out of bed, put on her slippers, and telephoned Dr. Balczynski.

"I feel all right," she said. "Only I can't sleep. Can you give me a sleeping pill?"

"I'd rather not," Dr. Balczynski said. "But I can send you a tranquilizer tonight."

"Thank you so much. I'm sorry to bother—"

"Not at all. That's my function."

Half an hour later Dr. Cooley walked in with a small cup of water and a tranquilizer. She watched Carlotta swallow the capsule.

"Would you like something to read?" Dr. Cooley asked.

"Don't laugh, but I only like to read westerns. The open range."

"Then we'll get you a western," Dr. Cooley promised.

She watched Carlotta closely. Dr. Cooley was torn between sympathy for the woman and the realization that the plan was working, that Carlotta was slipping into her previous emotional state, and that as she did so, the likelihood of *psi* activity vastly increased.

Kraft and Mehan observed the byplay on the TV screen in the dark observation room.

In that small annex they lay on cots installed under the overhanging screens. All around them, on shelves, hooks, and small metal trays, were wires, diodes, transistors, and sketches and blueprints.

After Dr. Cooley left, they watched Carlotta lie

down in bed once again. As her eyes became used to the darkness again, the tranquilizer set in. She relaxed, her mind grew weary, dulled but comfortable.

The light from some exterior point flowed in, making vague shadows on the distant wall.

She imagined strange shapes from the shadows. Rabbits. Geese. A lizard. A lizard with slanted eyes. Thick sensuous lips—coming forward—

Carlotta screamed.

"Are you all right?" asked Dr. Cooley.

Behind her were Mehan and a student Carlotta had never seen before.

"No, No—I—I . . . Where am I?"

"You're at the university. I'm Dr. Cooley."

"Oh, my God!"

Dr. Cooley sat on the edge of the bed. She felt Carlotta's forehead. It was slightly feverish.

"Would you like one of us to stay here with you?" Dr. Cooley asked.

"No. It's enough that you're nearby—I'm sorry."

From his desk in the dark observation room, Kraft watched, fascinated, as the light amplification units gave a surprisingly clear, light-bathed image of Carlotta in her bed.

For the thousandth time he meditated on the meaning of the experiment. They were actually seeking to provide first hand physical evidence of a "spirit," that is, having an objective existence in the physical world if only for a moment. All the gear, the expensive instruments, had a job to do, if and when—Kraft shifted his thoughts from the ultimate goal of their efforts. They owed it all to Dr. Cooley. To her faith and dedication. To every compromise she had ever been forced to make. To the hundreds of investigators around the world who had, in the face of ridicule, added their crumbs of data that now made this moment possible. He thought of his parents, without bitterness, who never for ten seconds believed in the worth of what he was doing.

He looked at his watch. 2:35 A.M. Mrs. Moran was

sleeping. He felt intensely curious to see the world through a different consciousness. Mrs. Moran's. For just a second. It must be so different it could not be imagined. Kraft was shot through with a strange personal feeling—jealousy. He so much wanted to see the frightening reality that Mrs. Moran perceived. It was annihilating. Obscene. Perhaps overpowering. But—

To Kraft, it was exotic. Forbidden. The last frontier known to man. He had seen lights before. Sparks. Sensations of cold. At a hundred seances. But never before a being . . . a fully formed . . . *entity*.

According to the subsequent logs of the experiment, it was in the late afternoon of the next day that the next major transition occurred.

Carlotta had finished, for the twelfth time, her lunch, brought to her from the cafeteria, when there was a knock at the door.

Cindy poked her head shyly into the room. Behind her were Billy and the girls.

"Anybody home?" Cindy laughed.

"Be it ever so humble," Carlotta said, and then picked up Kim and hugged her, carrying her into the familiar house.

Kim was confused. She did not know whether she was home or not. But nothing else in the adult world made sense either.

"They feeding you okay, Mom?" Billy asked.

Carlotta smiled. It was his way of asking how she felt.

"Everything's fine, Bill. Who wants some fudge?"

After half an hour they were sitting around the chipped table in the living room. Billy was telling an expansive tale of one of his friends who had stolen five tiles from a lumberyard and the police had made him put them back. Then there was another knock at the door.

Dr. Cooley entered.

"I'm sorry to interrupt," she said, almost in a whisper.

419

"That's all right," Carlotta said.

"There's a visitor—"

"Who?"

"It's your mother."

Carlotta felt numb. Suddenly she was very frightened.

"Mrs. Moran? I can send her away—"

"Oh, Christ!"

Carlotta looked back at the children, who by now wondered what was wrong. Cindy watched impassively, but her lips were tightened.

It was too late. Unbidden, footsteps approached down the corridor. Dr. Cooley had never seen such a strange transformation as that which traveled through Carlotta's face. A thousand ineffable sensations from fear to amazement bloomed and faded in an instant.

Carlotta's mother walked to the open door, escorted by a middle-aged woman holding her arm. Mrs. Dilworth wore a broad white hat. Under the brim the face was pink, the eyes surprisingly dark, and a mild demeanor set into that face as though into soft wax. Carlotta was thunderstruck, transfixed. Evidently the journey had been a difficult one, emotionally, for the old woman, for she seemed now to hesitate, afraid to raise her eyes to Carlotta's, afraid to take one step nearer.

Carlotta gazed at the wrinkled face, the familiar features crushed slowly by time's absolute hand, until it only faintly resembled the strong, vibrant features that Carlotta had remembered only too well.

Mrs. Dilworth looked at Carlotta, equally stunned, by the grown woman who was there, the features small but perfectly formed, the face worn by suffering.

For fully half a minute neither spoke. Cindy and the children understood, subliminally, what was happening. Dr. Cooley made a sign to Cindy, and discreetly they withdrew. Dr. Cooley wrestling with her conscience about turning on the monitors, and deciding this time not to. Julie and Kim became frightened, amazed at the silence.

"Carly . . ."

The voice was tremulous, shocked, yet intimate. She walked a step closer, with difficulty, to Carlotta, just inside the living quarters.

"Yes . . . Mother—" the word was difficult to get out—"It's been a long—"

Mrs. Dilworth reached forward instinctively to pull her daughter's face closer and kiss it, and she saw Carlotta stiffen. Carlotta recovered, presented her cheek. She felt a tiny kiss on the side of her mouth. When she looked again, her mother's eyes were moist.

"Sit down, Mother. It's warm in here."

Mrs. Dilworth sat gingerly on the edge of the couch. Her tired eyes scanned the large chamber, saw the semblance of a home and overhead, faintly visible, the gleaming of a multitude of observing instruments, all impinging on her daughter—the center of some bizarre petri dish.

"Then it's true," she murmured. "The newspaper—"

"Of course it's true."

"Oh, my God—Carly—how did it happen?"

Carlotta looked at her, angrily for an instant, then knew that the old woman was not being malicious.

"I didn't cause it," Carlotta said simply. "It just happened."

Against the wall, Billy, Julie and Kim sat or stood, as though instinct had taught them to present themselves formally to this elegant, distant person. They still did not know for certain who the elderly woman was.

"Billy, Julie, Kim . . . meet your grandmother . . ."

"Hello," Julie said stiffly.

" 'Lo," Kim echoed, uncertainly.

Billy said nothing.

"Excuse me," Mrs. Dilworth said, dabbing her eyes with a white linen handkerchief. "I didn't want to cry. I told myself I wouldn't, but . . ."

Embarrassed, her heart filled with pity, Carlotta watched her mother try to regain control.

"Julie," Mrs. Dilworth said softly. "Kim . . . Yes . . . You have Carlotta's eyes . . . so dark, so soft . . ."

The elderly woman put her handkerchief back into her purse. She looked at the girls almost objectively, though her eyes were limpid.

"Such dark, dark eyes . . . One never knows what is going on behind them . . ."

"Mother, I—"

"At least, I never did."

Carlotta suddenly perceived that everything the woman did in her life was motivated by timidity and fear. Fear of her husband, of God, of total strangers. Deep down, the old woman still did not feel that she had a right to exist. It was that whirlpool of uncertainty that Carlotta had fled, more than the cruelty, sixteen years ago.

How long had this woman suffered, first under the tyranny of her husband, and then under the tyranny of his memory? How long had she allowed herself to be sacrificed on his egocentric altar? Even now, it was plain to Carlotta, the woman was not freed and would not be freed in the short time left to her on the earth.

Julie wondered at the strange, fragmented conversation of her mother and this woman, this total stranger who knew them in some way. Was she really a grandmother? Where was all the laughter, the good cheer, like in the stories? Grandmothers were supposed to be kindly, friendly people.

"When I read the newspaper," Mrs. Dilworth said, "I had to—I only wanted to see—if I could help."

"I understand, Mother," Carlotta said, without coldness.

"I've examined myself, Carly, searched every last corner of myself, since you left—"

"Please, Mother—"

"But God gives us no signposts. None. We know the destination, but not which way to get there. Your father did not know any better than I."

Carlotta felt distinctly uncomfortable. She was afraid

the old woman was going to start talking about Pastor Dilworth, a prospect that threatened to flood them both with hideously unpleasant memories.

"Of course, Mother, I—"

"I prayed, Carly. For guidance. And there was no answer."

Carlotta softened in the enormity of that confession. God had been the cornerstone of the woman's entire adult life.

"I went to different churches, Carly. But there was no answer, only a terrible, horrible silence."

In the weakness of the old woman, her utter simplicity now, Carlotta found no room for fear, for hatred, only sympathy. The monsters who had imprisoned her, chased her, in that huge house in Pasadena—they were gone, and survived only in Carlotta's buried childhood. Carlotta felt a need to communicate with her, to bridge the gap that had cut them apart, seemingly forever.

"God forgives all, Mother," Carlotta said. "He forgave us many years ago."

Mrs. Dilworth seemed not to hear. She looked around at the strange surroundings, seeing in them some kind of proof of her own bitter failure and God's punishment.

"I regret that God did not fill our lives with purpose, Carlotta. Yours or mine. That would have made all the difference."

Carlotta smiled sadly, rose and kissed the old woman on the cheek, coming away with a scent of lilacs—the same scent she was fond of as a child. How much she had remained like her mother, Carlotta thought with amazement, in spite of everything.

"You should have believed more in yourself, Mother," Carlotta said gently. "Then it might have been easier to find God."

The nurse, nearly forgotten, coughed gently, a reminder that time was passing. How odd, Carlotta thought. Nothing truly stops in this world, no human relationship ever stands still. Even now, in only a few moments, I have changed in front of her, as she has changed in front of me.

Mrs. Dilworth gazed at the children fondly, then turned back to Carlotta.

"Might you allow them to visit their grandmother, Carly?"

In spite of herself, Carlotta hesitated. The thought of her own children in that house where she had suffered—

"It's such a large house—now it's almost empty—"

"Yes, I know . . ."

Carlotta looked at the children. It seemed as if she were approaching a deep chasm, a chasm she had shrunk back from for sixteen years. She was determined now to make the leap.

"Yes," Carlotta said simply, without turning back from her children, "it's a lovely home . . ."

"What do you say, children?" Mrs. Dilworth asked. "There's a tennis court, and croquet, and—"

"Billy, too?" Kim suddenly squeaked.

Mrs. Dilworth's face wrinkled into wreaths of smiles. "Of course. Billy, too."

It was settled. Carlotta wondered if she had cleared the abyss or had fallen into it. The more she thought about it, the less she liked the idea of her children on that estate. Yet it had seemed the only solution. There was no going back now.

Carlotta picked up Kim and held her close to the old woman.

"Kim is a curious little monster," Carlotta said smiling. "You have to watch her when she gets a crayon in her hand."

Kim found her cheek suddenly pressed by a gentle kiss, a scent of lilacs. She looked up, startled.

"Such beautiful children," Mrs. Dilworth said.

Julie returned her kiss gently, found herself embraced fervently.

"Well," Mrs. Dilworth said, winking, "that leaves you, Billy."

Billy stood stiffly, uncertain whether to retreat or advance. He found himself hugged by two thin, warm arms.

"My car is downstairs," Mrs. Dilworth whispered. "It's an old car, like me. But there's plenty of room in it."

"What kind of car is it?" Billy stammered.

Mrs. Dilworth turned to her companion. "Oh, Hattie, you tell him."

"It's a Packard touring sedan—1932," the nurse replied in a somewhat commanding tone.

"Wow!" Billy whispered.

Carlotta was so worried about the image of her children inhabiting the very rooms where she had been tormented that she found herself suddenly at the door, her children already out in the corridor. She kissed her mother lightly on the edge of her mouth. She could feel the light bones, the slight trembling in the arms. Mortality seemed to be present in the old woman's very breath.

All at once the house in Pasadena fell into reality. It was only an estate, with rose gardens and hedges. The terror was not there, in a physical place, but inside, in her own feelings, and they belonged to a little girl who might no longer exist.

She kissed her children softly goodbye.

"Isn't Mommy coming?" Kim said, as they walked slowly down the corridor, Mrs. Dilworth leaning on Carlotta's arm.

"Soon, Kim . . ." Carlotta said. "Soon, I'll come."

"God will be good to you, Carlotta," Mrs. Dilworth said. "You must not surrender your belief that you will be cured."

Carlotta turned, tears running down her face, as her entire family went into the elevator, and the doors began to close. Carlotta did not even see Julie waving.

That night, Carlotta could not sleep. She paced the room nervously. That hybrid room, so strangely like her own, so different-smelling, so alien, the way lights from distant fluorescent lamps spread through the translucent glass. Yet it was still her bed, her closet, her rug, her night table. As though everything but that nightmare had been transported into this closed-off wing of the university.

Everything is here tonight but him. *The aloneness, the being apart from the whole world, waiting, always waiting. Nothing is real. Everything has become separate from me, my own body, my children, my mother. Even my thoughts come and go as they please. Kraft is preoccupied with his electronic tests. Dr. Cooley keeps prying at me with questionnaires. Only Mehan takes the time to find out how I really feel. Doctors and scientists are always so cold, so distant. They never know what it is like to be afraid, really completely afraid.*

She stopped writing. There comes a point when it is better not to write, not to express anything, just hold it in. Because letting a little of it out only opens the door to other, deeper things, where the mind reels, flounders, like a feather falling in infinite blackness.

Then she sensed *him.*

Inexplicably, *he* was at the window. She turned. *He* was gone. She had seen nothing. Smelled nothing. It was silent. But *he* had been there, and now *he* was gone. For the moment.

She rang for Dr. Cooley.

Dr. Cooley shook herself awake. She looked up at the monitor, tuned in, and saw only Carlotta's shoulder and head at the lower half of the bed. Dr. Cooley wrapped herself in a laboratory smock and knocked at the door across the corridor.

"Mrs. Moran? Are you all right?"

Carlotta opened the door. Dr. Cooley could see at once that she had verged into a low level hysteria. It had happened so fast, within the half day that her mother had come and gone.

"Please come in," Carlotta said.

Dr. Cooley stepped inside. She noticed an odor in the house. Cooking odor, possibly. A very strange smell.

"I felt *him.*"

426

There was no need to ask who. Dr. Cooley felt the tension in the room. Perhaps it came from Carlotta. A nearly palpable, almost electric tension.

"How long ago?"

"A few minutes ago. At the window."

Dr. Cooley walked to the window. In the translucent glare, vague forms of dirt and surface bubbles stretched out like arms over the glass. She closed the draperies.

"It certainly must be difficult to sleep here," Dr. Cooley said sympathetically. "The light coming through these windows makes very strange patterns."

"I didn't see *him*. I *sensed him*."

"What did *he* want?"

"It's different now, Dr. Cooley—"

"What do you mean?"

"I'm afraid, Dr. Cooley. I'm afraid for all of us."

26

WITH less than forty-eight hours of tenure remaining, Dr. Cooley put in an urgent appeal to Dean Osborne's office for a one-week extension. It was submitted in memo form and personally delivered to Dean Osborne's office by Joe Mehan. One hour later she received the dean's reply—similarly formal, and on university letterhead. It stated that the fourth floor had to be vacated on schedule, to be overhauled and used for a National Science Foundation study on the effects of ultraviolet radiation on the retina of reptiles.

Somewhere in the night of May 23, Kraft dreamt that he saw blasted landscapes, twisted, forbidden tree-like forms, rolling clouds of some noxious gas—

Where had he seen those before? Those were the images Carlotta had recorded in her dream book.

"These dreams are very important," Kraft whispered to Mehan. "It shows there is a contact being made."

"Nonsense. It's just that you've become so involved."

"Maybe, but it also indicates a proximity—"

"I dream about my work all the time," Mehan said, lying back down on the cot.

Overhead, without images, the blank, silent screens of the monitors stared back.

Images of dark bird-like forms, which were not birds, floated in an unreal sky, high and far away in

Kraft's imagination. He so much wanted to see that strange, frightening world that Carlotta had seen. He almost felt it, forbidden, annihilating, but totally fascinating.

But in the night the scanning devices showed nothing. The hologram camera remained an idle statue. The tape ran endlessly, wasting miles of expensive material. Thermovision maps showed only the same living quarters, over and over, and the only change was Carlotta's form as she paced the floor, or stopped to write in the log book.

Time rushes like a wind. At one moment we are young, afraid of the dark, and then we are grown up, and the darkness is still with us. No adult comes to tell us it will be all right. No adult can soothe us with half-truths and stories. And yet, do we ever truly leave this darkness? Are we ever truly free?

As Kraft fell back into sleep, the lasers pointed at empty walls, empty halls, empty rooms. The ion concentration of the rooms was remarkably stable. There was no change anywhere.

But Carlotta gazed at the clock.

12:43 A.M.

Tonight he is back. How is it that no one else knows it? They run around making their tests as though everything were normal. Maybe the doctor was right—I am insane. Yet how could that be, since others have also felt his power?

Carlotta's mind began to fill with strange images, first of Pasadena, of the estate, and then it transformed as she began to dream, into a stranger landscape, a landscape she had never visited, blasted and twisted as though by some cataclysm of long ago, and it was bleak, unbearably frightening.

429

The day passed. Everyone felt a kind of charged anticipation in the air. Though everything they did was the same routine.

"I felt *him* last night, Mr. Kraft," she finally whispered, late in the afternoon.

"Yes, I know," Kraft said. "Dr. Cooley told me."

"*He* was outside."

"Outside? You mean, in the air? Outside the building?"

"No—outside, outside the world. *He* wants to come into the world where I am. *He* wants to destroy us all."

"You don't think *he* could be contained by anything we do?"

"Not anymore. *He*'s the strongest thing on earth."

Later in the evening, Dr. Cooley examined the log book. Carlotta's premonitions fit the classic symptoms of precognition.

No one slept well that night.

Then, on the morning of May 24, just before sunrise, Mehan heard a tiny beep. He opened an eye. On the monitor a red light flashed softly. Waking quickly, he walked to the screen, pressed a button, and saw only an empty bedroom.

"Please," he heard Carlotta's thin, static-ridden voice say, "come help me—Mr. Kraft—Mr. Mehan—"

Mehan padded rapidly across the corridor, pulling a laboratory coat over his pajamas. He knocked. There was no response. He heard Carlotta's voice whimpering far away inside, as though smothered. He took a key from his pocket and pushed the door open.

There was no one in the bedroom. The living room was empty. Mehan turned and went rapidly into the kitchen. It was cold. Carlotta was not there.

"Mr. Kraft—Mr. Mehan—" came her plaintive voice.

Mehan knocked at the bathroom door.

"It's me—Joe Mehan. Are you all right?"

He opened the door a crack. Carlotta was wrapped in

her red robe, huddled at the makeshift corner of the room, where the tub had been placed under the window.

"*He* came for me," she whispered.

"Just now?"

"Yes. I ran away."

"All right. Take it easy," Mehan said, wiping his lips nervously. "Let's get out of here."

They went into the observation room. Dr. Cooley, answering Kraft's call, came quickly down the corridor. Carlotta tried to explain what had happened.

"*He* threatened me—all of us—"

"Threatened?" Dr. Cooley asked.

"There was hate in *his* voice—"

"Against me? Against Gene?"

"Against everybody."

"What was *he* going to do?" Mehan asked gently.

"I don't know. *He's* afraid of being trapped by you."

Kraft and Dr. Cooley exchanged glances.

"Did you know that we had a method of trapping *him?*" Kraft asked.

"No."

"Did anybody mention that to you? A student?"

"I don't know what you're talking about."

"Because it is true," Kraft said. "We have engineered something. We are trying to work out a way so that it is not dangerous to you."

"It involves super-cooled helium," Mehan said, in a confidential whisper.

"If you try to trap *him* he'll kill you," Carlotta whispered in a low voice.

"Assume that the entity or apparition exists independent of its perceivers," Kraft lectured the class. "Then the next step is to determine the question as to whether it retains any physical properties, other than causing light transformations, aural phenomena, and tactile phenomena. In other words, has it a form? Is it composed of atoms and molecules? Does it exist of material in the way that objects or gases exist, does it exist in the form of energy the way that radio waves or light exist, or does it exist purely on the psychic plane, in which it is sensible only to the human mind, but not to scientific observation?"

The students, silent, were crowded into the small rampart over the living quarters. Down below, in a peculiarly brilliant light—the simulated morning light streaming in horizontally into the living room—Carlotta was speaking earnestly with Dr. Cooley.

"The monitors, which I have explained, will quickly analyze the electromagnetic or thermoionic properties of the entity. Assuming we can even get a piece of it," Kraft added, "the question of whether it physically has form will be answered by the equipment that Dr. Cooley is now explaining to Mrs. Moran."

A tiny light went on. Kraft had pulled open a double black door. Inside, illuminated by a small violet light, was an enormously complicated tangle of wires and copper tubing, equipped with trembling dials that read the temperature and pressure of cannisters packed and shielded in so much casing of metallic alloys that they were no longer visible.

"Whatever this entity is," Kraft continued, "the related cold spots suggest that it possesses properties similar to that of a heat sink, absorbing thermal energy in the proximity environment. Anything that consumes or absorbs heat is defined as endothermic and the most efficient and practical method of immobilizing it or rendering it inactive would be to supercool it." Kraft pointed to the dial of the assembly, and in a voice hushed with drama, said: "Liquid helium. Four hundred and fifty-eight degrees below zero. The coldest substance known to man. Except for the absolute zero of outer space itself.

"You would suffer burns and immediate loss of whatever part of you came into contact with the liquid helium. Forget about frostbite and gangrene."

The picture of an arm dropping from a shoulder, smashing into frozen crystals, flashed through their minds. Several class members edged closer to the rampart railing.

"The rationale behind using liquid helium is this," Kraft explained. "We want to put a handle on this phenomenon in any way we can. We know that by spraying any material substance with liquid helium, we will immediately bring its temperature down so low that its molecular and atomic activity will nearly cease. In which case it will be frozen."

The students seemed stunned by the implications of what Kraft was telling them. Suddenly it was becoming so real, so tangible, and not theoretical at all. It was like a door opening, a frightening door where no one could see what was on the other side.

"And if nothing happens?" a student finally asked.

"Then it suggests that the apparition is not composed of physical matter as we understand it."

"Another possibility," Mehan interjected, "is that this entity can move in and out of our spacetime framework, thereby eluding any physical attempt to restrain it."

Slowly, inexorably, the students turned their heads to look down below them. Carlotta now was looking up, not able to see them, but Dr. Cooley was pointing out various places on the rampart in the darkness above. Their conversation was very serious and intense, and Carlotta looked nervously at Dr. Cooley from time to time.

"This is incredibly dangerous," whispered a young lady. "What about Mrs. Moran?"

"The helium and a secondary liquid are both sprayed by high-intensity jets which are fixed to the outer wall below, roughly above Dr. Cooley's head. These jets will fire in only one direction—into the corner. As soon as Mrs. Moran is removed from the target area, two double-paned doors of tempered glass, with a vacuum between the panes, will slide into place, shielding her. That way she will be protected from direct and indirect effects of the spray."

"Do you really think you can maneuver the apparition into such a small area?" asked a student.

433

"Well," Kraft said. "It has a kind of intelligence. Our hope is to outwit it."

"You mean, use Mrs. Moran as bait?"

Kraft blushed.

"Yes."

Down below, Carlotta looked at the area over Dr. Cooley's head. She could not see the jets, installed into the steel ribs of the wall structure, but she retreated nervously from the area. Evidently she was mollified by Dr. Cooley's assurances, because she soon sat down again, at first jittery, and then even smiling as the two women talked.

The students watched, almost afraid to breathe. It was so quiet they could hear Carlotta talk in an undertone to Dr. Cooley.

"I'm not afraid," Carlotta said. "I'm not afraid. If you can catch the bastard, I'm not afraid."

But Dr. Cooley worried. She had never handled liquid helium before. She insisted that a test shot be made.

Inside a tiny laboratory on the fifth floor, Kraft turned off all but a single high-intensity lamp. He wheeled a cannister and its controls into place over a black, bakelite desk. Mehan, his hands and arms heavily shielded by reinforced pads, held a brass-like nozzle a foot away from his chest. Dr. Cooley placed a hamster, a red rose, and a small cloud of ammonia, steaming upward from a white chunk, into the target area.

"Let us assume that this area is the living room," Dr. Cooley said. "We will have shielded Mrs. Moran from the target area."

She nodded to Mehan and stepped back.

There was a small hiss, then a muffled roar, like the unbending of violently twisted metal. Only a thin vapor emerged, spread rapidly, dripping, expanding, then billowing suddenly into a steam-like cloud. The desk was obliterated with a freezing draft of air that pushed Kraft's hair back on his head.

434

"Jesus," he stammered. "Are you all right, Dr. Cooley?"

"I'm fine. How about you, Joe?"

"Okay, over here. Let's wait a minute for it to warm up."

"Is that thing off?" Kraft asked.

"Secured and locked."

"Put it back into its shielding," Dr. Cooley said.

Gingerly, Kraft touched the rose. He licked his fingers.

"It burns," he complained.

"Don't touch it for several more minutes," Dr. Cooley advised.

Mehan brought a pincers to the worktable. The steam was dripping a cold water down the sides of the desk, coating the hamster, frosted white, the tail rigid and curved, like a piece of white metal on the black surface.

"My God," Kraft whispered. "Frozen solid."

"Do you see here?" Dr. Cooley said. "The water in the cells burst in seconds."

"What a horrible way to die," Mehan said softly.

"No, it was anesthetized. And the death was instantaneous," Dr. Cooley said.

She reached for the flower. When she touched it, it shattered delicately, making a sound like a musical crystal. Like green and purple snow, the stem and petals fell as powder.

Mehan whistled softly.

"Notice the ammonia cloud," Dr. Cooley whispered.

"Where is it?" Mehan asked.

"It's that white rock on the desk."

Ammonia vapor rose rapidly as the temperature began to rise to normal again, noxiously, crumbling, hissing, spitting pieces of solid ammonia.

"Jesus—I've never seen it solid," Kraft said.

"Don't get near it," Mehan cautioned.

As the temperature of the chunk continued to rise, it spit more ferociously, bucked and heaved, nearly rose up

435

from the table, and vaporized into a vertically rising stream of gas.

"Phew, that stinks," Kraft said.

"The problem is this," Dr. Cooley said: "Are those glass shields really going to work fast enough to protect Mrs. Moran?"

"And is that vacuum between the panes really going to be perfect enough to keep the cold out?" Mehan added. "I don't want her hit by exploding glass."

"Then we should test out the glass," Kraft said.

They did so, that afternoon. The vacuum-separated panes held perfectly. They tested the apparatus that slid the shields into place. It worked within a second and a half. Kraft thought that was too slow. He replaced the ball bearings on the shielding apparatus, and found that the walls would slide into place within half a second. He doubted the glass shield could take the strain of being slammed into position much more often, so he tested them only once more. He figured they would only work once more and that was when the helium would be sprayed into the corner of the living room.

To aid Carlotta in remembering the position of the shields, Kraft placed red tapes along the carpet and the wall. He was secretly tormented that Carlotta would be hit by the barreling shield. The force would crush her.

But there was no reason to be worried. The laser-generated diffraction patterns were surprisingly stable. The helium cannisters were placed on a moveable dolly on the catwalk, to provide easier access in case the apparatus had to be moved suddenly. For the moment, however, the jets were loosely positioned in clamps, pointing uselessly at the living-room corner, angled down from above.

The day moved onward and nothing happened. Soon, Kraft mused, in the grip of an overwhelming despondency, they would be faced with the task of disassembly. It would be a wake—but worse.

Dr. Weber picked up the telephone and dialed. He

squinted out the window at the sunlight gleaming off the metal roofs and ducts of the medical complex.

"Graduate school? Dean Osborne, please. This is Henry Weber."

For an instant Dr. Weber tapped his fingers impatiently on the desk. Then he looked across the stacked papers to Dr. Balczynski, who sat there, tight-lipped.

"Hello, Frank. How are you?" Dr. Weber said jovially. "Fine. Just fine. Dr. Balczynski is here with me, and he informs me that they're moving in some pretty dangerous equipment up there . . . liquid helium and God only knows what else . . ."

Dr. Weber listened for several seconds. Dr. Balczynski crossed his legs, watching Dr. Weber.

"Nobody in that senate meeting really thought they were going to subject her to anything like this. It's one thing to ask questions, or roll dice down a plank, but when you take risks like that—"

Dr. Weber listened, with an expression of disgust.

"I know this is their last night, but Frank, how long does it take to kill a person?"

Dr. Weber listened, gazed heavenward, and hung up.

"Well?" Dr. Balczynski said.

Dr. Weber shrugged. "I can't figure him anymore. I think he doesn't know what to do."

"Do we really need his approval? I mean—isn't it within my authority to cancel the project?"

Dr. Weber smiled bitterly.

"You need to learn a lot about campus politics. Dean Osborne definitely has to approve."

27

At 9:30 in the evening, May 24, Carlotta was able to fall into a light sleep, the first sleep she had enjoyed in over twenty hours. Kraft watched her on the monitor screen, depressed, aware that in a few hours it would be all over.

Carlotta was visible on four separate monitor screens, tossing and turning in the bed. Needles quivered. At 9:53 Dr. Cooley noticed that a deviation had crept in between the "maintain" ion count and the ion count they had wanted to duplicate from Kentner Street. She instructed Kraft to raise the ion concentration by one half of one percent.

Fascinated, they watched in silence as Carlotta opened her eyes, sat on the edge of the bed, and jotted down several quick thoughts in the log book.

Kraft could not get the cameras to focus on the writing. Then Carlotta lay back on the bed, apparently unaware that several pairs of eyes were observing her every movement.

At 9:58 there was a crash.

Carlotta felt a draft of air. A cold stream of air. She did not even turn around. Her heart raced. She had the presence of mind to remember where she was. She knew now that they were watching. She turned slowly. There was nothing there.

How elusive he is. Like a cloud in winter. He rolls, rumbles like a cloud, but when you look, he's gone.

438

Into the air. Like the mountain stream when it melts, and it flows—flows—flows—

There was another crash. Carlotta gasped, looked up, turned around, and saw nothing.

"That dish—it flew off the ledge," Mehan whispered.

The observation room was a collage of staring eyes and perspiring faces, illuminated by flickering monitors.

Carlotta was slumped on the bed. Tiny jerks vibrated at the corner of her mouth. Quivers of exhaustion. Then she bolted upright, looked around as though surprised to find herself home again.

"She's forgotten she's at the university," Dr. Cooley said in a hushed voice.

Carlotta's body was tensed. She no longer looked up at the blackness that hid the scanning devices and cameras.

"I hope she doesn't forget about which area is safe," Kraft said. "In case we do get to use the helium."

"If she does forget, we just won't activate it," Dr. Cooley answered.

Their faces pressed closer to the monitor screens.

Carlotta seemed to smell something. Her face wrinkled up. She shivered.

"Temperature's dipped," Mehan said.

"Check the room controls," Dr. Cooley said. "Could be just our own thermostat."

Carlotta rose, explored the rooms. She peered into the bedrooms, as though looking for her children.

"They'll get you," she whispered. "If you come here tonight—"

"Why is she warning *him?*" Mehan asked.

"She may be challenging *him,* taunting *him,*" Dr. Cooley hoped.

They stared into the varied colors of the monitors, watching as a maroon Carlotta, tinged with green around the extremities, lay down and with difficulty tried to sleep. It was an eerie picture.

439

"I hope we're not underestimating this thing," Dr. Cooley said.

"What do you mean?" Kraft asked.

"I don't know—" Dr. Cooley framed her thought carefully in her mind before continuing. "It's just that we've gone to some pretty extraordinary lengths to invite a force into our world we know nothing about. I hope, if *he* should come, we don't live to be sorry."

The telephone rang. Dr. Cooley listened for a moment, then put down the receiver.

"It's Dr. Balczynski," she said. "He's on his way. With Dr. Weber."

Dr. Weber and Dr. Balczynski walked quickly up the stairways. They had attended a conference until well past 8:30, then had discussed the experiment for nearly an hour before agreeing on taking the bull by the horns and acting on their own initiative.

"I'll make you a wager, Dr. Balczynski," Dr. Weber said. "Either somebody claims to see it tonight, or else they come up with a pseudoscientific reason why nothing happened."

Dr. Balczynski frowned.

"I think you're being hard on them," he said. "They're like anyone else. They want to study the world. And leave no stone unturned."

"Some stones have a lot of worms when you turn them over. A good scientist knows when he has violated the boundaries of justifiable research."

Dr. Balczynski paused for breath as they reached the fourth floor.

"Well, it's been a very interesting few weeks."

"For you. How about Mrs. Moran?"

"She seems none the worse for it."

"Are you sure?"

"I'd wager my job on it."

"Don't be too sure you haven't."

When they got to the desk guarding the long corridor, a burly student there looked up sharply.

"Your resident has been causing trouble," the student said.

"My resident?" Dr. Weber said. "Who?"

"Sneidermann."

"He's here?"

"We can't get rid of him."

Dr. Weber tried to move forward, but was blocked by the student.

"Dr. Cooley will admit you to observe, on the sole condition that you agree to remove Sneidermann."

Dr. Weber whistled between his teeth. He turned to Dr. Balczynski.

"You see the kind of Nazis we're dealing with?" Dr. Weber whispered.

As they neared the observation room, they heard a caustic voice, quickly silenced by whispered pleas for quiet. Dr. Weber recognized Sneidermann's energetic form, pacing the floor in agitation.

"She's hysterical," Sneidermann said quickly to Dr. Weber.

Dr. Weber peered at a monitor.

Carlotta was roaming around what she thought was her house, dressed in a robe, nervously rubbing her elbow with her hand. She was frightened, as though waiting for a visitor, a sign, a sudden noise. She kept walking back and forth over an area marked off with tiny red tape.

"She certainly is high-strung," Dr. Weber agreed.

Carlotta suddenly stopped, looked around. In the darkness of the room only the bedroom light was on. It made her skin soft, but strangely colored, like pink-yellow wax.

"What's the matter—you afraid?" she suddenly said, loudly.

Kraft and Mehan jerked their heads back in surprise.

"She's talking to *him* again!" Mehan said. "She senses *him* there!"

Sneidermann leaned forward, whispering into Dr. Weber's ear.

"Let's just open the door," he hissed. "Rip it open if we have to, and get her the hell out of there."

"I don't know," Dr. Weber said, rubbing his lips nervously. "Let me talk to Dr. Cooley."

But Dr. Cooley was immersed in the final instruction to Kraft regarding the helium apparatus. Kraft was making contingency plans for climbing up onto the rampart to adjust the angle of the spray if he wanted a second shot.

"Elizabeth," Dr. Weber whispered. "How much longer is this going to go on?"

"A few more hours."

Dr. Weber checked his watch.

"She needs to sleep. I advise you to consider the medical ramifications of what you are doing."

"We've less than two hours left, Henry. Be so good as to grant me the right to continue."

Dr. Weber stepped angrily out of the observation room. He realized, in the darkness, that Sneidermann was nowhere around.

"He went to find a policeman," a student whispered.

"Oh, shit," Dr. Weber said. "I don't need all this."

Dr. Weber informed the corridor guard, who telephoned to a second monitor at the lobby close to the front doors of the building. Sneidermann was intercepted with a message. The message from Dr. Weber threatened immediate suspension from the residency training program if Sneidermann left the building.

"Is this a phony message?" Sneidermann said quickly.

"Absolutely not. Check upstairs."

Sneidermann raced into the elevator.

"You got my message?" Dr. Weber asked.

"Then you really did send it?"

"Of course, I did. We don't need a bunch of cops around here. What's gotten into you?"

"But they have to be stopped."

442

"This is a university, not South Side Chicago! You don't do things like that."

Sneidermann looked at the worn, flushed face of Dr. Weber. He knew that a line divided them, now and forever. It was true that a psychiatrist must protect himself from becoming involved with a patient. But now, common humanity required action. And if Dr. Weber was so crippled by a lifetime in the university, where politics and timidity insured survival—

"We wouldn't let her sleep in her own house alone," Sneidermann said heatedly. "Why the hell should we let her be preyed upon by these lunatics?"

"They're not lunatics, Gary. Besides, there are other considerations."

"Damn your other considerations!"

"Don't use that language with me, Gary."

"I've watched you for two months, pussy-footing around with these maniacs. And all in the name of academic relations!"

"Gary, I'm warning you!"

"Hell, that's just another name for cowardice!"

Dr. Weber glared at Sneidermann. What hurt the most was the look of disappointment in Sneidermann's eyes, as though a veil had fallen from his eyes, revealing his hero to be a tired, compromised old man. Dr. Weber swallowed nervously.

"Don't go to the police, Gary," he pleaded. "It's nothing to you, a scandal. But it's my whole career, my standing in the university."

Sneidermann glared back at Dr. Weber. Then Sneidermann said, "Are you going to stop it? Right now?"

"No. They have a right—"

Sneidermann turned on his heel and left for the exit stairway.

"Gary!" Dr. Weber called.

Dr. Weber raced to the top of the stairs.

"I'm warning you, Sneidermann!"

Dr. Weber caught a glimpse of Sneidermann going

443

down the stairwell. He felt he was sinking into a hole. He had not realized how much affection he had borne for the resident. After a moment he went to the end of the lobby and looked out the window. In the night the lights of the campus rose in odd places, pieces of bicycle parking racks, a parking lot, a night soccer game. How many years had flown by in the huge, ever-expanding complex of men and ideas. How painful all the sacrifices, the arguments, the devotion of lives.

Dr. Weber felt confused. He had never doubted the worth of it all until now. Sneidermann had pierced him with a glance, revealing to him the result of thirty years of too much security, of academic in-fighting, of isolation from the rest of the world.

Dr. Weber turned from the window. There was nothing left to do, other than go back and supervise the experiment until it was over, and make sure nothing worse happened, and then whisk Carlotta back into therapy. Probably not with Sneidermann, he thought. But the thought pained him too much to think about it anymore. When he got back into the observation room, Kraft whispered. "Look at her face. There's a fluctuation of light."

"That's just irregularities in the transmission."

"No, look! It's only in this area of the image—as though there were something just out of camera range."

Mehan peered more closely into the recorded image of the room. Carlotta was sitting in near darkness, a light glowing onto her from high overhead, waxing and waning, glistening off her smooth, black hair.

"Can't you swivel the cameras?" Dr. Balczynski asked.

"No," Kraft said, "their angle is fixed."

Carlotta backed up, crawled backward against the walls of the bedroom. She stared at a place out of camera range, over the closet doors. The thermovision scanner showed that area to be 7.5 degrees colder than room temperature.

"Now—if she would only lure it to the helium-freezing area," Kraft whispered.

Carlotta screamed.

A crackling sound flattened a needle against its peg. The microphones went dead. Kraft punched a button and the circuits were opened again.

"They'll trap you! They'll kill you!"

"She's definitely warning *him* now," Kraft said.

"Put more accurately," said Dr. Weber, standing at the door, "she is sliding into a psychotic hallucination."

"Absolutely not," Dr. Cooley protested.

"But you can see nothing, Elizabeth. Only an empty room."

"There were flashes over her head," Kraft insisted.

"That could have been anything: a stray light, an opening door—"

"It was angled down, from above, just like in her own house."

Dr. Weber was silenced. He suddenly realized he did not have the courage to demand the door be opened and Carlotta removed. He could not understand how his will had been sucked into this experiment. He watched the screens, fascinated.

In the hall, Sneidermann stepped quickly to the desk.

"I'm sorry," the student said. "Only authorized personnel."

"He's authorized by the university," said a gruff voice.

Dean Osborne stepped from behind Sneidermann, his jowls shaking with anger.

"I am Dean Osborne of the graduate school," he said slowly but clearly. "I would like to inspect your facilities."

"Yes, sir," the student gulped. "Right this way, sir."

They walked into the pitch black corridor. Dean Osborne made a face.

"What the hell is that stink?" he mumbled.

"What stink?" Sneidermann said.

"Smells like a locker of meat gone bad."

Inside the observation room it smelled of perspiration and cigarette smoke. Osborne cleared his throat.

"I believe the time has come," he said, "to end the experiment."

Dr. Cooley whirled around to see him with Sneidermann at the door.

"You can't succumb to pressure, Frank," she said. "The senate—"

"Screw the senate, Elizabeth," Osborne said. "This young man says you're torturing the woman."

"Absurd! See for yourself!"

"I'm looking—she looks in terrible shape."

Kraft whirled from his seat, his hands full of graphs and notes.

"The laser-generated diffraction patterns," he said excitedly, "they're changing! It's the presence of additional extremely low-frequency waves."

"The experiment is being suspended, young man," Osborne said with authority. "Turn off these machines and clear out of here."

"But we've got *him!* These graphs—they prove it. The low-frequency waves—as though from a living tissue—"

"You're insane!"

"Look for yourself, Dean Osborne," Mehan said.

On the monitors overhead there was an area of color hovering in front of the closet doors, settling very slowly to the floor. It radiated a translucence, glowing faintly pink, then orange, then slowly shifting toward a deep red.

"Is this a trick?" Osborne bellowed.

But no one heard him.

Carlotta stood uncertainly at the hallway. She was exhausted, terrified, her hair unkempt, damp from perspiration, staring wildly. She realized that the translucence was rolling, at a snail's pace, toward her.

"That's it," Kraft whispered. "Bring *him* into the living room!"

"Dean Osborne," Sneidermann said. "Stop this insanity now!"

446

But Osborne was transfixed by the screens. The red area seemed to have gained substance and was no longer transparent. It had rolled almost to the living room, but seemed unable to enter.

"All right," Osborne said, vacillating weakly. "Let's open the door."

At that precise moment, Carlotta screamed.

All eyes fixed on the flickering screens. The thermovision showed that the rolling mass had gotten colder and colder, approaching the freezing point. Then the monitors went blank. When they went on again, Carlotta was at the far end of the living room.

There was another flare of light. A monitor transmitted a white, blurred light.

"It's the camera!" Kraft said. "It's been shorted!"

"No! It recorded a bright flash, Gene," Mehan whispered. "That's what it was."

Carlotta stayed against the far wall of the living room, in the target area, catching her breath. She began to slump farther down against the wall, then caught herself and shook her head. Her face had the appearance of one whose reserves had been exhausted long ago.

Then it was ominously still.

"You bastard!" Carlotta screamed. "You foul stink of death!"

Carlotta huddled against the window. A globe of light, twice as big, hovered against the entrance to the hallway, coming ever so slowly into the living room.

"You bastard!" she hissed, again.

There was a low rumbling sound that shook the observation room causing tiny flecks of plaster to loosen and fall in a snow flurry.

Dean Osborne's eyes gaped in surprise. "What the hell is that? An earthquake?"

On the monitors, the light spread, as though circling for a place to find her, blindly groping. Carlotta edged toward the kitchen.

"Come!" she yelled. "Come and take me, now that I've got my army with me!"

447

"That's *him!*" Kraft whispered joyously, feverishly. "That's *him!*"

Now they all saw it—the globe of light poised slightly past the hallway entrance. It jerked, writhed under each of Carlotta's shouts, as though it understood.

"Get it into the target area," Kraft urged, breathlessly.

Sneidermann stared in amazement. She appeared to be looking directly at him and her robe had slipped so low her breast was nearly exposed. Her eyes, from lack of sleep, from insane fear, triumphant jubilation, suicidal daring, had a crazed glow—a glow Sneidermann detected as sensual desire. He watched her body as it moved sinuously along the wall, back into the living room, her back against the plaster, her legs thin but perfectly formed.

He found himself blushing, as though she were piercing his most inward thoughts with that stare, his most adolescent, most frightening self-doubts. For him, she had turned into the image of woman herself, unattainable, fearful, all-destroying, yet irresistible and alluring. His gaze was fixed on the smile that destroyed his manhood with its cynicism and bitterness.

"You little nothing," she giggled hoarsely.

Sneidermann felt himself lost in a black universe with no support anywhere.

"You nothing," she hissed. "You miserable stink!"

Kraft, agitated, knew she was much too close to activate the glass shields.

On the hologram, Mehan breathlessly watched as a miniature room, in three dimensions, made out of colored light, showed a tiny Carlotta taunting something just out of range, something that gave off a glow in the darkness.

He turned to Kraft frantically. "The hologram is missing it, Gene!"

Kraft swiveled over to a tape machine, wound the action back and replayed the scene on the tape monitor. To his dismay, it, too, failed to show the light form. He turned an anxious face to Dr. Cooley.

"Our cameras aren't seeing it, Dr. Cooley!"

But Dr. Cooley was too immersed in what was happening on the monitors, and softly urged: "Cajole it! Taunt it!"

Carlotta, oblivious of them, pushed herself flatter against the wall. The globe of light hung, motionless, like a cloud at sunrise.

For the next minute they watched the light form. It moved so slowly that it came as a small shock to realize it had begun to congeal. Extended areas were beginning to resemble the musculature of a powerful man.

"She's too close to the helium!" Kraft moaned.

"Then change the angle," Dr. Cooley whispered.

"I can't! Not from here!"

"Scream at it, Mrs. Moran!" Mehan shouted at the monitors. "Like you did before!"

Kraft turned to Dr. Cooley.

"I'm going in there," he said. "I'm going to move that helium nozzle."

"Yes," she said. "Yes!"

Kraft left the observation room and fumbled through the darkness of the corridor. His hand grabbed the doorknob of the experimental chamber. The handle turned. Suddenly he was paralyzed with fear. There was the sound of grating metal.

Kraft opened the door, slipped inside, and ran up onto the catwalk. He slipped down to the roller bars under the cannister and began freeing them. Then he heard the door below slam shut. He began to tremble so hard that his fingers were slipping all over the metal pieces. He was scared. In spite of everything, he was forced to look down.

Carlotta screamed at the globe against the wall. With each vile epithet, it jerked back, as though physically wounded, but nevertheless unmistakable arm-forms had congealed from the mass, and now shoulders were beginning to emerge.

In a daze, Kraft jerked at the cannisters and slid them down the rail. He leaned dangerously far over the rampart and began to free the jet nozzle from its clamp.

"Come on, you bastard!" Carlotta yelled. "Show your ugly face! Or are you afraid? Now that I've got my army!"

The form bucked and heaved, like a gesticulating minister caught up in his sermon, declaiming to an indifferent world . . . Carlotta laughed.

"Foul prick! Coward!"

She did not see Kraft above, did not see the nozzle swinging around toward her.

The interior striations of the light form turned over, in a myriad of subtle colors, Kraft could see through it all, to the furniture and the wall. But he was transfixed by the jelly-like mass that twisted into form, neither able to flee nor go any closer to Carlotta.

It was like looking into a hallucinatory splendor. The radiating interstices showed a thousand complicated forms, all of which evaporated as they congealed. It was like looking at thought itself, forming out of energy, returning into nothing . . .

It hovered there, as though waiting, groaning so softly the microphones did not pick it up.

"Die!" she suddenly screamed. "Die! *Die!*"

At that precise moment there was a shot, an explosion, from below. Pieces of ceramic flew past Kraft's ear. The remnants of a piece of crockery—a souvenir from Olvera Street—shattered against the iron railing of the catwalk, and a low rumbling caused the entire cavernous chamber to quiver and shake. The catwalk danced beneath Kraft's feet as the form writhed, beckoning toward Carlotta.

The deafening sound flattened the meters in the observation room. Mehan ripped the earphones from his thundering eardrums. Then it was silent again.

Kraft's right hand clutched the railing for support; his left hand aimed the helium nozzle at the entity's heart. His finger on the trigger, wanting to squeeze, but not daring to. Carlotta was on the wrong side of the tape.

"Where's your prick now?" she shouted. Her face was twisted with hatred, with a menacing look Sneidermann would not have believed possible. Carlotta had

450

never, in his presence, exhibited such behavior. She looked venomous, even dangerous. She resembled the castrating monster of classic literature. Her pretty face was unrecognizable, her eyes flashing with a bizarre sense of triumph. As though, in spite of them all and all their equipment, *she* had called *him* to her. Through the universe. Into the universe where she was.

Kraft watched her from above. Her body moved lithely. Seductively. Her back against the far wall, the robe slipped down from her shoulder, her breasts exposed . . .

The wall behind her shivered, a crack shot through it, until there was no more wall, only a falling of plaster and wooden studs, and the far laboratory wall was visible through the cloud of disintegrating material.

Kraft now realized what Dr. Cooley had meant. It was like playing with a lightning rod in the middle of an electric storm. There was no way they could handle the amount of energy that they had drawn into the laboratory.

He swallowed, gazing downward. The psychic force had come together. It had shape, volume. Yes, it was visible to the naked eye. Blunted features, powerful musculature, burgeoning phallus, a glowing, pulsating orb of desire incarnate, its single and sole objective, Carlotta Moran, writhing, twisting, as though in the grasp of a powerful man. It was as if he were staring into a dream. That what he was seeing was given form and shape by the psychic receptors of the brain. That what it was composed of—the kind of energy it was related to—must come from miles of data in the scanners. Certainly, it was powerful, maybe not even a wave structure at all, maybe it belonged to a different order. His brain was buzzing as the entity formed and gradually began to envelop the object of its twisted desire. And still Kraft remained, nozzle in hand, facing the entity with the tubing held in front of him like a harpoon, a thin-shafted gun, an absurd and ill-concocted weapon to challenge its awesome power.

"Die!" he heard Carlotta scream. *"Die!"*
There was a cracking of metal.

Out of the corner of his eye, Kraft saw the disintegration of the metal slats that led from the observation booth to the catwalk. Pieces of bolts were flying down into the environment. The pieces showered on Carlotta, spinning her out of the entity's heady influence to the far end of the wall.

Inside the observation booth, the monitor screens showed extreme deformations of shape, colored an ugly brown-purple, spreading to green, as the temperature began to fluctuate across the room toward Carlotta.

Dean Osborne swallowed, unable to comprehend what he was seeing.

"What the hell is it?" he mumbled to Dr. Weber, standing at his side.

Dr. Weber made an imprecise gesture. "A mass illusion," he replied, without conviction.

"For God's sake, Gene!" Mehan shouted at the monitors. "Now's the time! Blast him!"

At the same instant, Kraft was leaning over the railing, shouting, "Mrs. Moran! Move back!"

Carlotta turned, gazed upward. She had no conception who Kraft was.

"Move back!"

Carlotta stared at him, took a step backward, just beyond the tape. The white mass twisted slowly, neither liquid nor gas; the head, clearly apparent; the body, huge, sinewy, muscular; the penis, like an oblong fruit, protruding menacingly toward her.

Kraft, his eyes boggling with horror and amazement, raised the jet nozzle.

"Jump!" he yelled.

The glass shield slammed across her path. Kraft shot off a blast of helium. There was a vaporous roar. Freezing cold enveloped him, obscured the eastern sector of the laboratory. He saw nothing, heard nothing, his ears were ringing in pain, his body vibrating from the recoil. He realized he had been slammed backward against the far rampart wall. His shoulder ached in pulsing pain.

"Die, bastard! Die!" Carlotta yelled from behind the glass partition.

The entity writhed in seeming agony, then began expanding angrily. Growing, billowing, pushing the remnants of plaster walls to the ground like so much powdered sugar. The entire half of the house—the kitchen and bedroom—was covered in a frosted glaze. Chairs split and popped and danced madly across the floor. A lampshade fell, sparkling, shattering like glass, the fabric shooting outward like musical shards and disintegrating.

Carlotta laughed. In delirium, she imagined spacemen shooting *him* with ray guns. She imagined the far end of Kentner Street disintegrating in a snowfall. She imagined the world collapsing on top of *him,* burying *him* forever. She would kill *him.* Kill *him* that was somehow called up by her, though *he* was from a million light years away.

The television set was hurled through the living-room wall. Plaster flew up to the catwalk and the ramparts connecting the observation booth. Pieces of circuitry were left dangling against the niobium-shielded walls or bounced through to the corridor beyond the laboratory. It was the apocalypse of *his* reign, and Carlotta laughed.

Then, like a metallic roar, like the shaking of the foundations of the building, they heard the voice.

"Leave me alone!"

It was a groan from the depths of hell.

"Jesus Christ!" Dr. Weber said. "Who yelled that?"

"Her hallucination, Dr. Weber!" Mehan yelled triumphantly. "That's who!"

Suddenly, in front of them, the single translucent window broke inward, like a wave, showering small but heavy pieces of glass onto instruments, scanners, and observers. Dr. Cooley and Mehan fell back in their chairs. Dean Osborne fell against Dr. Weber, who held onto Gary Sneidermann for support.

"My God," Dr. Balczynski shouted, struggling to his feet. "Let's get the hell out of here!"

But no one moved. The entire room now glowed with a greenish haze. All the faces were lit from below with the weird glow of the distended light mass.

"Leave me alone!" the voice reverberated as the blue-green form stretched and grew, filling the chamber, reaching, distending, until it rose above the glass wall over Carlotta. She shrank into the corner, feeling the inevitable vacuum, waiting for the inevitable suck into his embrace.

Above her, the catwalk rippled like a ribbon in a high wind. Kraft saw the mooring of his narrow perch giving way, and clung to the railing, the helium nozzle welded to his clenched fist. The aura had filled the chamber, rising above the ruins, displaying a series of eyelets, like the embryonic brains of a fetus that glowed along what appeared to be the spine of the figure. The figure reached upward, ever upward, toward the observation booth, toward the catwalk, toward Kraft.

"Kill *him!*" Carlotta screamed.

Kraft slammed the valve open. The liquid helium for the second time burst from the end of the nozzle. Bits of icicles from the previous blast burst into a shower of powdery flakes. This time, Kraft steeled himself for the recoil. He saw the greenish liquid almost immediately change to white as it shot into space, into the aura, through the eyelets, into the very nervous center of the entity. There was a roar of thunder, a blast of cold air that penetrated to his marrow, and the lights went out. At the same moment, he felt the catwalk giving way beneath him.

Inside the dark observation booth, six figures huddled together waiting for the blow they were sure would come. The sound of breaking metal and the shredding of walls battered their eardrums, and the booth shook as though it were a toy in the hands of an irascible child. It seemed it must break loose from its feeble mooring for, after all, the booth wasn't an integral part of the laboratory, a considered element of the architect's vision, but a mere afterthought. A temporary part of what had certainly turned out to be an ill-conceived experiment. The room shook, but somehow held. Gradually, the shaking subsided and it became absolutely quiet. But still they trembled, waiting for the end. It never came.

"Dr. Cooley?" Joe Mehan whispered.

"I'm all right," she replied, but in a strange voice.

Someplace down below a fluorescence became visible. It was the incredible cold that buckled the floorboards, sent nails flying like bullets from breaking boards. Dean Osborne pressed himself against the back wall of the booth. Tiny explosions filtered up from below. Pieces of glass, of materials whose molecular structure was no longer the same, all shattering, one by one, like firecrackers. The walls of the laboratory—the outer walls—began to drop plaster onto the floors in the corridors outside.

Campus officers, attracted by the noise, came in through the lower corridors. Their flashlights played across the frozen ruins as they gingerly picked their way through the broken glass and tangles of twisted metal. Then, with ladders, they helped bring down the people trapped in the observation booth. Descending into what had been the simulated environment, Dr. Cooley's white-struck face showed in the beams of the traveling flashlights.

Hoarsely, she cried, "Gene? Gene?"

There was silence.

"Balczynski!" Dr. Weber growled.

"I'm here," said a voice, quavering.

Dean Osborne found himself standing shakily in the midst of a steel junkyard. Suddenly, he felt a movement beneath his feet.

"Somebody's underneath this mess," he yelled.

Joe Mehan and Dr. Cooley helped the officers extricate Kraft from the nest of cold metal. Kraft's face was swollen and there was blood seeping through his shirt. He was unconscious but alive. An ambulance was sent for. Joe Mehan dusted bits of glass and wire from his friend's face and hair, and wrested the helium nozzle, still clutched in his fist. Mehan's face was ashen. His movements were erratic. Like a puppet after the strings are cut. His eyes, woebegone, sought Dr. Cooley's.

"It's all over," he moaned. "And we got nothing."

"We got everything!" Dr. Cooley strongly corrected. "There were witnesses!"

Meanwhile, uncomprehending, Sneidermann fumbled through the wreckage, muttering to himself, stepping over pieces of frozen and still steaming fabric, trying to decipher in them the meaning of what he had seen, as he made his way to Carlotta.

But when he got to the glass partition and was able to force his vision to penetrate the dripping, clouded surface, he did not see Carlotta. She was nowhere to be found in the debris of the simulated environment. Nor was she, after a concerted search, to be found anywhere in the psychology sciences building.

Dazed, dumbfounded, totally unnerved, it seemed to Gary Sneidermann that, like every other bizarre happening on this most bizarre of nights, Carlotta, like the entity, had simply vanished in a cloud of smoke.

28

CARLOTTA stepped into what had been her home on Kentner Street.

(*How had she gotten here?*)

The house was devoid of furniture. The moonlight —the pale glow of low cloud cover over the city— gleamed on the floorboards. The air was still, the shadows deep and black in the corners. There were marks on the floor where the couch and television had been. Carlotta closed the door and locked it.

(*Had she walked?*)

She did not switch on the light, preferring the dark. She listened. Birds far away, calm, lonely, called their morning call—ineffable signals of nature's design, the interrelationship of all living things. Dogs barked—so late at night, so early in the morning.

(*No, there had been a bus.*)

The air was close, unmoving. She walked through the area in the center of the living room, where the glow of the moon had moved several inches since she entered. She opened a window, leaned pensively at the sill. The Greenspan house—lattice over the porch—the dark, heavy, protective frame of their house, reflected the pale light of dawn.

(*Had she paid?*)

How quiet it was. Carlotta gazed through the open door leading into the kitchen. The appliances were gone, rectangular irregularities imprinted in the linoleum where they had been. All those things they had done to make her better. To no purpose at all, in the end.

(*It was too much to think about.*)

Carlotta walked into the bedroom. Four round marks on the rug where her bed had been. (*How had they gotten it out?*) No curtains. No vanity table. The street light streaked in through dusty windows, suggested shapes in the shadows on the floor.

Opening the window, Carlotta felt the scent of her tiny garden. A soft perfume, heady, kinetic. The night insects on the stems, the leaves, and even crawling along the windowsill. The breeze ruffled her hair lightly. Restored her senses.

When she turned around, Julie was in the room.

Carlotta was not surprised. It wasn't real. Nothing was real. It was all a figment of her imagination. Julie appeared to observe her strangely, objectively, and then slowly subsided, grew transparent, and turned again into the shapes and stains on the wall. Carlotta looked around the room that had been hers for so long. The room no man had ever shared. Until Jerry. And then Billy became hostile. Vaguely floating, like strands of spiderwebs broken in the breeze, all these connections were there, somewhere, waiting to be woven together into a single whole. But Carlotta was unable to do it. The bedroom was quiet. The glow now shifted along the wall as she waited.

Carlotta felt the insects on her hand. She shook them gently back onto the garden plants. They observed her, antennae roving into the night. What magical realities did they possess? Carlotta knew they were driven by instinct; shielded, irresistible in their own way, for whom human reality was an ephemeral cloud compared to the solid substance on which they fed and the brutal drives which organized their lives. Carlotta watched them. It seemed that theirs was a more solid reality.

Now she knew why she *had* to come home. It was to come to the final place. The place where there was no more retreat.

A sound from the living room. Coughing. Carlotta

walked to the bedroom door. Jerry was in the living room, a suitcase at his feet. He smiled shyly. Guiltily. Confused. He looked at Carlotta as though begging forgiveness. He looked around, gesturing helplessly, then smiled, pleading with his eyes.

"Oh . . . Jerry!" Carlotta whispered.

Tears running down her cheeks, Carlotta ran forward. Jerry's arms reached out, enfolded her. His hands felt for her cheek. His eyes—soft—gazed on her face, which was trembling.

"Oh . . . Jerry . . ."

She kissed his hands over and over again. She stopped. She looked up sharply.

"Jerry!"

Jerry was gone. Instead, Carlotta saw Kim, with the body of a hunchback, crawl across the living-room floor, wheezing obscenely. A blue-green radiance filled the room from the center. Carlotta stepped back toward the bedroom, edged along the wall of the hallway. The room stopped undulating. She heard the distant call of different birds. Slowly she recovered her breath. The moonlight had now shifted another half foot, rising to the juncture of the floor and the stained wall.

Carlotta heard a noise. In the bedroom.

Billy, in the shadows, took off his undershirt. His muscles caught the gleam of the light. The shadows of the garden played over his chest. He looked at Carlotta. His eyes dark, brooding, and mocking. Billy fumbled at the belt buckle.

"Billy . . ." Carlotta whispered. "No . . ."

Billy stripped off his trousers, revealing his muscular, stocky legs, the full, weighty genitals.

"Two little ones and one big one—"

Billy laughed ruefully. He laid his trousers carefully down on the floor and advanced, facing Carlotta. His broad shoulders blocked out the glow of the dusty windows behind him. His hips moved as he came forward.

Carlotta screamed. She covered her ears with her hands. She ran back into the living room. To her surprise,

Billy did not follow her. She turned back. The street light reflected on the worn bedroom rug, shimmered, reaching almost into the hallway. It was empty.

Slowly, Carlotta calmed down. From time to time, the curves in the hallway walls—imperfections of cheap construction—suggested the shapes of boulders. Canyons. Mountains. And then they became the wall again. The nondescript, cream-colored wall, now tinted with the glow of the street light as it reached across the hallway.

Carlotta waited in her final refuge.

The moonlight shifted higher on the far living-room wall. Soon it had reached an area where it was blocked out by the top of the window. A black line across the rectangular glow. Carlotta could see, in the indentations of the wall, tiny butterflies, cream colored. Could hear a small chorus of voices—a confused hypnogogic babble of voices. Like children by the thousands, demanding, their voices blending. Then it died down.

Now the only sound was from the crickets in the vacant lot across the street. A chattering, musical scream that softly came through the windows. Carlotta could dimly make out the sunflowers in the vacant lot. Old wooden boxes. A broken fence. There was no sense of time. Time was a heavy blanket that was thrown over the house. Time was something that altered Carlotta's ability to discriminate among perceptions. Time was no longer a part of her universe.

It must be like this to die, Carlotta realized. That was why Garrett had accused her of leaving him. When it was he who was leaving life. She hadn't understood then. But now she did. Because it felt to Carlotta that Billy, Jerry, and all the others, even Kraft and Mehan, had left her, somehow. Gone and left her to die. When it was really she, Carlotta knew, who, in some way, was leaving them, was going under. Never to surface again.

The last refuge.

"Oh!"

A flash of light, then a shock. A trickle of blood

460

traced its way down her cheek. So sharp. So instantaneous. Like a snakebite.

Franklin angrily kicked his boot against the wall. He stood next to the window and ran his fingers roughly through his hair.

"How does it feel, babe, to go under?"

Carlotta watched him grope for words. His leather jacket hung uncertainly over his shoulders, revealing his powerful chest. His face was confused, hostile, unpredictable.

"Franklin—"

Carlotta was terrified. She recognized the mood he was in. He got that way when he was drunk, or stoned, or both.

Franklin came across the room in only a few enormous, eerie strides. He grabbed Carlotta and pulled her roughly up.

"Answer me, you lousy, stinking hole!"

"Don't . . . please . . ."

Franklin laughed. Then his features softened. He looked with longing at her. Her face, her small frame, her arms.

"Come, babe, come to me."

She resisted him, but his arms were strong. Carlotta was pressed into his embrace. His hands went under her dress. She pushed, stiffened. He was insistent. Then she realized that she could see right through him, see the distant wall and the window, right through the powerful shoulder, the stocky neck.

He was invisible. But Carlotta felt his strong legs press up against her. The warmth of his body, the growth of his need. The odor that was Franklin assailed her. Repulsive as it was, she desired him. Her body opposed her will, had needs of its own.

Franklin laughed—a cruel laugh—then was gone. Carlotta was alone against the wall. The echo of his sadistic laugh died away. Now the room appeared larger than ever, more empty than before.

461

The crickets screamed. They screamed to the world that Carlotta desired a dead man! Carlotta shook her head from side to side until the screams slowly faded.

"Franklin . . . ?"

There was no answer.

It was true, Carlotta thought. She needed Franklin. Depended on a man's physical strength. But there was no man.

For what seemed hours, Carlotta waited. The longer she waited, the more she slipped into a different reality. Finally, the glimpses she had of the house appeared in her mind's eye like imagination, and the intuitions she had of voices and appearances were her true reality.

"Carlotta. Turn thy face to me."

Pastor Dilworth strode among the gardens. Carlotta could see the hills beyond Pasadena. Lights vaguely shimmered in the night.

"Do you hear me, child?"

A musical voice, deep, almost metallic. A voice imprinted into her infantile personality. For Carlotta had entered that realm before the personality is formed, where the sounds and images float indistinctly, unstructured, and fearfully.

Pastor Dilworth held a strap in his hands. A woman —Carlotta's mother—moaned. In her hand she held a pair of underpants, befouled with blood and dirt. They advanced through a shimmering white of curtain. A gauze veiled all that they did. Their disgust was almost palpable.

"Carlotta!"

A voice not to be resisted. Whatever Carlotta was, she was obliged to obey that deep, rumbling voice. She felt herself drawn to it, in spite of every instinct of repugnance.

Suddenly, the strap lashed out.

The pain shot over the side of her shoulder.

"Father . . . !"

A sudden movement and Pasadena evaporated.

Pastor Dilworth was gone. The swimming pool was gone. It was all facade. There was only nothingness.

Was it a disguise? These hallucinations? Why did *he* send these chimera? To torture her? Or were they *his* messengers?

Or did she call them forth? And they in turn called *him* forth?

Carlotta stood, rooted in the darkness. Between the physical and the psychic world stood the realm of the imagination. Clinging to the windowsill for support, Carlotta felt the last restraints fall away. She rose, suspended, into the psychic planes.

"Carlotta . . ."

It was that intimate voice. One she dreamed of. Dreamed with. One that knew her in the deepest parts of her soul. It knew her . . . so well . . .

"Carlotta . . ."

Distant transparent walls glimmered like gauze, vaguely recalling the Kentner Street house—but infinitely extended: a soft glow along the lines of the rectangular windows; and through it all, the infinitude of black space, distant galaxies, veils of iridescent forms that evanesced as Carlotta watched. A negative world where sidewalks were translucent and shot in an infinite perspective among the stars—and there was neither ground nor gravity. A glow where the horizon appeared to rise, among magenta pools.

From distant sulphurous skies *he* came toward her, attended on either side by the dwarfs, their hair flaming red, coalescing into radiant, cold flame—licking coldly into the blackness that permeated them all. In one step *he* crossed a thousand miles, sharply outlined against the yellow clouds tinged with green—a forbidden landscape across which *he* came, directly toward her.

Breathless, Carlotta waited.

Flames of cold light licked up from *his* hair, shimmering eyes, lurid, unforgiving. In the blackness of space Carlotta saw the radiant interior of *his* being, the quick formation of eyelets, ganglia—as they changed, as *he* strode closer—closer.

Through the vaporous structures that resembled—but were not—the structures of the house, she sensed eternity gather itself, taking shape, a suction attaining visible form. Carlotta sensed, almost saw, *his* light stream through her onto revolving, floating horizons far below.

"I . . . I'm . . . afraid," she whispered.

"Carlotta!"

Carlotta stepped back, nearly blinded, enveloped in the cold odor. The perpetual, angry face, hard, without mercy—a powerful face, a face composed of a thousand faces, subtle masks, folding one into the next, but all with the same, murderous glare that filled Carlotta with a chilling cold.

"Please . . . I'm afraid . . ."

"Carlotta!"

"No . . ."

But she was sucked forward. All of her caught in the whirlpool of desire. A gravity—a law of the cosmos—irresistible, pulling her in to dissolve in his embrace. A thousand orgasmic fires, pinpricks of light, like mandibles, gnawed at her breasts, her thighs. Streaks of light burst behind her eyes as she was penetrated, pulled apart, filled, dissolved as never before.

"Oooooooooh . . ."

Her cry, continuous, musical, reverberated among the stars. Slithering forms shimmered before her eyes, whirling into her substance, growing colder, ever colder, burning with the cold that now flowered within her—faster and faster—all things disintegrating, holding onto *him,* dissolving, embracing, dissolving, disappearing into the void. A last awareness of light and darkness.

In the hissing, spitting void, the last refuge splintered, shot apart; and Carlotta, fragmented, became less than Carlotta, a vaporous substance—a last sound—like distant, dying thunder.

"My sweet . . . Carlotta . . ."

Epilogue

RECOMMENDATION FOR CONSERVATORSHIP

To:

COUNTY CONSERVATORSHIP INVESTIGATOR

Conservatorship is recommended for __Mrs. Carlotta Moran__
                                          (Name of Patient)

who is in my care. It has been determined that this person is gravely disabled as defined by the

Welfare and Institutions Code Section 5008 (h)

   *(a) as a result of a mental disorder

   ~~2 (b) by impairment of chronic alcoholism~~

and is

   ~~2 (a) unwilling to accept treatment voluntarily~~

   *(b) incapable of accepting treatment voluntarily

* (Strike out inapplicable classification)

Attachments: Medical Record Summary
               Including diagnosis, prognosis and reasons
               for recommending conservatorship

SIGNATURE OF PROFESSIONAL PERSON IN CHARGE OF AN AGENCY OR FACILITY PROVIDING COMPREHENSIVE EVALUATION OF INTENSIVE TREATMENT	DATE
Chas Sheidermann M.D. C. Sheidermann, M.D. Psychiatric Resident	6/11/77

RECOMMENDATION FOR CONSERVATORSHIP

<u>JUSTIFICATION FOR CONSERVATORSHIP</u>

Name: Mrs. Carlotta Moran

Address: 212 Kentner Street, LA. CA.   Telephone: KL5 1717

Birthdate: 8/3/44   Sex: F.   Marital Status: Widow

Interested Friend or Relative: Relationship: Mother
          Mrs. Harriet Dilworth
          743 Orange Grove Blvd.   Telephone: SM2 6464
          Pasadena, Ca.

Reasons and observations in support of patients inability to
provide for /x/ food, /x/ clothing, /x/ shelter. (check
appropriate boxes)

     (See below)

History of disability, current treatment, and recommendations
for patient care:

     Patient has had a schizophrenic disorder and for past
     weeks does not respond when spoken to, does not eat,
     and must be tube fed. She needs to be dressed by others
     and will not care for basic life functions without
     continual supervision. She has not responded to
     medication.

CL-1 issued 1-30-70

466

Diagnosis and description of patients mental status that
supports diagnosis:

    Schizophrenia – catatonic type.

Reasons to believe patient is incapable of, or unwilling
to accept help voluntarily:

    She does not appear to understand when asked if she
    wishes voluntary care, and does not react. Patient
    does not speak, therefore is not able to make verbal
    decision for voluntary care. Does not respond by
    gesture to offer of voluntary care.

    I therefore recommend that a temporary conservator
be appointed.
I declare under penalty of perjury that the foregoing
is true and correct.

              Executed on   6/11/77
              at West Coast University,   California

Gary Sniederman MD	*H. Weber M.D. Chief Psychiatrist*
SIGNATURE OF PROFESSIONAL PERSON WHO	SIGNATURE OF PROFESSIONAL
PERFORMED THE EVALUATION OF THE PATIENT	PERSON IN CHARGE OF REGIONAL
AND WHO RECOMMENDS TEMPORARY CONSER-	SERVICE PROVIDING COMPREHEN-
VATORSHIP PURSUANT TO SECTIONS 5352,	SIVE EVALUATION FOR INTEN-
5352.1 OF THE W & I CODE	SIVE TREATMENT REVIEWING
	RECOMMENDATION FOR TEMPORARY
	CONSERVATORSHIP PURSUANT TO
	SECTIONS 5352, 5352.1 OF THE
	W & I CODE

THROUGH the months that followed Carlotta's commitment to the hospital, Sneidermann tried to analyze what
had happened that night. But all his research into elec-
tronics, all his inquiries into chemical tricks, came to
nothing. There was no explanation for the vaporous substance that he himself had seen hovering along the walls
of the experimental chamber: no understanding the power, the force, the havoc it had caused which triggered off
the final collapse of Carlotta's personality. Even Weber
did not truly believe it was a mass hallucination. The
question buzzed continually in Sneidermann's brain like
an angry cloud of bees, refusing to be resolved. Whatever
it had been, it slapped Carlotta into a full-blown schizophrenia.

She had run home, guided by instinct, probably incoherent, Sneidermann mused, searching for some touch-
stone of reality, which, in her case, could only mean her
family. Sneidermann tried to picture her coming into that
house. That house that was no home, stripped bare of
every picture on the wall, every towel on the rack, every
remnant that might have given her some clue as to what
or who she was. And there was nothing but a shell. Even
the children were gone. Confused, frightened, under terrible pressure, she imploded like an inward volcano.

Arriving at the Kentner Street house early that morning, he had found her on all fours, in the living room. She

468

was nude. She gazed wide-eyed, seeing nothing, breathing very, very slowly.

He covered her with his shirt, put her into the car, and raced back to the emergency clinic. She was diagnosed first as a rape victim, but was unable to speak. Within the day, she was diagnosed as a catatonic withdrawal; three days later she was institutionalized.

It took six months until Dr. Weber and Sneidermann returned to speaking terms. When they did, an uneasiness still remained. Sneidermann wrote him an apologetic letter.

My youth constrained me to take measures which seemed at the time appropriate. I was guided less by the measures of medical prudence than by the promptings of deep feelings which I know now were not unmixed with lesser motivations. You will, no doubt, be justified in your refusal to consider my correspondence with you. But I am motivated, I assure you, solely by my effort to continue to uphold that solemn oath which I took upon leaving West Coast University.

Sneidermann did not return to the East. Instead, he assumed control of a ward in a state psychiatric hospital near Santa Barbara. One day he received a short note from Los Angeles.

My dear Gary, you will forgive my silence. It was the reaction of an old man who had forgotten the passions and mistakes of his own youth. Will you consent to meet me in Los Angeles? Please let me know.

It was signed by Dr. Weber.

Within three weeks, however, Dr. Weber was dead of a stroke. Sneidermann did not attend the funeral, as his duties prevented a leave of absence. He remembered a photograph of Dr. Weber from the class yearbook, found it, had it enlarged and framed, and set it behind his desk on the wall. He looked at it one afternoon, wondering whether one ever really finds one's way out of life's mazes, and felt tears streaming down his cheeks.

During the day Sneidermann supervised the ward and helped in others. The hospital was understaffed. Many of the patients had never been properly diagnosed, and Sneidermann battled the state legislature for financial assistance and legislative reform. In a surprisingly short time, he also managed to improve the security of the area. His wards were the only ones in Southern California which showed no rapes, beatings, or suicide attempts in the second two quarters of the year.

Many of the nurses and staff wondered, privately, why such a brilliant young doctor had ended up in a state facility.

Sneidermann opened a door after knocking gently.

"Good morning, Carlotta," he said softly.

"Oh, good morning, Gary," she said, closing her robe modestly around her throat.

Small lines had crept into her face, around the eyes, at the corners of her mouth. But the vitality was there. That animal-like grace that was so perfectly modulated. It was a face that had floated a thousand times through his dreams.

"I heard you had trouble sleeping," he said.

"A little," she admitted. "The sleeping pill was too mild."

"I'm trying to get you off sleeping pills, Carlotta."

"I get scared—just a little."

Sneidermann smiled. He looked at her with gray, sparkling eyes.

"I'd like to see you after breakfast," he said. "We could go out on the grounds."

"Yes. I'd like that."

He closed the door. The two ward nurses smiled. Sneidermann had a sweetheart among the patients, it was whispered. He was so studious, even curt, when the discipline faltered, when the wards were not run his way. But in room 114-B, Carlotta Moran, schizophrenic paranoid —when he opened that door, he softened, a kind of radiance emerged, and he became almost like a boy again, enthusiastic, with a sense of humor.

Sneidermann walked briskly to his private office. There was a group of newspaper reporters coming to inspect the facilities. Most psychiatrists hated such interference. Sneidermann welcomed it, even encouraged it. He wanted the state of public assistance to the mentally ill to become public knowledge.

Before lunch, he met with Carlotta.

"I received a letter from your mother," he said.

"Yes?"

"The children are fine."

"That's wonderful," she said.

She seemed abstracted today. Normally, during the day, she reacted with the instincts of any person. It was not until evening that she began to grow this way—distant and then afraid.

"Would you like to see them?" he asked.

"Yes. But I'd like to be better first."

"I can arrange a visit."

Carlotta smiled, shielding her eyes from the hot sun. The grass was green, watered by lazy sprinklers in rows. Children played under supervision, their laughter ringing out clearly and pleasantly.

"Soon, maybe," she said.

Sneidermann studied the face he had never touched, the neck he had never kissed. Yet he was far more intimate in a way, a kind of guardian angel to her now.

"I would like to decrease the sedative."

"No—"

"You're dependent on them. I don't want that."

"No, please—"

"Just a little. Little by little. That doesn't hurt."

"I'm afraid."

"Now, you know there's nothing to be afraid of." He reached for her hand, held it gently. "Will you do this

471

much for me, Carlotta? Try it. Each night we'll take a little less. And see what happens."

"All right," she said softly, smiling.

"What's so funny?"

"You really do care for me, don't you?"

Sneidermann blushed.

"I'm your doctor. Besides, you know I do—I told you."

"You shouldn't. You see what I did to your career. Winding up in this lousy—"

"I'm pleased to be here. I enjoy my work. Really. I do."

"Some part of you never grew up, Dr. Sneidermann. You're still like a little boy. You know, you should have married."

Sneidermann blushed more deeply.

"My private life is—quite satisfactory."

They laughed. As the afternoon sun dappled through the leaves of the trees overhead, Sneidermann wondered if he had not, in some inscrutable, odd way, found happiness on the earth. A prospect that few people believed in anymore. And in a place that most people would shun like the fiery circles of hell itself. Yet it was true. In a sense—at least during the day—now, together, in the soft breeze, there was no anxiety, no nervousness. They knew one another completely, without ambiguity. But as each afternoon grew, Sneidermann could see the changes come over her, bodily and facial changes. She darted her eyes about. She became obsessed with the shadows as they grew. She became nervous. She seemed to dread the coming of the night.

Or did she await it?

Later that evening Sneidermann strolled, as was his custom, by room 114-B.

"How is she?" he asked.

"A little restless," the nurse said.

"Did she take the sleeping pill?"

"Yes, sir. Only five milligrams."

472

"Good. Very good."

Sneidermann inspected the rooms down the hall. A boy who was severely autistic had injured his head against the wall. They had to brace him to protect himself. Sneidermann was trying to get a grant—a subsidy, anything—to get the boy off the ward and into the specialized care that he deserved.

He walked back to Carlotta's room.

"She's sleeping, sir. Very lightly."

"All right. You can go now."

Sneidermann walked to the tiny window at the door. His face pressed up against the glass.

Carlotta lay under light sheets. The moonlight came down, bathing her face softly. Her black hair was spread out, fanned over the pillow. Her nostrils appeared flared to him. He noticed that her hair was damp from perspiration.

She was whispering.

He could not hear. He opened the door a crack.

"Please, oh, please—oh, oh—"

It was an uncanny sound. Was she moaning in ecstasy or in protest—protest of some violation?

"Ohhhhhh . . ."

He swallowed; forced himself to observe, to note: she moves slowly, restlessly, almost suggestively, her face hideously grimacing—with pleasure? with loathing?

Transfixed, he watched until she was through and *he* was gone. Her moans subsided.

Humiliated, burning with jealousy, Sneidermann turned from the window.

He glanced at his watch. With only 5 milligrams, the nightmare had lasted less than ten minutes. He had worked her back into intelligible speech. He had worked her to where she could attend to her own bodily functions. She had regained every inch of grace, of charm, that had once destroyed his own vulnerable ego. And now he was decreasing the nightmares, bit by bit, day by day.

Sneidermann walked out onto the grounds to smoke.

The moon broke over his hands, guiding the lighter to the cigarette. He felt peculiarly full of emotion tonight. Small victories were the only important thing in his life now. He envisioned Carlotta, as he had so many evenings, chatting pleasantly, in some cafe, perhaps, in some beautiful place, her charming manners the envy of all. It would be enough for him.

But she hovered, beautiful and still unattainable, forever mysterious and elusive, before his consciousness.

He inhaled slowly. It had been a routine day. He was exhausted. He mulled it over again. A better sleep, under only 5 milligrams of sedation. It would take time, but—together, there was no limit to what they could do. He walked through the garden, remembering the day when it began, the day Carlotta first, trembling, walked into his office.

Out beyond the hospital was a highway, and beyond that the dried grass that led to the dark ocean. Sneidermann was content.

Addenda

A Multi-Phased Inquiry into the Physical and Psychical Components of a Discarnate Entity.

—Preliminary Observational Assessment Report.
—In preparation: Quantitative Study w/Data Reduction and Analyses.

by

EUGENE KRAFT
JOSEPH MEHAN

submitted as partial completion
for the Master of Arts in the
Department of Psychology,
West Coast University

DR. ELIZABETH COOLEY, Chairman,
Division of Parapsychology

The study of psychic events has, until now, been performed under field conditions of too random a nature to elicit definitive and incontrovertible data. Descriptions of "haunts," "apparitions," "ghosts," and similar noncorporeal visitations have never been reproduced under laboratory conditions. As a result, the entire area of investigation has been ignored by the scientific community, justifiably, as too unreliable to permit serious consideration.

A four-month investigation, however, recently concluded, has succeeded in inducing a psychic entity into a controlled field and has yielded rich veins of data concerning its nature.

A subject, known to have been visited by a singular entity, at times accompanied by two smaller entities, was placed in a shielded and sound-proofed environment (diagram appended). The environment was an exact duplicate of the home in which she had lived, save that the ceiling had been removed to permit direct monitoring and sensory scanning of the quarters below. In addition, the walls were buttressed with layers of shielding to prevent almost any extraneous electromagnetic interference from entering.

The subject lived in the quarters, which were furnished with her own carpets, drapes, chairs, bed, and utensils, for several weeks. During that time no variations in any of the monitoring devices were observed. Gradually, however, as she acclimated to the surroundings, she reverted to the emotional patterns that had dominated her life for the several months prior to the controlled experiment. This included extreme anxiety concerning her family, recurrent personal problems with her fiancé, and deeply buried memories from her childhood.

Gradually her log book began to fill with descriptions of repetitive dreams which suggested a psychic landscape that terrified her. On several occasions she reported in conversation her premonitions that a visitation was increasingly imminent.

As certain key emotional transitions occurred, the first definite readings were obtained in changes of the atmosphere's ion concentration, distribution and density. The first key emotional transition was the break-up, definitive and irrevocable, between the subject and her fiancé. The trauma was followed within eight hours by noticeable fluctuations in the atmospheric resistance, i.e., dielectric constant to ELF radiation, that is below 40 cycles per second, which is characteristic of human as well as all animal life.

The visit of her mother, from whom the subject had been estranged for over ten years, and the subsequent removal of the subject's children for their own safety, provided the second leap in the readings of the remote sensing physiological recordings.

As the isolation of the subject increased, she sank increasingly into her own memories, fantasies, guilts, and hopes for a better life. She became increasingly oblivious

476

to the laboratory origins of the environment. She began to speak to herself, at times to others not in the room, some of whom were known to be dead. In short, she began displaying the mannerism of a psychic in a state of receptivity.

Gradually, during a 42-hour period of intense emotional activity, visible phenomena began to be recorded. Most prominent was a white mass that extended along the wall, and which retracted into a ball over a three-hour interval, leaving a substance motionless, about two and a half feet over the carpet.

The subject began to shout at the apparition, vile epithets to relieve herself of the horror of having lived in terror of it for almost half a year. With each of her imprecations, the substance of the entity underwent dramatic changes, observable by the eye-witnesses, but failing, unfortunately, to make any impression on a number of highly sophisticated cameras and recording devices, including thermovision equipment, low-light level color video cameras, and a holographic-double pulsed laser. The most pronounced changes observed were of color and form as the mass evolved into a blue-green, light-emitting cloud. Also a distinct musculature began to form within the cloud, much as tiny blood vessels and organs can be seen in an embryo.

Immediately preceding the appearance of the apparition, there were distinctive and abrupt changes in the electromagnetic and thermoionic environment of the subject's immediate surroundings. It is not possible at this time to determine whether such changes caused the apparition, resulted from it, or whether both the apparition and the observable atmospheric changes were caused by a singular, underlying cause as yet undiscovered.

The last and most conclusive phase of the experiment involved an attempt to settle the most perplexing and persistent problem of the paranormal sciences.

Liquid helium, at temperatures approximating that of absolute zero, was sprayed, with a secondary liquid composed of a clear solution with minute particles in suspension, onto the blue, evolving mass. At the immediate instant of contact a scream was heard. Subsequent eye-witness accounts agree that the words were a deformation of "leave me alone!"

The entity was simultaneously visible to as many as eight persons, all of whom reported the identical sights and sounds at the same moments. Yet recording devices dependent on translating variable wave-length radiation into images all failed to pick up those events. Was it then a mass hallucination, born of the many weeks of fatigue, arduous effort, and sheer desire to see the entity? Such a possibility seems far-fetched because the observers included a dean of the university, a senior medical staff member, and a resident of the medical school, all of whom were highly skeptical of the proceedings. To suggest that they had, along with the highly disciplined team of Dr. Cooley, become "hypnotized" into believing in something that was not really there seems a dubious proposition at best. Even if something of the sort had taken place, it is impossible that all observers could have reported such identical findings without prior and extensive consultation. It goes almost without saying that such was not the case, and, in fact, several of the observers did not know one another or had little knowledge or even interest in parapsychology.

What then can explain the mystery? Is it the familiar tale, known in legend and myth for a hundred years, of the "ghost" that cannot be photographed? Is there not a more scientific explanation? The truth of the matter is that the entity did in fact exist, independent of those attending the experiment. This is proved beyond a possibility of doubt by the precise and continuous recordings of the temperature gauges, the ion concentration meters, and certain fluctuations in the electromagnetic atmosphere. Then what caused the relative failure of the visually-recording instruments?

It may be that it was perceived, *psychically,* by all the observers; and their minds, in order to translate the experience to a more readily understood level of awareness,

478

interpreted the events in visual terms. In other words, a severe storm of psychic energy, which may have been endowed with intelligence, was interpreted by human minds as though they had seen it, whereas in fact they had received the knowledge of that energy through *psychic* means. Hence the unanimity of their responses.

That there was an immense energy in the room is well known. It caused enormous stress on the structural timbers, pegged the needles on most of the dials, and finally caused the destruction of the entire chamber, resulting in extensive devastation and the injury of Kraft.

But exactly what the nature of this energy was is yet unknown. Was it electromagnetic, or did it only give off electromagnetic waves as a kind of secondary attribute? The truth is that no theory can yet account for the vast range of energy changes which were observed. What we may be dealing with here is a form of energy relatively new and unknown, one which is only now being placed under the scrutiny of science.

A secondary question, as to the origin of the entity, remains ambiguous. Given that the apparition exists independently of the subject, as confirmed by the data herein given, can it be determined whether it derives from the subject as a projected entity or, rather, does it derive from sources and space-times ("locations") as yet unexplored?

The latter appears to be the more likely solution, given the high degree of independence of the psychic entity from the psychological will of the subject. It would appear, however, that a highly receptive subject is an intermediary between the world of observable data and the planes of psychic experience. At best, further experimentation would be required to solve the problem once and for all.

To interpret these events as mass hallucination, fraud, or the collective imaginations of many dedicated workers flies in the face of all probability. The eye-witness accounts of too many individuals, some of them by no means sympathetic to the project, make the case incontrovertible that the entity existed, independent of other human beings, that it occupied space and time in our world, and that it interacted with physical matter.

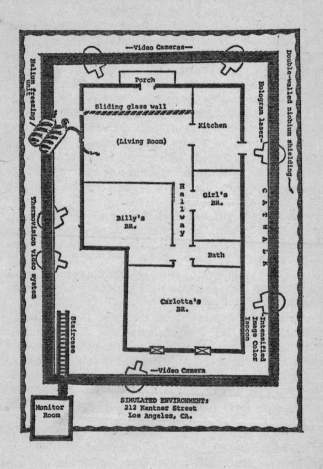

—Video Cameras—

Helium freezing unit

Double-walled niobium shielding

Hologram laser—

Porch

sliding glass wall

Kitchen

(Living Room)

C
A
T
W
A
L
K

Girl's BR.

Hallway

Billy's BR.

Bath

Thermovision video system

Carlotta's BR.

Intensified Image Color Isocon

Staircase

—Video Camera

Monitor Room

SIMULATED ENVIRONMENTS:
212 Kentner Street
Los Angeles, CA.